THE
EDEN
PROPOSITION

Kurt Dahl

ISBN: 1-4392-1567-7
ISBN-13: 9781439215678

Visit www.booksurge.com to order additional copies.

Acknowledgements

My enduring thanks and appreciation to all those friends who helped make this possible – Jon, Charlie, Bill, Larry, Dawn, Dick, Barbara, and many others.

Author's note

World population stood at 2 billion people in 1920. Eighty years later it had tripled to over 6 billion. We are now adding 1 million more every four days. By the year 2020 world population will grow to almost 8 billion, and reasonable projections vary from 9 to 11 billion people crowded onto this planet by the year 2050.

We wring our hands and speak alarmingly about the consequences of this massive growth – climate change, energy depletion, food shortages, resource wars, etc. – but these are only the symptoms, they are not the problem.

The real problem – *population growth* - is ignored, seldom even discussed.

No government or world body has the desire, much less the ability, to address this problem in any meaningful way. So mankind heads to the abyss, knowing why, and doing nothing.

August, 2018
Xinjiang Region, China
The remote town of Toli
This happened:

Late afternoon on a blistering August day, a rail-thin, weary-eyed bureaucrat sat facing a young doctor in the cramped basement conference room at the Toli People's Health Facility. A haze of cigarette smoke fouled the stagnant air in the seldom used room. No one spoke. Uneasy moments passed slowly.

Finally, the bureaucrat stirred. He stubbed out his cigarette, licked the end of his thumb, squeezed out the last ember, and threw the butt away. He paused, seemed to study the concrete floor where the butt had landed, then glanced back to the doctor and held his gaze but still did not speak.

He was well practiced in this art of intimidation, a necessary tool of his profession. Silence, carried to the extreme, can be deeply unsettling. But in truth, it was the skeletal bureaucrat, Zhang Sheng, the Director of Public Health Services for the Karamay district in western China, who feared the conversation that must follow.

Sheng knew something that the doctor didn't know. He knew it was his own life that hung in the balance, not the doctor's. If this exchange did not go exactly as he needed, he would face certain execution. Sheng's only hope was that this young doctor's ambition outweighed his ethics, much as Sheng's greed had brought him to this dangerous precipice.

Sheng continued to fix the doctor with his lifeless stare, and after several more uncomfortable moments he spoke: "Dr. Wei, you must be truthful and complete in what you say here. If you are not, then your career will be ended. Do you understand?"

"Yes, I understand," Wei said and tried to look obedient.

"Who else knows of the autopsy results?" Sheng asked.

"No one else knows. I did as you said after I called you yesterday."

"Are you absolutely certain that no one else knows?"

"Yes, I am certain."

Sheng nodded approval.

"And you understand that you must never discuss the autopsy results, or this conversation, with anyone?"

"Yes, Director Sheng, I do understand. You can trust me," Wei said, glancing down.

"Good." Sheng straightened up and placed his hands face down on the table. "Now, tell me everything about this episode. When did it begin?"

Dr. Li Wei, only three months into his first year of residency at the remote rural hospital, took a deep breath, stretched his neck and tried to relax. "The police brought him in two days ago," he began. "He was unconscious ..."

Sheng interrupted, "Did the police say if he was unconscious when they found him?"

"Yes, they found him lying in a doorway."

"Good," Sheng said, and wished he hadn't. "Go on."

"He was brought to the emergency room. He had no identification at all. He had a contusion on his left temple, so the police thought he had been assaulted. As our staff neurologist, I was called in. I did an imaging, and discovered the contusion was only superficial, that it would not have caused his unconscious state, and that it was probably a result of his falling. The police were satisfied that there had not been a crime and they went away."

"Did the police create a report?"

"Yes, it was a typical form, nothing to worry about. I signed off that no crime had been committed. They assumed that he was just a drunk peasant in from the countryside."

"What happened next?"

"He died."

"What were the symptoms?"

"There were no symptoms - he just died. I was curious. And since I had nothing to do that day, I decided to do the autopsy myself to determine the cause of death. I took him down to the morgue, and I started by working exclusively on the brain."

"You did no dissections of the trunk at all?"

"No, it is not my expertise. I just focused on the brain. At the time, I must confess, I really was thinking of it as an educational experiment. He was just an unknown peasant, after all."

"Yes, just a peasant." Sheng nodded and paused to light another cigarette. Smoking was, of course, not allowed anywhere in the hospital. Sheng took a slow drag, and in the absence of an ashtray, carefully perched the cigarette on the edge of the table.

Sheng continued, "And are you completely sure that he had no identification, no marks of any kind, nothing that would give anyone a clue as to where he came from?"

"No, nothing at all."

Sheng relaxed a bit at hearing this news. "Please go on doctor."

Wei tried not to look at the cigarette. A thin line of smoke was curling up behind Sheng and made it look as if the back of Sheng's head was smoldering.

"I removed the brain and began the dissection. Soon it was apparent to me that there were severe abnormalities. I had not seen these features in any of my work. But a little research revealed that these were the floral plaques associated with CJD – Creutzfeldt-Jakob disease, sometimes mistakenly called mad cow disease."

"And you are certain of this?"

"Yes, very certain. I can show you."

Sheng had been thinking about this strange discovery ever since last night, after Wei called him. He knew a little about CJD, but none of what he knew fit with the escaped man from the village. Still, he must assume the worst. And since everyone from the village was implanted with an RFI chip to identify them for the testing, Sheng needed only to take the body back to the village to find out. Still, CJD? It was supposed to be a flu vaccine that they were testing. How could this peasant have CJD?

"I'd like to go to the morgue now so you can show me the results. Can we do this without anyone finding out?" Sheng asked.

"No, we must wait for two hours," Wei said, glancing at his watch. "It will be after six then. We have no night staff in the morgue at this hospital."

"Fine, I will stay here. You are excused," Sheng said and reached for his cigarette.

Wei stood, bowed slightly, and backed out of the room.

Five hours later, the bureaucrat Sheng's state van approached the barricade on the remote mountain road that led to the isolated village. The dead peasant, zipped in a black body-bag and covered with a blanket in the back of the van, now made a final impact on his surroundings by issuing the vague smell of rotten meat typical of the recently dead. Sheng chain-smoked for the entire trip to keep the stench at bay.

Sheng parked the van twenty meters short of the barricade, lit another cigarette, and waited for his contact. The barricade was many miles from the village. Eight months ago the road had supposedly been destroyed in a mudslide. Since it was the only route into the village, the official story was that all of the villagers who lived there had been "relocated".

Sheng closed his eyes, took a long drag, and again cursed the foolishness and greed that had brought him to this point. But who could have refused so much money? He hoped that the money was now sitting in the promised Swiss account; he might need it sooner than he had planned. But the momentary pleasure of contemplating his dirty fortune soon dissolved into confusion about the bizarre incident with the dead peasant. Something must have gone terribly wrong at the village.

He should have asked more questions when the Indians approached him with the strange request to isolate an entire village to test their new vaccine. What a fool he had been. But they worked for a large and respected biotech company and had told him he would be helping them to fast-track a very promising vaccine. Still, it was too much money. He should have known that something was wrong.

Two vehicles pulled up on the other side of the barricade. His contact, a short and somewhat heavier than normal Indian man wearing an old-style white Nehru cap, approached.

"Do you have the body?" the Indian asked, grim-faced.

Sheng was surprised by the abruptness of the usually congenial man. "Yes, in the back," he said, gesturing absently with his cigarette.

The Indian signaled to the men standing by the barricade. Two came over and removed the body. One held up a device and quickly scanned the dead peasant, still zipped inside the bag. He nodded to the Indian in the Nehru cap.

"Good," the Indian said to Sheng. "This is the man that escaped."

The two men carried the body back to the vehicles.

"Director Sheng, we have bad news," the Indian said after the two men with the body were out of earshot. "Something went horribly wrong with the vaccine. I'm sorry to tell you, but all of the test subjects have died."

Sheng's stomach tumbled. He was now responsible for over a hundred deaths. What a fool! "What? How could that happen?" he stammered.

"The less you know, the better off you will be," the Indian replied.

But Sheng already knew about Dr. Wei's discovery of CJD in the peasant's autopsy. Should he mention it? He decided not to. It might be dangerous to know this. "What about the village?" he asked instead.

"We have removed it. It is just bare ground now. We will dynamite the road after we leave – sometime in the next few weeks."

Sheng took a deep drag on is cigarette. Well then, maybe this will work out after all, he thought.

"Director Sheng, we know how dangerous this is for you now. We will do what we can to make this event invisible, and to protect you." He had Sheng's full attention now. "In addition, we are prepared to triple your 'fee', and to provide you with papers for a new identity. However, these will not be available to you until two years from today - so we can be assured that you will be on the job and ready to squelch any leaks or rumors that might arise. Is this understood and acceptable to you?"

"Do I have a choice?"

"No."

Sheng took another drag and exhaled slowly. Two years? It would be a lifetime of fear. But he had no options. He looked away and nodded his acceptance.

The Indian waited for Sheng to look back to him. "Here are the instructions for your 'fee'," he said and then placed the envelope on the dashboard, as Sheng made no attempt to take it. "And from now on, there is no need for us to have any further contact. Good luck to you Director Sheng."

The Indian paused for a respectful moment to see if Sheng would say something, but Sheng remained silent and the Indian returned to his vehicle. The Indian conferred with the others for a moment and then they drove away.

Sheng sat motionless in his van, a tail of smoke snaked along the seat and up the far door, the silence no longer his ally.

Chapter 1

Twenty Two Months later
Sunday, May 31st, 2020
Astoria, Oregon, USA
The story begins:

Toby put the phone down, stared at it for a moment, then absently stood up and employed the international hand signal for "Holy shit". He put both hands, palms down, on the top of his head. "Holy shit!" he said. He sucked in a deep breath, his eyes rolled skyward and he stumbled back into his chair.

"Holy shit!" he said again.

The fateful call came during Toby's favorite time of day – while drinking his morning coffee and enjoying the view from the front porch of his Victorian cottage on the steep, north-facing hill above the Columbia river and the little town of Astoria, Oregon. The view rivaled any on earth. From his porch, the grand vista swept north across the four-mile wide expanse of the Columbia to the forested hills of southwest Washington, then west to the distant white-topped breakers that marked the violent collision of that massive river with the Pacific ocean.

Astoria had been Toby's refuge after the war. Undiscovered, its Victorian charm remained unchanged because it was simply too far from anywhere important. And in the chaotic world of the year 2020, Toby felt lucky to be living in this peaceful enclave of artists and rain.

But now his easy morning evaporated, replaced by a confusing contest of rapid-fire thoughts. For out of nowhere, Duval Dixon, the wealthiest human being on earth, had just called and talked to him for twenty minutes.

And to Toby's complete astonishment, Dixon knew him. Not personally of course, but he knew of his work, and in remarkable detail. But the moment that would change Toby's life forever, the moment that would sever the past from the future, came when Duval Dixon told Toby to meet him in Vancouver, British Columbia at seven o'clock the next night.

Toby sat motionless, stunned, his hands still holding the top of his head in place, and tried to remember everything that Dixon said. He stared out across the miles wide expanse of the river, vaguely in the direction of the remote logging town of Deep River where he had been born thirty-one years earlier, and once again he wondered – just who was the maniac driving *his* bus?

In his brief time on the planet, Toby had already experienced several lifetime's worth of unexpected events. Sometimes he blamed his parents, as they had conspired to give him such exceptional genes. Toby was a certified genius. So, unlike most of his friends from that remote town across the river, he had made an early escape from the logging life of rural Washington.

That escape, however, came with a set of deep scars - emotional and physical. Toby's parents died in a car crash a week after his graduation from high school. Pinned in the wreckage with them, Toby heard the gurgling last sound his father made as he struggled to reach out to his already dead mother. That memory would haunt him forever and the aftermath would begin a chain of events that would change everything.

After the accident, Toby delayed his college plans and spent a long, grim winter recovering alone in his family's house where, fueled by his unresolved anger and colored by his depression, he retreated to the world of fiction writing for relief. Like many young men of his generation, he also did some hacking, developed some websites, and eventually self-published his angst-born novel.

Then fate again intervened when he unexpectedly sold his book and website and received enough cash to abandon Deep River, and eventually his depression, and to pay for his undergraduate studies at Princeton.

There, his genius blossomed. The university rewarded him with a full ride for the rest of his education, all the way through to his PhD in mathematics. And now, this gift for math had given him the security of a full-time grant from CPS, the Center for Population Studies.

The grant allowed him to do his research, unencumbered by teaching or publishing, and it allowed him to live where he pleased – an appropriate payback for Toby's first three years as a CPS employee, three years spent in hell.

On the day of the surprising summons from Duval Dixon, Toby and Waino Huttala, an old boyhood friend from Deep River, had planned a kayak trip to Long Island in Willapa Bay. The trip would have to wait. Toby had no wife, no serious girlfriend, no pets, and no conventional job. It would take him only a few hours to get some clothes together, make a few calls, and hit the road for the six-hour drive north across Washington state to Vancouver, B.C.

Soon he was headed north across the four-mile long bridge that connected Astoria to the Washington coast. He had been anxious to get going, even if it meant spending an extra night in Vancouver. He would stop to tell his friend the story of that morning's amazing conversation, though Waino was unlikely to care, and might not even know who Duval Dixon was. Still, he had just spoken with Duval Dixon – the world's wealthiest human - he had to tell someone.

Waino was standing by the side of the garage getting the kayak gear together as Toby pulled up.

"Hey, man." Toby said.

"Hey," Waino replied. "Looks like it's going to be a good paddle, wind out of the north, but just a nothing breeze, and the tides are right for a trip around the island."

"Well, I hope you enjoy it, because I can't go."

"What are you doing here then?" Waino asked in his usual blunt manner. Finns liked to conserve their words.

"I'm on my way to Vancouver," Toby said and paused for dramatic effect. "Get this; I'm sitting on my porch this morning, having some coffee, the cell beeps, and guess who's on the other end?"

"Do I have to?"

"No. You couldn't anyway. It was Duval Dixon." Toby waited for a reaction.

Waino stopped fiddling with the kayak gear and squared up to get a better look at Toby. "Duval Dixon? Why was he calling you?"

"You know who he is, right?"

"Hell yes, I'm not retarded."

"Okay, sorry. Anyway, Dixon is having a conference on Vancouver Island at some retreat he owns. It starts the day after tomorrow and I'm supposed to be at the Oriental Hotel in Vancouver tomorrow night for the reception thing, and then fly over to the island the next day."

"So you actually talked to this guy?" Waino asked, still catching up.

"Yup, I actually talked to him, and for a full twenty minutes. He's a charming guy, but strange. You can feel the energy, or power, or something coming from him, even on the cell."

"Why you?" Waino was looking more concerned than confused now.

"Well, it's the probability work that I do. The conference is about possible population outcomes, or something along those lines. I didn't really get a good picture. I was in too much shock to ask any good questions. He's putting us up for six weeks, in order to get into 'substantial discussions' he said. And get this, Ben Mallory, 'Mr. Environment' and your former Senator, is going to be there."

"You're serious? Senator Mallory, Duval Dixon, and *you*? For six weeks?" Waino reached out and poked Toby on the shoulder. "Can I touch you?" he said, with a smile.

"Well, I don't get it either. But I found out one thing from the conversation with Dixon. He has been funding CPS, the people I work for. I guess he owns the thing. That's why he knows about my work."

Waino shook his head. He looked up at Toby with a sly grin, put his hands together, spit into them, rubbed them together, and stuck out his right hand. "Congrats to you buddy, this is a really big deal."

"Yuk, I'm not shaking that!"

"No, you got to. Here's the deal, shake my hand, then don't wash it or anything, and don't shake anyone else's hand till you meet Duval Dixon. That way we'll exchange DNA, and then I'll get rich like him."

"I'm sure that'll work." Toby smiled and stuck out his hand and they shook. Waino broke out in a big grin.

"But Waino, you know that the DNA exchange will just go one way – from you to Dixon. He'll just become a dumb-ass Finn. It won't do anything for you."

Waino nodded. "Well, I'd rather be me anyway. What's he doing today? I'll bet whatever it is, it's nowhere near as nice as a paddle on Willapa Bay on a perfect day."

Toby paused for a moment.

"You, my friend, make a very good point," Toby said. "So good, that I just changed my mind. Let's see if we can make it around the island. I don't have to be up there until tomorrow. I'll just stay here tonight. Okay?"

"Cool, ya sure. Just stay here. But we gotta hurry to catch the tide."

Chapter 2

The Centers for Disease Control
Sunday, May 31st, 2020
Atlanta, Georgia

Dr. Laura Sundgren, a forty-year old epidemiology analyst at the Centers for Disease Control in Atlanta, received the same summons on the same day. Maxwell Stanton, the director of the influenza division at CDC, called her at home with the news. Duval Dixon had requested her presence at his latest clambake. She was to be ready to fly to Vancouver by noon the following day.

"Damn it Max, do I have to do this? I have my vacation coming up in a week." Laura said. "Can't you send someone else instead?"

"Sorry sweetheart," Max said. "Dixon wants you. Take a look."

Max dropped Dixon's vmail message in Laura's inbox. Laura brought it up on her screen. Duval Dixon appeared, charming as ever, telling Max to have Laura on the plane tomorrow. He insisted that she would enjoy the session even more than the last one, and that he would personally be in attendance for the entire six weeks.

Even in a short, one minute message, Laura could see that she had no choice. The man simply expected everyone to do whatever he asked. And everyone always did.

Four years earlier, Laura had been summoned to Dixon's conference center on Vancouver Island for a session on the potential of a "Chestnut Blight" virus that could destroy the human species. "Chestnut Blight" was a term that some used at CDC to describe a disease with a one hundred percent mortality rate.

In the early decades of the twentieth century a fungus, *cryphonectria parasitica*, had killed off all of the American chestnut trees, an estimated three billion of them, accounting for more than a quarter of the eastern woodlands. It was a chilling example *that it could happen*.

The scary thing about it, in Laura's view, was that those big trees didn't travel much: no airplane rides, no crowded restaurants, no coughing, no handshakes, and no sex. They just stayed in one place and minded their own business. But the isolation didn't help them. The parasite found them all, and killed them all.

Dixon's Chestnut Blight conference had been attended by epidemiologists from around the world. Laura remembered that it began with twenty-four. She had been the only CDC representative. The three Chinese had left soon after the description of the "game" that Dixon insisted the scientists would play. The Chinese felt that it wasn't professional. As it turned out, the game, all twenty-four days of it, proved to be a fascinating experience. Laura's team had won; she liked that part too.

This time at least, Duval Dixon would be there in person the whole time and Laura couldn't help but wonder what bizarre mind-twisters the enigmatic billionaire had up his sleeve for this gathering.

Later that day, Laura should have been packing or getting her apartment ready for her absence. Instead, she again pulled up the second vmail that Dixon had sent her - the one with the eleven bios of Dixon's next marks.

This was an all-star cast. Because of the length of time demanded by Dixon (six weeks uninterrupted) it had several folks who were once-removed from the roles that made them important; an ex-senator of the United States, a former ambassador from Russia, and the former Secretary General of the U.N. from Kenya.

But Laura was also impressed by the collection of current luminaries that Dixon somehow prevailed upon. She recognized the popular video evangelist Dick Darby, and Martha Cartman Brown, a Supreme Court justice, and one of three other women. There was a professor of theology from Viet Nam, and Dr. Sessions Mothershed, the ancient East Indian cosmologist. Laura remembered him as the host of the PBS series "Conundrums" that aired some ten years ago. She was surprised to learn he was still alive.

The other two women were Sofia Contreras, an epidemiologist from the European Union, whom Laura knew slightly, and, of all people, Wyndi Rehn, the well-past-her-prime, former country and pop diva.

Then there was one more person, unknown to Laura: Dr. Toby Benson, a mathematician. Benson was younger than the others and had a kind of geeky appeal to him. In the vmail at least, he looked to be tall, with thick tousled dark hair, intriguing old-soul eyes, and wiry thin - her favorite type.

And even though she had never heard of him, he seemed quite accomplished. In addition to his mathematics credentials, he had spent three years in India after the war. She looked forward to hearing what he might have to say about that horror.

Chapter 3

Monday, June 1st, 2020
Deep River Washington

Once again, Toby and Waino had been thwarted in their attempt to paddle all the way around Long Island. The paddle north from the national wildlife refuge station to the northern tip of the island was smooth and beautiful as ever. After rounding the tip, the wind came up out of the southwest and soon became too much to handle - they had to give up and pull ashore on the Long Beach peninsula.

This was their fifth or sixth attempt at circumnavigating the island. Each ended with the same result. But, as always, it was a good day. Toby really didn't want to make it all the way around. He and Waino needed that goal to always be out there, giving them a reason to spend the day together.

Their paths separated long ago, and kept diverging. Never was this more apparent than the next morning. Waino was heading out to wrestle logs, and Toby was about to set off for Vancouver to have drinks and dinner with Duval Dixon. He and Waino were both uncomfortable, both on edge.

Toby felt, and suspected that Waino also felt, that this might be a final parting. It was just that the world seemed to be heading that way, things running down, things ending. It was the dark and prevaling mood of the times.

"So, tell me, hotshot. I've been thinking about this deal you're going to, and I can't figure out why they need a geekster like you there?" Waino said.

"Well, I'm not exactly sure either. But it's about population issues and with all the work I did in India after the war, I guess they must need someone to work out some projections. You know that I've been working on trying to make my probability-tubes equations easier to use, so that other people can apply them.

"That's why CPS has been funding my vacation in Astoria. But I'm a shitty coder, so all the computer stuff is taking way too long. I guess I'm still the only person who can work the equations and the programs effectively."

"You should keep it that way - job security," said Waino.

Toby got up and put his coffee cup on the counter. "Okay buddy, I'd better go. Here's the key to the house - take a look at it every week or so. It will give you an excuse to spend some time in Astoria. And feel free to sleep there any time you get too drunk to drive back."

Waino got up, walked over to Toby and gave him a hug. "I don't like where this is going. This is a big-time crowd you're hanging out with now. Who knows what happens next?"

Waino walked him out to the car. Toby didn't want to drag this out, so he quickly got in the car and pulled away. He glanced in the rearview mirror. Waino wasn't smiling. Neither was he.

"Probability tubes" were Dr. Toby Benson's claim to a place in the mathematical pantheon. He created the concept at Princeton. It formed the basis of his doctoral thesis and even in its early and somewhat crude form, it created quite a stir. Toby's fundamental insight was that probability distributions were, in many cases, not smooth, as had always been assumed, but instead tended to gather around specific numbers. His equations were complicated and required considerable input data. The analysis required fast computers because the equations needed to be executed in multiple iterations, millions of times. As the process unfolded, the magic appeared. Certain values became emphasized, and the bell curve vanished.

Even now, even after his name was occasionally mentioned in the same sentence as the words "Field Prize", Toby still had many detractors. But at the beginning, almost no one accepted his premise. The breakthrough came with the now-famous study of Canada geese family sizes in his favorite wildlife refuge – Willapa Bay.

After the publication of his astounding results, the world of mathematics took great notice of Toby. Duval Dixon also took notice and had his population think tank, the Center for Population Studies, make Toby an offer too good to refuse.

Dixon wasn't interested in geese populations. He was interested in the human species, and when the Afternoon War between Pakistan and India erupted, there was no better place to study rapid depopulation, and the subsequent population relocation and recovery, than in India.

Soon after his hiring by CPS, Toby was dispatched to Hell - the ravaged, radioactive, post-nuclear dead zone of the 2013 "Afternoon War" between India and Pakistan. Toby spent three years there, gathering the information necessary to run his equations by visiting the hospitals, the makeshift morgues, the food distribution points, the devastated cities and rural farmlands. He witnessed suffering on an unimaginable scale.

In theory, Toby was on loan from CPS to the provisional government of India, but due to their overwhelming difficulties, the government paid little attention to him. His probability tubes process was one of many predictors used to try to assess survival rates among the radiation-exposed survivors.

These predictions were necessary in order to project food and medical needs. But since the world health officials were not among the small handful of people who understood, or had even heard of probability tubes, his work and his projections were largely ignored, except by CPS, and Duval Dixon.

The war itself lasted only two hours - on the afternoon of September 30, 2013. More than three hundred million people were killed that afternoon. Another one hundred million perished over the next five years from starvation, cancer, and other diseases that swept through the weakened survivors.

Pakistan had fired first, after a series of statistically inexplicable technical failures, miscalculations, and bad judgments, had led the wrong person to think that Pakistan was under attack. The proximity of the two long-standing enemies meant that India had only a five-minute window in which to fire back, or else be annihilated. On the afternoon of September 30, 2013, many people made many wrong choices.

Ninety percent of the damage was on the Indian sub-continent, most of it in the south. Southern India still remained uninhabitable. India would never recover, and the rest of the world would continue to suffer the consequences of the overdose of radiation that swept the globe.

Like so many others involved in the massive relief efforts, Toby's health had been at risk. He had been given the best possible preventive measures, the best testing, and the best treatments available to mitigate his exposure to the high levels of radiation. He continued to undergo extensive testing every six months for the various cancers that might take hold. So far, all tests had been negative, but there would be no little Bensons in Toby's life. He was likely infertile, the result of a low sperm count.

There was, however, one positive aspect to Toby's experiences in India. He now knew more about human population dynamics than he did about geese. This knowledge, coupled with the continuing refinement of his equations, put him in a category by himself when it came to modeling the future population of the human species.

Recently though, Toby had questioned the value of that skill. CPS continued to put money in his bank account every month, but had not contacted him in over a year. He was beginning to wonder if his human population expertise was really anything important or useful. He was even considering returning to Princeton, if they would take him, to get back to basic research.

That was until the "Holy shit" moment the previous morning, when Duval Dixon finally demanded the presence of the expert that he had so patiently created.

Chapter 4

Monday night, June 1st, 2020
Vancouver, British Columbia, Canada

Toby pulled up under the massive wrought-iron canopy of the Oriental Hotel in Vancouver, British Columbia at 6:30 pm. The uneventful drive north from Deep River marred only by a tedious two hour delay at the border crossing. He tipped the valet and helped the bellhops with his suitcases, then turned to head into the hotel and was confronted by a stunning blond woman standing on the curb, arms folded, and flashing the most charming dimpled smile that Toby had ever seen.

"Dr. Benson, I presume," Laura said, extending her hand as he approached.

"You must be Dr. Sundgren," Toby said, paying extra attention to the handshake. He hoped to strike that perfect balance between strength and sensitivity. He thought it went well.

"Let's be done with the 'doctor' crap, Okay? Please call me Laura," she said, still smiling. "Shall we?" She turned and waited for Toby to walk with her.

Inside, they were surprised to see many of their fellow attendees sitting in the lobby. Toby was awestruck as Manute Solene, the recently retired Secretary General of the United Nations, approached.

"Ah, Doctors Sundgren and Benson, so nice to see you. I didn't know you were acquainted."

"Only for about thirty seconds," Laura said. "It is a great honor to meet you, Mr. Secretary."

"The honor is mine Dr. Sundgren," Solene said. "And Dr. Benson, it is a pleasure to meet you. I was very interested to read about your work in India. Someday soon I would like to hear of your experiences there."

Toby wanted to say: "And I would like to hear about your great work around the world over these last thirty years". Instead, he could only muster a mumbled "Thank you."

"Excuse me, but before you meet the other distinguished guests, I'm afraid we have a problem," Solene said. "We don't seem to be in the correct locale, or perhaps we are here at the wrong time. You see, we can't locate Mr. Dixon. There is no record of a reception here and no reservations for any of us at the hotel. We have tried to reach Mr. Dixon through his office, but to no avail. In fact, they have no knowledge of this conference, which seems very odd as Mr. Dixon was supposed to be here with us for six weeks," Solene said in a rush, out of breath.

It took Laura only a moment - then the light went on.

"Secretary Solene, I think I might know what's going on," Laura said. "I was at a conference hosted by Mr. Dixon four years ago. I've seen this before from him. Let's just say he amuses himself sometimes by being - how shall I put it – prankish?"

"Prankish?" Toby asked, and looked deservedly confused.

"Yes, prankish, as in he likes to fuck with people." Laura blushed and glanced at Solene. "Oops, sorry…"

"No need to apologize. I am familiar with that construct," Solene said and smiled. "And yes, you are correct, I have seen that side of Mr. Dixon."

"I have a copy of the vmail on my PDA," Laura said. "Maybe he misdirected us."

Laura retrieved her PDA and the three of them huddled together in order to see the small screen. She located the section with the directions and they watched the thirty seconds of Duval Dixon telling them where to go.

"It seems that we are at the correct location. He clearly said 'the Hotel Oriental'." The Secretary shook his head and clasped his hands behind his back.

"Actually, Mr. Dixon said 'oriental hotel', not 'Hotel Oriental'," Toby said, a little sheepishly. "Maybe 'oriental' is an adjective and not a noun."

"But he also gave the address as Pacific Avenue, and that is where we are," the Secretary said.

Laura waved for the concierge to come over.

"Is there another oriental hotel on Pacific Avenue?" Laura asked the concierge.

"In a way, yes," the concierge said. "The Fuji has just opened two blocks from here."

Laura nodded and gave Solene a knowing smile.

"Can you get the events coordinator at the Fuji on the line for me?" Laura asked the concierge.

It only took a moment for the concierge to return, with a cell in hand.

"This is Mr. Hachiya, events coordinator at the Fuji," the concierge said, handing the phone to Laura.

"Mr. Hachiya, my name is Dr. Sundgren and I'm with some folks over at the Oriental Hotel. We have a problem. We are supposed to be attending a reception hosted by Duval Dixon and we thought it was going to be held here, but that seems not to be the case. You don't happen to have an event tonight reserved by Mr. Dixon do you?"

"I'm sorry Dr. Sundgren, but I would most certainly know if Mr. Dixon was hosting anything at our hotel. I'm sorry, but it is not here." Mr. Hachiya sounded disappointed to give her the news.

"Okay, well, let me ask you one more thing. How many events are you hosting tonight?"

"We have four of our reception rooms in use - three anniversaries and a Bar Mitzvah."

"A Bar Mitzvah?" Laura looked at Toby and the secretary with a grin. "Would you be so kind as to tell me the name on the Bar Mitzvah?"

"Yes, it is posted as the Fujimora Bar Mitzvah."

"Do you host Japanese Bar Mitzvah's often?"

"To my knowledge, I believe this is the first one," Mr. Hachiya said, now sounding a little unsettled.

"Would it be possible for you to connect me with that room?"

"That would not be a problem Dr. Sundgren, and please call me back if I can be of any further assistance. Here is the Starlight Room now."

"Well hello there, who am I speaking to?" Laura immediately recognized the exuberant voice of Duval Dixon.

"This is Dr. Sundgren, Mr. Dixon."

"MacPherson, I win!" Dixon shouted to someone in the room with him. "He's an idiot - I took you, and gave him the field," Dixon said quietly to Laura.

"Well, I have an unfair advantage. I've seen you in action."

"Indeed you have, Dr. Sundgren, indeed you have. Well then, let's get this show on the road. Put the concierge on the line, will you?"

Within minutes, three limos pulled up in front of the Hotel. As the rest of the group piled into the limos, Toby leaned in and said, "I've had a long drive. It's only a few blocks - I think I'll stretch my legs and walk. I'll see you all in a few minutes."

Laura leaned in after him, "Me too," she said.

"So - hope you don't mind if I join you for the walk?"

"No, not at all. If fact, maybe you can answer some questions for me. This whole thing is way out of my league," Toby said, pausing a moment to collect his thoughts. "I just met Manute Solene, and I'm about to meet Duval Dixon. This is pretty heady stuff for a guy like me."

"I'm sure that there is a very good reason for your being here. Dixon may appear to be screwing around, but I expect that everything he does is completely calculated."

"Okay, then what the hell does that hotel trick mean?" Toby asked.

"Good question, and I don't really know. I suppose the simple answer is that it amuses him. My personal opinion though, and perhaps an even simpler answer, is that he does it because he can. I mean, who the hell else in the world could get away with pulling that stunt, on those people?"

"Seriously? Because he can? That gives him a wide open playing field, doesn't it? I mean, what can't he do?" Toby asked.

"Not much. And after this start, I think we are in for an extraordinary six weeks. Be ready, anything might happen."

They crossed the street and walked the last half block in silence.

"This is it, let's head on up," said Laura, flashing the hypnotic dimpled smile. "I haven't been to a good Japanese Bar Mitzvah in weeks."

Laura and Toby entered the Starlight Room together. Dixon spotted them and immediately broke off his conversation with Zelco Rabinovich, a former Russian ambassador to the United States.

"Dr. Sundgren, what an absolute pleasure it is to see you again!" Dixon gave Laura an enthusiastic handshake, held it for a moment, then leaned in with a conspiratorial smile and said, "You didn't tell the folks about our little bet, I hope. I just told the group that we changed hotels for security reasons. They seemed to buy it."

Dixon took a step back. "Damn, you are a good looking woman," he said. After a moment he broke off his admiring gaze at Laura and turned to Toby.

"Dr. Benson, I have been looking forward, for more years than you can possibly imagine, to getting to know you. Thank you for coming. I'm sure you won't be disappointed. I see you have already met Dr. Sundgren. Good. We'll talk later, but now that everyone is here I have some announcements to make to the group. Please excuse me."

Dixon ambled to the front of the room. Toby was overwhelmed, for the second time, by the man's extraordinary presence.

Duval Dixon's reign as the world's richest person began twelve years earlier when his company, Switch.Net, became a de-facto telecom monopoly. Dixon started the company in the mid-nineties after a distinguished career in the networking field. Much of his professional life, before starting Switch.Net, was spent at MCI in Dallas, where he was considered the data networking industry's high priest. This lofty status was reinforced by his easy Texas charm and legendary public speaking ability.

His reputation for "fucking with people", as Dr. Sundgren described it, began in those last years at MCI, spent mostly on the speaking circuit. In several of his late trade show keynote addresses he would propose elaborate, and very strange, future directions for the industry, only to conclude by saying something like, "I was just putting you all on. I really don't have a clue where we are headed." Which was also a lie. In those years (the early nineties) he had, in fact, a very clear idea where the industry was going.

Dixon knew that IP (short for Internet Protocol) was going to dominate networking for the foreseeable future. MCI had attempted to establish a propriety email system within their own network, but it became obvious to Dixon that email required ubiquity. The public Internet provided that, and IP was what made the Internet work. Dixon only needed to figure out how to horn in on what, he assumed, would be the staggering growth of networks using IP. However, the Internet had been built by the government and was a public facility, essentially free to all - a hard price to beat. This was a problem. But soon, the staggering growth of the Internet that Dixon had so accurately predicted provided the opportunity he had been looking for.

Switch.Net's business plan was to build a shadow network based on the same IP that ran the public Internet. But Switch.Net's network would be a better mousetrap. Congestion delays, packet loss, and security issues all were becoming part of the internet explosion of the late nineties. Switch.Net solved those problems by building a separate network, separate switching facilities, and by creating their own router software to run the whole thing. It was a slow process, and many times looked as though it would fail. But eventually, by 2010, the market capitulated to the need for the speed and reliability that Switch.Net provided. The other Internet, the public one, continued to exist, but in the world of corporate networking, Switch.Net dominated.

Predictably, Dixon became bored with running his monster. He left the company in 2012 and began selling off large chunks of his stock. Like others before him, he gave away hundreds of millions of dollars to charity. And after the war in India, that became billions, as he supported a good share of that devastated nation's massive recovery needs.

Dixon's current passion was biotech. Unlike the computer technology industry, where monopolies thrived, biotech remained a cottage industry. Small companies, with a tight focus on a specific area, were the norm. Dixon was reputed to own somewhere around thirty of these small labs, each working separately on some new drug or treatment. Most of these businesses were based in India, funded by Dixon to help with the country's difficult economic recovery. And it didn't hurt that many of the world's top biotech scientists were Indian.

Dixon never married, had no family and, to the best of anyone's knowledge, never had a serious relationship with a woman. Some speculated that with so much money, he could never trust any woman's intentions. But that did not account for the first fifty years of his life, before he became obscenely wealthy. It just appeared that Duval Dixon operated on a different plane, one on which love wasn't important.

After Toby's first brief encounter that night with Dixon, he was struck by what so many others had said about the man. Duval Dixon had a strong resemblance to his namesake, the old cowboy actor. Not as much in appearance, though that was certainly there, but he had many of the same mannerisms; the hand gestures, the head tilting, even the cadence of speech.

Toby was a fan of old movies, especially during these last three years in Astoria. He had seen many of the cowboy actor's classics. Toby didn't know if he was a Texan, but he played one in many of his roles, and a very charming one at that. Not a bad way for Dixon to get a compelling personality Toby thought - simply hijack one from the movies.

Dixon moved to the front of the room, clapped his hands once, and held them above his head momentarily.

"I have some bad news," he began. "Now I know that you're all exhausted from traveling and would like nothing more than to have a couple of smart cocktails and head up to your respective rooms. But, sorry to say, your rooms aren't here. Shortly, we will be ducking back into those limos, and we will go down to the inner harbor to board our float planes for the trip over to the island. I must, again, cite security concerns as the culprit. This is a very, *very* distinguished group that I am now responsible for." Dixon paused, looked around the room, and smiled. "Anyway… it's for our safety. So grab something to eat, get a drink or two, and remember to hit the head - the float planes don't have one."

"I am overdue for my evening sacrament," Solene said as he approached Toby at the drink table.

The Honorable Manute Solene put his hand on Toby's shoulder and studied the bourbon selection. "Toby," Solene said. "What's your pleasure?"

"I think I'll just have some water, Mr. Secretary … sir," Toby said.

"You're on your own for that," Solene said. "And please, call me Manny."

"Sir, I'm sorry, but I don't think I can call you 'Manny'," Toby said. "I spent three years in India after the war and I know what a great man, a hero, you are to the people of India and to those of us who saw the suffering first hand."

"Thank you Toby. I appreciate the kind words, but I was anything but a hero. The real hero is our Mr. Dixon," Solene nodded in Dixon's direction. "Of the little that was done to help India, Dixon did the most. He is my hero."

Manute Solene had been Secretary General for only six years, a short time when compared to some of his predecessors, but those six years were perhaps the most difficult ones that any person in his position ever presided over. Terrorism in all forms (religious conflict, tribal genocide, economic backlash) escalated in frequency and intensity during those years. But Solene's, and the United Nations', greatest trial, perhaps even mankind's greatest trial, had been the Afternoon War of 2013. With a death toll approaching half a billion, it accounted for more deaths than all of the conflicts in the long terrible history of mankind's wars combined.

Solene had convened the General Assembly of the United Nations a week after the war. He delivered what many consider to be one of the greatest speeches ever made to that body. A stirring call to action, it was "a watershed opportunity for the international community to come together to support the victims," he said. "It was the moment to once, *and for all time*, free mankind from the terrible burden of nuclear weapons."

The debates, the speeches, the agendas, the prejudices, and in many cases, the disgusting insensitivity and simple stupidity of the members of the United Nations assembly filled the media screens for days, then weeks, and finally months. In the end - they did nothing. It was left up to private organizations, with some help from the World Health Organization, and Duval Dixon (the largest single contributor to the relief effort), to save what they could of India.

The "watershed opportunity" was lost. The reputation, power, and influence of the U.N. was forever compromised. Solene remained as Secretary General for several years afterward, doing what he could to secure private contributions for the relief efforts. Still, he considered himself a failure.

"Ah, Dr. Sundgren," Solene said to Laura as she approached the bar table. "May I make you a drink? And please call me Manny from now on. May I call you Laura?"

"Yes Manny, you may."

"This is going to be a very interesting few weeks. Quite a cast Dixon has assembled," Solene said.

"What do you think he is up to?" Laura asked.

"I thought it had to do with population issues. That's what he told me," Toby answered.

"Does this look like a group that would spend six weeks discussing population problems?" Solene said, waving his hand vaguely in the direction of their fellow attendees.

"No, that doesn't make sense to me either," said Toby. "But why else would I be here? Why am I included in this group?"

"I don't know, Toby, but I'm sure there is a reason. Laura, do you have any ideas?"

"I don't, and I'm not going to waste much time trying to figure it out. I was at one of Dixon's gatherings before, a few years ago. A group of epidemiologists, like myself, from around the world. We expected one thing, and got something quite different. Even so, it was a great experience and I'm curious to see what he has in store for this group." Laura said. "But now, I think we should go meet the others. Come with me Toby, we'll do this together."

Toby stepped back and shot a curious, but intense look at Laura.

"What?" Laura asked. She could see that something she had said had jolted him.

Toby shook it off and relaxed. "Nothing, sorry."

Laura paused for a moment trying to figure out what it was she had said, then shrugged and flashed her stunning smile, gently grabbed him by the arm and led him to the buffet.

Chapter 5

Early morning, June 2nd, 2020
Vancouver, British Columbia

Dixon called it a Twin Otter. It was the biggest float plane Toby had ever seen. Two of the over-sized, twin-engine float planes were brought up to the dock, although it appeared that the entire group could have fit in one. Dixon said two would be safer, and that as it would be a long flight; the planes needed to weigh less to conserve fuel.

It all made sense to Toby except the long flight comment. Toby sailed in these waters often. His parents had been avid sailors and owned a nifty little 32 ft. Island Packet sailboat that they moored in Anacortes, Washington. Toby still had the boat, named the "Gull", and still kept it in Anacortes. Since his return to the Northwest, Toby spent many fine weeks sailing aimlessly about in the waters surrounding Vancouver Island.

Anacortes was directly across from the San Juan Islands. From Anacortes you could simply hang a right and sail up the Georgia Strait to the inside passage around the east side of Vancouver Island, or go left and sail out the Juan de Fuca Strait and then around the ocean side of the massive island. A sailboat could take several days to get to the west side of the Island, but Toby knew that a plane flying from the city of Vancouver (which was not on Vancouver Island, but across the Georgia Strait on the mainland) directly over the middle of the island, should be able to reach almost anywhere on the west side of the island in about an hour, so no "long flight" would be necessary.

Zelco Rabinovich nodded at Toby as he eased into the seat next to him. He and Toby hit it off at the reception. Rabinovich was the starting point guard on the 1992 and 1996 Russian Olympic basketball teams, facing slightly better competition than Toby had at Deep River High School. Nonetheless, basketball was a bond and a safe conversation starter. Rabinovich was thirty-four at the time he played in his last Olympics, and a national hero, mostly because he didn't leave Mother Russia to play in the NBA like so many others had done. He had parlayed that good will into a successful political career.

Rabinovich was a likeable man; well-spoken and modest, with an easy smile. He left the United Nations at the same time as Solene, and Toby suspected it was for the same reasons: disgust with its inability to do anything for India. For the last five years, he had been working for a think-tank in Washington D.C.. Toby hoped for a bit of conversation with Zelco, but the plane was too noisy. Instead, he pulled out his PDA and reviewed the bios of the people that he just met.

Wyndi Rehn was interesting. She had been a star country and pop singer for many years, but her voice wasn't good enough to keep her on the charts as the years wore away at her once spectacular looks. As Toby read from the bio, she was about the same age as Laura, but in person, she looked ten years older. Wyndi was currently a vice chairperson for PETA, the animal rights group, and their chief public spokesperson. But even with the PETA connection, Toby still couldn't figure how she was connected to population issues.

The Reverend Richard Darby was shorter and smaller than Toby had pictured. On TV, Darby appeared to be the size of an NFL offensive lineman. In a brief conversation with the Reverend, Toby got the uneasy impression that Darby didn't want to be at this event.

Martha Cartman Brown, the Supreme Court Justice, was a total cliché - slight, tight, and boring.

Tony Nguyen, the Vietnamese theology professor, was a surprise. Toby spoke to him at the buffet table, and learned that Nguyen was Vietnamese in ancestry only. He was born and raised in Minneapolis, received his doctorate from the Harvard Divinity School, and he even spoke with a slight Minnesota accent. He had returned to teach at Augsburg College, near the University of Minnesota, where he was a leading voice in the One Faith movement.

The One-Faither's were attempting to find the spiritual equivalent of what physicists had been searching for since the 1930's: a "unified field" theory. Similar to the physicists' attempts to unify the seemingly incompatible four forces of physics, the One Faith movement was attempting to unify all of the incompatible beliefs of the world under a comprehensive, one-size-fits-all religion. How great would that be, Toby thought, and wished them success, though he knew it was futile.

Sofia Contreras, the other epidemiologist, had gotten a lot of Laura's time at the reception. She was slightly older than Laura, in her early fifties, but well preserved, with smooth dark southern European skin. Also like Laura, she had an aura of confidence and professionalism about her.

Toby had met Dr. Sessions Mothershed before, briefly, in India. Dr. Mothershed was a small, and now at age eighty-five, stooped native of Delhi, with a PhD in theoretical physics from Oxford. Ten years earlier, after a distinguished career in cosmology, he became famous as the host of a TV series called "Conundrums". The series tried to explain, in "advanced" layman's terms, a few of the controversies that were bringing the world of cosmology and particle physics to a state of ultimate confusion. Toby had closely followed the three shows that were dedicated to the unraveling of String Theory.

Last was the retired senator from Washington, Ben Mallory. Mallory was one of Toby's heroes. In his two terms in the Senate he was an uncompromising voice for the environmental movement. Now he was a director of the Nature Conservancy, a group that Toby often fantasized about working for. Toby only got to shake Mallory's hand and say how much he admired him, to which the Senator replied, "Thank You," and quickly turned back to the animated conversation he was having with Wyndi Rehn.

Toby counted them up, twelve in all, including Dixon. The variety, fame and the accomplishments of the group reminded Toby of those old English murder mysteries. Toby put away the PDA, reclined in his seat, closed his eyes, and imagined the possibilities. Sleep came within minutes.

Hours later, Toby was jolted awake. He looked out the window to see that the plane was now bouncing lightly along the water. The big Otter slowed and settled down into the light chop. A few minutes later they were tied up at a dock.

As the second plane approached, Toby walked to the end of the dock, stretched, and tried to wake up. He could see that they were on a protected sound, with three or four tall islands surrounding the large body of water they had just landed on. It seemed deserted. The only lights he could see were from the compound where they were docked.

This didn't look to him like the west coast of Vancouver Island. Even Barkley Sound, the biggest protected water on the west side, didn't have islands this tall. This place looked more like the inside passage of southeast Alaska.

The second plane landed, docked, and emptied. The four pilots were joined by two other men from the lodge. The two men, both of East Indian decent, were a perfect "Mutt and Jeff" pair, Toby thought. The tall one stood casually and wore standard western clothes, but the shorter, unusually heavy one wore a traditional white robe and an old-style Nehru cap that Toby had occasionally seen in India on those who wanted to be known as important.

Dixon waved, and assembled the group around the pile of luggage. "My apologies to all of you for the long day. I see it's a bit after midnight Pacific Daylight Time, and just now getting dark. We are quite far north," Dixon paused for a moment, letting the sleep addled group get focused on what he was saying. "If any of you stayed awake during the flight, and I don't think anyone in my plane did, you may have noted that the flight took almost three hours."

Dixon paused again, smiled, and looked around at the group.

"Dr. Benson, you are well acquainted with this part of the world, are you not?" Dixon asked.

"Yes, I guess so," Toby replied, surprised to be called upon.

"So ... Dr. Benson, what say you?"

"Well," Toby said. He straightened up a bit and looked at the now curious group, "I'd say that this is not the west coast of Vancouver Island. The islands are too big, and the flight took too long. Most likely we are in southeast Alaska, somewhere in the inside passage."

"Good deductions," Dixon replied. "But wrong conclusion. We are in Haida Gwaii - the Queen Charlotte Islands."

Toby's eyes widened. He had always wanted to go to the Queen Charlottes some day, but they were so hard to get to. Now he was here. This incredible day just kept getting better.

"Probably most of you know little, or nothing at all about this part of the world, " Dixon continued. "Tomorrow, we will have a geography lesson and some history too. I am certain that you will find it interesting. But, enough said about that for now."

Dixon walked over to where the four pilots and the two other men were standing.

"Tomorrow, when we can see and think better, we'll do proper introductions. But for now, let me just say this," Dixon said, gesturing toward the pilots. "These four gentlemen will be with us for the duration of our meetings. In addition to being skilled pilots, they will serve as captain and crew of the two fine fishing boats you see tied up on the other side of the dock. They are also our security team. Believe me when I say that they have the training, the knowledge, and the technology to deal with most anything that could come our way," Dixon said, stepping past the pilots.

"And these two young men," Dixon said and put his hand on the shoulder of the short Indian, "who have been here for several weeks now, are our researchers. We have set up a very comprehensive digital library here at the compound. If any questions of fact come up during our discussions, and I suspect they will, these men will get us the answers."

Dixon stepped back to the middle of the group. "Oh, about Mr. Patel, and Mr. Jain," Dixon waved his arm back towards the two researchers. "They are not our 'household staff'. By that, I mean that for cleaning, cooking, fetching, and all the rest of it, we are, I fear, on our own. There is no staff here. We will figure all that out tomorrow as well.

"One last thing, and then we can go get some sleep. This was a fishing resort when I acquired it some time ago. The accommodations are not plush, but I think you will be comfortable enough. You can see behind me that it is on four levels. Can everyone see?" Dixon looked over the group to see if they were paying attention, then turned to face the buildings on shore.

"There is a boathouse at water level at the end of the dock. Two of the pilots will be sleep there. Next, up the hill about a hundred feet, is the main lodge. That is where we will eat, drink, and hold our discussions. On the next level up, directly above the main lodge, you should be able to make out three cabins. That is where you all will sleep. Each has a sitting room with a fireplace, four small bedrooms and a bathroom. Then, if you look above and off to the left a bit, you will see a single, larger cabin. I will sleep there, with our two researchers, and the other two pilots.

"Since I forgot to bring the Harry Potter sorting hat, you will have to figure out who stays where on your own," Dixon said, then turned to face the group again. "Are there any questions that cannot wait until tomorrow?" He paused for only a nanosecond. "Good - our security team will lead you up the hill; they have the flashlights. You must grab your own luggage. One more thing: we will convene tomorrow once everyone is awake, so sleep in as long as you like. See you all in the morning."

Dixon waved one hand in the air, grabbed his small bag, and headed up the dock.

The group spoke little as they groped around for their luggage, but by the time they reached the cabins, the sorting hat was unnecessary. The two men of God, Reverend Darby and Professor Nguyen, and Dr. Mothershed chose to room together in the first cabin. The four women, naturally, ended up together in cabin two. That left Toby with Secretary Solene, Ambassador Rabinovich, and Senator Mallory. If there were to be competitions among the cabins, as at scout camp, Toby liked cabin three's chances.

Toby entered the cabin first and turned on the lights. The front room was classic fishing lodge, circa 1945. Two overstuffed chairs of undetermined age, a couch, and two end tables with fishing-motif lamps, were all arranged around a low table facing the stone fireplace. On the other side of the room sat an oval table and six chairs, with a cabinet along the back wall, containing playing cards, poker chips, puzzles and games. Above the cabinet was a large bookcase filled with leftover paperbacks from decades of visitors. The front wall had solid-paned windows, looking out on a spacious, covered porch, and then North over the water.

The hallway to the bedrooms split the back wall of the sitting room. There were two bedrooms on the right, one bedroom and a bathroom on the left, and a bigger bedroom in the back. The big bedroom in the back had a door to the outside. The other three bedrooms had only a window, and were quite small.

Ben Mallory entered the cabin last, headed straight down the hallway inspecting the bedrooms, returned to the front room and informed his cabin mates that he would take the back bedroom, muttering something about his prostate and having to pee a lot. Toby thought instead that it was because the Senator was hoping for heavy weather to blow in, perhaps some "Wyndi Rehn".

Toby took the room next to the bathroom, stowed his luggage, and walked back to the front room.

After Solene had discovered the liquor cabinet, and Toby had lit a fire, the four men of cabin three assembled around the fireplace. The topic of discussion became fishing. All four of the cabin mates were experienced fisherman, and like all dedicated fisherman, they had stories to tell. Toby could do little but grin, listening to these distinguished men swap fishing stories, with their feet up in front of a warm fire, sipping 20 year-old scotch. It just kept getting better and better.

In cabin two, the four women were also gathered around the stone fireplace. Laura, in her Georgia Tech t-shirt and sweats, was seated on the couch with Sofia Contreras, who had on pajamas under a heavy quilted robe, as she wasn't used to the chill of the far northwest. Wyndi Rehn, seated on the fireplace hearth, was also prepared for the chill, wearing a hooded sweatshirt with a picture of Dave Mathews on it, over sweatpants and a turtleneck. Justice Brown entered the room last, wearing a stunning black and red silk, high-buttoned Chinese evening set.

"Justice Brown, that is gorgeous! You put us to shame," Laura said.

"Thank you, I bought it in China last year, and this is the first time I've worn it. I thought this might be the kind of event where someone, other than me, might see me in my nightclothes," Justice Brown said, in her usual serious manner. "But please call me Martha. I suggest first names all around from this point on," Martha said, sitting down in the chair to the left of the fireplace. "Well, I expect Duval has something very interesting planned for this group."

"Duval?" Laura said, "You sound like you know him."

"I do," Martha said plainly. She paused for a moment. "I have known him for a long time, since the eighties when I was working as a lawyer for MCI in the telecommunications area. AT&T had just been broken-up by Judge Green. There was a lot of law to be decided in that area at the time. It was my first job out of law school, and I was very fortunate to have stumbled into such a dynamic industry.

"Duval was the head of strategic planning for the data communications division of MCI. I was assigned to his group. It was non-stop," she said and paused, searching for the right description, "excitement, hard work, mayhem. I'm not sure how to describe it. Duval convinced us we were on a quest, you know - 'inventing a new industry'. He was right, of course." Martha looked away, a bit wistfully, Laura thought.

"Wow, you actually know him," Laura said, amazed. "So tell us some things. What do you know about his youth, parents, etc.? There isn't much available about him on the Net."

"I don't know much, probably the same things you have found out. He was born and raised on a ranch outside Dallas, only child. His parents were strict Methodists. He was home-schooled, left home at fifteen and worked his way through the University of Texas, getting a degree in electrical engineering. After he left home, I don't think he ever spoke to his parents again. I have no idea what happened to them. He went to work for EDS after college, then MCI some years later. And, the rest," Martha paused, "is history."

"What about that blogger rumor from a few years ago?" Laura asked. "You know what I mean, don't you?"

Martha paused, trying to decide how much she should disclose. The strange events of the last few hours had somewhat unnerved her and she was concerned that she not unnecessarily alarm the others. But she concluded, as always, that full disclosure would be the simplest approach and continued with the story, as she knew it, of Duval Dixon.

"Yes I know the rumor," Martha said and took in a deep breath, exhaled slowly and leaned back in her chair. "In fact, I'm one of the few who actually read the blog before it disappeared."

"Do you guys know the story?" Laura asked, glancing at Wyndi and Sofia. They shook their heads "no".

"Five or six years ago, maybe more," Martha began, concentrating now on trying to remember the details. "Yes, it was five. Anyway, a blogger did some digging into Duval's past. The blogger claimed to have found a neighbor who knew Duval's parents - or to be more precise – knew the people who Duval claimed were his parents."

"Okay, yeah I remember that now," Wyndi said. "Whatever happened with that? I don't remember hearing how that came out?"

"Well, nothing happened," Martha continued. "The blogger claimed that the neighbor knew the couple, and that the neighbor also knew that they never had any children, even though the blogger did find a birth certificate at the county seat. The couple had both died, so the alleged neighbor was the only source. Then, the blog just disappeared. And nothing more has surfaced since."

"Probably Dixon's lawyers threatened to sue," Wyndi said.

"No, I don't think so," Martha said. "If it were adversarial, it would have stayed in the news. More likely, Duval just bought him off."

"Or worse," Wyndi said.

With nowhere to go from there, the group went quiet for several moments.

Sofia broke the tension. "What was he like then, when he was a regular person? Did he date?" she asked, changing the topic to a lighter note.

"No, he was too driven," Martha said. "But we worked very closely," she said, again trailing off.

"And?" Sofia leaned forward, anticipating what might come next.

"Well," Martha said slowly, "What the hell? This isn't a complete secret, several members of the media are well aware of this. I expect they have been holding back all these years waiting for the right moment to use it. Duval and I had a brief, how shall I say it … tryst."

Eyes widened all around. There was, to Laura's knowledge, no one who had ever been publicly identified as having been a lover of Duval Dixon.

After an awkward silence, no one knowing how to continue with the questioning, Martha spoke again.

"But I'm sorry to say, I won't be able to shed much light on the inscrutable Mr. Dixon," Martha said, looking down, feet together on the floor, leaning forward with her elbows on her knees. "We only trysted … a few times," she said. "Four, to be exact."

Martha stared at the floor for a moment. The other women waited silently, knowing more was to come.

"It was on one of the many trips we had to take to Washington DC, where MCI was headquartered. We were in DC for a week. And that's where it all took place. It was 1984. I was 28, and Duval was, I think, 35. My God, I can't believe it's been 36 years."

"Duval and I were working hard at trying to understand every nuance, subtlety, and possible unintended consequence of Judge Harold Green's consent decree which broke up AT&T's monopoly. Duval was a very focused man, and for many years, that is what I attributed his abrupt 'cessation of trysting' to."

Martha paused, took a sip from her drink and continued. "But, my view now, after watching his success over the years, is that it goes beyond an intense focus on his work. Duval would not allow himself to become personally involved with anyone. I'm not sure how to describe his relationships, because he is kind and generous to the people he knows. He has many friends. But, he has a way of being a friend, and still staying above the relationship. He operates always, on the big picture, on a distant and higher plane."

"So then, how would you explain the game playing, the manipulations, the little tricks he plays on people," Laura asked. "I know I didn't describe that exactly right. What he does isn't really describable, but you know what I mean, don't you?"

"Yes, I do know what you mean."

"Like this change of plans tonight," Laura interrupted, before Martha could go on. "Do you think 'security concerns' were the real reason?"

"Probably not," Martha answered. "Though I imagine we will find out sometime soon. And, like many of Duval's manipulations, there is always a portion of reasonableness in his after-the-fact explanations. What was that phrase the Nixon people used during Watergate?" Martha thought for a few seconds, getting no help from her younger companions.

"'Plausible deniability', that was it," Martha said, smiling at having remembered. "He always has plausible deniability."

"Sometimes he does these things to push people, help them think in new ways, sometimes to reward them," Martha continued. "And, I think, sometimes he does these things for his own amusement. In the end, the victims, though that's probably not the right term, often seem to feel positive about what he did to them.

"But he can be ruthless, even scary, when operating in his own best interest, working toward some major goal." Martha leaned back in her chair. "I'm getting a little carried away here, I should stop."

"No, no, not at all, please tell us more. It's beginning to feel as though something very unusual is afoot. Whatever you can say about Dixon might help us," Sofia said.

"Yes Sofia, I agree with you," Martha said. "This is quite a gathering that Duval has assembled here, even by his standards. And the isolation he has created in the last few hours, I mean, how could anyone besides us know where we are?" she asked.

"I tried my cell, it doesn't work here," Wyndi said.

"My point exactly," Martha said. "But, now I am done. It is late and I am tired," Martha said, standing up. Soon after, cabin two retired for the night.

In cabin one, Reverend Darby sat up for a long while, not bothering to light the fire, drinking alone.

Chapter 6

Tuesday, June 2nd, 2020
Haida Gwaii – The Queen Charlotte Islands

Toby woke before his cabin mates, took a quick shower, and stepped out onto the porch of cabin three just as the first rays of the sun warmed the hilltops of the tall islands to the west. Toby rubbed his eyes and gave himself a brief face massage in preparation for the thrill of finally seeing the Queen Charlottes in the daylight.

He leaned into the porch rail and took in the sweep of water and green islands that had been waiting all night for him to witness and appreciate. Only two mornings ago, before his life had changed lanes, he had been enjoying a view of similar scale and with the same elements of water and steep green hills – the view from the porch of his Astoria house. But that was in the civilized world. This was different. This was in the Queen Charlottes Islands, one of the most beautiful yet unknown and consequently unspoiled regions of North America. It was as spectacular as he imagined.

The three cabins and the main lodge faced northeast, looking out on a protected sound. It looked to Toby that there were three or four large islands ringing the sound, perhaps a mile or two away, but it could be more, he knew that distances over open water were hard to judge. The islands were steep, tall, and uniformly green. There were no signs of civilization anywhere that he could see, not even scars from past logging operations.

There appeared to be a convention of bald eagles on the rocky outcropping that guarded the right side of the long dock. Dozens of the great birds perched on spruce limbs and dozens more swooped down to the shoreline where others were tearing apart a large fish. In the bay and around the dock groups of ducks kept a wary eye on the noisy proceedings.

Toby squinted, concentrating on some movement along the far shoreline of the island across the sound directly to the north. He watched intently for a moment, then smiled when he recognized the arching rhythm and the holstein coloring of a pod of Orcas working their way along the shore. They were heading west, toward a passage that Toby presumed led to the open ocean.

The mystical moment was interrupted by activity down at the dock. The two big float planes on the left side of the dock were now facing toward open water. The pilots had been working early this morning to get them turned around. They were just now tying them up to the dock. Toby hadn't heard the noisy engines being fired up, so they must have roped them around, not an easy task.

A quick glance at the boathouse told Toby that the tide was out. The boathouse was built on pilings, about fifteen feet above the current water line. The shore was rocky and steep. Most of the islands of the northwest were like this - tall, steep, and dropping straight into water. Beaches were rare. Getting to the dock from the boathouse required walking down a long ramp that changed its degree of incline based on the tides. The dock itself floated. At low tide, the ramp was steep, and at high tide it was almost flat. The ramp was steep now.

Toby knew that the tides in this part of the world ran from about twelve to fifteen feet, taking a little less than six hours to go from low to high, and vice versa. Those big tides moved an immense amount of water in and out, four times a day. In confined spaces like the narrow passages between these big islands, the currents were very strong. Toby had sailed in places, especially in the inside passage on the northern half of Vancouver Island, where the currents were so fast that when you were in them it was like being on a whitewater rafting trip.

This was dangerous water, and cold. Toby knew there would be no swimming parties at this event. Anyone who had the misfortune of ending up in the water here would become crab bait in no more than a few minutes.

He headed down the path to the main lodge. Coffee would be good, and he was looking forward to seeing where the group would be spending much of their time over the next six weeks.

"Good Morning" Toby said, as he entered the lodge and spotted one of the pilots at the kitchen counter making coffee.

"Hi, good timing, the coffee is ready. Cups are over here," the pilot pointed to his left.

"Toby Benson," Toby said, extending his hand. "We didn't meet officially last night. I think you were the pilot on my plane."

"Good to meet you Dr. Benson. My name is Mark ... Mark Dunn."

"Is anybody else up and around yet?"

"I haven't seen anyone except us worker bees. We had to get the planes turned around. It saves about half an hour if we need to leave in a hurry. And now we're getting the boats ready. It looks like it's going to be a great day to get out on the water."

Toby grabbed a cup, and poured some coffee.

"Make yourself at home. I need to get back down to the dock. Mr. Dixon said we will head out to do some fishing at about two this afternoon," Dunn said walking toward the door. "See you later."

Toby looked around. The main lodge was a classic - one large open room, with a long kitchen counter all along the east wall. Parallel to the kitchen counter was a long eating counter at bar-stool height, with a dozen or so stools. Opposite, the west wall featured the requisite massive stone fireplace. Mid-room, and in front of the fireplace, a dozen or so overstuffed chairs and sofas were spread out in various configurations.

The lodge walls were the original three inch, ribbed tongue and groove boards, laid horizontally. They had aged to a dark coffee brown. Toby guessed the place dated from the nineteen-forties, and had changed little since it was built. The walls were covered with fishing photos - pictures of happy men, holding up huge salmon. Toby had never seen salmon that big.

One man, who must have been the original owner, was in many of the pictures. Toby didn't recognize him, but he saw several people that he did recognize. In one, Hemingway was standing next to the apparent owner - both men sporting giant grins with cigars sticking out of them, while each held up one of those mammoth salmon. In the back corner, there were even some pictures with Duval Dixon in them.

Toby looked closely at the picture of Dixon. Wasn't that Solene in the background standing by the boat? It had to be him, he was hard to miss. Toby realized that he hadn't asked the Secretary what he had been doing these last few years, since he left the U.N. He would now. And during the fish tale swapping last night, why hadn't Solene mentioned that he had been here before? Senator Mallory had done most of the talking, so perhaps he hadn't wanted to get into it then. Still, it seemed odd.

No one else had come down to the main lodge yet, so Toby grabbed another cup of coffee, and headed outside to explore. He looked at the rocky point to the left, on the west shore of the cove and decided it wouldn't take him long to scramble over it and see what the big bay on the other side looked like. Maybe there was a beach, and up in this wilderness, that would mean seals and eagles.

When Toby got back to the main lodge an hour later, almost everyone was up and milling about the kitchen. Only Reverend Darby was missing. The kitchen was a mess, the coffee was gone, and someone had burned something that looked like it might have been eggs. Toby could see that this group was going to have trouble at meal time.

He stood by the front door, mustered his courage, and addressed the group in a loud voice. "Hey everyone. I have an idea about how we can handle this food thing."

Dixon, seated by the front window, looked up from his coffee, a little surprised at Toby's bold attempt to lead this distinguished group. Although, in the midst of the mess they had just created, they didn't seem quite so distinguished.

"We used to do this when we had a group sailing, and it worked great. It's really very simple. We have four cabins, so we take turns. Each day one cabin is responsible for everything, and I mean everything, having to do with food and drink. They make each meal, serve each meal, clean up each meal, make snacks, hors d'oeuvres, make drinks, serve drinks – everything. So, every fourth day, in this case, you work hard. But the other three days you get excellent service. And, it always works out that the teams get competitive and make some terrific meals," Toby finished, now a little embarrassed by his outburst.

Several people nodded, several others looked at Dixon for approval. And the four women of cabin two applauded. Everyone knew what that was about.

Laura was the first to speak.

"Moved, seconded and approved!" Laura said, nodding at Toby.

"Hey, wait just a minute there," said Reverend Darby, who had just stepped in a few seconds before Toby made his suggestion. "I don't think our cabin can do this."

"Reverend Darby," Professor Nguyen said, "I would enjoy the 'competition', as Dr. Benson described it. Cooking is my hobby, my passion. If you can chop without hurting yourself, we will do just fine," Nguyen said.

"And I worked, when at Oxford many years ago, very many indeed, as a busboy. I am considered quite talented with a dishtowel," Professor Mothershed added.

"Well, in that case, and since I do know my way around a well stocked bar, it seems that I spoke too soon," Darby replied, and gave Toby a slap of approval on the back.

"Okay, great," Toby said. "Let's go in order. Our cabin will do today, including cleaning up this mess … and making more coffee. Cabin two, tomorrow, and after that we will experience the culinary artistry of Professor Nguyen." Toby smiled and gave the professor a nod. "Then Mr. Dixon and the security team."

Toby looked over at Dixon.

"Is that ok? Will they be able to do this?" Toby asked.

"I'm sure they will be happy to, even relieved. Like some others in this room, they were worried that it might fall entirely in their lap," Dixon replied, inwardly pleased to see that Toby could hold his own in that group.

Dixon drank the last of his coffee and stood up. "Good, thank you Dr. Benson, I'm glad we have that settled. This was beginning to look a little worrisome," he said and waved toward the kitchen.

"Here is how I'd like to see the day progress," Dixon said looking at Solene now. "Lunch is to be ready at 12:30. But not too heavy, we will be going out fishing in the afternoon."

"Yes sir," Solene said, saluting.

"Thank you Cookie," Dixon said. "So, this afternoon, I propose fishing in two groups. The real pros can go out in the small boat and troll for salmon. This isn't a very good time of year, but you may luck upon a spring Chinook. You'll have some fun then. The rest of us will go in the larger boat. We have a place we go to where we drop anchor and jig for halibut. I do suggest that everyone here goes fishing. This is a rare day, sunshine and light breezes. We will probably enjoy this high pressure for a few more days. But the rains will return; this time of year can be very cool and wet.

"Right after lunch I'd like to tell everyone about this exquisite fishing lodge, so I only have to do it once. As for now, you have a few hours to look around and get ready for our fishing trip," Dixon said and shuffled around, getting ready to launch into another subject.

"We will start our discussions, the serious ones, directly after dinner. Tonight they will be brief. And, lastly, you may have noticed that your cells don't work here. We also do not have access to the net, so no vmail, or even email for that matter. We will discuss what that means after dinner. I think that's it," Dixon concluded, leaving no opportunity for questions.

Most of the group went down to the dock to inspect the fishing fleet. Doctors Contreras and Sundgren remained in the lodge looking over the fishing photographs that lined the walls.

Toby joined them. "That's the actor, Sterling Hayden," he said. "He was in a lot of movies in the forties and fifties, and some in the sixties."

"Aren't you a little young to remember him?" Sofia asked.

"I've been watching old movies lately, since I got back from India. I like them because there is so little in them that reminds me of the world today. Simple plots, good folks, happy endings. It's a good escape for a few hours."

"Lucky for you that you have a few hours to escape," Laura said. "I can't remember the last time I saw any movie, old or new."

"You should get out more," Toby said.

"Yes I should, and thank you for that perceptive suggestion."

"You're welcome," Toby said with a smile, and walked away several steps.

"Look over here." Toby directed them a few feet down the row of photographs.

"Hemingway stayed right here, in this lodge. I'll bet he got drunk sitting on one of those very stools," Toby said, waving toward the bar.

"How about that," Laura said, inspecting Hemingway. "You know, this lodge does have a kind of strange energy. Maybe Hemingway's ghost will join us for a drink some night."

"I think ghosts hang out where they died," Toby said. "Hemingway shot himself in Idaho."

"Well then," Laura said, and returned her gaze to Hemingway's picture. "We better find out from Dixon who *has* died up here."

During lunch, the security forces and the researchers were busy setting up the main seating area for the meeting. They had placed a small desk, with one chair, under the front windows to the right of the fireplace. A longer desk was placed along the back wall, facing out toward the front of the lodge. Two chairs were behind the desk, and two keyboards and screens were set on the desk. Obviously, the researchers would sit there, in that relatively dark and out of the way corner. A large flat panel screen was hung on the wall just to the left of the fireplace.

After lunch, with everyone seated, Dixon stepped to the fireplace. He clasped his hands, looking at the group, and flashed the co-opted crinkled-eyed cowboy actor smile.

"Good," he said and paused for a few more seconds, making eye contact with everyone, capturing his audience. He is really good at this, Toby thought.

"This is how we will be set up for our real discussions, starting tomorrow," Dixon began. "Mr. Patel, and Mr. Jain, will be seated as you see them. Those funny-looking devices they are wearing are sound-deadening headgear. When they speak to their machines, you will not be able to hear them. Say something Mr. Jain," Dixon instructed the researcher.

Mr. Jain's lips moved, but a quiet muffled hiss was all that could be heard.

"Cool, isn't it," Dixon smiled, and turned toward the front windows.

"I have this little desk over here by the window. Low tech, as you can see. I need the notebook (gesturing at the thick, three ring notebook on the desk) to remember things. Age will have its way." Dixon paused, then walked over to his desk and sat side-saddle on the corner.

"So now, I've got a little slide show to show you. I feel a little like a nineteenth century schoolmarm in a one-room school house standing up here. All I need is a switch, to swat you with so you don't fall asleep," Dixon said, to some quiet laughter.

"Actually, I could use a pointy thing for the slide show. Mark, see what you can find," Dixon said to the security man who had slipped in and was now standing behind the bar.

Mark stepped outside, went around to the south side of the lodge, and returned within seconds, fishing rod in hand.

"How perfect is that?" Dixon smiled, taking the rod from Dunn.

"Thank you, Mark. Did everyone meet all the pilots this morning?" Dixon asked.

"Good," he said, hearing no objections.

"Okay, first screen," Dixon walked over to the flat panel. "This is the west coast of Canada. And these are the Queen Charlotte Islands or, more accurately, Haida Gwaii. You can see that Haida Gwaii is considerably north of, and farther out to sea than Vancouver Island. Here is the city of Vancouver. Now you know why the flight took so long." Dixon paused, and the next screen appeared, a bigger map of the Queen Charlotte Islands.

Dixon turned back to the group. "Haida Gwaii is the ancestral home of the remarkable Haida nation. It is said that at the peak of their civilization - and as with most Native American peoples, the peak being that time just before we brought them the gift of smallpox," Dixon paused. "Anyway, at the peak there were as many as thirty thousand Haida living in these islands. After our generous 'gift', that number was reduced to only a few hundred. All because we coveted otter skins, and the Haida coveted iron.

"There are some good books on that early history over there on the bookshelf. I recommend 'Raven's Cry', if you can handle the sad truth."

The fishing pole aimed back to the map. "Here is where the lodge is," Dixon pointed to the southern section of the islands. "As you can see, we are in a National Park Reserve called Gwaii Haanas. And amazingly, these are the only buildings in this vast reserve. It's quite a story of how this came to be – you can ask me about it later, if you are interested."

"Gwaii Haanas," Dixon said as he walked over to the window and waved his pole in the direction of the water. "It is as pristine and beautiful a place as you will find anywhere on the coast of North America. One Haida story claims that this is the place where the first human being emerged. So ... Gwaii Haanas is the Haida Garden of Eden. And well it should be."

Dixon stared blankly out to the sound for several long moments. "Ironic to be sure …" he said softly.

To Toby, it felt like Dixon spoke that last bit to himself; he might not even have known that he had said it out loud.

Dixon composed himself, walked back and faced the group. "Now, about the lodge itself. I purchased this island from a man named Bucky Webster. Bucky ran this place as a fishing lodge for many years. And as you can see," Dixon said, pointing his fishing pole at the photographs on the wall. "He hosted a number of famous and wealthy people over the years.

"Unfortunately, since becoming the owner, I have failed to be as good a host as dear old Bucky. Though you can see our own Mr. Secretary General Solene, standing on the dock in the background of one of those photographs on the wall … you'll have to look close. Manny was up here five years ago, I believe."

"It was four," Manny corrected.

"Four, that's right, it was after you resigned from the U.N.," Dixon said. "It was a recruiting trip really. I signed Manny up to be on several of my boards. And we had the first discussions that eventually led to the formation of 'WorldView', the organization that Manny heads up now, and where he spends most of his considerable energies. We also caught some damn fine fish that trip. Tales of which I'm sure Manny has already shared with his cabin mates."

"Well no," Solene said. "We did discuss fishing last night. But I wanted the Senator to finish with his lies first, so I would know how far I had to go to top him," Solene said with a smile, nodding at Senator Mallory. "But I neglected to properly consider that Mr. Mallory was in fact a Senator. I'm afraid now that it may be several days before he concludes his remarks."

Another mystery quashed, Toby thought.

Dixon walked to the window and looked out, and up at the sky. "You know, this is too perfect a day. I think I'll skip the rest of what I intended to say. Let's go fish," Dixon waved his fishing rod like a saber, and pointed it to the front door. "Grab your hats; it's bright out there."

Professor Nguyen, Rabinovich, Mallory, and Solene chose to take a chance on finding a trophy salmon, hoping to be immortalized on the lodge wall. The women stuck together, not being fisher-persons. They were more intrigued by the thought of hauling up a hundred pounds of halibut. Dixon decided to work his charm with the women. Toby volunteered to be the 'cookie' on the halibut boat, though he was really planning on choosing whichever boat Dr. Sundgren boarded.

Dr. Mothershed begged off, claiming he could not swim. The Reverend Darby said he did not feel well, and needed to lie down. Toby was surprised that Dixon said nothing when they excused themselves. He expected that Dixon would somehow charm or shame them into coming. Toby concluded that one reason Dixon always seemed to win was that he knew how to pick his battles.

The calm winds and relatively flat water allowed the pilots (now sea captains) aboard the "V. Cerf", the larger of the two boats, to put full throttle to the powerful twin diesels. In a matter of minutes they had crossed the sound to a shallow shelf in front of a crescent-shaped beach. They anchored in twenty feet of water and, after Dixon had showed them the simple art of jigging for halibut, they all began to whoop and holler as they raised one after another of those ugly flat creatures into the boat. The hours passed quickly until the pilots announced that they had enough fish aboard.

"Sometime soon I'd like to hear more about your time in India," Laura said, as she slumped down next to Toby, exhausted after hauling up an astounding amount of halibut. "That is … if it's something that you don't mind talking about."

"I as well," said Dixon, who somehow managed to be standing right next to Toby without his noticing. "In fact, I think that we may have some time this afternoon for a chat. What time is your cabin planning for dinner?"

"We hadn't discussed it yet; probably sometime around seven."

"Make it later. My remarks will be short tonight, and I'd prefer it if everyone was tired."

"Okay, but I don't think tired will be a problem. I'm there already," Toby said. "We'll make it eight then. It may take a while to bake up the Halibut anyway. I've got a decent family recipe I hope to use."

"Good. I'd like the two of you to wander up to my cabin at five, or a little after. That'll give you time to get cleaned up. Not that I don't find your strong scent of fish alluring, Dr. Sundgren. It's just that it works best on a boat," Dixon said.

Laura was already seated on the porch of cabin four, Dixon's high roost, when Toby arrived.

"Just in time Toby. We're having a Tom Collins. Long on refreshment, very short on alcohol. Some of us still have work to do tonight," Dixon said. "I'll make you one ... be back in a jiffy."

"Thanks, that sounds good," Toby said, walking past Laura to a comfortable-looking wicker chair. "You do smell better," he muttered, not looking at her.

Laura stuck out her foot, attempting to trip him.

After jumping to avoid the outstretched limb, Toby thought that maybe this flirting stuff wasn't so hard after all. It seemed to him that his junior high repertoire might still work. Next time he had the chance, he planned to push her down.

Dixon returned and sat down across from his two guests.

"Cheers," Dixon said, to no one in particular, while looking out over the sound. "Great view, don't you think?"

He turned back to Toby.

"Toby, as I told you on the cell the other day, I do know some things about your work, and about you, because of CPS," Dixon said, then turned to Laura.

"CPS stands for the Center for Population Studies, Dr. Sundgren. Toby has been employed by that group for the last six years. The first three were in India, and the last three on an open-ended grant that allowed him to continue working on his probability theories in Astoria, Oregon. What Dr. Benson didn't know until two days ago, was that I was the primary - well, sole funding agent for CPS." Dixon paused for a sip of his drink. "Manny Solene is also on the board of CPS, so he too is aware of Toby's work."

"Secretary Solene ... really? This is all pretty amazing," Toby said. "You won't believe this, but you and Manny are the first people I've ever seen in person with a direct connection to CPS. I've never met another person who works for the center."

"Well, I might as well come clean," Dixon said, turning on the charm. "There is a very logical explanation for that."

"What's that?"

"You haven't met any other people from the Center because there aren't any. You are the only employee."

Toby could not think of what to say. He looked out over the sound, wondering what the hell could that possibly mean. No other employees? He'd been working directly for Manute Solene, the former Secretary of the United Nations, and for Duval Dixon for the last six years, and he didn't even know it? Why?

"Toby, there is nothing sinister here," Dixon said. "I just took an interest in your theories after the goose thing. You know that the goose study even made it into the popular press. Anyway, I felt that your theories had tremendous potential in the area of human population studies, and I was correct. India was simply an opportunity for you to be in a real situation to expand your work, and your knowledge."

Toby shook his head as if to remove some cobwebs. "Well, thanks, I guess, for helping me. But, to be honest, I'm more confused then ever about why I'm here," Toby said, looking at Dixon and hoping for some explanation.

"I can imagine," Dixon said. "Some day, before this is over, I truly do want to talk about your experiences in India ... but it probably won't be anytime soon. I really had a different agenda in mind when I asked you two up here," Dixon smiled and looked over at Laura. "Are you surprised, Dr. Sundgren?"

"Well, yes. You continue to surprise, even when it's expected," Laura said.

"I'll take that as a compliment," Dixon said, lifting his glass to Laura.

"The reason I asked you both up here is that I want to give you a heads-up about tonight. You two are a little different from the rest of the group, at least in my view. I can predict the reaction from the rest. But I'm concerned about you two," Dixon said, then stood up and walked to the railing, leaning over it and looking out to the sound.

Laura glanced over at Toby and shrugged her shoulders, baffled as ever.

Dixon turned around and faced them, suddenly serious.

"So, I give you these brief words of advice - don't overreact to what you hear tonight. Eventually, things will get clearer," he paused. "I said 'clearer'," Dixon added with sudden intensity. "Not easier. What we will be about these next few weeks will be very hard. I ask you to just stay with me. Okay?"

"Sure, okay," Toby said, not knowing what he was agreeing to.

Laura nodded as well.

"Good. Now drink up. Finish the Collins. Lots of good vitamin C," Dixon said, more of an order than a request.

In silence, they walked down the path from Dixon's cabin. Toby completely forgot about his plan to push Laura down.

Solene helped Toby prepare the Benson family halibut recipe, baked with lime and a cheese sauce. Outside on the porch, Senator Mallory was holding court with Professor Nguyen, Wyndi Rehn and Sofia Contreras. The others, Toby presumed, were still getting cleaned up, or, more likely, catching a quick nap.

"How's the Reverend doing? Is he feeling better?" Toby asked Solene.

"You didn't hear?"

"Hear what?"

"Mothershed asked Sofia to come up and look in on him as soon as we docked. After a brief examination of the Reverend, and of the evidence - that being an empty bottle of Jack Daniels - Sofia concluded he had drunk himself into a stupor and had passed out. We managed to get him up and into bed. There was another empty bottle in the trash, so he must have done the same thing last night," Solene said, shaking his head.

"Holy cow," Toby said. "Poor guy. You know, I didn't think he looked very good from the beginning. But that kind of drinking goes beyond being an alcoholic. It's self destructive," Toby said.

"I agree," Solene said. "He's clearly not a well man."

The halibut dish received high praise. Reverend Darby appeared part way through the dinner. He had showered, shaved, and changed into clean clothes. Although Toby saw this as a good sign, it was only momentary.

Darby grabbed a plate of food and promptly poured a large glass of whiskey from the bar. Round three was underway.

Thirty minutes later, the twelve participants, the four pilots and the two researchers had been fed, and were now finding a spot to sit. This time the pilots were staying with the group. One had taken a dining table chair and put it in the corner behind Dixon's desk, another one sat in one of the overstuffed chairs, directly in front of Dixon's desk. The other two were sitting at the bar in the back, behind everyone.

Toby had noticed something else. They were armed. They all wore cardigan sweaters, and a bulge, obviously a holstered gun, was visible below the shoulder. The rest of the group took notice as well, as they all silently found places to sit.

Dixon stood up and surveyed the group for what was, under the circumstances, a very long time. The Texas charm was nowhere to be found. His expression was deadly serious.

"So," he paused. "Now it begins."

Toby had the distinct impression that Dixon was again speaking to himself.

Dixon took a few steps to the right, and looked down at the floor.

"First, let's deal with the absolutes, the non-negotiable items," Dixon said and gestured towards the pilot seated by his desk. "From now on, the security team will be present at all of our proceedings. In fact, some of them will always - and I mean always - be with me."

Dixon paused and stared down at the group with an even greater intensity. "To protect me," he paused again, and made a sweeping gesture around the room, "from you."

Dixon watched the startled group, a slight smile emerging. "You see, as these proceedings progress, some of you may decide that I need to be killed. The too-bad-Hitler-wasn't-assassinated strategy. I understand why you will feel this way, but don't try it. These men are trained, dedicated professionals. They have been informed about what is going to occur here, and they are in agreement with my goals for this session. They will not hesitate to kill you, should you make even the slightest threatening move."

The room held its collective breath, stunned into silence as Dixon again stared them down.

"Please believe me about this. I don't want anyone to get hurt. And I believe that eventually you will see that killing me would be a mistake. This is not because I hold my own life in such high regard. I've lived a long, eventful, fortunate life. I'm seventy-one years old. I will die soon anyway.

"Instead, it is because we have the most important task imaginable in front of us, and I know that I am the only person on Earth who can accomplish the goal. Now, don't become pop psychologists here. When I say that *only I* can accomplish this … I say it because it is true."

Senator Mallory Stood up and angrily shouted, "What the hell do you think you are doing? You can't threaten me! Look around this room. Do you understand who you are talking to? What the hell is this? Have you gone completely insane?"

The security man directly in front of Dixon moved quickly to Mallory, another from the back of the room moved up behind him. Both put their hands on Mallory, firmly forcing him back into his chair.

"No, I assure you I am not insane Senator, but if you will be quiet and listen to the rest of my remarks, I think you will have a better understanding," Dixon said, gesturing to the security people to return to their seats.

"Let me finish the security issues. None of you is carrying a weapon; we checked your luggage. The knives will be counted and locked up after every meal. I won't be eating with you. But don't worry. Cabin four will take its turn fixing meals. Just don't give the security team any silly orders.

"Occasionally, I will ask one of you, or some of you, to come up to the porch at cabin four to talk with me privately, but that will be the only contact that I will have with you, except for the proceedings themselves.

"Now, as to your participation in these proceedings … it is required. You have no choice in that matter. You will remain here until the proceedings are completed. I know that you have all blocked out six weeks for this event. I think it will be over sooner - a small consolation. You already know that your cells do not work here and that we have no access to the net. There is simply no way for you to contact the outside world.

"All of your administrative assistants, or closest associates, have been contacted, under your name, and told that you will be unable to contact them, and they should not attempt to contact you, except in cases of extreme emergency," Dixon's intense gaze swept the room looking for a complaint and saw none.

"If someone has an emergency, we will figure out a way to deal with it. But, it has to be dire. Sickness, even death, doesn't qualify. Perhaps if Washington D.C. was destroyed, and Justice Brown was needed to assume the presidency ... even then ..." Dixon's voice trailed off. "I think you understand.

"Now – perhaps our little adventure getting here becomes clearer. The only folks who know our true location are still here with us. Certainly if the FBI got busy, they would probably find us in short order, but there is no reason now for anyone to look that hard.

"The island itself is completely isolated and there is nowhere to walk to. Don't try to go over the top. There is only a maintenance facility on the other side. First, it is very unlikely you could find it. And if you did, remember, the people there work for me. They have been instructed to disable their boats - as our two boats at the dock will be when not in use," Dixon paused, thinking.

"I guess that does it for security stuff. If I've missed anything, it is because I forgot to mention it, not because we didn't think of it. But you get the idea. You are here until we finish. You have no choice."

"Now, when we do finish, you will be free to go. We will fly you back to Vancouver, and that will be that," Dixon said, hands on hips, looking straight at the Senator. "You may do what ever you want at that time. You will be free to have me arrested, contact the press, write a book, contact the FBI, CIA, AARP ... whatever you want." Dixon said, exhaling dramatically.

"I am betting, however, that when the time comes, and you are back at home, that none of you will do any of those things," Dixon said, smiling for the first time.

"Now, having heard that, many of you are thinking that the security stuff is unnecessary, and that it is just another game - another Duval Dixon manipulation to get your attention," Dixon said, switching deftly back to his high intensity persona. "And, again, I assure you that it is not. I guarantee that you will discuss killing me. You will be absolutely committed to going to the authorities, right till the end.

"The battle, my battle, will be won or lost in those last few hours before you leave. And – you have my assurance on this - the outcome will be completely in your hands."

Dixon continued standing, breathing hard. He surveyed the group, trying to get a feel for what they were thinking. Then he exhaled slowly and seemed to relax a bit.

"Take a short break everyone, just don't leave the building. I have one more thing to discuss," Dixon said, and walked out to the porch to get some air. Two of the security people followed.

Toby felt dizzy. He stood up, closed his eyes, and took a few deep breaths.

"Here, have some water Toby. You look a little shook up."

Toby opened his eyes. Solene was standing next to him, a bottle of water in hand.

"Thanks," Toby said. "I don't know what to say. I'm beginning to wonder if my friend Waino slipped me a pouch of mushrooms a couple of days ago, and all this is just going on inside my mind."

"Duval certainly knows how to 'fuck' with people, as the lovely Dr. Sundgren so accurately put it," Solene said. "My advice is to just settle down, try to relax. It will eventually sort itself out, it always does. Well, perhaps I should amend that … it always has," Solene concluded.

It took only a few minutes for the stunned group to reassemble. The Reverend Darby remained seated, pouring the last of the Jack Daniels bottle into his glass. That makes three full bottles in less then twenty-four hours, Toby thought. This man is in deep trouble.

Dixon walked back to the fireplace, flanked by the gunmen in cardigans.

Suddenly, from the back of the room: *"You are a conjuror, an agent of Satan!"* the Reverend Darby boomed from his seat, startling everyone. "And you are not so smart. I know what's going on here and I will not allow it," the Reverend continued to roar, as he had done so many times from the pulpit. "In your foolish heathen ways, you have missed your only real danger. You may control this earth, but God has no master! I will summon him, and he will answer … *and you will be destroyed*! Try to stop that with your armed devils in sweaters!!"

With that crescendo, the Reverend finished, now looking somewhat dazed. He drained his glass, which was still half full, closed his eyes, leaned back, and slipped into a stupor.

Can this get any weirder, Toby asked himself. Just remember to breath, relax, and stay focused. Do what Solene said.

Dixon looked at the security people, to make sure they weren't getting jumpy. He knew he had put everyone on edge, including his well trained security team. After all, he had ordered them to shoot a Supreme Court Justice, or the former Secretary of the U.N., should it prove necessary.

"My apologies for Reverend Darby - who now seems to be napping," Dixon said. "I was unaware of his drinking problem. Just leave him in the chair for now. He can sleep for a while. We will deal with him by tomorrow."

Dixon motioned for the security men to sit back down.

"Well, that didn't take long did it? The first attempt on my life," Dixon said, not smiling. "The Reverend has called upon his God to smite me. And so soon, we haven't even started yet." Dixon said, shaking his head. "And who knows, it might work; I don't discount his chances ..." Dixon trailed off, clearly troubled about the Reverend's outburst.

"You know what," Dixon finally continued. "I can do the rest tomorrow. I've already said the important stuff, and I think the last thing that I was going to say tonight will have a better impact on rested people. I'm tired, and I'm guessing you are too," Dixon paused, and stared the group down for the last time that night.

"Again, I ask, be patient, you will come to understand soon. And, I would advise you against 'speculation'. You have no chance. Good night," Dixon said unceremoniously, and walked out the door with two of his bodyguards in tow.

Laura rose from her chair and walked over to Toby, who was standing with his eyes closed, trying to restart normal breathing.

"Come with me," she said. "Walk me out to the dock."

"Can we do that?" Toby asked.

"I'm pretty sure that he said we weren't allowed to escape, and we weren't allowed to kill him. He didn't say anything about walking on the dock," Laura said in her best smartass tone. She took Toby's arm and led him out the door and down the walkway. They walked to the end of the dock, each wondering if somehow Dixon could hear everything they were saying.

When they reached the end of the dock Laura turned to Toby, her arms tightly folded in front of her.

"Look, as much as I told myself to expect anything, I didn't expect this. It wasn't what he said - though that was horrifying enough. It was how he said it, how he handled himself. And that outburst from Darby, and how Dixon reacted to it. He actually looked scared. And did you hear what he said about dealing with Darby by tomorrow? How the hell is he going to do that? Kill him?" Laura said in a rush, upset.

Toby didn't reply. He didn't know where to start.

They stood on the end of dock, not speaking, just looking out on the sound. Even at this late hour, the long evening rays of the northern sun were still shining on the tops of the islands.

"This is such a beautiful spot," Toby finally said. "I have a sailboat in Washington … in Anacortes, just across from the San Juan Islands. Do you know anything about the San Juans?"

At first Laura was upset that Toby had abruptly changed the topic. But then she realized that Toby was just trying to get her to settle down a bit, and knew that it would be a good idea.

"I've been there, actually," Laura said, still looking out at the water. "We had a conference in Seattle, and a bunch of us went up to Friday Harbor for the weekend. The ferry ride through the islands was the highlight. It started from Anacortes as I recall."

"That's right - Anacortes," Toby said. "I've sailed all around this part of the world - the San Juans, the gulf islands, the west coast of Vancouver Island, but I never got up here, to the Queen Charlottes," Toby said. "It was just too much open water to cross with my little sailboat."

"Well, at least that's something positive about this event. You made it to the Queen Charlottes," Laura said.

"I guess that's right," Toby said, and smiled.

"You should smile more," Laura said, turning toward Toby.

"I'd like to," Toby said, his face returning to its more normal intense look.

Laura took his hand, held it and then blessed him with that heart-stopping smile. Toby could only grin back at her.

"There you go - that wasn't half bad," Laura said, letting go of his hand and briefly touching him on the mouth with her finger. "Okay then, let's get back."

They turned and walked back up the dock.

From the front window of cabin four, shaded from view by the deep porch, Dixon watched the exchange at the end of the dock, and broke into a little smile of his own.

Chapter 7

Early June, 2020
Malabar Research Farm
Central Oregon

"What *is* this place? What's going on here?" Jan shouted out over the postcard-perfect pastures that fell away in layers to the west below her hillside cottage. She sighed at the silent response, leaned on the porch rail and tried again to find a context for the bizarre reality she had uncovered only hours ago.

No living parents? What could that possibly mean? But the dots wouldn't connect, and this time it frightened her.

Not just frightening, this was also wildly unexpected. Only four months earlier, Dr. Jan Burnside Watson had fled the chaos of New York City to accept the position of resident physician at Malabar Farm, a new agricultural research facility built in the foothills of Oregon's Cascade Mountains. She thought she had found tranquility there, in the idyllic remoteness of rural Oregon. It had all seemed so perfect then. A bit too perfect, she now knew.

Jan turned away from the rail and contemplated what to do next. She knew she had to tell Professor Vanderham, the director at Malabar Farm, though it wouldn't be easy. She had been down that road before and it hadn't ended well. But this time it can't be explained away, she told herself. This time it's not me.

She checked her watch - almost five. It was a two mile walk to Vanderham's office - she had to hurry if she wanted to catch him.

Twenty minutes later, Jan arrived at the administration building and stood outside long enough to attempt, with only moderate success, to calm down. She found Director Vanderham and Doc Seifert, the other physician on staff at Malabar, in the director's office chatting casually.

"Good - both of you are here," she said, bursting into the office. "I know we've discussed this before, and I know what you're going to say, but this time it's just *too* weird."

"Again?" asked Professor Vanderham.

The former Dean of the agronomy school at Oregon State University and now the head person at Malabar Farm, Gil "Vandy" Vanderham untangled his long legs and stood up, in what seemed like a dozen unrelated movements, to get Jan a chair. At close range Vanderham's height always startled her. The five foot two inch doctor felt no more than waist high to the six foot ten inch Vanderham.

Vanderham glanced up at the clock on the wall. "Hold the 'too weird' discussion for a minute, Jan. As part of my leadership responsibilities, I'm required to get to know our new young scientists. It says so right here on my calendar: 'After 5pm - mingling at MacDonald's Pub'. I fully expect the two of you to participate as well."

"Perfect," said Jan. "Good, that's perfect. I can prove this to you first hand. I have to go over to the infirmary and get my laptop. I'll meet you there in five minutes."

"Hey Abe, how's the war going?" Maggie MacDonald asked, as Vanderham and Doc Seifert walked into MacDonald's Pub.

Even without the signature beard, Vanderham's gangly walk, booming voice and craggy features, often put people in mind of the original Mr. Lincoln. Maggie MacDonald had been calling Vanderham "Abe" since she had opened up the Pub two years ago. To his great relief, no one else had picked up on it.

"I think the South's going to win it," Vandy said.

"No way, I read the book and you're gonna win. But this time you're gonna live too," MacDonald said.

Vandy smiled at MacDonald's little prophecy. "I hope you're right."

"Damn straight I am. Wanna wear the hat tonight?" Maggie asked. She had found an old stovepipe hat at an antique shop several years ago and kept it on display behind the bar for the sole purpose of annoying Vanderham.

"I'm never wearing that hat," Vanderham said, for the two hundredth time. "Bring us each a Guinness and a glass of that wine that Dr. Jan drinks."

Vanderham looked over the room and was pleased to see that many of the young scientists had discovered MacDonald's. The place was packed. Though it was a quieter crowd than the recently departed construction workers, there was a good solid buzz in the room. Vandy and Doc Seifert found a table in the back just as Jan walked in.

"Good crowd here tonight," Vandy said as she sat down. "I don't know how all these folks could have gotten to know each other if we didn't have MacDonald's Pub – definitely one of my best ideas."

"It wasn't your idea. It was hers," said Jan.

"Yes, but I had to approve it."

"Like you were going to say no?"

"A legitimate point," Vandy concluded as Maggie approached with the drinks.

"Cheers!" He held up his glass. "Here's to finally getting this show on the road."

They all took a drink.

"Okay then Jan, what's your latest conspiracy?"

"In a minute. First, let me ask you something. Professor Vanderham, are your parents still alive?"

"No, Dad had a heart attack and Mom got cancer, many years ago now."

"Doctor Seifert – yours?"

"Also no, both died from cancer."

"Let me add that mine are gone as well. My dad was killed in Iraq and Mom had a stroke," said Jan.

"So what's your point?" asked Seifert. "We're old, our parents are gone, it happens to everyone."

"I'll get to it in a moment. I think we should meet some of the new student scientists first," said Jan as she opened her laptop.

She stood up and waved at MacDonald, who was standing by the bar. "Maggie, could you come over here?"

Vanderham and Doc Seifert looked at each other and shrugged.

"Maggie, we want to meet some of the new folks. Could you do us a favor and pick out a person and ask them to come over here to chat with us? And when they leave, just grab another person at random and send them over until we ask you to stop?" asked Dr. Jan.

"I can handle that," said Maggie.

Maggie's first recruit approached the table. "Hi, I'm Kirby. The waitress said you wanted to speak to me."

Seifert and Vanderham stood up to greet the young man.

"Kirby, I didn't get your last name, could you spell it for me?" asked Jan, after all the introductions had been made.

"Zeigler: Z-E-I-G-L-E-R"

"Thanks," she said, returning her attention to her laptop.

Vandy decided to lighten the mood a bit, as Kirby looked a little worried. "Kirby, what's your field?" he asked.

Jan let the small talk go on for a few minutes and then at a pause in the conversation asked, "Kirby, I'm looking at your medical admissions form. You say here that your emergency contact is a friend from college, is that right?"

"I think I put down Joel Hansen. He was my college roommate."

"Can I ask why you didn't use your parents?"

"Unfortunately, they are both gone - I mean deceased."

Vandy and Seifert looked first at each other, and then at Jan, who was now wearing a slight smirk.

After a bit more casual conversation, Kirby was dismissed and Maggie sent over a young black woman from Africa. The conversation went along the same lines as before, and eventually Jan asked the question about her emergency contact on the medical form and got the same result: parents deceased.

Maggie MacDonald was in a United Nations mood, so the next two she sent over were from South America and China, both with the same story: parents no longer living.

"Okay, enough," Vanderham said. "Are you seriously convinced that everyone here has both parents dead?"

"I've gone through every medical form, all one hundred and sixty of them. Not one person listed a parent as an emergency contact. That's how I first spotted it. I just happened to notice it on the first few I reviewed, and then I checked the rest. I thought it was more than a little odd, so I started asking them about it. I've probably talked to forty people now, and it's true of everyone I've asked. Including us, I might add."

"I don't get it. What's this about?" asked Seifert.

Vandy took a sip of his Guinness and leaned back in his chair. "It was before you got here, Doc. The first time Jan went through the scientists' medical records, she came to me because she had some concerns."

"More than concerns – I was spooked," said Jan.

"Okay, spooked. Anyway, she was concerned because of the profiles. Even though it was a diverse group racially, the profiles of the scientists were all so similar."

"They were all the same!" Jan interrupted.

"Well okay, they were virtually the same. They were all very healthy, no illnesses, no genetic problems, no chronic disabilities of any kind. All in their twenties or early thirties, all single, all unmarried and childless," said Vandy.

"This was not statistically possible in any randomly selected group of this size," added Jan.

"So Jan convinced me to email the executive director and ask him what this was all about. I did, and he sent back a completely reasonable answer. He also revealed more about what was expected from Malabar Farm than I had gotten from him in all of the previous four years."

"Great, why do we exist? It's never really been that clear to me either," asked Seifert.

Vandy paused for another sip of beer. "Well, the executive director went on to say that we should stop thinking of ourselves as an educational institution. Instead, we should think of ourselves as a private scientific laboratory. He said that this group of young scientists was chosen with this specific profile as a means to reach optimal production without any distractions. And as a private business, as opposed to a university, for instance, we have the right to hire the most productive people we can find. In his experience in the biotech business, people with this type of profile were the most productive."

"I don't get 'productive' I thought we were doing research."

"Good point. And that's the part that finally made some sense to me," said Vandy. "His expectation is that this group will start churning out patents that can be licensed to the big agricultural conglomerates. He thinks agriculture is a large, untapped opportunity for biotech patents."

"So, I bought it," said Jan. "Single, young, healthy, childless - all are characteristics that would reduce the competing demands on the scientists' time and energy. They would have no difficulty turning in eighty-hour weeks. I don't necessarily agree, but it's at least a logical argument," said Jan. "But, *this* ... what possible reason could there be for having *no* living parents?"

"Hmm, it is strange. And if what you say is true, it can't be a coincidence," said Seifert. "It's clearly a requirement in his profile and it's not an easy one to satisfy. Think how many applicants you would need in order to find one hundred and sixty healthy thirty-year olds, with both parents dead."

"But why?" asked Jan. "Why is that a requirement? I can't come up with one possible outcome, or result, or benefit of any kind, of having no living parents. Not one. I'm completely stumped!"

"Okay, we'll ask. I'll send an email," Vandy offered.

"And, I take it you still don't have any idea who this mysterious 'executive director' is?" she asked.

"Haven't a clue," Vandy said, hoisting his glass to MacDonald for a refill.

Chapter 8

Wednesday, June 3rd, 2020
Haida Gwaii

The morning after Dixon's frightening discussion of his being assassinated, Toby got up early again, needing more than ever to walk along the shore. The day before, while working in the kitchen, he found a small thermos. He filled it with coffee at the main lodge, made by one of the security guys who never seemed to sleep. Toby noticed that the Rev. Darby must have gotten up in the night and wandered up to his cabin, as the chair he had been sleeping in last night was now empty.

Toby climbed up and over the pile of rocks, and headed out along the beach to the west. About a hundred yards down the beach he found a large rock, about the size of an automobile, tucked up against the tumble of driftwood. Many northwest beaches were bordered at the high end by huge piles of driftwood. Large logs floated throughout these waters, blown in from high winds, or more often, lost from log-tows going to the mill. Eventually they washed up on the shore where the tides moved them up to the top of the beach, and the storms arranged and rearranged them into a pick-up-sticks wall of interlocking wood.

The rock was an inviting place to sit and survey this wild beach and drink coffee. It was like being back in Astoria – coffee in hand, great view to enjoy, and time to contemplate.

And contemplate he did. But as hard as he tried to sort through the many compelling, confusing issues at hand, his thoughts returned to the even more compelling Dr. Laura Sundgren.

After what seemed to be no more than a minute, Toby noticed the coffee was gone, checked his watch, and saw he needed to hustle back. God help him if he was late – Dixon might have him shot.

As Toby emerged from the brush by the main lodge, he could see Dixon, along with all four of the security team, and both of the Indian researchers, gathered at the end of the dock, apparently engaged in a staff meeting before the day's event. Inside the lodge, the cabin-two cookies were hard at work. And it smelled great, pancakes and bacon, a perfect fishing lodge breakfast.

Solene was standing with Sen. Mallory by the fireplace. He gestured to Toby to come over.

"Have you seen Reverend Darby this morning?" Solene asked, skipping the usual polite morning small-talk.

"No, I haven't, I've been at that beach over there since I got up," Toby said, pointing to the leftmost front window. "Why? Has he invoked God to smite us all now?" Toby asked, with a smile.

"He seems to be missing," Solene said.

"Oh, sorry," Toby said, embarrassed about his foolish remark. "He wasn't in the chair when I came down here this morning, and I think I was the first one here except for the security guys. I just assumed he woke up and went up to his cabin sometime in the night. Maybe he woke up and wandered into the woods and got lost. Has anyone been out looking for him?" Toby asked.

"The security man, Mark, came in a little while ago and asked ..."

"More like told," Mallory interjected.

"Told would be more accurate," Solene agreed. "Mark told us to stay here, that they had the situation under control, and that Dixon would be up in about fifteen minutes to get started. Have you eaten?"

"No, I'll go get something. It smells good," Toby said.

Toby grabbed a plate, and walked over to the stove, where Laura was flipping over three pancakes.

"The last of the batch, you got here just in time," she said, but without the usual smile.

A few minutes later Mark appeared at the front door. "Mr. Dixon will be here in five minutes, please get your coffee and find a seat," he said.

Toby thought it sounded a bit like a presidential news conference announcement. Dixon was certainly going out of his way to separate himself from the group. What a change from the first two days, when he was Mr. Texas Charm.

Finally everyone was in place, and within a minute Dixon walked in and stood in front of the fireplace. He looked slowly around at everyone and exhaled ominously.

"I have very bad news to report concerning the Reverend Darby," Dixon said. "He has committed suicide."

Toby immediately looked at Laura, who was looking at the floor, arms crossed in front of her, and shaking her head. She looked up at the ceiling, and then over at Toby.

"Phil, would you please tell everyone what you saw last night?" Dixon said, gesturing to the back bar where Phil, one of the security team, was standing.

"Yes sir. Sometime around three o'clock I heard a loud thud, it woke me up. It sounded like it was coming from somewhere down the dock. I got up to investigate and saw The Reverend Darby walking down to the end of the dock with a small anchor from one of the boats in his hand. I should have reacted faster, but I was still a little groggy. Anyway, he got to the end of the dock, unfastened his belt a couple of loops, ran it through the anchor ring, and then re-hitched it.

"I started running down the dock. He looked back at me, then looked up for a split second, and jumped into the water. He was gone by the time I reached the end," Phil said, his voice faltering. He was obviously shaken by what had happened. "I should have run after him immediately. I'm really sorry."

"Not your fault Phil. There is no way you could have gotten there in time," Dixon said.

"I will go straight to heart of the matter," Dixon said, then paused. "Let me re-state that. Of course the real heart of the matter is the inexplicable tragedy of a man as great as the Reverend Darby taking his own life."

Dixon walked to the window and stared out at the water, "You recall what I said last night regarding unforeseen events?" he asked, and turned back to the group. "I didn't expect something like this so soon. But there it is. And now, as I said last night, we will continue on as planned."

Several people started to protest at once.

"Stop, let me finish," Dixon held both hands above his head. "Reverend Darby's tragic choice will not affect our work here at all. We will proceed. That point is not up for discussion ... understood?"

Dixon looked around the room, challenging anyone to protest. No one did.

"Now, as for the details; we cannot find the body. The currents are strong here. By the time we had enough light, the currents had swept him away. Soon, the crabs will make it impossible to find anything other than the anchor," Dixon paused and returned to the window.

"His family and the authorities will be informed when we return. Whatever consequences that ensue from this decision will be dealt with at that time. Unfortunate for his family ... yes it is. But necessary, as you will soon realize."

No one said a word.

Toby looked around the room, no one moved. The group was in shock. The threats Dixon made last night were upsetting, but Toby felt that no one had taken them seriously. Now it was different. This was no longer an intriguing game that Dixon was playing. Reverend Darby was dead, possibly murdered. Toby was certain that, at a minimum, Dixon's decision to not report the death had to be a crime. Duval Dixon was not above the law. How could he avoid trouble when they returned? And everyone here was a witness. Were they all now in danger?

Dixon walked to the center of the room and nodded to one of the researchers. A picture of the Earth appeared on the screen behind Dixon.

"We start now," Dixon said.

"I am going to ask you a question. For the rest of our time here we will discuss this question - argue it, look at it in every way that we can. This is a question that I have been focused on for over a decade. And now, I've decided it's time to seek outside help. That's why you are here," Dixon paced a few steps toward the windows.

"But this isn't a jury, you won't have a vote in the outcome. Ultimately, I will answer the question on my own. I believe you can help me, but I don't know that for certain ... I could be wrong. In which case, nothing is lost."

Toby had no idea what that meant, "nothing is lost". But it sounded ominous.

"The question then," Dixon stopped and looked at the group. It seemed to Toby that Dixon made, and held, eye contact with each person in turn. Toby had to remember to breathe.

"The question is," Dixon paused again for several more moments, as if he didn't want to go on. Finally, after what appeared to be a brief pep talk inside his head, Dixon nodded several times to no one in particular, and continued, "The question is this: Is it now time, here in the year 2020, to reboot the human species?"

Many in the group relaxed, some even smirked. Collectively they all had the same thought – this is just going to be one of those pointless, think-tank, future-of-the-world panel discussions.

Senator Mallory, predictably, was the first to react. "Are you kidding?" he bellowed. "This big build-up and then this turns out to be another of those stupid, future-of-mankind bullshit conferences? You can't be serious."

"Let me finish. Then ask that question again if you like," Dixon said. "However, I do understand the Senator's point. As a theoretical question, it is a pointless debate. But the question I am asking is no longer theoretical."

Toby froze. This can't be, he thought. It can't be … it's not possible. After all this time - it was Dixon?

Dixon continued, "To become a real question, *and not theoretical,* it requires that three conditions must be met," he said. "First, it must be possible to do. Let me restate that. *I* must be able to demonstrate to *you* that I can do it – and that I can do it *right now.*

"Second, I must be able to prove to you that I am *willing* to do it.

"And third, in order for you to consider the question at all, you must believe that you will not be rebooted yourselves. In other words, you will not die. You could not be expected to objectively consider any action that resulted in your own deaths, or even the deaths of your loved ones," Dixon said.

"Mr. Dixon, maybe I'm the only one, as English is my second language, but I don't think I understand. What is this 'it' you are talking about? What do you mean by 'reboot'?" asked Dr. Contreras, looking confused.

"Let me be more specific, Dr. Contreras," Dixon said. "Here is what I can do. I can release a biological agent which will cause the death of every human being on Earth. I have created this agent, and I have the means of distribution. I can vaccinate several hundred people, including this group and a number of your families, so that they will survive. In a matter of a year, the total population of human beings on Earth will be less than one thousand. That is what I *can* do. The question I am asking is "*Should* I?""

"Come on now Dixon," Mallory said. "I don't believe you. It can't be done. I was on the counter-terrorist sub-committee in the Senate. We were briefed on all of that biological terrorism bullshit. It was never taken seriously, not even by the CIA. You remember SARS and the Bird Flu panics? Nothing ever happened. It can't be done ... period. And since it can't be done, this '*question*' of yours is stupid. Frankly, you are starting to sound like a total nut-case."

"As I said Senator, to make the question legitimate, I need to prove to you that it is real. Let me try to do that. You are all aware of my significant business interests in the biotech industry. You have likely heard that I have as many as thirty facilities in India alone.

"The actual number is fifty-one. I have invested over twenty billion dollars in these facilities in the last decade. I'm sure you can agree, that if such an agent could be invented, that I have the ability to produce it." Dixon looked at Mallory for confirmation.

"Okay, I'll give you that," Mallory said.

"So now I need to convince you that I have invented such an agent. Four years ago ..."

"Oh, fuck," Laura gasped, putting her head in her hands and looking up at the ceiling.

"Dr. Sundgren, I'm surprised it took you that long to connect those dots," Dixon said with a slight smile, his first of the day. "Perhaps you would like to explain?"

"No ... go on," Laura said in a barely audible whisper.

"As you wish," Dixon continued, and gave a nod to the researchers.

A group photo of about twenty people popped up on the screen. "Four years ago I hosted a conference on Vancouver Island. The purpose of the conference - well, the purpose the attendees were told - was to explore some "outside-the-box thinking" with regard to global pandemic response protocols.

"The process we employed at the conference was a bit unusual: we played a game. The group was divided into three teams. Each team was either on offense, defense, or judging. The team on offense described a situation which included some information, but not all, regarding a rapidly emerging biological threat. The team on defense had twenty four hours to craft a response. The judges decided who 'won'. It was more complex then what I just described ... but you get the picture.

"Speaking of which, there is the group picture," Dixon pointed to the screen. "And you will notice Dr. Sundgren in the first row. This explains the 'Oh, Fuck' that you just heard."

Toby stiffened, a bolt of electricity shot up his spine. It *was* him. He looked at Dixon, hoping for eye contact, a sign perhaps. But Dixon was looking at Laura, ignoring him. Maybe Dixon didn't know about him, Toby thought, he had used an alias. Toby decided not to say anything. Dixon would surely say something to him if he knew.

"Shall I go on, or would you like to add something here?" Dixon asked Laura.

Laura gave a barely perceptible shake of her head.

"The event wasn't going well," Dixon continued. "The game turned out to be a bit boring. Perhaps boring isn't the right word. It was too predictable. One group would describe a situation that turned out to be smallpox, and another group did pandemic flu of some kind. They all knew the characteristics and responses for all of the usual suspects. So, this event was turning into nothing more than a review of existing protocols, clearly not something that these distinguished epidemiologists needed to do.

"Then Dr. Sundgren changed the game. She convinced her team to 'think backwards'. Rather than describing a threat that was already known, she asked them to create the worst possible agent. In other words, if you were God and you wanted to eliminate the entire human species, what characteristics would you want in a biological agent, regardless of whether or not that agent existed, or could even be created."

Laura sat rigid, staring at Dixon, terrified that he was going to identify her as the designer of the weapon that he would use to kill eight billion people.

"I will put your mind somewhat at ease, Dr. Sundgren. We did not use your team's specific agent. You see at that time, we ..." Dixon stopped in mid-sentence, and looked down at the floor.

"I'm going to digress a bit, to tell you who the 'we' is. Initially, there were five of us. For obvious reasons it had to be a small number. Mr. Jain, now seated at the computer, was one of the original five. He is, in fact, not a research assistant, but one of the world's most talented biotech scientists. At various stages, several additional people became involved. The number has since gone down. Now I believe, though I suppose I can't be entirely positive, that everyone who knows about this is on this island."

The group's collective head was spinning. It took them a moment to process what they just heard.

"The number has since gone down"? What does that mean Toby wondered? Did they know about it at one time and then forget? Not likely. Dixon seemed to be admitting to murder. But then, what's wrong with a few dozen killings if you are planning to eliminate eight billion people anyway? That wouldn't even be considered collateral damage – it would just be an early start. The horrifying conclusion came to Toby that Dixon, just by the act of having this idea, or plan, or whatever this thing could be called, had given himself permission to do anything he needed. Everyone is going to die soon anyway, so Dixon was now free to do anything, or kill anybody, he wanted.

Dixon continued, "The group I just described had been working on the problem of finding such an agent, but we had fallen into the same way of thinking as the teams at the conference. We explored various strains of smallpox, modifications of flu virus, delivery systems for anthrax - all existing agents. But, after the conference, we focused on Dr. Sundgren's approach - thinking backwards. We had the luxury of time, as we were not limited to twenty-four hours as had been the case for Dr. Sundgren's team. So we came to a very different conclusion.

"Therefore Dr. Sundgren, you need not share Oppenheimer's angst; you are not the designer of the agent of doom."

Toby looked over at Laura. She didn't look relieved.

Dixon went on, "We made the list of the characteristics that would be necessary to make an agent that would do everything we wanted. I'll mention a few of the obvious ones. It had to be highly contagious - person to person, through the air, and by contact. It had to have a long incubation period, so that it couldn't be quarantined until it was too late. It had to be 100% fatal. And we had to be able to create an antidote, either a vaccination, or a treatment protocol. There were many other requirements, related to production, distribution … things like that. For instance, the development and production had to be able to be broken up, and done in several facilities so that the real purpose would not be discovered.

"The list was daunting, as you can imagine. But we had some miraculous breakthroughs. We thought it would take another five or ten years, but … well, here we are. It's done."

"Bullshit, bullshit, bullshit!" Senator Mallory exclaimed. "You couldn't do this with five people. It's not possible."

"Senator, I understand your skepticism. Let me address your specific point. We were able to break up the development into pieces. Each piece could be shown to be an important step forward in biotech science by itself, so no suspicions would be raised by the work. I had multiple labs working independently on each piece. The final assembly of the agent, and of course the purpose of the agent, was known only by a few," Dixon said.

"But I don't expect you to believe this simply because I am telling you. I have a better way to prove this. May I assume that none of you believes that Doctors Benson, Sundgren and Contreras are part of this plan? By that I mean that they have heard about this plan right now, the same time as the rest of you? That is correct, is it not, Doctors?"

Toby, Laura, and Sofia all nodded but did not speak.

"Senator?" Dixon looked at Mallory. "Do you agree they are not shills in my little con game?"

"Okay, I'll bite," replied Mallory.

"Good," Dixon said. "Here is what I propose. As I mentioned, Dr. Jain is a biotech scientist. He was our chief scientist on the project. He will take Doctors Contreras and Sundgren aside for the rest of the day and give them an in-depth briefing on the agent. This briefing will be way too technical for the rest of you to follow. I will ask you to trust their judgment when they report back to you tomorrow."

"Dr. Benson, I would like you to spend the rest of the day with Dr. Patel. Dr. Patel is also not a research assistant. He is, in fact, an accomplished mathematician and the world's foremost authority on Probability Tube equations. Well, foremost, save one - Dr. Benson, who created them. Let me explain one thing, so that you don't leap to any conclusions, and so that you understand the look of complete confusion on Dr. Benson's face. Dr. Benson has never met Dr. Patel, and in fact, had never heard of Dr. Patel until this minute. Correct Dr. Benson?"

"Yes, correct," Toby said.

"Good. It is one thing to prove that this agent will be as effective as I have just claimed. But, it is another thing altogether to show that it will cause the result we expect on a worldwide basis. Dr. Benson's equations can give us the best indication of what might occur, provided that he has sufficient data on the input side to produce a valid result. Of course, Dr. Benson could not accomplish this in a day if he was starting from scratch. But, Dr. Patel has been using the equations for years now, as we focused in on the characteristics of the agent. So, Dr. Benson, we are simply asking you to review what Dr. Patel has already done, and then to assure the group here that, to the best of your knowledge, Dr. Patel's predictions are accurate."

Toby exhaled, and nodded at Dixon.

"Mr. Dixon", Dr. Mothershed said. "I too am a scientist. More importantly perhaps, I am a critic of scientists. While I am not an expert in these specific disciplines, I believe I could be of value as a listener during these reviews. I would appreciate being able to remain and observe these presentations."

"Good idea Dr. Mothershed, I agree, please stay behind," Dixon said.

Dixon moved back to his little desk, and slumped down in the chair, hands folded in his lap, and stared blankly out at the water. After a moment he looked back to the group.

"I can't imagine what is going on inside your heads just now," Dixon finally said. "I apologize for delivering this news so clinically, but you must remember that I have been living this idea for more than ten years. I have been able to distance myself from the intense emotions that I expect you are now experiencing. That may be a good thing, or it may be a bad thing."

"This is another way to look at why you are here. I don't trust my perspective, or my context anymore, especially now that the quest is over and the decision must be made. I'd guess, at this point, that you think that I am a madman, or insane, or that I have succumbed to the influence of my extreme wealth and have become a raging megalomaniac. History certainly provides many examples of personalities warped in this manner."

Dixon rose from the chair and stepped again to the middle of the room.

"Years ago, when I first encountered this idea, it was, as the Senator suggested, an exercise in mental masturbation. It is not a unique idea. There are literally hundreds of books, movies and videos in the "end-of-the-world" genre. I'd venture to say that almost everyone has fantasized about being a lone survivor in a world where everyone else is gone.

"But now, as the world has spiraled downward over these last ten years, the idea of massive population reduction has began to have more merit. The problem was always the same though - it couldn't be done. Asking for volunteers wasn't going to work. Governments could not conceivably even consider the question. Ditto the United Nations. One day it dawned on me that I might be the only person in the world who could make this happen. And not only was I, alone, able to do this, but this also might be the only moment in time when it could be done," Dixon said. "I'm not a young man."

Dixon paused, and studied the group. Toby felt the rise in Dixon's intensity.

"I will make the case for 'why me - why now' later in these discussions," Dixon said. "Right now though, just try to follow me. It doesn't matter if you believe this to be true. It only matters that I believed it to be true, and I did. At that point, it was clear to me that I had an obligation to prove that it was true – that I could do this. I had an obligation to get to the point that we are at right now - today. That it can be done.

"And now that I can do it, I have a further obligation to ask the question: should I?"

"What do you mean by 'obligation' Mr. Dixon?" asked Dr. Mothershed, too politely, considering the circumstances. "Obligation to whom?"

"Obligation to the future, Dr. Mothershed, to the future," Dixon said. "Let me make this clearer. While these sessions with Mr. Patel and Mr. Jain are going on for the remainder of the day, I have an assignment for the rest of you. I hope this will give you a starting point for the serious and thoughtful contemplation of this question - as opposed to having you go back to your cabins and rant about what a madman I am.

"Here is your assignment. It is another question," Dixon said. "Given the two possible scenarios for a year from now, those being; one - that nothing has changed, or two - that only several hundred human beings remain on Earth. What will the state of the world be in three hundred years?

"Three hundred years from now ... consider each case, in which one will humans *and* the earth be better off?"

Dixon paused, rubbing his hands together. "As you are all well aware, science began telling us decades ago that we had long ago overshot the earths carrying capacity. There are simply too many people consuming too much. And we are, of course, now seeing the early stages of the resulting ecological collapse. Food shortages are upon us.

"Though, in terms of human awareness, sustainability problems always seem around the corner – never quite impacting the present, so nothing is ever done. But if you look three hundred years down the road you can no longer ignore the overshoot issue and the inevitable collapse it will create."

Dixon paused again and turned back to Mothershed, "Dr. Mothershed, this is the future that I speak of. This is the obligation that I have, to at least ask the question. And now, this is the obligation that all of you have - to seriously consider this great question, and give consul to me ... about what I should do."

Chapter 9

Wednesday afternoon, June 3rd, 2020
Haida Gwaii

Late that afternoon Justice Brown and Wyndi Rehn slipped into the main lodge to prepare dinner.

"Okay if we start getting some food together?" Justice Brown said to the two groups huddled in opposite corners of the main room. "We thought we'd do a cold veggie pasta thing and leave it on the table so people could come and go as they wish."

"Please do," Toby said. "I've heard enough anyway. Dr. Mothershed, should we call it a day?"

Dr. Mothershed nodded approval and stiffly rose from his chair.

"We have heard enough as well," Dr. Contreras said. "Can we help you with the dinner?"

"No, no ... Wyndi and I will handle it. I'm sure you guys could use a drink and some fresh air," Justice Brown said.

Laura put her hand on Dr. Contreras' shoulder, gave her a tight lipped grimace, and walked out to the porch. Toby followed her out.

They stood together for a while, not speaking. Toby leaned on the rail, looking out at the water. Laura stood in the shadows behind him, arms folded tightly in front, holding herself together.

Jain and Patel gathered up their documents, shut down their systems and quietly headed up the path to cabin four. Dr. Mothershed found a comfortable chair by the fireplace, sat back down and closed his eyes.

Finally, Laura took a deep breath, exhaled slowly, and walked back to the doorway of the main lodge. "Sofia ... let's go up to the cabin and freshen-up and then talk for a bit." She turned and walked back to Toby. "Could you meet me down at the dock in about an hour?"

Toby nodded and continued his empty stare out over the water.

An hour later, Toby stopped by the main lodge. Dr. Mothershed was in the same chair and seemed to be napping.

"I'm grabbing a bottle of wine. Laura and I are heading down to the dock for a minute. Can I open a bottle for you two?" Toby asked.

"You bet," said Wyndi. "How did it go today ... or shouldn't I ask?"

"Well, I don't know what to say right now," Toby said. "It's a little complicated. But first thing tomorrow Jain and Patel will present an abbreviated version of what we heard today. After you hear them, whatever I have to say will make more sense."

"Sorry. I knew I shouldn't have asked," Wyndi said.

"No, no ... that's okay. I don't mean to keep you in suspense so I'll just say that as far as I can tell, Dixon can do what he claims ... as I'm sure you expected."

Wyndi stared at Toby for a moment and then nodded.

"I'm over here," Toby said as Laura came down the ramp to the dock. Toby was seated in the afterdeck of the "V. Cerf", the larger of the two boats, a half empty glass of wine in hand. He filled Laura's glass and handed it to her as she sat down.

Laura took a long swallow. She leaned forward, elbows on her knees, staring down at her feet. Toby waited for her to collect her thoughts.

"Did Patel go into the details of this agent that they have created?" Laura asked after a moment, and straightened back up in her chair.

"No, not the biology of it, just the effects," Toby replied.

Laura looked away from Toby and started to tremble. "My God ... this is beyond, beyond I don't know what ... beyond anything. I don't have the words for it. I don't have the emotions for it."

Toby said nothing and waited again for Laura to compose herself.

"Ever heard of prions?" she finally asked.

"I don't think so," Toby said.

"I'm sure you've heard of mad cow disease."

Toby nodded. "But I've just heard of it, I don't know anything about it."

"That's not unusual. mad cow was never a big deal. There was an outbreak in England in the mid nineteen-eighties. It was attributed to using ground-up sheep as feed for the cattle. They stopped doing that, and it was never a problem again. There was a rumored outbreak in rural western China a year or two ago but the Chinese weren't very forthcoming about it, so we never knew for sure," Laura paused for another therapeutic drag on the wine glass.

"Anyway, the agent that causes mad cow disease is called a prion. Prions are very unusual. They are neither bacteria nor virus, but basically just a strange protein. Somehow a normal protein gets folded improperly and becomes pathogenic. This mis-folded pathogenic protein is called a prion. I don't know much about this, it's not one of my areas. But I know that the mechanism for how it becomes mis-folded in the first place is, or was, unknown. Some people suspected that an undiscovered virus did it, others claimed it was the protein alone that acted. In any case, once the prion exists in your system, it causes other normal proteins to fold improperly, and then the new ones do the same ... creating a chain reaction. Then the prions start destroying brain cells, eventually turning the brain into Swiss cheese. The result is like an accelerated form of Alzheimer's."

After another swallow of wine Laura went on. "Mad cow disease in humans is called CJD, for Creutzfeldt-Jakob disease. CJD can take as little as a year to run its course, or it can take considerably longer. But it always results in death. There is no cure or treatment. It's not even detectable. So, you can see why Dixon chose prions," Laura said.

"That matches with the criteria they gave me - 100% fatal," Toby replied. "And that explains the long delay between the initial contact and death. But they told me death occurred in three to five months, not a year to eighteen months."

"Well, they have modified a number of things. One of the modifications was to increase the initial number of prions, so that death came sooner - in three to five months," Laura said. "And, of course, the biggest modification was to make it contagious."

"I'm no biologist but that doesn't make sense to me. How can a protein become contagious?"

"You've got that right. A protein cannot be contagious in the normal sense. In the past, people contracted CJD by eating meat from an infected 'mad' cow, in other words, ingesting the prions. But Dixon's scientists found out how the prion was created, and isolated it. And it's a mystery to me why it didn't get any publicity. This would have been a major discovery."

"Well, given what he intended to do with it, there isn't much mystery," Toby offered.

"I understand that, but a fairly large number of people had to be involved. Remember, Dixon told us that only five people knew. So how did he get the others to keep it a secret?" Laura said. "But, maybe I don't want to know."

"Can you tell me how contagious you think this Prion virus is?" Toby asked. "They told me that everyone on Earth would eventually contract it, except those who remained completely isolated from human contact."

Laura took another large gulp of wine, put her glass down, stood up, and turned to look out at the water. She put both hands on the rail and looked straight up.

"My God," she muttered under her breath. She took several deep breaths and returned to her seat. "Sorry ..." she said and looked at Toby with a sad smile.

Toby nodded and waited for her to go on.

"Okay ... well first, it's not the prion virus that's contagious. What they have done is cobble together a new virus that includes the protein-folding genetic instructions from the prion virus and the contagious aspects of the typical flu virus. Have you ever heard the term 'reassortment'? Laura asked.

"Not in a biological sense."

"Well, this is an area that I am acquainted with," Laura said. "Reassortment is the mechanism that causes the common flu virus to mutate almost every year into a new strain. Flu viruses have eight RNA segments that contain their genetic instructions. It is actually quite easy to exchange these segments with outside segments, often from animal flu viruses. The ability of the flu virus to create these new 'Reassorted' combinations is why we need a new flu vaccine every year."

Laura leaned forward and went on. "Reassortment is actually a fairly easy process to do in the lab. But who would want to do it? There is no upside to creating a new strain of flu. It wouldn't even be useful as a biological weapon. The flu doesn't normally have a high mortality rate, and once it's released it can't be contained. Everyone would be at risk, even the people releasing it."

Laura paused and picked up the wine bottle to refill Toby's glass. "You are behind, drink up. Might as well - the end is near."

She continued. "We actually spent the majority of our time looking at the reassorted virus. With the large variety of genetic material available to them, from both existing human and animal flu viruses, they were able to create the perfect monster. It is highly contagious, but the initial flu symptoms are somewhat mild, so that they don't cause any alarm or create a quarantine situation. My guess is that the CDC and WHO, after assessing the outbreak, might give up, and recommend that everyone expose themselves to it in order to get it over with. Kind of like parents deliberately exposing their children to chicken pox just to get it over with.

"The problem is, after a few months, the secondary symptoms appear, courtesy of the prion creating genetic material. But as I said before, with no cure or treatment for prions once they are in your system, it will be too late. End of story," Laura leaned back in her seat and stared out at the water.

"Are you sure everyone will get the initial virus? Toby asked. "Most of the time, not everyone gets the flu. I haven't had it for years."

"We covered that. The normal 'Reassortment' process that each year creates a new flu is usually a mild change. It's built on a platform that we have already experienced. So we have some built-in immunity. But every so often, like fifty to one hundred years, a more radical Reassortment takes place and a more dangerous pandemic flu is created. The Spanish flu of 1918 is a good example. Dixon's people have created one of those pandemic viruses on a radically new platform. None of us has any built-in immunity."

"My God …"

"It gets worse," Laura said. "Just to be certain, they actually created *five* of them! Each one is different enough to breach any possible immunity. It's obscene - *he's* obscene," Laura said, shaking her head.

Laura continued, "Let me tell you a little about the 1918 Spanish flu. Except for a few very isolated places, everyone on Earth was exposed to it, and half of them got sick. Remember, that was in 1918. Travel was slow and rare. And it started from only one point, a military base in France."

"I did get one piece of information along those lines. I don't know if I can believe it though," Toby said.

"Really, what is it?"

"I was told that the virus would be released in three waves, about a week apart, in more than fifty thousand locations worldwide."

"What?" Laura exclaimed, looking puzzled.

"I know, I know … how do five people do that? I asked and they said Dixon would address it sometime, but they assured me it was true."

"Amazing. So what else did you discover in the mathematical-prediction world?" Laura asked. "What did Mr. Patel have to say?"

"Pretty simple really. Everyone gets sick, and then everyone dies. As long as what Patel told me is true … and according to you it is."

"What did you do all day then?"

"We worked mainly on secondary and tertiary effects. What happens to the hermits, people at the South Pole, sailors in submarines, and those that somehow miraculously survive the virus," Toby said.

"Huh … I hadn't thought about that. What does happen to them?"

Toby shook his head, "Same thing, they all die."

He went on. "I was told the virus will lurk for many years. They wouldn't tell me where or how, but again they assured me it would. So most of the hermits and sailors will eventually be exposed to it, get sick and die. As for anyone with immunity – should there be any - they will die from secondary events. Like shooting each other if they come in contact. Maybe drink themselves to death, commit suicide, have an accident, or die from natural causes since there will be no healthcare.

"Even if a few survive all of those problems, the odds of them creating a sustainable breeding population are essentially zero. It's possible that a completely isolated tribe in the rainforests of the Amazon or New Guinea may survive intact. But they will simply remain an isolated tribe in the rainforest. If they haven't changed in ten thousand years, there is no reason to think they will change for another ten thousand. So they don't count."

Toby paused for a sip of wine.

"But I don't get this part. Why won't everyone die, including us and Dixon?" Toby asked.

"Jain claims they have a vaccine that will prevent the prion-folding genetic material from activating, and another vaccine to prevent the five flu types. Belt and suspenders, a good practice, considering what's at stake," Laura said.

"Are you sure they can do that?"

"Not completely, no. But they did isolate the virus, and they learned how to extract the genetic information. They have enough knowledge. If it's at all possible, then they could have done it," she said.

"Well I guess it doesn't make much sense for Dixon to proceed unless they are pretty confident about the vaccines. Dixon wanted to 'reboot' the human species, not eliminate it. I do believe that's what he intends."

Laura got up again and leaned on the back rail, staring out over the water.

"I haven't told you the worse part," she said.

"There's something *worse*?"

"Yup," she said, turning back to where Toby was seated. "It's not just that people will die ... sorry ... that *all* the people will die. I still can't really grasp that."

Laura's voice faltered. She sat back down.

"It's the way they will die. It's going to be horrible ... beyond horrible."

Toby thought Laura might need a short break.

"We're out of wine. I'll run and get another, stay put. I'll be just a minute," Toby said.

He returned, out of breath. Laura looked up at him with tears in her eyes.

Toby squatted down in front of her chair and stroked her cheek and hair. "You don't have to go on, we can go back up if you like."

"No, you need to know this, right now. We have to do something," Laura said gently brushing his hand aside. "But thanks."

Toby opened the bottle and filled her glass.

Laura took a sip and went on. "I mentioned that CJD … remember that's the name for the prion disease. CJD is like an accelerated form of Alzheimer's. The phases of CJD start with depression, then confusion, and then most people will experience psychotic thinking and psychotic episodes and insomnia. Followed by loss of motor skills, staggering, falling, etc. and then nervous system collapse, incapacitation and finally … certain death. It is a horrible, protracted death even with good and loving care from family and doctors. But think of this: everyone will have it at the same time. The entire world will go from depressed to psychotic, all at the same time!"

Laura paused. She looked at Toby, shaking her head.

"Babies, three-year olds, teenage girls, the army, healthcare professionals, the President, everyone psychotic, all at the same time. Can you even imagine the chaos? And anyone who survives that hellish experience will then face several months of progressive incapacitation with no one to care for them. Think of the children …" Laura couldn't go on.

Toby didn't know what to say. Who would? After a few moments he stood up in front of Laura and gently took her hand. She stood up, buried her head in his chest, wrapped her arms around his waist and began to sob. He held her tight for several minutes.

"Sorry," Laura stammered, trying to get her normal breathing back. "My God, I've never done that before, and I've seen a lot of bad stuff, a lot of suffering. I'm supposed to be a trained professional. I shouldn't have done that."

She wiped her eyes on her sleeve and stepped away from Toby. Toby couldn't think of anything to say. Laura took a few more moments to compose herself.

"So … one of Dixon's predictions has already come true," Laura said. "We need to kill him."

Once again, Toby's mind began to spiral. Three days ago he had been sitting comfortably on his front porch in a nowhere little town leading a nowhere little life. Now, here he was, on a boat in the Queen Charlotte islands with a beautiful woman from Atlanta telling him that he had to kill Duval Dixon, the wealthiest person on Earth, or else everyone in the world would die. And it might be his fault. Could this rabbit hole get any deeper?

"Sit down," he said finally. "Let's think this over."

Laura sat.

"I don't think we could kill him," Toby said. "There are ten of us, and five ... no seven, with Jain and Patel, of them. Four of them are highly trained and armed, special forces types. None of us has any kind of weapon. I doubt we could even hurt one of them, much less get to Dixon."

"Could we sneak up at night, or something like that?" Laura asked.

"Maybe, but we would have to get by two of the guards and the two other guys, who I bet are also armed. Only two of us are young enough for anything strenuous. I guess I just don't see it."

"How about poisoning him?" Laura said.

"With what?"

"Snakes, scorpions, wombat blood ... I don't know. You're from around here, what's poisonous in the northwest?"

"Well," Toby replied. "That's always been one of the benefits of living in the northwest. There isn't much danger in the woods. There are no poisonous snakes west of the coast range, where we are, and no scorpions or any poisonous insect that I know of. There is a spider, the brown recluse, but I don't even know what it looks like, and I'm not sure if it's bite is even fatal. Sometimes kids die from eating the wrong mushrooms, thinking they have found psilocybin. That might be our best bet. But I think the mushrooms grow in short grass or fields, and this area is mostly rocky, besides, it's not the season for them. They come out in the fall, after the first rains."

"How about putting something in his food. Somebody might have a prescription that would work, or bleach, or ground up glass or, I don't know ... anything," Laura said, starting to sound desperate.

"I don't think we will ever see Dixon eat with us again. With all the careful planning that they put into this thing, I'm sure they would have thought about the food poisoning possibility."

"Well *fuck* ... oops, sorry," Laura said, followed by a long sigh. "Maybe Reverend Darby's God has the best chance after all, maybe we should all pray for Darby's murder to be avenged."

"We don't know he was murdered," Toby said.

"Really? You actually think it was just a very convenient suicide?" Laura asked, angrily.

"No, I don't know … you're probably right. But Let's rethink this. Our goal here isn't to kill Dixon. Our goal is to stop him. We wouldn't be here if we didn't have a least a small chance of talking him out of it. Why else would he have gone to all the trouble - not to mention the risk - involved in bringing this group together? If he already had his mind made up, he wouldn't have done this. It would be pointless. He must be serious about seeking our counsel. Maybe our best chance is to do exactly as he requests, and to try and talk him out of it."

"Quit being so damn logical. I still want to kill him," Laura said, only half joking.

"Let's talk him out of it first, then you can kill him."

"So Dixon wins again. We do exactly as he wants. That's your best plan?"

"Look, he's had a long time to set this up. He knows how to do this … how to manipulate people, industries, governments even. I'm sure he has thought through all of the possible reactions we might have. I doubt he missed anything. I don't see any other choice. Not only that … but we, all of us, will have to be damn good to talk him out of this. He has put the last ten years of his life, not to mention most of his wealth, into this project. It's going to be very hard to get that train off the tracks."

"Ok smart guy, got any ideas about how to convince him?" Laura asked.

"No, not really. Well, maybe one to start with," Toby said. "I think you and Sofia should focus your remarks tomorrow on what you told me about how horrifying the last six months will be. Skip the part about 'will it work'. We have to assume it will. I know this will be tough, but spend time tonight thinking about the worst, most graphic way to describe the event. In the end, maybe Dixon won't have the stomach for it. And it might help to get the rest of the group cranked up."

"I don't know if I can do that again."

"Think about it anyway. Talk to Sofia. See what she says."

Laura stood up and put her arms around Toby. They held each other tight for several long moments. "God, I'm glad you're here," she said. "Too bad sex isn't in the picture. But under the circumstances, it doesn't seem … appropriate, if you know what I mean."

"I do, but hold the thought," Toby said.

Wyndi Rehn and Zelco Rabanovich were alone in the main lodge when Toby and Laura walked in. Wyndi was cleaning up the kitchen and Zelco was sitting at the bar keeping her company.

"There is still some pasta salad in the fridge," Wyndi said. "Are you guys okay? You don't look so good."

"I've been better, but I think I'll eat something. Toby, you want some pasta salad?" Laura asked, heading to the fridge.

"Sure. Where is everybody?" Toby asked.

"Most everyone is up in cabin three, drinking and debating," Wyndi said. "Sofia just helped Dr. Mothershed up to his cabin. She may be in cabin one with him. Dixon's army boys came by briefly, made up some sandwiches and headed up to the commandant's high roost. I guess they aren't eating with us anymore. And Zelco stayed behind to hit on me."

Zelco smiled, clearly charmed. Laura glanced over at Toby and gave him a nod.

"Did anyone say what time we start tomorrow?" Toby asked.

"Yes, sorry, I forgot to mention it. They said we won't start until noon, so you guys, and Sofia and Mothershed can spend some time in the morning comparing notes," Wyndi said. "Can I ask again? How's it look?"

"I think he can do it if he wants to," Laura said with a grimace.

"My God … someone please wake me up. This can't be happening," Wyndi said.

"I'll wake you up," Zelco said, a little too brightly.

Wyndi looked over at Laura and said in mock disgust, "Some things never change."

Chapter 10

Thursday, June 4th, 2020

Haida Gwaii

The next morning Toby, Laura and Sofia met for several hours. Sofia then briefly attended to Dr. Mothershed, who stayed in his room.

The session started promptly at noon without any commentary by Dixon. Jain presented the prion story with such complete dispassion that Toby thought he could have been at a college bio-chemistry lecture. After two hours of diagrams, slides of molecular structures, and unpronounceable terminology, the group was anesthetized. Dixon then announced a one-hour break and was quickly escorted out by his security team.

One hour later, Dixon returned, flanked by his guards. Patel started immediately with a short presentation of the timeline and final outcome. Patel's presentation had the opposite effect. The group was stunned by the graphic reality of Dixon's plan. Then Dixon finally rose to speak.

"Doctors Sundgren and Contreras would you please offer your thoughts on Dr. Jain's presentation," Dixon said, and immediately sat back down.

Toby was starting to shake. The atmosphere in the room was beyond oppressive. The group was in shock. Even Mallory was silent, staring straight ahead, his mind apparently locked up. After the clinical presentations by Jain and Patel, and now Dixon's fierce, no nonsense presence, it was at last clear to the group that this was not a game. Dixon was serious. He intended to kill eight billion people.

Laura spoke first.

"My God Dixon, what kind of a monster are you?" she stammered, fighting for composure.

The security team came to full attention. Dixon didn't move.

Laura remained seated. She blew her nose. Finally, after several deep breaths, she continued, "First, for the groups benefit, I will say, and with Sofia's complete agreement, that I believe Dixon and his team of asshole freaks can do what they claim. The science appears to be sound. This prion-based agent that Dr. Jain just showed you is as contagious and as fatal as they say. To make this quick, I'll speak for Dr. Benson as well. He says the mathematical projections confirm Dixon's statement. Everyone gets sick and everyone dies. And even those who don't, will also die. Everyone dies...*everyone dies*.

"So, except for the very few that Dixon anoints with his vaccine, based on what we saw yesterday and what we know from our professional experience, Dixon can do exactly as he claims." Laura paused for a moment, then added, "Dixon, you were right about the prediction you made the other night; if I could kill you right now I would."

The group stirred uncomfortably. After some sort of signal from the back, the security men slowly removed their guns from the shoulder holsters and held them in their laps, finger on the trigger - now on full alert. Toby watched Dixon intently, waiting for him to speak, or for him to somehow have Laura stopped. Dixon sat still, showing no emotion, and said nothing.

Laura spoke angrily, "Put your guns away boys. There isn't any way that I could kill the bastard, at least not now. So *put your fucking guns away*!" she shouted.

The group stared wide-eyed at Laura. Dixon nodded to someone in the back and the army boys slipped the guns back into their holsters.

Laura, energized, continued, "Dixon's freaking Stepford scientists gave you a nice little presentation this morning ... very clinical, very scientific, and completely inhuman. I'm now going tell you what they didn't. I'm going to tell you how this thing is going to go down. It's already beyond any comprehension that Dixon is considering wiping out everyone on Earth. Let me tell you how everyone will die. It is going to be *horrible*."

She rose slowly from her chair, and walked over to the back wall, "I'll just stand over here. Don't shoot." She leaned against the back wall, arms tightly folded.

Laura stared at the floor for a moment and tried to regain her composure.

"I have a friend at the CDC," she began. "A fellow Doctor, her name is Hanna Wold. She's pregnant with her fifth child. Great family, great husband, the kids are terrific. They made me an honorary aunt. Murray is the oldest, he's eleven, then Justin, he's eight now I think. Then Danny, a girl, very smart, very outgoing. She thinks she's in charge of the whole group. Danny's seven. And then Amanda, four, who has perfected the art of cute. Hanna is eight months pregnant, so she will give birth to number five while we are here," Laura said with a slight smile as she thought about the kids.

Laura noticed Dixon stirring uncomfortably. He could see what was coming.

"God damn it Dixon," Laura blurted out, sensing Dixon might stop her. "You listen to this. Don't you dare try to stop me."

After a tense, momentary stare down, Dixon gave her a nod of approval to continue.

"I'm going to tell you, in as much detail as I can, about what Duval Dixon is going to do to this wonderful, loving, innocent young family. These are good friends of mine," Laura paused and looked around the room. "All of you have friends like these, try to imagine them as you listen to this horror."

Toby thought – great idea Laura, make it real, make it personal.

She started the story of the Wold family's five months of hell. No one moved. Tears welled up and finally just ran down her cheeks as she described the things that would happen to this family – to the children – as the world became depressed, then totally psychotic, and then incapacitated.

Toby tried hard not to engage with the story so he could see what was happening in the room, especially with Dixon.

The group was mesmerized by Laura's account. Many shared her tears. Dixon, however, remained stoic. He didn't move. His expression never changed. But Toby did feel like one or two of the security team were struggling to stay composed. Maybe this was a crack that could be exploited. Perhaps they could get to one or two of the security team. They might then have a chance at getting to Dixon.

Laura finally finished, exhaustion showing as she slumped down in her chair, covering her face with both hands. Sofia got up to speak.

"It's hard to imagine a worse way to die," Sofia said. "Your brain will rot and there is nothing you can do about it. Almost before you know you are sick, you will not be thinking right. Depression and psychosis mixed, not only for you, but for everyone else, all at the same time. And, there will be nobody to help you and nobody to maintain your world.

"Laura talked specifically about a single family and what horror they will go through," Sophia said. "Who knows if she is accurate. It's totally unpredictable. I think it will be worse. I think a mass hysteria, a mass paranoia will quickly emerge, - worldwide, everywhere, all at the same time. The brutality and cruelty will be unimaginable. Laura talked on the small scale. I want to bring up some points we came up with this morning having to do with the large scale."

Sofia paused to look down at a note card that she had prepared, "It has been only a few years since the Afternoon War between India and Pakistan. That was only one small exchange between two secondary nuclear powers, but the devastation was immense. What will happen when everyone who has a finger on the trigger of a nuclear weapon goes crazy, all at the same time? We saw what happened in Pakistan when only a handful of sane people made a series of misjudgments. I have to believe that when everyone who controls every weapon goes crazy, the result will be enough nuclear weapons exploding to destroy all life in the world.

"This is not what I assume to be Mr. Dixon's objective. The same will be true of all the nuclear power plants. Who will shut them down if no one is sane? How will the contaminated fuel be dealt with? What will happen after ten years, a hundred years, a thousand years, to this radioactive fuel and waste products? Who will shut down the refineries and oil wells? Who will put out the inevitable fires ... not only in the oil wells and refineries, but also in the cities? Won't they eventually *all* catch fire and burn down? Couldn't the smoke clouds from all these fires blot out the sun and end all life on Earth? Won't the chemical factories that make all the dangerous pesticides and herbicides eventually leak their poisons back into the environment? Wouldn't it be possible that the world, one hundred years after this event, would be far more polluted than today?"

"The fact that everyone will be essentially crazy at the same time makes it completely impossible to predict the outcome of this event," Sofia continued. "Mr. Dixon asked us the question about the status of the Earth three hundred years from now. My guess is that, based on the concerns I have just stated, the earth will be far worse off, and most likely devoid of any life at all. Mr. Dixon's guess may be different. Regardless, both are guesses, no one could possibly see beyond the inevitable chaos that will take place. Not even Mr. Dixon." Sofia said, and sat down.

Hope flashed through Toby, but lasted only for a moment. The powerful, emotional presentations by Laura and Sofia had the expected horrifying effect on the group.

For Dixon though, Toby quickly realized, this was not new news. Dixon has known how this would go down for many years now, and proceeded anyway. The "quality" of the death must not be a concern to him. And then Toby realized - it wasn't one of the requirements that Dixon had mentioned earlier. The tired old "end justifies the means" argument must be his refuge.

Dixon slowly rose to speak.

"I'm encouraged," he said. "I think these discussions may be of real value … judging by the insight and intensity of the two doctors' remarks. They are correct in much of what they said. The death process will likely be even worse than they described and beyond anything we can even imagine. Billions will suffer, many of them children, all of them innocent. If the doctors had not brought this up, I would have."

Dixon looked up at the clock. "Take a short break, be back in ten." He walked quickly out the door and up to cabin four, flanked by his bodyguards.

Justice Brown tapped Toby on the arm. "Come outside for a minute," she said quietly. Toby followed her out.

"I think he's serious," she said. "I know him a little, and I don't think this is one of his charades. I don't know who to trust. Since you obviously only met him a few days ago, I'm going to assume you are not involved in this. We have to do something to stop him. Can you figure out any way to get a message out?"

"No, I've tried, but I can't think of any way," Toby said. "What do you mean about whom to trust?"

"Knowing Dixon, I'm assuming one or several of us is in on this. It would only make sense. Remember, he said all of his co-conspirators were on this island. For some reason, that caught my attention."

"I hadn't thought of that," Toby said. "Maybe we shouldn't be talking like this out here. I'll come over to your cabin tonight with Laura. We can talk then."

"Are you sure she's not part of it? That picture with her and the other scientists is a little disconcerting."

Toby reeled at the thought. "God, I hope not. No, no, I'm sure she's not." He reflexively looked back at Laura, who was standing by the door with Sofia. He caught her eye. She had been watching him talk to Justice Brown.

Dixon returned with his entourage. The group reseated itself.

Dixon began, "As I said, if Doctors Sundgren and Contreras hadn't brought up that awful vision of the dying process caused by the prion agent, I would have. And Doctor Sundgren's very personal account of the horror that will come to the Wold family is vital for you to keep in mind. And for me to keep in mind as well. It makes the contrast between choices as stark as possible. The disturbing and unpredictable way that this will happen presents a very high hurdle for us to overcome. And that's a good thing."

Dixon took a drink of water and continued.

"*Please* pay attention now," Dixon stopped and methodically made eye contact with each person. "This is important. One of the hardest shifts in your thinking that I will ask from you, will be to get you to step back. To step farther back than you have ever, in order to gain a greater level of perspective. The question I asked you yesterday about the prospects for the human race three hundred years out for example." Dixon paused again to survey the room.

Toby could sense him warming up to deliver a prepared lecture. The group sensed it to, and seemed relieved to listen to a little "philosophy of thinking" instead of the non-stop, horrifying body blows that had been delivered this morning. Everyone relaxed just a bit, and settled into their chairs.

Dixon continued. "Let's talk about the deaths and the suffering brought up by the Doctors. Rather than looking at the six months during which this event will occur, how about expanding that horizon to one hundred years."

Dixon gave a nod to Patel and a graph appeared on the big screen.

"Ah," Dixon said, looking up at the screen. "I have forgotten to explain this. You see the two lines are labeled "status quo" and "Eden". Please excuse my - our presumptiveness, but "The Eden Proposition" was simply a short and descriptive name for this event."

Dixon put his arms in the air, palms up and looked around the lodge.

"So ... all of this 'event', that you are now a part of, is called 'The Eden Proposition.'"

This time Toby gasped audibly. Several people looked over. Dixon stopped his lecture and asked, "Dr. Benson, are you okay?"

Toby looked up at Dixon, who was staring back, looking concerned. Toby studied Dixon carefully, looking for something - a sign, anything - but got only a blank look in return. Maybe it wasn't it him? But how did he know? The rabbit hole had just gotten much deeper.

"Sorry," Toby said. "Please, go on."

Dixon nodded, and pointed back to the screen.

"Back to the first graph; it's very simple," Dixon continued. "We will start with total deaths over the next one hundred years. The 'Eden' projection is obvious. We have been throwing around a lot of numbers for the total population of the world in the last few days. The actual number is about seven billion four hundred million. So, obviously, total deaths over the next one hundred years under the Eden Proposition will be that number – plus an inconsequential few hundred out of the surviving group.

"In contrast, total deaths over the next one hundred years, under the status quo, are projected to be about twelve billion, barring any unforeseen major disaster. So, from a very simple-minded perspective, and if you believe that death is the ultimate suffering, you can see where the most suffering is. There will be five billion more human deaths in the status quo scenario."

Dixon looked up at the next screen and then back at the group.

"A daunting title for sure," Dixon said. "'Total suffering days for five-year olds over the next one hundred years' - I'll explain. Doctor Sundgren talked about the Wold children. I don't remember if they had a five-year old … no matter. We intended to have this discussion regardless, as evidenced by this slide."

Dixon moved back to his desk and perched on the corner.

"We took quite a few liberties in putting this together because real data was seldom available. You may dispute the actual numbers we used. But the general result is the same in any case." Dixon looked back up to the screen and paused, apparently lost in thought.

"Children suffer every day right now," Dixon said, and looked back at the group. "Wars, sickness, starvation, abuse, neglect. There are countless ways that innocent, defenseless children suffer awful fates each and every day.

"There are one hundred twenty million five-year olds in the world right now," Dixon continued. "When we added up all the possible abuses present in their world today we came to the disturbing conclusion that, at a minimum, ten percent were in a situation we would call suffering. That works out to roughly twelve million five year-olds suffering each day, or about four-billion four-hundred million 'five-year-old-suffering-days' each year. That number will stay roughly the same each year over the next one-hundred years."

Dixon stood and pointed up to the screen. "As you can see, the 'Eden' line is again flat. At the beginning, we figured one hundred days of suffering per child - that's the period between serious symptoms appearing, and death - times one-hundred-twenty million five year-old children. So, that would be twelve billion total suffering days this year, and none worth noting in the next ninety-nine years. Therefore, twelve billion total five-year-old suffering days over the next one hundred years.

"Now - and this shows the dramatic impact of perspective - compare Eden to status quo 'suffering' days. As you can see, there are four-hundred forty billion suffering days in the status quo over a hundred years - *almost forty times as many as the Eden scenario!*"

Dixon walked back to the center of the room. "I apologize again for the clinical nature of this discussion. I know you probably have many objections and problems with this argument. For instance: how about calculating 'lost-days-of-bliss' - those days when a happy five year-old chases a butterfly across the yard? We will get into all of those discussions, I hope, over the next few weeks. But earlier today, the good doctors brought up the specific issue of suffering. I wanted to try to show you how 'perspective' can change what you think – even what you are certain to be true.

"If the Eden Proposition happens, there will be a six-month period of intense suffering, followed by ninety-nine years of almost none. The status quo simply spreads out the suffering. Eden compresses it into the first six months. So, the question is: where are you watching from? What is your time horizon? Is it truly one-hundred years? If so, it is indisputable that there will be far *more* suffering in this world if we do nothing."

Dixon nodded to Patel. The screen went blank. "Take a break, stretch your legs, get some air. We will continue our discussion of perspective in one hour."

The group was silent, some stayed in their chairs trying to make sense of what they had just heard. Toby watched as Laura got up and walked toward the door.

"Fuck," she said angrily, and kicked over a small table with several drinks on it. Glasses shattered as they hit the wall beneath the large front window. She headed down the path and out to the dock. Toby caught up to her a few moments later.

She turned to Toby, with not so much anger as confusion in her voice.

"How did he do that?" she said. "After our little speeches this afternoon, Sofia and I even thought we might have convinced him right then to give this nonsense up. Now … somehow, he's made everything we said go away. And what scares me, is that *I'm* not sure now. He might be right. But I know he can't be!"

"Look," Toby said. "This is just beginning. We've got several more weeks to convince him. There are ten smart, capable people in that room. Somehow we will have to figure out how to derail this 'Eden' thing. There has to be an argument that can get to him. We just need to find it."

Toby reached out and touched her arm, but she wasn't in the mood for consoling.

"I don't believe it," Laura said. "He's already decided. That's why he's so prepared to counter every argument we throw at him, like we just saw."

"Okay ... then why are we all here? He doesn't need our approval to proceed."

"I don't know. Maybe he wants us to share his guilt, or to confirm that his thinking and motives are pure. Maybe he expects us to make him God and worship him. How the hell do I know?" Laura said, her anger returning.

"Or ... he desperately wants us to convince him not to do it," Toby said.

Laura looked up at Toby and sighed. She turned and walked a few more steps out toward the end of the dock, then came back.

"What did Justice Brown want?" she asked.

Toby thought for a moment before speaking, "I think she was finally convinced that this thing we are doing here is real. Until you guys spoke, she still believed Dixon was just doing one of his staged events. When she saw that you all thought it was real, she got scared. She wants to get together tonight and talk about how we can stop him."

Toby watched for Laura's reaction, hesitating to tell her about the rest of his conversation with the Justice.

"Great, maybe she can issue an emergency injunction," Laura said sarcastically.

"A couple of quick announcements," Dixon said after the group had reassembled. "You may have already noticed, but the group in cabin four will not be dining with you anymore. We will prepare our own meals and eat separately. And, after noticing the glass pieces on the floor, the security folks have replaced all glassware with plastic cups. I guess they are worried that someone might slash my throat with a broken glass. Or perhaps they are just worried about Dr. Sundgren hurting herself."

Dixon looked around the room then paced a few steps toward the windows.

"I want to get back to the issue of perspective. It is crucial to our discussions." Dixon signaled to Patel to put up the next screen. "This is from a survey we have recently done. Secretary Solene, as many of you know, has been running a company that I own called 'WorldView'. The simple description of WorldView is that they conduct surveys about all kinds of things, from all kinds of people. I believe, and so does Secretary Solene, that WorldView has captured more, and better, information about the attitude of the world's people than we have ever had before."

Dixon paused for a drink of water.

"All of you are aware, intuitively and anecdotally, that attitudes around the world ... well, suck. Not exactly a scientific term, but you know what I mean. Ever since the Afternoon War, some seven years ago now, attitudes have been sliding toward despair. Though many people point to the utter failure of the international community to help in India and Pakistan after that war, and the subsequent collapse of the influence of United Nations, as the turning point in the collective psyche of the species - it is more likely that it was destined to happen in this time-frame anyway, and that the war was simply a well-timed catalyst.

"But, no matter the reason, we know that attitudes are at an all-time low. The topic provides endless fodder for the Blogs, the TV news organizations, and what remains of the print media."

Dixon made a gesture in the direction of Solene. "And who better to understand this phenomena than the man in the middle of that watershed event - Secretary Solene? His insights, and his ability to move freely about the world because of his reputation, have led to WorldView's remarkable accumulation of information documenting the current mindset of the human species."

"And It didn't hurt that WorldView's budget was bigger than the United Nations' in this area," Solene added.

"I suspect it was more efficiently spent as well," Dixon said.

Dixon stared intensely at the group and continued. "I can't emphasize this enough ... perspective, perspective, perspective ... with my apologies to the real estate profession," he said. "We will never be able to fully explore our obligation here unless you can step outside the perspective box that has governed your thinking throughout your life. This question - *this absurd and frightening question* - demands that we adopt a much longer, deeper and wider, perspective."

Dixon walked back to the windows and stared out over the brilliantly sunlit sound. He paused there for several minutes. It seemed to Toby that

Dixon had become stranded on his own rhetoric – "*this absurd and frightening question*". It hung in the air for everyone in the room to absorb. Toby thought it should be put up above the fireplace in a blinking, bright-green, neon sign.

Finally Dixon took a deep breath, as though reentering his body, and turned back to the group.

"I hope the example of suffering five year-olds from earlier today gave you an idea of the impact that a shift in the time-frame can make. Now, look at these screens from our WorldView data. I'm going to run through them quickly. These will show you just how short a time-frame the average human being has these days," Dixon waved to Patel, who quickly flashed about a dozen graphs on the screen.

"Don't worry about absorbing this information right now. We will get back to it in more depth during our discussions. I just want to use them to, once again, emphasize this point about perspective."

Dixon waved in the direction of the screen. "Understand what this means. If you have such a short 'time frame of concern' - as you have just seen from these screens - then why should you care about using up resources, or polluting the environment, or AIDS in Africa?" he said. "With such short time-frames, these problems simply become someone else's problem. I'm astonished every time I look at this data. The world has a surprising short view don't you think? And, disturbingly, it's getting shorter … as we will show later.

"Until yesterday, were any of you concerned about what the world would be like in three hundred years?" Dixon paused to see if anyone was foolish enough to answer. "Do you think anyone has ever seriously considered that question before now?"

"Nostradamus perhaps … and you," Dr. Mothershed offered, startling everyone.

Dixon cocked his head and paused, not sure if Dr. Mothershed's spontaneous comment held a deeper criticism by linking him with Nostradamus.

"Perhaps," Dixon said quietly, walking back to the tables where Jain and Patel sat. Toby thought Mothershed's comment had derailed him. After a minute Dixon returned to his desk and sat down.

"I hope I'm not driving you all down that road," he said finally. "I've read a little Nostradamus. It's mostly gibberish, psychotic delusions. I don't buy the so-called mystics, especially those who predict the 'end-times'. Do you know, for example, where the Christian 'Rapture' story comes from? Mr. Nuygen, care to answer?"

Mr. Nuygen came to attention, surprised to be called upon. "I'll try. I believe it was first preached by a Scottish Clergyman in the early nineteenth century. It is speculated that it initially came from a deranged teenaged girl in his parish. But your point, I believe, is that it is not Biblically based. There are a few tenuous allusions in the Bible that people stretch to interpret as support, but it is based almost entirely on the 'Revelations' - or delusions, depending on your point of view - of a disturbed teenage girl from Scotland."

"Thank you Mr. Nuygen," Dixon said. "And, the book of Revelations, if read objectively, is also more likely to be the product of mental illness rather than divinely inspired. And let's hope the mental illness resided in John, the author. If not, then the mental illness moves up the food chain to the Divinity - an even scarier thought," Dixon said, becoming more animated.

"This is one of the best places to apply Occam's Razor – which I'm sure you all know well. The simplest explanation, without question, is that these mystics were mentally ill. And of course that begs the question; "Why then have these *specific* mentally ill people become so revered? After all, there are a lot of raving lunatics out there. And the simple answer for that, per Occam's Razor, is: dumb luck, somebody had to."

"So, in case you had any doubt, you can see that I am not a religious person. I am also not divinely inspired. God has never spoken to me. And most importantly … *most importantly* … I am not mentally ill. Or so I believe."

Dixon leaned forward, his elbows on the desk, his chin resting on his clasped hands. After a moment he continued.

"You know, there have been times when I've had my doubts. In fact, soon you will hear some things that will disturb you greatly. They have disturbed me, and almost destroyed me as well," Dixon said, gravely. "So, every six months for the last few years, I've gone through comprehensive psychological testing. Without revealing the Eden Proposition of course - perhaps a significant omission. In any case, the results were clear: no sign of psychosis."

"I expect you can imagine that I have had many moments of doubt, of bewilderment and confusion even. But I have always returned to the dogged pursuit of the Eden Proposition, only because of the overriding *obligation* to the future, not because of mental illness."

Dixon stood up and returned to the middle of the room.

"So, the point of my little digression - and thank you Dr. Mothershed for sidetracking me - the point is, that you should guard against dismissing this event, and of dismissing me, as the delusions of a mentally ill person, in any form you might select; psychosis, paranoia, megalomania ... whatever. To do so would be too easy. It would be a cop-out. I'm asking you to do a *hard* thing. Don't take an easy way out."

Dixon stared down the group, making individual eye contact until he saw a sign of acceptance. In turn, each gave him back a short, grim nod.

"Thank you again Dr. Mothershed. Okay now, one more big step backward in the perspective area is required. I've beaten to death the time-frame issue ... the depth part of perspective. Now I want you to think width," Dixon said, pacing back to the windows. Toby sensed another prepared lecture coming.

"Another trend has been gathering momentum over the last few decades. Secretary Solene has studied this trend as well," Dixon said. "It goes like this: as our world has spiraled downward, as hope for the future has diminished, not only have people shortened their time-frame of concern, but they have also narrowed their *area* of concern. There was a time when the United Nations held out hope for many people as an institution that could produce a positive future. One world, one government. We all saw that dream disappear after the Afternoon War. Under the current stresses, the world is becoming more and more fragmented. There were, even just a few years ago, people who still believed in a worldwide community of mankind. We even had a name for them. We called them 'Statesmen'. Jimmy Carter, Secretary Solene even - but I can't name any now, can you? The world doesn't want them."

Dixon paused for a drink, and continued. "Instead, people have been retreating into smaller and smaller groups. 'Tribalization' is the term the media is fond of using. Here is a shocking survey from WorldView. Dr. Patel, could you put up the new United States map?"

The map appeared on the screen. It was the United States with seven different colored areas.

"According to our surveys, if a vote were held today, without any campaigning, over sixty percent of Americans would vote to dismember the United States into these seven new countries. I think this is inevitable. It's happening everywhere else in the world, why not here? Their reasons ... well, the people in the Northwest don't want to share their abundant water and cheap power. The people of New England want to close their border to the hoards moving up from New York. The farmers in the Midwest want to get better value for their food - the OPEC strategy. The people on the high ground are afraid of the people that are about to be driven back by the rising ocean. And so on, and so on."

"And just as a shorter time-frame of concern makes the big problems into someone else's problems, so does reducing one's area of concern. Eventually, when every problem becomes someone else's problem, nothing gets done. To make matters worse - and this is my own belief and I hope we have a good discussion on this topic - this is not a cyclical event. It is, instead, a slippery slope. Once it starts - and you could certainly say it has started - there is no way to turn back. In the future, time-frames and allegiances will not expand, they will continue to shrink. Things will get worse and people will continue to retreat," Dixon said, and sighed deeply.

"Sorry about the preaching. That can wait. But, let me get back to the perspective issue one last time," he said, and returned to his desk for a drink of water.

"One last perspective shift. Human beings are not the only 'stakeholders' - to use a business term - in the health of this planet. We are but one of untold millions of species who live here. So I ask you: Who speaks for them?'"

"I can," said Wyndi Rehn, brightening a bit at the prospect of suddenly having a role in the proceedings.

"Yes, you can, and that's why you are here," Dixon said. "So Ms. Rehn, let me ask you this. If each species were given a vote on … *our absurd, frightening question* … how do you think it would come out?"

"Well … maybe ninety-nine to one in favor of getting rid of us," Wyndi said. "Some actually would want us around - dogs, cats, crows, head lice, dump gulls, cock roaches, rats. But overall, we'd lose bad."

Dixon paced back across the room and continued. "Now think of it this way. If we could step back far enough and have such a wide view as to become truly species independent, then this question becomes a no-brainer, and these proceedings become pointless. If the other species could do it, they would throw us off this island planet as soon as possible. To most of them … *we* are the pandemic."

"Therefore, one issue we have to resolve in our discussions is just how 'species independent' can we - or should we - be while looking at our question. Please make that part of your thinking."

Dixon went over to say something to Jain and Patel. They began to pack up. Dixon turned and addressed the group. "Take two hours to get some food, but not too much. And don't drink a lot either. What you will hear this evening will not sit well on a full stomach or an alcohol-addled brain," Dixon said and then quickly left the building.

The emotionally battered and intellectually exhausted group remained motionless until most of Dixon's team departed. Two security men stayed behind for a few minutes. One gathered up some food while the other watched his back. Mallory, Wyndi Rehn, Sofia, Solene and Nuygen immediately disobeyed Dixon's directive and gathered at the kitchen bar for a round of drinks. Dr. Mothershed remained seated and closed his eyes. Toby wasn't sure if the ancient physicist was napping or thinking.

Somehow Rabinovich and Justice Brown ended up together outside at the far end of the porch. Toby watched the conversation for a moment. Rabinovich did most of the talking and Justice Brown occasionally nodded solemnly. Toby's first thought was that they were up to something, especially after hearing Justice Brown's concerns earlier in the day.

"I need to get some exercise," Laura said to Toby, who was still engrossed in watching the odd couple on the porch.

"I'm sorry, I missed that. What did you say?" Toby said.

"Stop staring. You're too obvious. I don't think you have a future in the spy trade," Laura said quietly. "Come on let's go walk back and forth on the dock. I really do need some exercise. It's been too many days with my butt planted in that chair," Laura said. "If we are going to be here for a few weeks, I need to figure out a way to get some heavy breathing going."

Toby gave her the raised eyebrow look, but restrained himself from making the obvious comment.

"Good for you for not jumping all over that," Laura said.

On the way down to the dock Laura grabbed Toby's arm. "You'll like this," she said, stopping just short of the boathouse. "I found the book Dixon mentioned about the Queen Charlottes – 'Raven's Cry'."

"Cool. How was it?"

"I can't say, I just scanned it last night before dropping off," Laura said. "But get this – do you know who it was that first sailed into Haida Gwaii and started the trade for otter skins, and so presumably gave the Haida the gift of smallpox that wiped them out?"

"No, don't know, sorry," Toby said. "I'd guess Vancouver?"

"Nope," Laura said. "It was Dixon."

"Huh?"

"Yup, Dixon - Captain George Dixon - July of 1787."

Chapter 11

Thursday Evening, June 4th, 2020
Haida Gwaii

Dixon reconvened the group at eight. Though late, this far north there was still daylight and would be until almost midnight.

"If you recall," he began. "The esteemed Senator from Washington expressed concern that our purpose here to discuss 'this absurd frightening question' was nothing more that an intellectual circle jerk. I responded by saying that in order to move from the theoretical plane of the circle-jerk to hard reality, I would have to prove three things to you. The first was that I could do it, it would work, and that I could do it right now."

Dixon engaged Senator Mallory in a stare-down.

"It is my belief that you are all in agreement that this first point is proven. Do you agree? Senator Mallory?" Dixon paused, expecting no objection, and getting none.

"On to the second point then. Which is: am I willing to do it? Do I have the stomach for it? Can I pull the trigger and do this horrifying thing?" Dixon said, and paced back to the window.

"I will address that now." Dixon nodded to Patel.

Nothing happened.

Patel looked at Dixon, hesitated, looked at the group, and then at the back wall. "Mr. Patel, please put up the screen ... now!" Dixon said forcefully. Patel glanced at the group again, gulped, said something to his machine, and a picture of a small rural village appeared on the screen. There were large mountains in the background and it appeared to Toby to be somewhere in the high country of central Asia.

"This is an unnamed remote village in western China," Dixon began. "It had a population of one hundred eighty when this picture was taken, two years ago."

Dixon gave Patel a stern look. A second screen appeared, taken from the same vantage point. It showed nothing but freshly plowed soil where the town used to be.

"This is the village as it looks today," Dixon said, and continued staring at the screen, momentarily lost in thought.

Dixon composed himself and turned back to the group. "As you all know, I am a technology person. A technology person would not attempt any major project - especially one like the Eden Proposition - without a full systems test. This was the test."

Toby was stunned. Dixon couldn't have done this to a whole village. Toby looked at Laura, she was staring at the ground. She must have known. Then it hit him; he remembered that she had said something about a rumored mad cow outbreak in China. This must be it.

"We were able, with the proper application of significant bribes, to completely isolate the village for more than a year," Dixon continued. "The local authorities - the ones who we bribed - were told we were testing a new flu vaccine. After the event, we told those same authorities that the test had gone horribly wrong, that everyone had gotten the flu from the new vaccine, and had died. Since they were culpable, having taken the bribes, they agreed to cover it all up, eventually identified it as a bird-flu event, and quarantined the area."

Dixon exhaled through pursed lips and glanced briefly out to the water.

"The system test was completely successful," he continued, once again without any discernable emotion. "We were able to test the efficacy of the agent. It proved to be one hundred percent fatal. We were also able to observe the length of time between the first exposure to the virus and the onset of the prion based symptoms. And we learned exactly how long it took to die, as well as the behavior of the victims as the symptoms progressed. In addition, we were able to test and verify the success of the vaccine. It also proved to be one hundred percent effective."

Dixon paced again, walking toward the fireplace. After a moment, he continued. "This test has verified everything Mr. Jain and Dr. Sundgren have told you about this agent. But I am not telling you this in order to verify the ability of the agent to do what we said it would do - you have already accepted that it can."

Dixon stared at his feet and then looked back up. "I am telling you this to prove my second point; that I am completely *willing* to do this."

"Next screen, Mr. Patel." Patel paused only a moment, and the new screen appeared. "This is the anti-viral complex, building numbers three and four, at one of my biotech facilities in India.

"I assume you are all familiar with these buildings from news reports. Almost a year ago now they were bombed by Pakistani terrorists. Both buildings were completely leveled, and over a hundred and seventy employees were killed."

Toby was familiar with this event. It had occurred in an area that he had spent time in and it had always puzzled him. There had been very little terrorist activity by Pakistanis in India since the war. It was Toby's experience that most Pakistanis felt guilt and remorse about the war, not lingering hatred.

Yet the authorities were certain that the Pakistani terrorists were the bombers. A Pakistani terrorist group had even taken credit for it on their blog.

"What you don't know however," Dixon said, looking directly at Toby, "is that these are the facilities that were responsible for isolating the virus that created prions, and then for making the vaccine. As I had stated before, much of the work had been compartmentalized in order to hide our real objective, but the final assembly and testing of the vaccine needed to be done in one place. Many of the people in these buildings had some knowledge of this project, though nothing close to complete knowledge."

Dixon stood silent, surveying the group, letting this latest horror sink in. "Many good people died here," he finally said, looking back at the screen. He walked over and sat on the corner of his little desk.

"As you will come to understand, control of the vaccine is very important." he said. "The person who controls the vaccine can design the future of the human race simply by choosing who gets the vaccine and who doesn't. Therefore, I could not take a chance that this vaccine could fall into someone else's possession ... anyone else's possession."

"I now have about four hundred doses of the vaccine," Dixon continued and pointed up to the buildings on the screen. "The rest was destroyed in the bombing of these buildings. The formula for creating the vaccine was also destroyed. And, unfortunately, every scientist who had any knowledge of how to create it was also killed.

"This should answer several questions you might have had. For instance; the fact that right now only a handful of people have a full understanding of the Eden Proposition. There were others, as I alluded to earlier, but they died in these buildings.

"And now you can understand how I intend to 'reboot' the human race. I will choose several hundred people to receive the vaccine. They will be together, in a protected place, while the horrifying event takes place. It is my belief that these several hundred people, most of breeding age, will form a sustainable new population of humans."

Dixon walked slowly over to the windows. "As I have just shown you, I've already caused the death of several hundred people as part of the Eden Proposition. So, in case there was any lingering doubt about whether this security team will use immediate lethal force should anyone try to attack me, then that should be clear as well; they will."

Dixon stood looking out over the water for a moment, framed by the strange long twilight of the far north glowing on the forested hills of the islands across the sound.

Toby watched Dixon and began shaking. Here he was in the Queen Charlottes, a place he'd always wanted to see, sitting in the most perfect lodge that he'd ever been in. To his left, he could reach out and touch Manute Solene – perhaps the most respected person in the world, and he was listening to a presentation by Duval Dixon – the most successful person in the world. What could be better? How could he be so lucky? Except, *except* ... the message he was hearing was so obscene. Not only that, it might end up being his fault. What kind of fucked-up nightmare could this be? Please wake me up he begged. Anyone?

Solene reached over and put his hand on Toby's shoulder. "Breathe," he said, and gave Toby a look whose power somehow brought him back into control. Toby nodded and inhaled deeply.

Dixon finally turned around. "Okay. We are now done with the 'revelation' phase of this confab. You've heard enough - more than enough, I imagine. I will close with the same benediction that I delivered before."

Dixon gestured to Patel and Jain. They turned off their machines and prepared to leave.

Dixon moved to the fireplace, center stage.

"Here me well," he began. "I am not God. I am not a messenger or emissary from God. I have not spoken to God. I am not an alien. I've not been abducted by, spoken to, or been directed by aliens. I'm not insane or mentally unstable. I don't have a psychological disorder. Not megalomania. Not even insecurity. I'm as sane and balanced as any of you. Yes, hundreds have died at my direction. Hundreds die every day for so-called legitimate reasons. An American president sends troops to the Middle East for reasons less important by orders of magnitude than this. Thousands die. And he is a hero to some. Less heroic to others, but no one believes he is insane."

He walked over to his desk and turned his back on the group to get a drink of water.

Toby stared straight ahead but somehow missed Dixon returning to the fireplace. And though it seemed impossible to Toby, Dixon's intensity level shifted into an even higher gear.

Dixon fixed the group with a stare that left them wide-eyed and breathless.

"Do not take the easy way out and think I am the problem. The problem is out there. I am proposing a solution to the problem. I have gone to extreme lengths to make this a viable solution. And now, you have a great responsibility. You are here to help decide if this is the right thing to do. You must take that responsibility seriously."

Dixon took a deep breath, signaled to his team, and walked to the door. "One last thing. Tomorrow, I want to hear from each of you exactly how willing you are to accept this greatest challenge. Good Night."

Once again, Dixon had paralyzed the entire group. For several long moments, no one moved. Finally Toby stood up and spoke. "Can we all stay here for a while and talk about what to do?"

"Yes, a good idea," Senator Mallory said and rose from his seat. "Let's get a drink first."

Toby approached Solene who was making a scotch rocks for Justice Brown. "Can you come with me for a minute?" Toby turned and walked toward the door where the last one of the security team was posted. Solene followed.

"We'd like to have a private discussion, would you please excuse us?" Toby asked the security man, whose hand had gone to his holster as Toby approached.

"Sorry sir, I was told to stay here until you all left."

Solene stepped forward, uncomfortably close to the security man.

"Soldier, you know who I am?" Solene said. "I am the former Secretary General of the United Nations. I know you are very good at what you do, otherwise you wouldn't be here, so you understand the chain of command. You understand and respect the proper authorities. Isn't that correct?"

"Ah, yes sir, I do," said the newly reconstituted soldier.

"Good. You go now. Tell Dixon I said to leave us alone. And tell him to turn off any listening devices that he has planted in this room. If he has a problem, tell him to come down here."

"Yes sir, I will," said the soldier, and headed out the door.

Toby gave Solene an astonished look. "I'm amazed that worked."

"Surprised the shit out of me too," Solene said.

A moment later, the security man stepped back into the room with Dixon on his heal.

"You may confer in here alone if you wish. I'll remove the security person," Dixon said. "Secretary Solene also asked me to turn off any recording devices that I had planted in this room. Let me assure you, there are no recording devices planted. None of this is being recorded. Think about it. Do you think I would want an electronic record of these discussions?"

Dixon grabbed the security person's arm and they quickly exited.

Toby took control again after everyone was reseated.

"Let me ask this first," Toby said. "Does everyone here agree that this is real, in other words, this is not one of Dixon's staged theater events? Does everyone agree that he is seriously considering this?"

"There's no doubt in my mind," Laura said.

"I've known him and watched him for almost forty years. I have no doubt that he is serious," Justice Brown added.

"But isn't this how he always does these tricks of his?" Senator Mallory asked. "Doesn't he completely convince the suckers and then, later, pull the rug out? I mean, think about this - he's going to kill eight billion people? Really? I'll bet he's filming this and then he'll sell the video; 'Ten prominent people fooled into thinking they will save mankind – listen to their lame, and sometimes hilarious reasoning'. It would be a big hit, the ultimate 'punked'. Everyone would love to watch us make fools of ourselves."

No one spoke. Mallory had injected a virus of doubt into the mix.

"I don't think so," Toby finally said. "Just look at him. Listen to him. He'd have to be the greatest actor of all time to have done what he has over these last few days."

"Maybe he is," Mallory said. "In some ways, his whole life has been an act."

Solene stood to speak. "I suppose the whole thing could be a charade," he said. "Though, at this point, I think all of us would agree that that possibility has a slim chance of being true. But I don't think it matters. We must assume that Dixon is not acting, that this is real. If we are wrong, and it is an act, well then that's great! The worst that happens then is that we may be a little embarrassed. So therefore we have no choice, we must believe he can do this."

Mallory spoke. "I just wanted to point that out – the charade thing. I actually do believe it's real. And Secretary Solene is correct. We have no choice but to believe it's true."

Toby looked around at the others. "Anyone feel differently?"

No one spoke.

"Okay, then I assume that all of us can also agree that we must find a way to stop him?" Toby asked.

Toby looked to Dr. Mothershed, who was once again seated, motionless with his eyes closed.

"I see three choices," Toby continued and looked around the room, suddenly unsure if he should be taking the lead in this conversation.

Solene sensed Toby needed a little nudge. "Good - go on," he said.

"Okay, three choices. First we can try to kill or capture him. Second, we can try to find a way to get a message to the outside world to send someone to rescue us. Or third, we can do as he has asked, and spend the next few weeks trying to talk him out of this thing," Toby said. "What we need to do is decide which one of those has the best chance of success."

"Let's go after him. There are more of us, and we have the element of surprise on our side. We can pick the time and place. That gives us a big advantage," Ambassador Rabinovich said. "With a good plan, we might be able to get him."

"I don't know Zelco - just look at us," Solene said. "We don't exactly look like the magnificent seven ... or nine. Half of us are over fifty. None of us, except maybe you, has had any training in this stuff. I doubt we could even get out of our chairs before they shot us. Those guys are complete professionals. I don't think we would have any chance."

"Zelco, I agree with Secretary Solene," Toby said. "And think about this: what happens after we fail? Then Dixon will decide this session is a bad idea after all. And then what choice does he have? He will have to kill everyone that survived the attack. And because the deaths of this distinguished group cannot possibly be explained, he will have no choice but to put the Eden Proposition into motion. In other words, our actions would insure that he proceeds."

"Sound reasoning, Toby. I see your point," said Senator Mallory. "So choice number one is gone. Then what's our chance of getting a message out somehow?"

"I've seen a few boats motor through the inlet," Wyndi said. "Maybe one of us could sprint down the dock and yell and wave at them. The security guys wouldn't shoot us in plain view of the people on the boat."

"No, they would probably let them come in and dock, and then shoot them and you. Remember what he did to his own scientists in India," said Rabinovich.

"How about someone heading into the woods, and going over to the other side and trying to hail a passing boat over there?" asked Laura.

"I know these forests," Toby said. "They can be almost impenetrable, this is a rainforest after all. And, I suspect they have planted electronic monitors on the obvious trails. I wouldn't try it. A decent tracker and a good hunting rifle would get you every time.

"But ask yourself ... why are we here?" Toby continued. "The only reason I can come up with is that Dixon actually wants to talk about this. I don't think he needs us to help him deal with his guilt or for us to share in the blame. I think he's way beyond that. He simply wants to give the current culture of the human race, now represented by the ten of us, one last chance to make its case. One last chance to avoid being 'rebooted'. I say we take him at his word and try our best to talk him out of it."

"Toby, I completely agree. I think we should commit to having Dixon's discussion," Solene said. "And, it has the added benefit of buying time. If the great debate isn't going our way we can always take another road in three or four weeks."

"Buying time is a good thing," Mallory added. "Who knows where this will go in a couple of weeks? So far, it seems to take a new turn every few hours."

"Are we in agreement then?" Toby asked. "Dixon said he wanted a commitment tomorrow, it sounds like we are ready to do that. Everyone agree?"

Toby looked at Rabinovich. "Zelco, are you okay with this?"

Rabinovich took a deep breath, exhaled and stood up. "I don't know ... this man's a criminal. An admitted mass murderer who is planning the worst atrocity in the history of mankind. And you suggest we sit down and chat with him about it for a few weeks?" Rabinovich walked to the door. "I'll think about it. I need some air."

"I'm concerned about what Zelco might do," Justice Brown said after Rabinovich went outside. "He was asking me all kinds of questions about Duval this afternoon."

"What kind of questions?" Solene asked.

Justice Brown glanced at Toby, then looked hard at Solene. "Oh, nothing important, I shouldn't have said that. I'm sure he's just upset and confused like the rest of us. Really, it was no big deal," she said.

Toby studied Justice Brown and suddenly realized that she had, in that moment, decided Solene was in on it. Solene was the "mole" she had mentioned earlier today. That's why she backed off just now. At least, that made more sense than Laura.

Wyndi Rehn raised her hand as if in school. "I have a question for you all", she said, diverting Toby's attention away from Solene.

"Go ahead," Toby said.

Wyndi stood, somewhat uncomfortably, to address the group, "I believe, like I think you all do, that Dixon proved those first two points of his. You know ... the ability, and the will to do this awful thing. But do you remember the third point? I don't want to seem selfish here, but you remember the third point was that we wouldn't be rebooted. I think that's still pretty important for us to know. If he can't make us believe we will survive, then maybe I would side with Zelco and give it the old flight-93-rush-the-cockpit try. Did I miss something or has he ignored that issue so far?" Wyndi said.

"Well, after what he told us today about those buildings in India where he killed one hundred and seventy of his own employees, I think you've raised a very good point Ms. Rehn," Senator Mallory said. "Why *would he* keep us alive after this session is finished?"

"He would have to keep us alive if we talked him out of it, wouldn't he?" Toby said. "He's gotten away with those events in China and India, so as of now, he's still clear of any serious wrongdoing. But I don't know how he could get away with killing all of us. That's another very good reason to try to talk him out of it."

"But how could he trust us not to tell what he did in India and China?" asked Laura.

"Those events have already been dispensed with," Solene said. "The governments of China, Pakistan and India all have decided what the cause was. So, case closed. And with India and China, the governments also have a stake in the explanations given. Because of the bribes, they are complicit. And besides, can you really imagine going to the press with this story: 'Duval Dixon wants to kill everyone in the world? I think Duval realizes that if he does decide to relent, there is very little we can do."

"Back to my point, and I hate to ask this again," Wyndi said. "Maybe it's because there is a part of me that might be sympathetic to Dixon's idea. Remember, I like to think I can speak for the other species. But, what if he decides to go ahead with the Eden Proposition? Do you think he will give us the vaccine then? How can he assure us of that?"

"Would you really want to stay alive if he does it?" Laura said. "I'm not sure I would."

"Well, *hell* yes, if that's my only choice. I want to stay alive. Don't you all?" Wyndi said. "Come on now, be real, you'd rather be alive then dead, wouldn't you?"

The group silently pondered Wyndi's primal question.

Finally Toby spoke, ".I don't have an answer for you about the vaccine and how can he assure us that we will get it," he said. "But, before we make our commitment tomorrow, I think we should ask Dixon. He may have an answer."

"He always does," said Laura.

Toby studied the group, trying to decide if he should press further.

"Is there anything else we should talk about?" he finally said.

"Perhaps I should not say this," Dr. Mothershed said from his chair, surprising most of the group, who thought he was asleep.

"What I have to say may take several minutes. You are all tired. It's best if I remain silent," Mothershed said.

"No, no, by all means, please let us know what you're thinking," said Justice Brown. "We need to hear everything that could help us."

"Thank you Madam Justice, I will go on then," Dr. Mothershed said rising from his chair to get a more direct look at the group.

"Let me get that for you," Sofia said, adjusting his chair.

"Again, thank you. One of the few benefits of becoming old and decrepit is that people do nice things for me," said Dr. Mothershed. "So … I will now play the role of the advocate of Satan."

"You mean 'the devil's advocate'?" asked Laura.

"Yes, yes, of course, the devil's advocate. That is the correct idiom," said Mothershed in his lilting Indian-British accent. "This is what I am thinking: It doesn't matter what we do. This *absurd frightening question* of

Mr. Dixon's has already been decided. He will do it. He may not know it yet, but it most certainly will happen."

Dr. Mothershed waited until the stunned group could muster a question. Finally Laura spoke: "How do you know this?"

"Let's call it 'future history,'" said Mothershed. "Sometimes the future can give us clues about the present."

It had been a very long day. Toby was exhausted and was sure that everyone else was too. He hoped the day had run out of surprises. But once again, the bottom fell out of the rabbit hole, and he resumed the tumble.

The group looked around to each other, wondering if the others had heard the same thing they had.

"I will explain," Mothershed continued. "Are any of you familiar with the 'Thorne Hypothesis'?"

"Time travel?" asked Toby somewhat sheepishly.

"Yes, time travel Dr. Benson, very good," Mothershed said with a nod to Toby. "Thorne has proposed in his hypothesis that time travel is possible. His hypothesis has gained considerable credibility over the past decade as we have learned more about gravity waves and other such things that you wouldn't want me to try to explain. Let's just say that, based on our current best knowledge, it is now accepted that time travel is indeed possible. Of course we are nowhere close to devising the means to do so, but sometime in the future those means will be accomplished. Interestingly, it doesn't matter if the means are available in one hundred years or in ten thousand years."

The astonished group could not imagine where Dr. Mothershed was going with this. But they didn't want to miss it, wherever it might lead.

Mothershed continued, "But as we have become accustomed to the acceptance of the Thorne Hypothesis, we have had a problem. A conundrum, if you will," Dr. Mothershed said, smiling at the reference to his own TV series.

"The conundrum is quite simple: where are the time travelers?" Mothershed paused to allow the implications set in.

"I had always assumed that our culture would continue in the future roughly as it is today. Perhaps we would have bumps along the way, but we would continue to strive for increased knowledge, and that our technology would continue to progress. So, eventually, even with unforeseen delays ... *still,* eventually, we could achieve the means to fulfill Dr. Thorne's hypothesis. Now if this was true, then the only explanation for our not being able to identify actual time travelers would be that Thorne's Hypothesis was wrong - that time travel wasn't possible. Except we had come to the conclusion that it was correct. If it was correct, then we should be able to identify time travelers in our midst. And round and round we went.

"Mr. Dixon has now solved this puzzle for us. As a result of his Eden Proposition, he has changed the culture of the human species. Either he has miscalculated, and everyone dies, or his resulting society rejects technology, or somehow uses it without the headlong striving, as we do now, for 'more and better'. In either case it doesn't matter to this discussion. What matters is that the Eden Proposition likely occurs, or else we are back to our original conundrum ... where are the time travelers?"

"I'm sorry," Mothershed said, clasping his hands in front of him. "You have heard too much already today. Please accept my apologies for bringing this up. But now you see now how odd we theoretical physicists are. We think about silly things like this," he said and bowed slightly. "Let us all retire now before anything else happens."

Not knowing what to say, the brain-weary group said nothing, obeyed Dr. Mothershed's request, and silently walked up to the cabins.

Chapter 12

Early Morning Friday, June 5th, 2020
Haida Gwaii

Before he had time to think, Toby found himself standing by his bed.

Shots? He heard gun shots. Two of them, very loud, very close. As he reached for the door, a third shot rang out so loudly that he jumped back into his room.

Toby reached the front room of the cabin just as Solene and Mallory opened their bedroom doors and stumbled into the hall.

"Where?" was all Solene could say.

"It was close, maybe up at Dixon's roost," Mallory said.

"Where's Zelco?" Toby asked.

"Oh shit," said Mallory, turning around and quickly heading to Rabinovich's room. "He's not in here."

The front door opened and Laura burst in, followed by Wyndi Rehn and Justice Brown.

"Those were shots weren't they?" Laura asked.

"Yes, I'm sure they were," said Toby. "Where is Dr. Contreras?"

"She went to check on Mothershed and Nguyen."

Sofia opened the door and came in, professor Nguyen and professor Mothershed followed.

"Zelco is not here," said Solene. "Anyone know where he is?"

"Maybe he's down at the lodge," Mallory said.

"Let's stick together and all go down there, it's too crowded in here anyway," said Toby.

"What time is it?" asked Sofia.

"It must be three-thirty or so, it's starting to get light outside," Toby said and headed for the door. "Let's go."

As they reached the path that lead down to the lodge they could see one of the security team standing in front of Dixon's cabin, His gun drawn. There appeared to be smoke coming from Dixon's front porch. Another security man stood guard by the boathouse.

"Zelco, are you in here?" Toby shouted into the main lodge as he entered. "Zelco?"

Toby checked the bathroom. Mallory went into the pantry.

"He's not here," Toby said to the group, now assembled around the kitchen bar. Rehn and Nguyen started some coffee.

"Has anyone seen him? Did anyone see him after he walked out last night?" Toby asked.

"Yes. I did," said Solene. "I went back out to the porch for a while after we returned to our cabins. Zelco came up the path from the dock. He asked me what he had missed after he walked out. I tried to explain Dr. Mothershed's time traveler thing, but I'm afraid I didn't do it very well. He said he was hungry and went back to the main lodge. It was starting to get quite dark, so it must have been past midnight. I went to bed a short time after that and didn't hear him come back in."

Toby's first thought after hearing Solene was that it sounded a little like a rehearsed speech. He needed to get Justice Brown aside and ask her what she thought about Solene.

"I'm so sorry, I should have said something," said Justice Brown. "I just didn't think he would do it so soon, especially after our discussion last night. I thought Toby was very convincing in his analysis about the futility of trying anything violent."

"I don't understand," said Mallory. "What should you have said?"

"Zelco talked to me out on the porch during one of our breaks. He suggested that we needed to do something to stop Dixon. I must admit that when he asked, I was inclined to agree. I don't now of course. He asked questions about Duval."

"What questions?" Asked Mallory.

"Things like … when does he sleep, where, how deep. He must have heard about our former relationship. I told him it had been more than thirty years since I had any personal knowledge about Duval, so I couldn't help."

"Did he say what he was going to do?" asked Toby.

"No ... that was it, just the questions."

The door to main lodge opened. First one and then a second security person cautiously entered. The first had his pistol drawn. The second was carrying an automatic weapon.

"We need you to all move over to the fireplace," said Mark.

Is this it, Toby wondered, the mass execution prior to the real mass execution? He suspected the others thought the same thing. But there was nothing to do but obey and hope for the best.

After they gathered in front of the fireplace, Mark addressed the group. "For the moment, we are in a very serious situation. We don't know what is going on with all of you. Until we have clarity, please understand we have to take substantial precautions. Don't do anything foolish. First, we need to pat everyone down. Please cooperate."

The security guy with the automatic weapon took a position by the bar. Mark walked back and gave him his pistol and then approached Solene. The former Secretary General of the United Nations raised both hands above his head. Mark quickly checked him for weapons and then proceeded to pat down the rest of the group. Laura, like all the others, was still in her sleeping clothes. Hers were considerably skimpier then the others' however, just a t-shirt and panties. As Mark approached her, she lifted her t-shirt a few inches, exposing her panties, quickly spun around so he could see the back, then gave him a brutally defiant stare. He just nodded, and moved on to the next person. Toby's concentration in this dangerous situation became seriously compromised.

"Alright, now I'm going to escort each of you, one at a time up to your rooms so you can get dressed," Mark said.

"Before you do that, please tell us what has happened," said Toby.

"Yes, please do. Before we do anything more, tell us what's going on?" asked Solene.

"Okay ... I'm sure you all heard the shots. A half-hour or so ago, Ambassador Rabinovich snuck up to Mr. Dixon's cabin. He threw a crude Molotov Cocktail onto the front porch to create a diversion. As we came out to deal with the fire, he broke down the back entrance and tried to attack Mr. Dixon with a large barbeque fork that he had found somewhere. He was shot before he could get to Mr. Dixon. Ambassador Rabinovich did not survive."

Just then, one of the boats started up. Another meal for the crabs, Toby realized.

Several hours later the group, now fed and dressed, was seated in the main lodge. Two security men were stationed nearby with automatic weapons at the ready. There was no opportunity for any group discussion or planning, so they only engaged in subdued conversation, but mostly they sat silently, wondering if one of the possibilities that they had discussed last night might come true. Dixon might decide this conference was a bad idea and proceed with the Eden Proposition immediately. In which case, they were expendable. Worse then that, they were witnesses - to Darby's, and now to Rabinovich's suspicious deaths. And, even more damning, to the admission by Dixon that he had wiped out a Chinese village and two Indian biotech buildings. They all realized that there lives now hung on Dixon's whim.

Dixon entered the lodge alone; the other two security men were apparently on the boat, which still hadn't returned.

Solene spoke first. "Duval, we want to assure you that Zelco acted on his own. None of us knew what he was planning. We did, in fact, have a long discussion last night about our options. And we did consider every approach, including aggressive actions like that attempted by Zelco. But we came to a clear decision that our best, and really our only option, was to engage you in this important discussion and to try our best to talk you out of this disturbing ... Eden Proposition. I can only speak for myself, as we haven't conferred since the news about Zelco, but I feel just as strongly now, as I did before, that we should begin the important discussion that you brought us here to do."

Dixon looked somber. He surveyed the group slowly and with such intensity that Toby felt - and was sure the others felt as well - that their fate was, in that moment, being decided.

Finally Dixon spoke.

"Does everyone here agree with Secretary Solene?" he asked, and proceeded to interrogate, in turn, each of the nine remaining defenders of the human race. Toby was the last to speak. After assuring Dixon that he agreed, Toby realized that no one had asked Dixon about the point that Wyndi had brought up the night before. The thought of dying within the hour had pushed the thought of dying next month out of their minds.

Toby decided to see if he could get this train onto a different track. "We did have a question for you," he said, mustering his most confident tone.

"Yes, what is it?" Dixon said, without emotion.

Toby, suddenly unsure about asking Wyndi's question, looked over at Solene. Solene gave him a almost imperceptible nod of approval.

"Wyndi brought this up last night. Wyndi, is it ok if I ask it? Or do you want to?" Toby asked.

"You go ahead."

"Okay. We have all now been convinced that you have the means to do this thing, and after what you told us yesterday, we are also convinced that ..." Toby paused, not finding the right way to describe that Dixon was crazy enough to actually do it. "That you have the will power to carry out the plan should you decide that it is necessary."

Toby took in a deep breath and exhaled slowly, then continued. "But remember, when you told us about moving the question from the theoretical to the real, that there was a third point. And the third point was that we wouldn't be rebooted ourselves. That we couldn't be asked to consider an action that would result in our own death," Toby said, now warming up to his little speech. "In light of what we heard last night, and of course what happened to Zelco - this point is now critical."

Toby waited for Dixon to say something, but Dixon remained silent, staring blankly at Toby.

Though now somewhat unnerved, Toby went on. "We would like you to somehow assure us that we will survive. Survive this conference for starters. And, should you proceed with the Eden Proposition, that we will be among those who receive the vaccine. You were right when you said that we couldn't conceivably support a proposition that included our own death."

Dixon stared at Toby for a few more moments, then took a quick glance at Solene.

"Here is what I'm going to do," Dixon said. "I'm going to have a meeting with Jain and Patel and Mark. I'd like for Secretary Solene to join us, to represent you all."

"That will leave the rest of you here with only one security person until the others return. Don't go anywhere, and please don't do anything foolish. I'm sure you have figured out the consequences should you try and fail. Be assured though, the consequences would be the same even if you tried and succeeded."

"Manny, Mark, please follow me up to my cabin," Dixon said, and walked out the door.

After they left, Mallory sat fuming for a few minutes. Finally he decided to try something. He cautiously approached the remaining security man.

"What's your name again?" Mallory asked.

"I'm sorry sir, but please do not talk to me," said the unnamed security person.

Mallory studied him for a moment. "When we leave here, there is going to be hell to pay. You are looking at substantial jail time. This is now a kidnapping situation. That is a life sentence all by itself. We also have the two deaths to be reckoned with," Mallory paused. "But if you help us, I'll see that you get pardoned. That's a full pardon, not just a good plea deal. I can guarantee you a full pardon. The President owes me."

"Sir, let me explain something to you," replied the security man. "We are trained professionals. Please accept that. Because of last night's activity, we have moved to a heightened security level. This is the last time I will ask you to not talk to me. If you persist, I can guarantee you that I will take action. That is the protocol. Please return to your seat ... right now."

Mallory sighed and returned to his seat.

Dixon, Solene, and Mark returned within thirty minutes, accompanied by Jain and Patel. Patel was carrying what appeared to be three small laptop computers.

"Please be seated," Dixon said as he reached his small desk. Solene took his usual chair with the group.

"I have decided to accept the idea that Ambassador Rabinovich acted on his own. Therefore, with the assurance from Secretary Solene that everyone here supports proceeding with the discussions, we will finally start this great debate tomorrow," Dixon said and walked to the front of the fireplace.

"First, though, let me say how we will deal with this situation. We will now claim, with all of you supporting our claim, that Darby and Rabinovich died in a boating accident. It is not all that uncommon for two inexperienced boaters to capsize a small boat while trying to retrieve large crab pots," Dixon said and raised his hands above his head, palms out, squelching any premature protests.

"I will remind you that both Darby and Rabinovich are completely responsible for what happened to them. No crime has been committed by us. These two men were famous, highly respected individuals. The boating accident story will protect their legacy. It will protect their families. You will be doing them a great favor by supporting this version of the events. The bodies, of course, will not be found," Dixon said. "Are we in agreement about this?"

"Do we have a choice?" Mallory asked sarcastically.

Dixon stared at Mallory. "Of course you do. But I want you to understand there is room for another person on that crab boat."

"Is that a threat?" Mallory shot back.

"You're Goddamned right it is!" Dixon shouted angrily. "This morning, one of you just tried to kill me. What exactly do you expect, Senator Mallory ..."

"Whoa! Okay," said Mallory, leaning back in his seat with his hands up, palms facing Dixon, employing the international hand signal for "Whoa ... I give".

Mallory, now conciliatory, spoke calmly, "I'm sorry. I do understand that it is in everyone's best interest, especially Darby's and Rabinovich's, to support the boating accident story," Mallory said, using his best politician's "I know when I'm beaten" tone. "My apologies, but please understand, I'm a little on edge. We are all a little on edge. But the boating story will have my full support. And, please be confident that I - really all of us - are ready to have this great debate. I'm looking forward to the challenge."

Dixon studied Mallory for a few moments while working on regaining his own composure. "Ah, as always Senator, the consummate politician. I'm surprised it has taken you this long to understand which side to support."

Dixon looked up to address the whole group. "My apologies as well for that little outburst. The Senator is quite obviously correct about all of us being on edge."

Dixon got up from his desk and stepped back to the front of the fireplace. He pursed his lips and blew through them, then nodded several times to himself, obviously trying to release the tension that had built over the last few hours.

"Okay then, let's get started. I have one more thing to discuss - to show you actually. This will answer Ms. Rehn's question concerning my assurance that you will get the vaccine. Then, we will break for the day, and I will put the large boat at your disposal. You may go fishing, or take a cruise around the inlet. I will instruct the security team to stand-down from their heightened security posture. I hope that things can get back to a less stressful state."

Dixon walked over to Patel and retrieved one of the three small devices that he had just brought in. "I wasn't going to show you this until we were all done here and about to leave. You may remember a statement I made at the beginning about how, in the last few hours, I would convince you that you would not reveal what we had discussed here. Well, this is why I knew that would be true," he said and held up the small computer.

"You all are aware how difficult it is to protect intellectual property these days. Most of the international treaties that were established in previous decades have either expired or are being ignored. In the biotech business, we have to go to great lengths to protect our drugs. Especially in the early stages, and especially when we need to move the actual product. Sometimes, we need to move the product across borders without detection."

Dixon held up the small computer, "We built this device several years ago. It looks like, and is in fact, a working laptop/video player device. You know what these are. They are very popular, and you each probably own one or several of these. On the outside, it is an exact replica of a major brand from several years ago. Therefore, it is easy to take across any border as a carryon. Occasionally they will ask you to fire it up, but since it does work, that's not a problem."

Dixon placed the device on his small table and entered a few keystrokes. The keypad popped up a bit, enough to grab and open it up. Dixon held the device up, showing the interior under the keypad.

"Inside you can see the five vials in a row," Dixon said. "There is a vial in the middle, the one with the red "X" on it. That is a vial of a very corrosive material. If broken, it will dissolve the plastic of the other four vials. It will compromise the contents of those vials to the extent that the material inside will not be usable. And, more importantly, the material will not be able to be re-engineered. It will be useless to anyone who tries to analyze it.

"So, the way this works is that the courier does *not* have the code to open up the device. Therefore the courier cannot steal it, or cannot reveal it to someone else who might steal it. If someone steals it and tries to force it open, the mechanism inside will break the corrosive vial, and ruin the contents. The code can only be sent via satellite, in a heavily encrypted mode, to the device from our headquarters."

Dixon removed one of the vials and held it up to for the group to see.

"Each of these vials contains enough Eden flu vaccine ..." Dixon paused. "We have been calling the consequences of our agent the 'Eden flu'. Again, please don't try to find any meaning in that designation other than it's convenient and short."

He went on, "Each vial contains enough vaccine for three doses, provided that you are very careful with measuring out each dose. The four vials therefore contain enough vaccine for twelve doses. But, I will add that you might consider using two doses per vial instead of three, enough for eight people, to be on the safe side. We do believe that this will work for twelve people, again, only if you measure it precisely. But, it will be your choice as to how to use it."

Dixon closed the V-box. "Now, this is the most important part for you to understand. First, each of you will get one V-box with the dosage I just discussed in it. Remember I said that the box can only be opened from an encrypted code sent to it via satellite. In this case, I will be the only person who has the code to open them."

Dixon paused and paced a few steps to the fireplace, waiting for what he had just said to sink in.

"I need to make something else clear," Dixon said. "When we conclude our session here, I will not announce my decision about releasing the Eden flu. It's likely that I will *not* have made a decision by then. But even if I have made a decision, I will keep it to myself. And I do not have any timetable as to when I might make a decision. However, It would be logical to conclude that after some substantial period of time, probably measured in years, that it would be difficult for the Eden Proposition to proceed. But other than that, you will never know what I have decided, *unless…*"

Dixon walked back to the desk and entered something on the keyboard. The V-box began to chirp loudly and a green LED began to flash on the left side of the box. Dixon entered something else and the chirping stopped, but the light continued flashing.

"Unless," Dixon continued. "Your V-box alarm goes off. The audible tone will continue for two minutes. But the light will continue to flash forever, or until the battery goes dead. So, remember to keep your V-box with you at all times, and remember to keep it plugged in or have sufficient battery power."

Dixon held up the V-box, slipped the battery out, and held it up for the group to see.

"Remember to keep it with you at all times. When the alarm goes off The V-box can be opened in the normal manner without damaging the vaccine. Like so …" Dixon held up the box, and demonstrated.

"Now listen carefully. This is Important. You will have only that first day to take the vaccine. The Eden Flu virus will be released the next morning. If you plan to share the vaccine with family, or anyone else, they must be vaccinated that first day also. If you can't get to them that day, the only thing you can do is call them and tell them not to leave their houses, not to let anyone in, not to drink tap water, and not to talk to anyone until you can reach them. Make sure you yourself take an ample dose of the vaccine first."

"Obviously, you should not tell them, or anyone for that matter, what is going on. Only bad things can happen if the authorities learn what might happen, and if they understand what is in these boxes. First of all, they cannot get around the tamperproof engineering. So they will gain nothing by having the box. And more importantly, you will lose everything. You will not have the vaccine for yourself or for your family."

Dixon looked around the room, "Is everyone with me so far?" No one spoke.

"Good. Then let me add one more thing," he said, pacing back to the windows.

"If I find out through any means available to me that any of you have gone to the authorities, or have done anything at all to compromise my ability to launch the Eden Proposition. Then, I will not send the code to *any* of you. In other words … everyone here, including everyone's families, will not get the vaccine. One person's actions will cause the death of everyone here, and the twelve others that each of them could have protected."

Dixon paused to see the reaction. The group sat motionless, still processing the implications.

"Not only that, you must understand the position you will put me in if the project becomes threatened. It is likely that I will be forced to proceed. If I don't, I will assume I will never have the opportunity again. That will substantially skew my decision to favor launching the Eden flu immediately. Bottom line: if you go to the authorities, the Eden Proposition will commence, and you will not get the vaccine. Is that clear?"

The group remained silent.

"Let me go further," Dixon continued. "Be assured that if something dramatic were to happen to me, the Eden Proposition would be immediately launched. Let me give you an extreme example. Let's say you were able to go to the government without my finding out. And that the government decided to wipe me out as quickly as possible by sending a submarine to launch a tactical nuke on this island. I would die, everyone still on the island would die, and it would be so quick, that we wouldn't even know what had hit us, much less have had a chance to give any orders to anyone. But even in that case, we have a contingency plan that would release the Eden flu. And, I would not be around to send the code releasing the vaccine to you. We have thought of everything, please trust me on that."

"Mr. Dixon may I ask something?" Toby said solemnly.

"Yes, go ahead"

"First, I have to say, that this is ingenious. I was wondering what you could possibly do to keep us from going to the authorities after we leave, but this…" Toby said, and just shook his head.

He continued, "This still doesn't answer Wyndi's question. How do we know if there will be any real vaccine in the box? Or if you will even send us the code if you decided to launch the virus?"

"Good questions. I'll deal with the last one first," Dixon said. "If, from the beginning, I did not intend to send you the code, it would not make any sense for me to put the vaccine in the V-box in the first place. There would be no point in wasting the vaccine, or taking any chance that it could fall into the wrong hands. So, I would accomplish the same result by not putting the vaccine in the V-box in the first place. Correct?"

Toby got it, and nodded.

"So, your two questions are really only one question - how will you be assured that there is real vaccine in the box?"

Dixon looked around the room to make sure everyone was following him.

"And the answer to that question is … it doesn't matter," Dixon said and paused to let it set in.

"Let's assume that in the first case, that there is real vaccine in the V-box. That means, as we have just discussed, that it is my intention to release the vaccine to you if the Eden Proposition goes forward. And provided that I am alive and free to act, I will do just that. You have my commitment."

"Now, what if the box doesn't have any real vaccine in it," Dixon said and walked slowly back to the fireplace. "That means that I never had any intention of giving you the vaccine in the first place."

"So, listen carefully now. What if you decide, when you leave here, that there is no vaccine in the box? Then what should you do?" Dixon asked and paused for a moment.

"If you go to the authorities the most likely result - by a long way, I might add - is that you will force me to launch the virus. And since the box does not contain any vaccine, then it will have no value to you or the authorities. Think about it. If you believe there is no vaccine in the box, your best course of action is *still* to do nothing and simply hope that I decide not to launch the virus. Understand clearly; that remains a very likely possibility.

"Or maybe you are just wrong about the vaccine *not* being in the box. So … that's why I say it doesn't make any difference as far as what course of action to take. Under *all circumstances*, you're best choice, the only reasonable choice, is to do nothing – simply wait and see."

Dixon walked slowly over to the windows and stared out at the water.

"You need to make a shift in your thinking right now," Dixon turned back to the group and continued. "Understand, and accept as absolute fact: that the launch of the Eden Proposition is assured unless I decide otherwise. The weak link in this chain is not the virus, or my ability to make the virus, or my ability to distribute the virus, or the end result of the virus being released. Those things are already set up and cannot be stopped. The weak link is the vaccine. As I mentioned before, whoever controls the vaccine, has the ability to save themselves, and shape the next culture of the human species. The vaccine is the most important thing now."

"Then why risk putting it in this stupid box," Wyndi asked. "Why don't you just give it to us now?"

"Toby just said it," Dixon said. "Control. If I gave you the vaccine now, many of you would go the authorities immediately after you left here, regardless of how these discussions go. And the irony of that is, of course, the likelihood that it would force me to launch the Eden flu. So in a very real sense, I need that control over you in order to preserve my right to *not* … listen carefully, I repeat … to preserve my right to *not* launch the virus."

"I'm sorry, but I guess I don't get it," Wyndi said. "It helps me to say it out loud. So you are saying, that if any of us goes to the police, or FBI or the press, or anybody like that - and you find out about it - then you won't give *any* of us the secret code for the vaccine box?"

"Yes, that is a promise."

"You would kill all of us and our families if any of us went to the authorities? Really?" Wyndi said, scrunching-up her face.

"Yes. Absolutely," Dixon answered without hesitation. "And with good reason. I absolutely need to protect my right to *not* launch the Eden flu. All of you would want me to have that right as well, don't you?"

"Let me ask you, Wyndi," Dixon continued. "Will the idea that you would cause the death of everyone here and their families keep you from going to the authorities? Of course you have to combine that with the fact that I would launch the virus as well. And remember, that if you go to the authorities, you will force me to do just that."

"Probably. But what if you didn't find out?" Wyndi replied.

"But what if I did? How can you know for sure I won't? That is a huge risk to take, and a risk that has very little chance of having any reward. And it will cause the virus to be released."

Dixon paused, rubbed his face, ran his hands through his thinning hair, paced over to the windows and again stared out at the water. Toby glanced over at Laura. She was already looking back at him, shaking her head slowly from side to side, a tight-lipped grimace on her face. Toby interpreted it as resignation. Game, set and match to Dixon.

After a long minute or two, Dixon reentered his body and turned back to the group.

"First: does everyone understand how this works?" Dixon asked, picking up the V-box and holding it up. "I repeat, you will each get one when you leave here. Keep it with you at all times. Make sure it is plugged-in or has a good battery. Check the light if you have been away from it for any length of time. Understood?"

Dixon looked across the group, trying to discern if everyone understood.

"Duval, I get how the box works, but I'm trying to sort out what you expect from us," Laura said. "Are you expecting us to go about our lives as if nothing has changed - except we will study this little box every few minutes to see if the light is on and the world will end? What kind of life will that be? Living in fear of this little green light ... forever?"

Dixon looked down at the floor for a moment, troubled by the question.

"You know, Dr. Sundgren," Dixon said. "The point you make has always been a concern of mine - the open ended nature of my decision making process. I think it's time I resolved that issue. For my sake as well as the point you have just made."

Dixon started walking again, stroking his hair.

"Here is what I will do. If I haven't reached a decision in a year, then I will consider my lack of a decision to be, in fact, a decision not to proceed," he said, and paused to think. "No - make that eighteen months. I may want to call you all back into session next summer, after we have had a year to digest this. So, eighteen months, the first of January, 2022, if nothing has happened by then, go ahead and throw away these boxes. I will give up control over you at that point, and you will be free to do as you like with the information that I have given you."

Dixon let out a big sigh, and nodded up and down a few times, agreeing with himself that this was a good plan.

"Dr. Sundgren," Dixon said. "Does that work for you?"

"It's better, I think," Laura answered, somewhat reluctantly.

Toby was quickly trying to work through the implications of the latest rule. Toby waited for Dixon to do what he always seemed to do: spring a trap.

Dixon continued. "Thank you, Dr. Sundgren for asking that question. I like this new approach much better. Not only does it address your concern. It also forces me to decide, but in a reasonable time frame. And - this is the part I like best - it gives you a reason to make considerable efforts to affect my decision after we leave here."

"You see," he continued. "If you don't want me to proceed, all you have to do is to continue to give me reasons to delay. In fact, this will give you motivation to try to take important positive actions – 'save the world' kinds of actions."

Dixon was warming enthusiastically to this new idea.

He waved his arms at the group and continued. "You are a very accomplished, very powerful group. You can actually do things that can make a difference. After you leave here, you might take the position that you have eighteen months to save the 'seven billion.'"

"You know I will be watching," he continued. "And, you know that I am likely still to be undecided - unless, and until, the little green light comes on. Perhaps this will inspire you to do things that might give me a reason not to turn on that light."

Toby's head was spinning, his thoughts were careening around. Was this the ultimate trap? Did he just come up with this now? Maybe this was the plan all along. And this whole event was nothing more than a way to motivate these world-weary people to get off there ass and to go forth and do good.

But then he remembered. Darby and Rabinovich were dead, the village in China, the buildings in India. No, he should take this at face value. Dixon had simply come up with a new twist.

Dixon surveyed the group once again, looking for any other questions.

"Good," he finally said. "Now, you know it all. We can proceed."

Dixon walked back to the kitchen bar to have a quick conversation with Mark. After returning to the fireplace, he began again.

"Believe this ... if you believe nothing else ... *believe this*," Dixon said with solemn intensity. "I am telling the truth when I say that I want your help. I've been inside this project for too long. I need to know if my thinking is valid. This is the reason, the only reason, that I have gone to all this trouble to set up this session with you all. I did not anticipate that it would be so ... so ..." Dixon paused, searching for the right word. "Such a chaotic few days getting to this point. I knew it would be difficult, but not in this way. Regardless, we have now reached the point where we are ready to proceed. It is my impression that all of you now understand and accept the situation you are in. I do not anticipate any further unusual things to happen."

Dixon turned on the charm switch. The Texas smile returned.

"Get some food, try to relax and enjoy the afternoon. We will start in earnest tomorrow," he said. "Any last questions?"

Toby took a deep breath. "I have one," he said.

"Go ahead," Dixon said, surprised and sounding somewhat apprehensive.

"Is Secretary Solene part of your Eden Proposition group? Has he been a part of this from the very beginning?" Toby asked, in a rush.

Dixon stared at Toby for only a split second. He nodded to himself and the smile returned.

"That's quite a question, young Skywalker," Dixon said, amused by his little reference. After a brief pause, he continued, "Let's ask the Secretary."

Dixon turned his gaze to Solene, who was now staring down at his feet. Dixon waited a moment for Solene to look back up at him.

"So, what say you Secretary Solene? Are you part of this?"

Part 2

Chapter 13

Four weeks later
Wednesday, July 1st, 2020
Haida Gwaii

Toby filled Laura's glass and then his own. They had come down to the cockpit of the V. Cerf to have one last moment alone before rejoining the real world. After four weeks of agonizing and exhausting discussion, Dixon had surprised the group with the announcement that they would be flying back to Vancouver the next morning. They were done.

"I can't believe it's over," Laura said. "I guess I'm relieved, but what happens now?"

"Well, tomorrow morning they put us in those two planes over there and, we hope, fly us back to Vancouver," Toby said.

"Thanks," Laura said, slightly irritated. "That clears up everything."

Laura got up and walked to the back rail. A warm breeze out of the north had built up a moderate chop that rolled into the gap between the dock and the stern of the V. Cerf. Sporadically, a small plume of salt water misted into the cockpit. Laura put both hands on the rail, tilted her head back, closed her eyes, and let the wind blow through her hair and let the fine spray drift on to her face. She stood there for several minutes, deeply inhaling the ocean-scented air.

Toby watched, even more smitten now then when he first saw Laura waiting for him on the curb in front of the Oriental Hotel some four weeks ago.

"You know something?" she asked, and abruptly turned back to Toby. "I regret that I haven't taken the time to appreciate how beautiful it is up here. You have, with your walks over to the beach, and I see you down here on the dock sitting and soaking up the air and the water and the sun and the beauty of it all. And now, just hours before we leave, I finally want to see and feel this place like you do."

"Well then maybe this is your lucky day," Toby said, and got up and moved to the rail next to her. "I've been thinking about this since Dixon announced the end of the discussions this afternoon."

"Let me guess," Laura interrupted. "You are going to propose, and then we are going to escape into the woods and build a log house and eat slugs and raise squirrels and have eight kids."

"Amazing," Toby replied, straight-faced. "Except for the slugs, you got it exactly right. How did you do that?"

"Easy – Mothershed told me our future history."

"Or, maybe you're the time traveler Mothershed's been looking for."

"I wish," said Laura with a sigh. "If I was a time traveler, I'd go back ten years and seduce Dixon into marrying me. I don't think he'd be doing this if he had a bunch of kids."

Laura turned and put her hand on Toby's shoulder, "Sorry - I interrupted. Tell me what you were thinking about."

"Well, it is a proposal of sorts. I've told you about my sailboat in Anacortes?"

"Of course, we talked about the San Juan Islands. Beautiful, just like here."

"I don't know if you have realized this yet, but Dixon has released us two weeks ahead of schedule. Your calendar is clear for the next two weeks and so is mine. So ... tomorrow, how about we head straight for Anacortes, buy a little food and sail away for a while?" Toby said, hoping the heat he felt on his face didn't give away the fear and uncertainty he felt about his bold proposal.

"Well my goodness Dr. Benson," Laura said in her best imitation southern accent. "What kind of woman do you take me for?" And then quickly added, "Don't answer that."

Laura, now serious, looked into Toby's eyes and paused for just a second. "Are you sure?"

"Completely, absolutely, ya-sure-you-betcha sure."

"I could have done without the ya-sure thing. But, we can work on your proposal skills, and some other things, over the next two weeks," said Laura. "Okay, let's sail away! I would absolutely love to go. Besides all of the other good reasons, I think it'll be good for us to have some time to decompress after this … this … obscene event."

Toby, struck speechless at the prospect of two weeks alone on a sailboat with this extraordinary woman, could only nod and grin.

"But let's not tell anyone, okay?" Laura said. "In case Dixon wants to call us back, or the word gets out that the session is over and the CDC wants me to report to Atlanta immediately."

"Or the police want to question us about Rabinovich and Darby," Toby added.

Laura grimaced, "I forgot about that …"

They stood for a moment, shoulders touching, looking silently out at the water. Toby wondered if this was the right time for that first kiss, but chickened out. It could wait one more day.

"We need to go back up to the lodge." Toby said. "I'm guessing the group will disperse quickly tomorrow after we land. So this will be the farewell thing tonight."

"Do you think Dixon will be there?"

"I doubt it."

Laura grabbed her glass and the empty wine bottle, took one last wistful look out at the water and smiled at Toby. "Sailing in the San Juans, huh. I like *that*!"

A minute later, they joined the somber group assembled in the main lodge. At the door, Laura gave Toby a see-ya-later light squeeze on his elbow and walked over to the kitchen where Sofia and Justice Brown were talking. Toby headed to the bar to replenish his wine.

"Now, as I recall, it was under similar circumstances some weeks ago that you and I first made our acquaintance," said Secretary Solene with a grin as he stepped up behind Toby.

"Weeks ago? It seems like a lot longer."

"Yes it does. Why don't we take a little stroll out on the dock?"

Toby nodded, and followed Solene out the door and back down the path to the dock.

'So," Solene finally said as they stood at the end of the dock looking out at the golden glow of the evening sun on the islands to the north. "Were you surprised today when Duval decided to end the discussions?"

Toby thought for a moment before replying. "No, not really. I've had trouble concentrating the last few days. I suspect everyone has. I'm not sure if it's just mental exhaustion or simply that the group has said everything they are capable of saying," Toby said. "But I think it's probably the latter."

"I agree, I think it's the latter," Solene said, still staring out across the sound.

After a minute, Toby looked directly at Solene and asked the question that everyone wanted answered. "What's going to happen now?"

Solene reached back and placed his glass on a dock post then turned to Toby, folded his arms in front of him, and looked down at his feet for a moment before answering.

"Well, I guess tomorrow we get on those airplanes over there and fly back to Vancouver."

Toby grinned and shook his head.

"What's the matter? It wasn't that funny," Solene said.

"Well, ten minutes ago Laura asked me that same question, and I gave her the same answer."

"It looks like we're fresh out of profound answers, doesn't it," Solene said with a wry smile.

"You'd better not be," Toby said.

"Okay, you're right, I'll give you a better answer. But I warn you, it's going to fall far short of the profound."

Solene reached back, grabbed his scotch, drank it down and turned again to face out to the water.

"It will be just as Duval described it," Solene continued. "Tomorrow, we go back and resume our old lives and Duval will think over what was said here. And then at some point, he will make his decision. That's it."

"Resume our old lives?" Toby asked, incredulously. "I don't see how we can do that."

"What else can you do?"

Toby just nodded.

"What about you guys?" Toby asked after a moment. "How can you avoid getting in trouble over Darby's and Rabinovich's deaths? Do you really think that story about drowning while picking up crab pots is going to hold up? We'll all be questioned and I don't think this group will be very consistent. The authorities will be suspicious, and the media will go nuts. I just don't see how even someone like Duval Dixon can control the consequences of those deaths."

Solene turned and looked directly at Toby. "Trust me. Believe me about this," he said, tapping Toby on the chest with his index finger. "This is not an issue at all. There will be no difficulty with Rabinovich and Darby when we return."

"I guess I wouldn't put it past Dixon to wiggle out of it, but it will be interesting to see how he does it," Toby said.

"Yes. It will be that."

"Can I ask one more question?"

"Go ahead."

"Did Dixon get what he wanted out of this session?" Toby asked. "And I'm sure you have a better idea of what he wanted than I do."

"Not true, not true," Solene said. "He wanted exactly what he said at the beginning. He wanted this group to help him with his decision. Exactly as he said. Nothing more."

"Well then, maybe I asked the wrong question. Let me try again," Toby said. "Did we help Dixon with his decision?"

Solene folded his arms, looked down at the ground and shook his head slowly from side to side. Finally, with a sad grimace, he said, "Truthfully … I don't think so."

Toby could only look at Solene. His chest tightening once again with the fear that always came from directly confronting Dixon's "absurd frightening question".

"You cannot imagine the conflict … the war, that is raging inside of Duval Dixon's psyche," Solene went on. "I guarantee you that he doesn't want to do this thing. Who would? But he cannot escape the conclusion that it is something he must do."

Solene paused and looked intently at Toby.

"Dixon is not a religious man. I'm sure you have become convinced of that over these last four weeks. He has never felt that some outside force has been acting on him. That is his claim. I've never heard him say or act differently, so it's clear to me that he believes it. He knows that there is no God, and therefore he *knows* that no God is inspiring or requiring him to pursue this."

Toby nodded, "I can see that."

"Dixon believes, as he said during the 'Why me – why now' discussions, that this awful decision has fallen to him simply because of a convergence of history and circumstances," Solene paused and looked skyward. "I'm not a religious person either. But who knows? I'm not sure if it's that simple. Maybe this is how it has to be. Maybe this thing could only be done through an apparently sane, stable and logical person. Maybe Dixon is just the means, like Noah, but he isn't part of the real discussion. The one going on up there," he said, and again glanced heavenward.

Solene paused, took a deep breath and looked back at Toby, "Sorry, I digressed. Your question was; 'Did the session help Dixon?'. I know he wanted it to. He hoped desperately that it would. And I don't want you to think you, or the group, failed because you didn't say the right things."

"Failed?" Toby said emphatically. "Don't put this on us. How could we *fail*? We did our best to engage Dixon in this discussion. But Dixon himself said it was not up to us to decide."

"Yes … yes, sorry. You are absolutely right. I used the wrong word. Please don't think that you have any responsibility for the outcome of the Eden Proposition. That's not what I intended to say. You see, Duval suspected going into this event that it was unlikely that it would result in the discovery of anything that he hadn't already thought of.

"I think there was one thing that helped, though. And that was the deadline that he agreed to. I fully expect that he will take that one more year before he finally decides. Maybe meet with some of you again. Maybe he will just watch to see what happens, within the context of some of the discussions we had here. But nothing will happen right away, unless …"

Solene's voice trailed off. Toby waited a moment then asked, "Unless what?"

"Unless something unexpected happens and he is forced to decide. That's always been the big risk of getting this group together. I advised against it in fact, for just that reason," Solene said.

"What do you mean by 'unexpected'?" Toby asked.

"Someone goes to the FBI, or tries to find out things they shouldn't know. Duval has discussed this, and you have even mentioned it: the unintended consequences of some unforeseen action by anyone who knows about this. Too many people know right now. The 'unexpected' is a distinct possibility."

Solene gave Toby a stern look. Toby wasn't sure if what Solene had just said was a warning, or a prediction.

"I hope you all understand that if Duval feels his ability to pull the trigger is threatened, he will have no choice but to do it, and do it immediately," Solene added solemnly.

"We all understand that. I am pretty sure that no one in this group will do anything to cause Dixon to act."

"I hope you're right," Solene said, and turned his gaze back to the golden-topped hills across the water.

After a moment, Solene stuck his hand in his left front pocket and brought out a small slip of paper. "The real reason I asked you out here was to give you this," he said and handed the paper to Toby.

Toby took it and looked it over. It had a long string of numbers on it, perhaps fifteen or so, and nothing else.

"What is it?" Toby asked.

"I have no idea," Solene said. "Duval asked me to give it to you. He said to keep it with you at all times, and said that if things started happening, and you had some trouble, it might help. That's all I know."

Toby looked at it again - he had no idea what it could be.

Solene put his hand on Toby's shoulder, "Toby, if we don't get a chance for a proper goodbye, I want to say it has been a pleasure to get to know you over these past few weeks. Duval was right when he first told me about you. He said you were an important person. I agree. I hope our paths will cross again."

Toby, flustered by the unexpected anointment from the former Secretary General, could once again only manage a mumbled "Thank you".

"Oh - I almost forgot," Solene said. "Dixon told me that to get to the real number on that slip you would have to do a transformation. He said to start at the first number and write eight, seven, eight, seven, and so on, underneath the digits, then to subtract the eight sevens from the number on the paper, and that that would yield the real number. Sort of a simple encryption, I guess. He told me you would figure it out."

Toby looked back at the paper and then put it in his pocket.

"I guess we should go back up," Solene said, and put his hand on Toby's shoulder. "Lead on ..."

Chapter 14

Thursday, July 2nd, 2020
Haida Gwaii

As he had done every morning for the last month, Toby rose early and headed down to the main lodge to make coffee. He wanted to spend one last time on his beach, but decided that this morning he would stay in the lodge. He didn't want to miss anything on this important departure day. Several hours earlier he heard one of the boats fire up and leave. Now, as he looked down at the dock, he could see it was the smaller, faster boat that was gone, and also that two of the security people were fussing around the airplanes, preparing them for the flight back to Vancouver.

The group began to trickle in. Soon everyone was there, breakfast was underway, and the somber atmosphere of last night's farewell event was replaced by a sense of relief and an energetic anticipation of the return to the real world. Almost as if they believed that once they all left here, this nightmare could be forgotten.

Toby wasn't as sanguine as the others, particularly after last night's conversation with Solene. He couldn't stop thinking about the "unintended consequences" comment. After several hours of contemplating it, he decided that Solene was right. With so many people in the know, the unexpected should be expected. Toby even gave some thought to the possibility of applying mathematics to the concept of "unintended consequences" by somehow combining probability, game theory and the uncertainty principle to come up with a likelihood of unintended consequences for any complex act. Probably a silly idea, but he planned to give it some more thought after returning to Astoria.

Dixon and Solene entered the lodge together, a few minutes after the breakfast clean-up was finished. Solene had been staying up at Dixon's high roost ever since Toby had "outed" him four weeks ago at the beginning of the discussions.

"Get a seat, let's get started," Dixon announced, and headed for the coffee pot.

After everyone had settled in, Dixon began. "Even though this is the last morning, I think you will find it to be quite interesting."

Toby heard the boat approaching just as Dixon entered the lodge. It was now at the dock, its engine shut off. Dixon paused to drink from his coffee for a minute.

A few minutes later, the door to the lodge opened. Audible gasps filled the room.

Ambassador Rabinovich and the Reverend Darby entered, smiling broadly. The group jumped up, Dixon nodding, smiling, and obviously enjoying his latest trick.

These were two very fit looking ghosts, Toby thought. Especially Darby who looked thirty pounds lighter and now sported a healthy tan. Darby worked the room, saying "hi" and shaking hands with everyone. Zelco stopped to whisper something in Justice Brown's ear. She nodded without a smile.

Finally, Dixon stood and raised his hands above his head, "All right, all right, let's sit back down and I will tell you what the hell is going on here.

"First, in all this commotion, you all probably didn't notice that someone else slipped in along with the ghosts of Reverend Darby and Ambassador Rabinovich. That large handsome Native American man back by the bar is Jacob Threelodges. Jake is the person in charge of maintaining my properties in this part of the country. He has been staying on the island, over on the other side," Dixon said, as Jacob Threelodges stood up and nodded to the group.

"I'm sure that Reverend Darby and the Ambassador will tell you that Jacob has been an agreeable host for them over the last few weeks. In the case of Reverend Darby, Jake went way beyond the call of duty, especially in the first two weeks," Dixon said. "The Reverend had no choice but to go cold turkey. It wasn't pretty, as I'm sure he will tell you. What is it now Reverend? Thirty days?"

"Yes sir – something like that," Reverend Darby said. "I understand you all thought I was dead. I'm sorry about that. But in a sense, I was dead. And now I am beginning to feel like I'm living again. Thanks to Jake, and of course to Mr. Dixon. God does indeed work in strange ways!"

"I'm sure it was obvious to everyone that Reverend Darby was in deep trouble when he got here." Dixon said. "We felt that for him, and - more importantly - for the discussions, we had to isolate him. It worked out that he had a chance to get sober and I wish him success in continuing to win that battle.

"Ambassador Rabinovich was another matter. As you can see, he was not shot during his attempt on my life. He was subdued, and then drugged. We had a lively discussion with the security team as to what to do with him. They convinced me that it would set a good precedent for the rest of you if you thought that we were *willing* to kill. I think they were right. It certainly set a tone. Ambassador – anything to add?"

"Well, on the one hand, I'm sorry I missed the proceedings," Rabinovich said. "The whole attack thing was a dumb idea. Those guys are good. I was down, face-first on the ground, before I even knew what had hit me. On the other hand, the Reverend and Jake and I got in some world class fishing."

It began to dawn on Toby that maybe none of this was real. What a relief it would be if this whole event were nothing more than another elaborate Duval Dixon stage creation. For a moment or two he let himself believe it, and a great wave of euphoria started to wash over him. He could feel the hairs stand up on the back of his neck.

But then he remembered last night's conversation at the end of the dock. Solene had all but told him that Rabinovich and Darby were still alive, though Toby had been too dense to figure it out. However, Solene was deadly serious when discussing the Eden Proposition itself. He would not have spoken that way if it wasn't real. As quickly as hope had spread, the grim reality of the last four weeks returned.

Dixon continued, "Just to tidy this up a bit – I will ask Reverend Darby and Ambassador Rabinovich to stay here one more night so that Secretary

Solene and I can brief them on what they missed. The rest of you may think this strange, but it should only take a few hours. Tomorrow they will return to Vancouver. We will not file charges against Ambassador Rabinovich, for obvious reasons. And I believe the Reverend Darby will be heading directly to a clinic in Arizona. Is that correct Reverend?"

"Not quite," answered Darby. "I'm returning home to see the family for a week or so first. But then, with God as my witness, I am going to check myself into the clinic for the help I need."

"Good for you," Dixon said. "As I said, I'm sure all of us wish you success with that difficult task."

Dixon moved to center stage in front of the fireplace, put his palms together and rubbed them slowly back and forth as he thought about what to say next.

"Right now, I'll bet you are asking yourself – what *is* real, and what's not," Dixon said. "Let's make it simple. I'll tell you."

Dixon signaled to Patel, and the pictures of the village in China appeared on the screen - the village where the purported test of the Eden flu occurred.

"What do you really know about this?" Dixon asked and then answered. "Nothing really. All you have seen are before and after pictures of a village somewhere. As we all know, these days pictures are not always truthful. You know how easy it would be to doctor up an image and make the village disappear. So, you really don't have any idea what happened here. I will tell you this now. I have no idea where this particular village is. I simply asked Mr. Jain to find a picture of a village and then make it disappear."

Dixon signaled again for a new screen. The picture of the Biotech complex in India came up.

"And what do you know about this?" Dixon asked and looked around the room, pausing for dramatic effect. "What you do know with certainty about this is exactly what everyone else in the world knows. That it was blown up by terrorists. Both governments have said so, and the terrorists themselves have taken credit for it."

Toby began to realize that these were non-denial denials. Dixon never said he didn't do these awful things. So what if the picture of that village in China was doctored. Dixon could still have wiped out another village – the one that Laura and the CDC had heard rumors about. And he hadn't denied that he was the one who blew up those buildings. All he said was that the blame had already been assigned and that the world thinks terrorists had been responsible.

Toby had to ask: "So are you saying these two events, the one in China, and the one in India, never happened?"

Dixon, looking somewhat surprised at being questioned, replied, "No, I'm not saying that. I'm just telling all of you what you really know."

Toby pressed on, "So then are you saying that you did wipe out that village and bomb your own company?"

"I'm not saying that either, and furthermore, I'm not going to say anything else on that topic," Dixon said, looking annoyed.

"Next screen please," he said. "This is from the detailed presentation we gave to Doctors Contreras and Sundgren. This is a diagram of a prion, a mis-folded protein. Notice anything about it, doctors?"

Laura couldn't believe what she was seeing. How could she have missed this in the first presentation? It wasn't right - the protein in this diagram could never actually exist.

"I don't understand," she said. "I don't see how I could have missed this. This isn't a real protein. Are you sure you didn't switch this diagram with the first one?"

"Are you sure? That's the important question," Dixon said.

"I'm not too sure about anything right now."

"Good. That's precisely the point! None of you can be sure of anything. You know nothing that could be of any help to the authorities. But before you begin to think this whole thing was a hoax, let me tell you what is real."

A screen, which simply said "The Eden Proposition" came up on the big flat panel. Dixon turned around and pointed at the screen. "This is real," Dixon said, with such scary intensity that Toby felt chills run down his back.

Dixon walked over to Dr. Jain's table and picked up the sample V-box, "These are real." He held it up above his head and looked slowly from person to person.

"In just a few minutes I will pass out a V-box to everyone here. They are operational and they now contain the actual vaccine. Mark loaded each box with the real vaccine in the last half-hour. It had been stored on the other side of the island and Jacob brought it over this morning along with our two ghosts.

"And earlier this morning, I personally loaded the release codes. That way only I know what code to send to you. So, if something happens to me, no one else will be able to send you the correct code and release the vaccine."

Dixon nodded in the direction of Reverend Darby, "Don't worry, I will explain the V-box to you and the ambassador later this afternoon."

"Everyone else here understands about the V-box, correct? Remember to keep it with you at all times, to check the green light frequently, and to keep charged batteries in it. And understand that you may have only one day to take the vaccine after the code is sent.

"Mark, will you go up to my cabin and bring the boxes down please," Dixon said. "On second thought, I'll give you a hand. The group can take a short break."

Laura caught Toby's eye and signaled to him to meet her on the porch.

"Un-fucking-believable," she said, jaws clenched, shaking her head.

Toby glanced back inside the lodge. Darby was continuing to glad-hand his way around the group. Toby was struck by the contrast. Darby was energetic, relaxed, happy. The others looked shell-shocked.

"I'm curious about something," Toby asked. "Are you sure about that slide of the protein? Do you really think you could have missed it the first time?"

"I've been thinking about that. I'm pretty sure I would have noticed it," Laura said. "But you know, it really doesn't matter. Dixon did what he wanted. He created doubt in everyone's mind – even mine."

"What about the Chinese village? You had mentioned there were rumors about a mad cow outbreak. Do you remember any more about that?" Toby asked.

"No, I've been trying, but I can't recall where I heard it. I plan to follow up when I get back to the CDC," Laura said.

"Unreal," Toby said and took a deep breath. "I'm still in shock. Rabinovich and Darby are alive. I didn't see that coming. Did you?"

"No, and I don't know why. After all, we know Dixon does this kind of thing. We were looking for his games all along. I guess that's why he's so good at it."

"He is," Toby said. "He's completely off the rails. And at this point, there is nothing we can accuse him of. I honestly don't know if any of this is real. Do you?"

Laura shook her head, "Nope, I'm having trouble even thinking about it."

"Well, the good news is - we don't have to think about it for a while," Toby said. "You still want that escorted tour of the San Juans don't you?"

"More than ever," Laura said, dimples fully deployed. "More than ever."

Mark and Dixon returned, each with an armload of V-boxes.

"Please have a seat. I have some brief closing remarks to deliver before I pass these out and you all fly back. I trust everyone is packed?" Dixon asked, looking around for any packer slackers. "Good. Mark, go tell the boys to have the planes ready to go in 30 minutes.

"Dr. Jain and Dr. Patel will be flying back with you. As I said earlier, Reverend Darby And Ambassador Rabinovich will be staying an additional day. And, as my good luck would have it, Dr. Mothershed has asked to remain here with me for a while," Dixon said, waving at Mothershed.

"I am simply an itinerant," Dr. Mothershed interjected. "I have nowhere else to go. The view is good here, the food acceptable, and the conversation stimulating. I am very thankful to Mr. Dixon for taking in a homeless old cosmologist."

"And I'm very much looking forward to the conversation as well," Dixon said. "I hear Dr. Mothershed has a great knowledge of time travelers - a subject that I have some knowledge of myself. I'm anxious to hear his views."

Dixon moved to center stage one last time.

"I don't know what to say right now. 'Thank You' is woefully inadequate. The great debate we have engaged in over the last four weeks has been intense, intelligent, emotional, and often profound," he said with a nod of appreciation to the group.

Dixon walked over to the window, stared out over the water, and seemed to leave his body again, as he had done so many times over the last few weeks. The group had learned to wait for him to return.

"You are probably wondering," he said, then smiled broadly and faced the group. "Well … you are probably wondering about a lot of things, aren't you? Obviously, that's by design. And I forgot to mention one more thing along those lines."

Dixon pointed out to the water. "Dr. Benson, you are the resident navigator of this part of the world, are you not?"

"Well, not really," Toby answered. "I've never been up this far before."

"Okay, then I will forgive you for not noticing," Dixon said. "On that first day, I showed you all a map and then told you the story of where we were in Haida Gwaii. I'm sure that most of you don't recall, but in any case, the location I gave you then wasn't correct. We are actually somewhere else. You see, I didn't want to give you any help if you decided later to escape.

"But the story about Bucky Webster, from whom I bought this place, was essentially correct, so if you want to do a little digging when you get back, you can probably figure it out." Dixon said. "Unfortunately, there is substantial cloud cover to the east of us today, so the plane trip back won't be much help."

Dixon moved back to the fireplace, faced the group and rubbed his palms together, obviously enjoying disclosing his latest deception.

"So, where was I?" he said.

"'You are probably wondering …'" Solene offered.

"Yes, that's right, thank you again Mr. Secretary," Dixon continued. "You are wondering, what will I do now? The answer is the same as before. It will take time to consider what was said here. I may consider other approaches to solve this dilemma. I may even ask some, or all, of you back here to ponder this some more. Or, I may decide sometime soon. In any case, I will decide within the eighteen months that I have committed to you. But remember: the only notification you will get if I decide to proceed, will be via the V-box. And that is all I will say on that topic."

Dixon walked back to the bar, where the V-boxes were stacked.

"These boxes are individualized. Make sure you take the one with your name on it," he said.

Dixon moved to the front door, then turned to the group with his arms extended above him, as though giving a benediction. He slowly made eye contact with each person, then smiled and said a simple "Thank You." He paused a moment more, closed his eyes, clasped his hands and bowed to the group, then turned and walked out the door.

Chapter 15

Thursday, July 2nd, 2020
Departure, Haida Gwaii

After having spent the last month in silence, away from the sound of cars, phones, freeways, and the background din of civilization, the noise was a shock, painful even. The pilots had put full throttle to the big float planes, taking off one behind the other so that all four engines, amplified by the echoes off the hills, roared at a level approaching the threshold of pain.

Toby looked out the window, catching a glimpse of the compound as the planes banked away to the east. Soon, as Dixon had predicted, they were above a low-level summer on-shore flow that made it impossible to make out anything below. Toby was seated next to Dr. Jain. He and Laura had taken separate planes in order to avoid any suspicions about their immediate plans.

Toby looked over at Jain and gave him a cursory smile. It was too noisy for any reasonable conversation. Toby settled into his seat, closed his eyes and allowed himself to daydream about a world where he and only two hundred other human beings were alive, specifically, where he and Laura and some others, were alive. That daydream took its obvious course, and then focused primarily on the next two weeks aboard the "Gull". If Jain had looked over, he would have noticed a very contented smile, and perhaps other physical anomalies, as Toby indulged in a fantasy that was about to come true.

The planes floated up to the dock in Vancouver around noon. Several taxis were waiting to take the majority of the group directly to the airport. Sofia's international flight didn't leave until the next day, so she needed to return to the hotel. Laura explained to the others that her flight didn't leave until later that night and that she was going back to the hotel to spend a little time with Sofia. Toby had to go back to retrieve his car, so the three of them shared a taxi.

Several hours later, Toby stood up and put his hand on Laura's chair. "I think it's time to go," he said, after a lunch with Sofia that had gone on far too long for both Toby and Laura.

"Laura, how about I give you a ride to the airport?" Toby asked, trying to sound casual.

"Well, it's a little early ..." Laura teased her impatient future lover. Toby had a moment of fear. "But I guess it would be easier. Where's your car?" she said, after holding out as long as she could.

Sofia looked at Laura with a knowing grin. "Well, well," she said.

"What?" Laura asked in mock disgust. "Like we're going to go make-out in the airport parking ramp?"

"Hourly rates?" Sofia said. "I'm sure they have this concept in North America."

"You Europeans - all you think about is sex," Laura said, rising from the table to give Sofia a hug.

"And this is a problem?" Sofia asked, with a chuckle.

Toby retrieved the car and, after another round of farewells under the great iron portico of the Oriental Hotel, he and Laura were finally alone, pulling out on to Pacific Avenue for the two hour drive to Anacortes.

Laura gazed silently out the car window until Toby pulled onto the freeway for the thirty-minute ride to the border. "You know what's funny?" she finally asked.

Toby looked over at her. "What?"

"Being back in the world like this, and after only a few hours, the whole event just doesn't seem real to me anymore," Laura said. She raised her voice and turned to Toby. "It can't be real! Dixon wouldn't do this, he couldn't do this! It was all bogus. How did we all fall for it?"

"You think all of it was bogus - really?" Toby asked.

"It sure feels like it now. What do you think?"

"I hope you're right ..." Toby said, quietly.

"I'm right," Laura said emphatically. "And now, and for at least the next twenty-four hours, I don't want to talk about it - or Dixon - *at all*. Deal?"

Toby smiled, and reached his right hand over for a shake. "Deal," he said. "Excellent plan."

"Okay, so listen up Dr. Toby Benson," Laura said and shifted in her seat to better face Toby. "Being that I don't know squat about you, we are going to play one hundred twenty questions. I'll start."

"I thought it was twenty questions?"

"Twenty is not nearly enough. But when I'm done, you can ask me something."

Two hours later, Toby pulled into a grocery store in Anacortes. "Question eighty-nine will have to wait," he said. "Our first real test awaits us."

"What's that?"

"Shopping together."

"Just a second. Before you go in, I have to ask you one more thing," Laura said, now somewhat unsure of herself. "You said something to me about what happened to you in India – the radiation thing?"

Toby smiled, and figured out where this was going. "Sperm count," he said. "Low sperm count."

"So – how low? Do we need to get some protection?" Laura asked sheepishly.

"I don't think so. I mean – no, we don't. The doc told me it was extremely unlikely."

"One-in-a-thousand unlikely, or one-in-a-million unlikely?" Laura asked.

Toby laughed, "Like there's a difference?"

"Okay, well what the hell, I hate rubbers," Laura said, and got out of the car.

"*Hate* rubbers? I hope that's not an official CDC position?" Toby asked and followed her into the store.

"No, it's not. I'll show you the official CDC position tonight."

Late that evening, with a full tank of diesel and with the boat amply provisioned, they motored out of Anacortes harbor into the Rosario strait.

"I love this boat, Toby," Laura shouted up from the galley. "It's beautiful – it's perfect."

"Are we going to raise the sails?" Laura asked as she climbed up the steps from the main cabin to the cockpit..

"No wind," Toby replied. "Besides, it's late, and we don't have far to go."

Laura knelt on the cockpit bench, faced forward and leaned on the cabin roof. "Do you know where we're going?"

"I have an anchorage that I always go to on the first night. Decatur Head – dead ahead. Should only take thirty minutes."

"Thirty minutes? I thought I had a little more time. I should go below and put on my pretty underwear," Laura said, flashing her most seductive smile. Toby had to remember to keep breathing.

"You know, I don't understand that part," Toby said. "Usually the underwear doesn't stay on long enough to get noticed."

"Really? Well, let's see about that …" She went back down below. A few minutes later she emerged wearing only a short see-through-thin sleeveless tank top, and tight, lace, almost-thong, panties.

"I don't think the Captain can leave the helm right now. So, I'll just sit over here. This will give you time to appreciate the beauty of fine undergarments," Laura said, and walked up to Toby.

Toby's hands were still on the wheel, Laura leaned forward, their bodies separated by the large steering wheel, so that only their lips met. Toby thought it was the sexiest kiss he had ever experienced.

"I've wanted to do that for so long!" Laura said, with a radiant smile, and sat down on the cockpit bench in a spot that was still in the sunlight. Toby, sporting a stupid grin, could not stop staring. Laura was one of those rare women who clearly felt at ease about her body. In her case, this was not difficult to understand. She was beautiful - long legs, smallish, but shapely breasts, and the pale flawless skin of a true Scandinavian blond.

"Don't you have to watch where you are going?" she asked, enjoying her effect on Toby. "And you better step back a bit, you don't want to get that bulge caught in one of the spokes."

Toby's eyes rolled back. He took a deep breath and tried to look over at his destination. He began to worry that he might not make it another twenty minutes.

"Baseball," he said. "Let's talk some baseball."

Laura giggled, "Baseball, okay. So – do you bat righty, or lefty?"

Toby thought even that sounded sexy, though he wasn't sure what it meant.

"It's so nice and warm in this sunshine," Laura said, then leaned forward and deftly shed the little tank-top. She closed her eyes and leaned back to get the full effect of the sun – and Toby's gaze.

"Oh shit," Toby said, under his breath – he hoped. "Did I say that out loud?"

"You mean the "Oh shit" part?"

Toby pushed the throttle ahead to full speed, the boat vibrated at the sudden acceleration.

"In a hurry?" Laura asked. She stood up and moved forward for a better look at the destination. Toby got a better look at her other side. Still perfect.

"How much longer?" she asked.

"Five minutes, maybe ten."

"Do you need help with the anchor?"

"No, I have an electric windlass, I can get it myself."

"Good, then I'm going down to the aft cabin bunk. I'll be there if you need me for … anything," she said. "Here, you keep these." Laura slipped off her panties, and handed them to Toby. She caught her breath, bit her lower lip, then turned and stepped down into the main cabin.

There was one other boat in the bay behind Decatur Head. Toby had to maneuver over to the southern, shallower end to get as far away as possible from the new neighbors. Even at a hundred yards, he knew they would be in for a auditory treat over the next two hours. But then, he didn't really care.

It was the most efficient anchoring Toby had ever made. Within minutes, he leapt into the main cabin, peeled off his clothes, and finally, finally, and finally again - consummated this long courtship. Much to the delight of the neighbors.

Chapter 16

Friday, July 3rd, 2020
Decatur Head, San Juan Islands

Toby was seated in the cockpit with his morning coffee in hand when Laura finally emerged from the cabin. "Hi," was all he could manage to say. He wished he had come up with something more romantic. Laura, now wearing a loose fitting sleeping t-shirt, slumped down next to him.

"Well," she said. "That was quite a workout. Sofia was right," she smiled at Toby, and reached up and kissed him on the neck, cheek, and quickly turned onto his lap and then kissed him with surprising intensity on the mouth. Toby held her tight, rocking her back and forth, as they exchanged lovers' noises.

Finally, Laura sat up and smiled. "Okay I'd better move. I don't want to get you going again. I'm a little worn out." She got up and headed back down to the galley. "More coffee?" she asked.

Toby smiled, pleased with himself - he had managed a perfectly acceptable romantic moment without having to say a word. "Yes, thanks. The coffee is in the thermos; just bring it up."

A few minutes later, Laura emerged from the cabin. "Wow – what a beautiful morning," she said after pouring Toby's coffee. She sat down on the cockpit bench opposite, not wanting to risk the consequences of actual physical contact. "I thought it was always rainy and cold up here. This is spectacular, it must be seventy-five already. What time is it anyway?"

"It's about 9:30. It's going to be warm today – too warm if you ask me. I just checked the weather report and a mid-summer Pacific high pressure ridge is going to be stalled above us for a while."

"Sounds good to me."

"Well, it's good news – and bad news actually. When a high pressure system stalls around here, the San Juans get dead calm. Look out there." Toby pointed back to the east. "The water is like glass, no wind at all. And no wind means no sailing. Not only that, but I've been up here before in this kind of dead air, and it actually gets smoggy because of all the boats motoring around. They call it an inversion."

"That doesn't sound good. So what do you want to do? Go back?" Laura asked.

"No way. I'd rather sit right here for the next two weeks than go back."

Toby picked up the marine atlas he been looking at, and moved over to sit next to Laura. "But I have an idea. This is where we are," he said, and pointed to the map. "Originally I thought we could just putter around the San Juans. But now, with this weather, and since we have two full weeks, I think we should make a run for the west side of Vancouver Island, up to Barkley Sound – right up here."

"It looks like a long way," Laura said. "You sure we have enough time?"

"I think so, it could be a little tight, especially if we hit some bad weather, it can get foggy on the west coast."

"Great, then let's do it! And, I have a confession to make."

"No. You mean you weren't a virgin?"

"No, I mean yes - whatever," Laura said laughing. "The confession is that I actually have two more weeks beyond the original six before I have to go back to Atlanta. I was about to take a vacation when Dixon summoned me. So I just tacked it on to the end of the session. I decided not to mention it to you, just in case you were woefully inadequate in the bunk."

"I'm not sure – but was that a compliment?"

"Yes of course, a compliment," she smiled, and patted him on his personal parts.

"You mean I'm at least a step above woefully inadequate?" he asked, grinning.

"Yes, at least a step above," Laura said. "But if you pay close attention to my instruction, and you practice hard, one day soon, you may find yourself a step above moderately-acceptable."

"Okay then, I'll do it! I'll practice every day, morning and night!"

"Oh – oh! I think I've just been out-bantered. It doesn't happen to me very often. I'd better retreat to the galley and make some breakfast."

Toby brought up the anchor and motored slowly out of the bay. He turned the Gull west into the main passage through the San Juan islands. Laura emerged a half hour later carrying two plates of scrambled eggs. She had changed into a small black bikini.

"It doesn't get any better than this!" she said, gesturing out at the steep forested rocky shoreline of Orcas Island slipping by only fifty yards to the north. "Wow!"

They spent the rest of the day lazily motoring around Orcas, Lopez and Shaw islands, anchoring off Deer Harbor for a lunch break, followed by a little kissing and teasing. Around dinnertime, Toby brought the Gull in neatly to a spot on the inside of the guest dock at Friday Harbor on San Juan Island.

"Let's try our hand at going to a restaurant," Toby said, after tying up the boat. "How long has it been anyway – four weeks? I'll bet that's a record for you."

"This is good too," Laura said, over a bowl of clam chowder, and gazing out of the restaurant window at the charming village of Friday Harbor. A large Washington State ferry boat was approaching the terminal only a few yards away to the south. "It's all good so far. Thank you again, Dr. Benson."

Laura put her spoon down, "So. What is our plan again, Captain sir?"

"Tonight we stay in Friday Harbor at the dock. Tomorrow we go to Sidney on Vancouver Island. It's just a little north of Victoria. We need to go through customs there, and we can stop at the Gardens. You'll love them - they are spectacular. Tomorrow night we'll anchor in Sidney harbor, and then, bright and early the next morning, we'll make a run for Barkley sound."

After dinner, Laura reached out for Toby to take her hand. "Take me for a short walk," she said with the dimples at full sail. "Then you can take me."

"Seriously?" Toby asked.

"Yes - you should definitely take me seriously."

"I do."

"I like the sound of that!"

Chapter 17

Sunday, July 5th, 2020
Bethesda, Maryland

Dr. Sanjay Jain knelt behind the stainless steel barbeque, his heart pounding, and wished that somehow he could walk away. He had no choice now; he must do this. If only he and Patel had succeeded at Haida Gwaii, this wouldn't be necessary. But Dixon had kept the vaccine on the other side of the island with the big Native American, and then had sent Patel and Jain back with the others. They simply had no opportunity to get their hands on the quantity of vaccine that they needed.

This is Dixon's fault, he told himself. What happens now is on Dixon's head. Damn that man! Dixon could be so clever, and yet so oblivious. It was his fatal flaw, Jain thought. So perceptive in many things, he was blind to one important thing: he could never see into another person's heart.

How could he not expect that Jain and Patel would be devastated by his brutal bombing of their friends and countrymen? For Jain and Patel, Dixon was no hero to India. He had used devastated India to create his horrifying five-headed monster flu, and then had disposed of the creators as if they were garbage. And afterwards, Dixon showed no remorse. There were no apologies. What could he possibly expect?

From the moment that Jain and Patel heard about the destruction of the biotech buildings in India, they had started plotting their revenge. They had recruited four countrymen as conspirators. Their plan now was to acquire as many V-boxes as possible, figure a way to extract the vaccine, and then, knowing that Dixon would immediately launch the Eden flu, to retreat to the foothills of the Himalayas and form an Ashram - a survivable community for their fellow Indians. Hindis would then be the survivors, not Dixon's people. That would be the best revenge. Karma would be served.

From his spot on the patio Jain could see the Reverend Richard Darby, televangelist to the masses and former drunk, in his den hunched over a computer. It was late, well past midnight on a Sunday morning. He had been watching Darby for over an hour, making sure everyone was asleep, and hoping that the Reverend didn't have a dog. They hadn't talked about how to deal with a dog. They weren't experienced in these things. This would be their first.

He had to go now. The two others, waiting in the bushes by the front door, must be worried about him. He took one last look at the Reverend and then crept back to the front of the house.

"What took so long?" one of the others whispered from the bushes.

He didn't answer.

"Let's do it," he said. He needed to move quickly, before he lost his nerve.

The two others slipped out of the bushes and got in position, flattened against the wall on either side of the front door.

He knocked softly, not wanting to awaken anyone. He could hear Darby approaching. His heart raced. He hoped he would be able to speak.

Darby looked out through the glass, recognized him, and opened up the door.

"My goodness, what are you doing here?" Darby asked, looking confused.

"I'm so sorry to bother you, forgive me," he said. "I have been sent to give you something."

"Well... come in then," Darby said.

"No, no, I don't want to wake anyone," he said. "Please, just step out here so I can show you this."

Darby hesitated for a moment at the strange request but decided that this man posed no danger, and stepped out onto the porch.

Then - from behind - the first man dropped a noose over Darby's head and yanked it tight. The second man bear-hugged him, pinning his arms.

Darby's eyes bulged grotesquely. His mouth opened, but no sound could escape his crushed windpipe.

The three of them wrestled Darby to the ground, face down, the noose-man's knee in Darby's back for leverage as he pulled hard and took another inch of rope from the loop around Darby's neck. Darby twitched for only a moment, then went slack. It was done.

Jain slipped into the house as the other two carried the body around to the back. They would string Darby up in the maple tree near the patio – an apparent suicide.

He looked around the den and quickly spotted what he had come for. Jain grabbed the V-box, quietly slid open the patio door, and joined the others in the back yard, watching Darby swing silently from the maple branch.

Dr. Sanjay Jain wanted to vomit, but forced himself not to. The fake suicide had to hold for at least a few days. They had more work to do, more boxes to retrieve.

Chapter 18

Two days later
Tuesday, July 7th, 2020
Barkley Sound, Vancouver Island

The small sailboat snugged up on its anchor line and began to swing in a slow arc as the tide changed from slack to flood. Toby noticed the slight movement and glanced over at the tide table taped to the wall beside him. "Low tide – 5:15 am", it said. Toby checked his watch - right on schedule. He looked again at the PDA screen, hoping it would suddenly display something different – it didn't, so he reluctantly walked back to the aft cabin and put his hand on his bunkmate's shoulder. "Laura, wake up. You have to see this ... wake up."

A few minutes later a sleepy Laura, wearing only a t-shirt and sporting a gaping yawn, stumbled over to the chart table where Toby was intently studying his screen. She leaned in against him and put her arm around his shoulder. "What's up?" she asked.

"Hey," Toby said and gently put his hand on the small of her back. "Look at this. I set my PDA to alert me if it found any news about the twelve of us. It went off a half-hour ago." He turned the small screen so Laura could see it.

She took a moment to focus. "Rabinovich is *dead*?" She looked at Toby, confused by what this meant.

"That's not all," Toby said. "Rabinovich was supposedly killed in a break-in robbery. Senator Mallory is also dead, a heart attack they claim. And this is beyond bizarre. The Reverend Darby has committed suicide. This time for real."

"Oh no," Laura gasped. A mask of true horror crossed her face. "Dixon ... it's Dixon, oh my God, it's happening ... it's *happening*."

Laura slumped on to the end of the couch across from the chart table, holding her face in her hands, staring at Toby.

Toby put his hand on her knee. "I don't think so."

"What?"

"I don't think it's Dixon," Toby said calmly.

"What? A coincidence then? You can't possibly think that?"

"Oh no, not a coincidence – definitely not. But not Dixon. Why would he want to kill us now? He could have done that more easily up at the lodge?"

"Because he couldn't get away with it there."

"But still, he didn't need to invite us there in the first place. Why would he take us there, let us go, and then have us killed?" Toby asked. "It doesn't make any sense."

"Well, who then? If it's not a coincidence, then it must be someone who knows what went on up there."

"Right. It has to be someone who knows what went on. And, so far as we know, Dixon wasn't a target." Toby stood and walked to the galley and back. "Which means that they weren't trying to stop the Eden Proposition. And there is no benefit to killing us – the participants – except ..." he stopped, looked down at Laura and nodded for her to fill in the blank.

"The vaccine!" Laura said. "Of course, that's the only thing of value that we have."

"And if it's the vaccine that they're after," Toby said. "That rules out Dixon, he already has the vaccine. And if he didn't want any of us to have it, he simply wouldn't have put it in the V-boxes in the first place. It has to be someone who knows about the Eden Proposition, and who knows about the vaccine."

"Okay, who?" Laura said. "Give me a piece of paper."

Toby ripped out a sheet from an old log book and handed it to Laura.

"Are you sure those guys in the news stories are really dead?" she asked.

Toby glanced at the stories again. "From what they say, they must have bodies – heart attack, suicide, break-in. They must have identified the bodies."

"Okay, it's not them. It's not Dixon and Solene. It's not us. That leaves Sofia, Wyndi Rehn, Justice Brown, Mothershed, and Nguyen. I don't see it being any of the women – sorry – but I can't imagine it. How about Nguyen? He was very quiet during the proceedings. I never got much of a read on him," Laura said.

Toby looked at his PDA, "Let me do a search. How do you spell his name?"

Laura held up the piece of paper where she had written the names. "Oh shit - I've been misspelling it. Let's see." Toby typed in the corrected name, and sorted the results by most recent date. "Here it is: he was killed in his apartment the night before last. It just got reported. I guess that rules him out. And, whoever it is, they do get around. Two killed in D.C., one in Chicago, and one in Minneapolis, all in about forty-eight hours."

"Well, I still say it isn't the women. It couldn't be Mothershed, could it?" Laura asked.

"No, besides the obvious reasons, he stayed with Dixon. But we're overlooking some people. There's the security team, and Jain and Patel."

"Duh, of course. It's early, my mind isn't quite up to speed yet," Laura said. "The security guys, they're trained killers. Maybe they're working for the CIA or something."

"Could be them, or the Indians, or maybe some other people that knew about this that Dixon didn't tell us about. I don't know who, but I do know this – we are in serious danger, right now."

"Why? We still don't know if this is real. What if Dixon never intended release the virus? Or maybe he never really created it. It's still possible the whole thing was just another bogus Dixon theater production. Isn't it?"

"Whoever is killing us for the vaccine thinks it's real. They must know."

"Oh my god … I can't believe this. It's going to happen then - and right away, isn't it?" Laura said, beginning to choke up. "Dixon's going to release it, or maybe he already has. My God, how did it get here so fast? God damn that man! He thought he had it all figured out."

Toby shook his head. "Unexpected consequences, just like Solene predicted," he said and put his hand gently on Laura's knee. "I'm sorry …"

She took his hand and squeezed, "Not your fault Dr. Benson, not your fault."

"I'm not so sure," Toby mumbled absently.

"What?"

"Nothing ... sorry."

Laura took in a deep breath and exhaled slowly, "Okay, enough of that," she said, and stood up. "Let's figure out what to do. Where are our V-boxes? Maybe Dixon has sent the code."

"Not a chance. If the vaccine was in the boxes, and after what's gone on with the killings, he wouldn't send the code to anybody."

"Why? He said he would. He did promise."

"Look ... he knows that all these people have been killed for the V-boxes. He doesn't know who has them now, or what shape they are in," Toby said. "Us, for instance, he doesn't know if we've been captured or killed. I'm sure he assumes the worst. And that applies to any others who are still alive. He doesn't know who has any of the V-boxes right now. The last thing he would do is unlock them."

"So we're just screwed then?"

Toby stood and put his arms around Laura. Laura tried to fight the fear. She held Toby hard and wouldn't let go, swaying a bit as the boat gently rocked. After several long minutes, she pushed away far enough so that she could pull her sleeping t-shirt over her head. She grabbed Toby's hand and stepped urgently to the aft bunk. "C'mon," she said. "The world's going to end soon."

Two hours later, after honoring the end of the world with a spirited celebration of life, and after breakfasting in the tight, stunningly beautiful Barkley Sound anchorage, with the morning sun rising above the trees to the northeast, and serenaded by the sound of water lapping on the close-by shore, and the always present background punctuation of distant gull squawks, the reality of their incongruous situation returned.

"My god," Laura said. "It's so beautiful here! Everything, I mean not just the scenery, but the smells, the air, the solitude. Even the movement of the boat. It's just ... perfect. Thank You Dr. Benson."

"You are more than welcome," Toby said and leaned over to kiss the most incredible woman he'd ever been with. "But we have to figure what to do next. We can't just sit here."

"Why not? We're safe, they could never find us here," Laura said.

"Yes they can."

"Oh, c'mon. We didn't tell anybody about going sailing, and even we didn't know where we were going until after we left Anacortes."

"We left tracks."

"On the Water?" Laura said, with a chuckle.

"No – not on the water. In my bank account. I used my debit card to get supplies in Anacortes. And the day before yesterday, I used it to get fuel in Kildonan. That puts us in Barkley Sound. Anyone could figure that out."

"They don't have access to your bank account, do they?" Laura asked, now worried.

"No, but it would take them about a minute to hack into it."

"Well, still, this is a big area out here - it would be really hard to find us."

"That's true, and that's probably why we're still alive. They went after the easy targets first. But now, if they haven't been successful getting any of the vaccine out of the V-boxes, they will be desperate and come after us."

"I'll bet by now the others, if they are still alive, have gone into hiding, or have hired some kind of security," Laura said.

"You're probably right, and that could mean ..." Toby hesitated. "That could mean that we're next on the list."

"C'mon Toby, can't you please say something hopeful?"

"Okay, well ... at least we have figured out some things. And maybe we can come up with a plan to stay ahead of the game."

"This is so freaking bizarre, isn't it?" Laura said. "Here we are, sitting all alone it this gorgeous place, talking about getting killed by an unknown hit squad, not to mention the imminent end-of-the-world. Good God ..." she said, shaking her head in disbelief.

Laura stood up and slowly turned in a circle, taking in the full sweep of the wild shoreline. "So pretty ... why now?" she asked herself. She looked back at Toby, sighed and then said, "I'm going down below to get cleaned up. Need anything?"

"No, but I'm coming down too. I'll clean up the dishes and get it buttoned down. I think we should get out of here as soon as possible."

"Really, you want to go right now?" Laura asked. "Where?"

"Maybe I'm paranoid, but I think we're better off out in the ocean. I want to go back out and head north as fast as we can. I'll tell you why later. Make it a quick shower; I'm going to pull out in about ten minutes."

"Okay, Captain sir, and remember what they say," Laura said, saluting.

"What do they say?"

"You're not paranoid, if they really are after you."

Twenty minutes later, out on the open ocean, Toby could see they were in for a challenging day of sailing.

"Laura, look in the closet behind the chart table and bring up two life jackets," Toby shouted. "It's going to get a little rough."

Laura brought the lifejackets up and then banged around the cockpit, hitting the wheel hard as she tried to hand Toby his jacket.

"Sit down over here for just a minute," Toby said and pointed to a spot next to the wheel. "I've got to get sails up. It'll make a big difference. We won't roll as much. Hold on to the wheel and just try and keep this same heading. Do you know how to do that?" he asked.

Laura gave him a look as though she didn't exactly understand the question. After all, she thought, how hard could it be to steer straight ahead?

Toby smiled, "It's not as easy as it looks. The swells will push you around. See that compass there?" Toby said, pointing at the round black globe mounted just in front of the wheel. Laura nodded. "Try to keep that same heading, and try not to over-steer. I'll be right here in the cockpit, so don't worry. I don't have to go on deck to raise the sails. This boat is rigged for single-handing. All the lines come back into the cockpit."

Toby wished now that they had practiced some sailing during the last week, but there had never been enough wind. He also wished that these swells weren't so damn big.

He struggled with the sails. The rolling of the boat, combined with the erratic steering of the first mate made it more difficult than it should have been. Eventually, he got the jib unfurled to about seventy percent, and raised the main up all the way. The boat steadied as Toby adjusted the sheets, and the Gull surged ahead. Toby cut the engine, re-took the wheel from Laura, and then experienced the thrill that all true sailors can relate too; that exhilarating first moment when the engine goes silent and the boat is making way smartly under sail.

He stood behind the wheel, getting a feel for the rhythm of the swells, the pressure and direction of the wind, trying to determine how high he could comfortably point the Gull into the wind. It was a bit of a balancing act. This wasn't a race, he didn't need to pinch it up to the max, but he did need to take the swells as much off-center as possible.

The good news was that the breeze was steady at fifteen knots out of the northwest. The Gull powered its way up and over the swells, healed-over at a noticeable but not uncomfortable angle.

Laura had moved over to the high side of the cockpit for a better view ahead. She was up on her knees, on the cockpit bench, facing forward, leaning on the main cabin roof, enthralled. "Whoa! You never told me about this," she shouted back, so to be heard over the sound of the salt water parting and flying by as the Gull knifed ahead. "All this time I thought sailing was just motoring from beautiful anchorage to beautiful anchorage, eating, drinking and screwing. But this is the best part!"

Toby smiled. "I have to admit, it's at least a close second!" he shouted back, secretly thinking the other thing might actually be second. But he also knew that moments like this, under sail, were rare.

Toby stood silently for the next twenty minutes, doing nothing but enjoying the feel of the helm. He focused on keeping the Gull pointing perfectly and pushing ahead at the maximum speed possible. He could, and many times had, spent several hours standing right in that spot, transfixed. Finally, after enjoying his guilty pleasure as long as he could, he yelled at Laura to come back and sit by him so that they could talk.

"Wow, that was just spectacular! I was hypnotized!" she said, smiling broadly.

"I'm glad you like it, and I'm especially glad you don't get seasick."

"Me too - never have," Laura said. "So what's your big plan – other than taking me out here for the thrill of a lifetime."

"I don't want to shout, so maybe you could stand up here by me," Toby said.

Laura got up and grabbed a handful of Toby's right butt cheek. "I need to hold onto something," she said with a smile.

"Down girl. You can hang on to the rail behind you."

Toby shifted to the high side of the wheel, so he could turn a bit and face Laura, who now stood directly behind the helm, hanging on tightly to the back rail. "Here's what I think we need to do," he began. "If we are right about the vaccine and why they are doing this, then we need to expect them to come after us soon. They've had almost forty-eight hours to get to Kildonan. They could even be there now.

"They probably went to Anacortes first and found out about the Gull, so they can identify it. If I was them, I'd charter a big float plane and search for us from the air. That should be our first warning – if a float plane flies anywhere close to us. That's why I wanted to get out here in the ocean. I don't think they could land a float plane in these swells. But if we were at anchor in a sheltered bay, we'd be sitting ducks."

"Makes sense. But we can't stay out here forever, or were you planning on going to Hawaii?"

"That thought actually crossed my mind. Unfortunately, I don't think we have enough provisions, definitely not enough water." Toby said. "But I'm thinking that maybe we can make it back to the Queen Charlottes and find Dixon's lodge."

"But won't they go get a boat, after they find us with the plane?" Laura asked. "With a big power boat they could chase us down pretty quickly, couldn't they?"

"Good point. So we had better pack up some things, in case we need to escape into the woods."

"The woods?"

"Okay: listen to this. Tell me what you think," Toby said, as a plan emerged in his head. "If we spot them coming after us, we'll try to get ashore without their seeing us. Then we get off the boat and go into the woods but we leave the boat where they can find it, and in the boat we leave the V-boxes. Then, they'll go aboard, find the boxes, and if they can't see us, they'll just leave. After all, they really only want the V-boxes."

"But what about us? If we leave the V-boxes, we won't have any vaccine."

"Doesn't matter. Dixon's not going to open them anyway. Whoever those bad guys are – either they've figured out how to break in to the boxes, or they're still trying to figure it out. We don't have their resources, so I don't think we'd have a chance at breaking in."

"But maybe we could reach Dixon somehow - phone him, or email him. If we can assure him it's us then maybe he'd send the code," Laura said.

"Well okay, I guess that's possible. So, we could take one and leave one," Toby said. "In fact, they may not know for certain that you're with me. Maybe they think I'm alone. All they would be going by is my debit card."

"Okay, it's a plan, I guess. The woods are better than dead. What do you want me to do?"

"Down below, in that same closet that had the life jackets, probably on the bottom, is a small backpack. It's my day-hike and survival-gear pack. I've got a good GPS, dry matches, whistle, knife, first-aid – stuff like that in it. Put a little food in too. Oh, and look in the top drawer of the chart table. There should be some batteries right in front. Throw those in too."

"How about some clothes?" Laura asked. "How long will it take us to get somewhere on foot?"

"Good idea, get a change of clothes, we may need something dry. I don't think it will take us long, maybe a day or two at most. Just grab anything of mine, nothing's clean anymore. And get me my hiking boots, and remember yours too. Put them in a plastic garbage bag. Make that two bags, to keep them dry. Then bring them out on deck with the backpack."

Fifteen minutes later, Laura emerged from below looking a little green around the edges. "That was harder than you think," she said. "I got bounced around good, getting the clothes together. Where do you want these?" She threw the backpack and the garbage bag of clothes on the cockpit bench to Toby's right.

"That's fine," Toby said.

Laura sat down, needing to settle her stomach. After a minute she reached into her pocket, pulled out a slip of paper and held it up for Toby to see. "I was going through your pants pocket, and I found this. It looks like it might be important. What is it?"

"Going through my pants pockets?" Toby asked with a wry grin.

"You bet. I can do that now. I've got total pants privileges. I can get in your pants any time I want to."

"Whose rule is that?"

"Mine," Laura answered. "So what is this, your Swiss bank account number?"

"Let me see it," Toby said, and reached over for the piece of paper. "Oh, that's something Solene gave me just before we left," he said looking at the numbers on the slip.

"Okay, so what is it?"

Toby looked over at Laura and smiled. "Actually … I don't know."

"Why did he give it to you then? Didn't he tell you what it was," she asked, now curious.

"Solene said that Dixon told him to give it to me. Solene also said that he had no idea what it was, but that Dixon told him that if … " Toby paused, trying to remember what Solene had said. "Something like: 'If things start happening, and I needed help, this would help'. That's not exact, but it's close. I figured it might be a phone number or a password. To be honest, I kinda forgot about it."

Laura looked puzzled, "Well, things are happening and we need help. Maybe we should try to figure it out."

"Here, you take it, I have to steer," Toby said, handing the paper back to Laura. "Count the digits. How many are there?"

She counted. "Fifteen. It doesn't look like a phone number, I don't think you need that many numbers even for an overseas call."

Laura looked at the slip again, and then at Toby, "Tell me again what Solene said?"

"Okay, let me think," Toby said, pausing. "He said: 'If things start happening, and you get in trouble, this will help.' That's pretty close, I think."

"'Things start happening and you get in trouble …'" Laura said looking perplexed. "You know, Dixon said something like that to me a day or two before we left. It was the last time I talked to him."

Laura looked skyward, scrunched up her face, looked back down and tried to replay the tape from that brief conversation. "Damn, what the hell was it he said?" She stood up and leaned on the cabin bulkhead, looking out to sea, thinking.

"Wow! I've got it!" she said and turned back to Toby. "I just remembered what he said. At the time I thought it was meaningless, just some kind of sailor's farewell message. You know, like when actors tell each other to break a leg."

"So what did he say?"

"You won't believe this," Laura said, still thinking. "My God - that man. This is vintage Dixon."

"Alright already, what did he say!"

"He said, in a very off hand way, like some kind of sailor's catch-phrase. He said: 'If things start happening and you need help, just think latitude and attitude.' That's what he said."

"Huh?" Toby said. "That doesn't make any sense."

"I know. That's what I thought too, but then 'break a leg' doesn't make sense either. That's why I thought it was some kind of old sailor's farewell."

"Or an old Jimmy Buffet song."

Laura held up the slip and waved it at Toby, "Latitude and longitude – that's what this is!"

"Let me see it again," he said, reaching for the slip. He studied it for a minute and looked back at Laura. "Sorry, but I don't think so. There are too many digits, and the numbers don't make sense as either latitude or longitude."

"You sure?"

"Wait - just a second. I forgot something. Solene also told me it was encrypted, sort of. These aren't the real numbers. I've got to do something to them first. Go down and get me a pencil and another piece of paper."

Laura came back up on deck a minute later and handed Toby the pencil and paper.

"Come over her and help me steer, I need both hands to do this. I'll stay right here and correct if you need help."

"Aye, aye, Captain," Laura said and moved to the wheel.

"Okay, just keep it right here," Toby said and let go of the wheel. He wrote the "eight, seven" alternately below the numbers on the slip, did the subtraction, and wrote down the transformed number on the other piece of paper.

He studied it for a moment. "Well, it looks better - these first seven look alright, but the last eight don't make sense. There should only be six digits – not eight. Unless ..."

Toby looked up at Laura and smiled. "Eight, seven – it's not only the encryption key, it's a clue! Eight digits, and seven digits, that's how they are divided. So that makes the latitude and longitude go to a tenth of a second. That's why each one has an extra digit. He's such a clever bastard!" he said, shaking his head.

"Can you figure out where it is on the map?"

"I sure can, probably down to a few feet. But I have to go down to the chart table to use the nav-computer. You need to steer for a few minutes. Grab the wheel, we'll do it together for a while so you can get the feel."

Laura stood at the helm, Toby pressed behind her, all four hands on the wheel. He let her steer, gently correcting her if she strayed off the heading. They stood there, silently enjoying the wind, the boat pushing along under sail, the sound of the water, and the warmth of the full body contact. Toby was in no hurry to go below. He wished he could stay right there forever. Finally, Laura said she could handle the helm by herself and reluctantly told him to go below to find the mystery location.

"It looks like you're right," Toby said, as he came up the ladder to the cockpit. "The spot is north of here, but still on the west side of Vancouver Island."

"You're kidding," Laura said frowning. "It's actually near where we are right now?"

"It's not exactly near where we are, but I think we might get there or close to it in a day or so. It's not on the water. It's at the end of a bay, about three miles up an estuary, in the woods."

Toby glanced up at the sails - the jib was luffing. He figured Laura had strayed off course. He put the marine atlas down on the bench and moved quickly to the helm. "Here," he said. "Let me take that."

"I think I did okay," Laura said. "According to the compass, we're still going in the same direction."

Toby checked, she was right. Instead, the wind had shifted a bit around to the south. He would have to fall off a little. He wasn't pleased with the new heading for the leg out to sea, but the wind shift would help them coming back in. Down below, at the chart table, he had plotted a course that would give them a shot at making it to Dixon's secret coordinates by late evening. He didn't want to do any more tacking than he had to, so he decided to head the Gull out to sea for another three hours. Then, if the wind held steady on the return leg, they would be on a heading that, depending upon the currents, might just barely take them into the right bay.

"Where is it?" Laura asked, looking at the marine atlas.

"Look on the west side of the island, about two-thirds of the way up. See that big bay just south of Nootka Island? Just east of there. I circled it for you."

She looked. "Got it. So where are we now?"

"About twenty miles out to sea, almost due west of Tofino, maybe a little south."

"This is fun," Laura said, studying the map. "So what direction are we heading?"

"Almost due west. We'll keep heading west for three or four more hours. Then tack ninety degrees, and head due north. If we're lucky, that will take us into that big bay right by Nootka," Toby said. "While I remember it, put this slip in the backpack," he said, handing her the paper with the coordinates on it.

Laura stood up, opened the backpack, and put the slip inside. She moved over by Toby, so she wouldn't have to talk so loud. "I'm a little freaked out by this thing with the coordinates."

"What about it?"

"Let me ask you something," Laura said. "Do you think you could have figured out that those numbers were latitude and longitude on your own?"

"Maybe ... but probably not."

"And what he told me would not have done me any good at all, if not for the that slip with the numbers. So, Dixon gave us this information - information that we could only, *really only*, have figured out if we were together," Laura said. "That's a little bizarre don't you think?"

"Bizarre? Dixon? Where, exactly, is the news flash there?"

"No, c'mon, think about this. What if we go to this place, and we hide there and survive. What if there is the real vaccine there? What if Dixon's there? I mean, this place might be our only hope to stay alive."

"I sure hope so."

"But if it is, that means Dixon was *only* willing to save us if we were together. If we were apart, we'd never know about it. He only wants us alive if we are together! Isn't that even more strange than Dixon's usual strangeness?"

Toby hadn't thought about it in those terms, but she was right. Dixon wanted them together.

"Huh," Toby said. "I don't know, maybe it's something simple. Maybe he just likes us and thought we would be good together."

"And, apparently, he only likes us when we *are* together. You have to admit it's very weird."

"Put it on the list," Toby said and turned his attention back to the helm.

Two hours later, Toby turned the helm over to Laura. He went below and recalculated the Gull's position and charted the course that he wanted to take to get to Dixon's mystery spot. He made sandwiches and brought them up to his new helmsperson.

"Oh, oh. I think I see a plane," he said, looking due east, over Laura's shoulder as he approached with her lunch. He put the sandwiches down next to her, and quickly checked the sails and boat's heading. "Looks Good. You doing okay?"

"I'm fine. Where's the plane?"

"Back over your right shoulder, pretty far away, probably flying over the coast. I'll get the binoculars," Toby said, and headed back down to the chart table.

A minute later he was on deck, scanning the sky to the east. "There it is, I've got it. It's heading north, along the coast. But it could be anybody. I'm sure lots of planes fly along there."

"Is it a float plane?" Laura asked.

"Yup," Toby said, putting the binoculars down. "I'll take the wheel. Why don't you sit down and eat?"

"Okay, but I want to steer again sometime. What a rush!"

"I knew you'd like it." Toby took the wheel, made some minor adjustments to the jib sheet, and settled into the zone. Thirty minutes later he gestured for Laura to take the helm again. He took up the binoculars to see if he could spot the float plane.

"See it?" Laura asked.

"Not yet."

Toby lowered the glasses, and scanned the sky without them one last time.

And there it was again. This time it was north of them, but heading south. And it was closer, they were no longer flying along the coast. The paranoia in Toby thought they might be flying a grid – looking for something.

"There they are, coming our way," he said, pointing to the north.

"Can they see us from up there?" Laura asked.

"I think so. We can see them, and we're about the same size," Toby answered, keeping them in sight with the binoculars. "Shit! I think they're coming in closer."

Toby put the binocular strap around his neck and let the glasses hang. "Laura - I'll take the wheel. Go below and see if you can find one of my hats - anything is fine. Look in the closet. And then stay below; don't come out."

Toby wished he had thought this part out more thoroughly. He could have covered up the big "Gull" stenciled on the side. He could have had on a better disguise on. He had just never expected that he was actually right about the bad guys looking for the Gull by float plane.

Laura tossed out a hat, "Is that okay?"

"Fine, and stay back from the ladder."

Toby pulled the hat down over his ears and watched as the float plane circled above them and then turned, banked and headed steeply down, right toward the Gull.

"Shit! Laura - stay way back. They're coming in for a close look."

"Are they going to land?" Laura shouted out from the hatchway.

"God, I hope not," Toby shouted back.

The plane kept coming, straight at them. It reminded him of those old World War II films of kamikaze's flying straight into the camera. At the last moment, it banked slightly to the right and roared by. It was ear-shattering, shaking his entire body, less than a hundred yards off the starboard beam and no more than fifty yards above the water. Toby could see two sets of binoculars peering out the windows at him. At least it didn't look like they intended to land.

The big plane roared by, then rose and banked to the right. Toby watched it until he was convinced they weren't going to make another pass. No need to, he figured. He was sure that they had identified him.

"Can I come out now?" Laura shouted.

"It's okay: come on out."

"Who was it?" Laura asked, sounding worried.

"I saw two of them looking at me with binoculars. I'm not entirely sure, but they looked like they were Indian. After they buzzed us, they headed east. My guess is that they chartered the plane out of Tofino. They're heading back there now. Then they'll get a boat and come out and get us."

"Can't we just head off in another direction? Maybe they won't be able to find us if they're in a boat. It's a big ocean," Laura offered.

"Maybe, for a while, but eventually they'd find us. And if they catch us out in the open ocean – we're dead. They'll kill us for sure."

Toby bit his lip, and wondered again, for the millionth time, about how he ended up in this bottomless rabbit hole.

"Shit, shit, shit!!" he shouted, suddenly realizing his potentially fatal mistake. "I shouldn't have taken us this far out. We have to turn around and head to shore as fast as we can."

"How long will it take to get back?" Laura asked.

"Well, it's one o'clock now and we've been on this heading for about five hours. It'll be faster going back in, so probably four hours, maybe three. I'll know better after we get headed in and I can see how fast we're going."

"How long will it take them to get a boat and get to us?" asked Laura.

"Three hours maybe – but it could be less if they have a boat standing-by, or if they get a very fast boat."

"I hate to tell you this Captain, but that math doesn't work. They'll catch us before we can get ashore."

"Maybe. But they have to find us. They might head out to sea where we were spotted by the float plane. That could add another hour," Toby said. "But we don't have any other choice, so let's go."

"Okay, let's go," Laura said. "What can I do?"

Three white-knuckled hours later, Toby could see land coming up fast. He scanned the coast with the binoculars for an opening of some kind, something that could hide them for a few minutes while they jumped ship and slipped into the woods. Luckily, to the north and just a bit off their current course, he spotted a small bay with what appeared to be several islands in the middle of it. It looked perfect for his plan.

Laura had been sitting silently for the last hour. Toby had been fully engaged in keeping the Gull from being slammed sideways by the trailing swells while trying to catch and surf as many of them as possible. His shoulders ached. But as hard as the last few hours had been for him, he could only imagine what Laura was going through - sitting there in a ball, holding on to her knees, silently contemplating her imminent death.

"Hey," he said, breaking the silence. "Are you okay?"

"No, not yet," she said, looking straight ahead. "Get me to shore and I'll reconsider."

"Well maybe I will. It looks like we win the whose-lucky-first sweepstakes. I think we're about a half-hour away from a perfect spot. Look a little to port – to the left, sorry. See that opening? I think we can get in behind those islands in the middle and get to shore without being seen. But maybe it won't matter. I don't see their boat yet."

"Should I look for them with the binoculars?" Laura asked.

"Good idea." Toby handed the glasses to her. "If you feel you can do it safely, go up and stand by the mainmast. It's the highest point, you can see farther out. But hang on tight to the mast with one hand."

Laura scrambled up onto the cabin roof and stood by the mast with one arm wrapped around it. It took her several minutes to get her feet set just right in order to keep her balance long enough so that she could get a few seconds of viewing. "This is hard to do," she shouted back to Toby.

Toby watched her scan to the south, along the coast, "See anybody?" he asked.

"No, I think we're good."

"Look over this way, too." Toby pointed behind him. "Maybe they went out to sea – where we were when they flew over."

Laura adjusted her position and waited for the Gull to reach the top of a swell. Toby could see her stop scanning the horizon and fix on one location. At the top of the next swell she held the glasses down and looked back at Toby. "There's a boat directly behind us. It's coming our way!" she yelled.

"Alright," Toby said, trying not to sound panicked. "If they aren't too close, I think we can still make it. Listen carefully – I'm going to blast into that opening ahead at full speed. We need to be lucky again and not hit any rocks. Then I'm going to head to the left, behind that island and go right up to the far shoreline – see it right there?" He pointed to a steep slope that came straight down to the shore.

"Okay, I see it," Laura said, her breath coming fast now.

"If I can spot a rock or a log on the shore that's big enough, I'm going to try to pull right up to it – like a dock. I want you to undo the safety rail, and stand there with the backpack and one of the bags. I'll take the other. When we get close, throw the bags on shore and jump onto the rock. I'm going to be coming in fast, so you will need to be quick. Got it?"

"Got it."

"I'll be right behind you. I'll set the steering wheel before I jump and then the Gull will motor away by itself for a while. That way they won't know where we went ashore."

"You're kidding. This isn't a James Bond movie, Toby."

"I'm not so sure about that," Toby said. "And if there isn't a big rock that will work, I'll just beach it as best I can, and we'll scramble ashore through the water and then see if we can outrun them."

Toby braced himself. The opening was only a few seconds away.

"Laura," Toby said. "Hang on tight – we may hit a rock."

The Gull barreled into the small bay, both sails taut with the stiffening breeze, engine at full throttle. Lucky again, the water in the opening was deep. Toby couldn't even see the bottom, much less any rocks.

"Laura - go roll up the Jib, like you did before, only faster," Toby shouted, and released the jib sheet. Laura furled the sail in as fast as she could.

Toby loosened the main sheet and turned to port, behind the little island, and now only a hundred yards to the big rock on the steep bank of the far shore.

"Laura, can you see the boat? Are they in the bay yet?"

"No - I don't see them."

"Good. Take off your life jacket and throw it in the cockpit – it's too bright." he yelled, and did the same. "Go down and get one of the V-boxes. Leave the other one for them - maybe they'll be satisfied with the one."

Toby approached the rock, hoping it was going to be deep enough to pull alongside. Twenty yards – ten yards, Toby turned hard to port and glanced back over his shoulder – still no boat in sight. He decided to try to bring the Gull to a stop at the rock. It would be safer. He shoved the gearshift into reverse - but he had waited too long; he was too close. The Gull slammed hard into the rock.

"Jump!" He yelled to Laura, unnecessarily. The impact had catapulted her out of the boat. She was now scrambling up and over the rock.

Toby put the throttle at half speed, and slipped the gearshift back into forward. He set and locked the wheel to a very slight turn to port, away from the shore, and waited till the last possible moment to jump ashore – to make sure the Gull would head back into the bay. At the last second he grabbed the V-box and the backpack, and jumped from the stern rail onto the rock.

"Quick, we have to hide somewhere. Can we wedge down behind this thing?" Toby asked.

Laura slid down the backside of the rock into a narrow opening.

"We've got to get down more!" Toby said, now in a panic. He could hear the boat approaching. Laura had to contort herself to get further down into the narrow space between the rocks. Toby wedged down on top of her.

"There they are," he said in a loud whisper.

"Wouldn't it be funny if it was just a fishing boat coming in to anchor?" Laura said, in a voice strained by her awkward position.

"No, that wouldn't be funny. A good thing maybe, but definitely not funny."

Toby adjusted his position so he could see the boat. It looked to be a fifty-foot ocean going sport-fisher. Lucky again, he thought - that is a fast boat. They must have gone out to the place where the float plane had first spotted them. If they had come directly up the coast, he knew they would have caught the Gull in the open ocean.

By now the Gull had motored several hundred yards away, toward the north end of the bay. The big sport-fisher pulled up behind it and then alongside. Toby watched as two people boarded. He couldn't tell for sure, but thought they carried rifles.

In a minute or less someone emerged from the main cabin of the Gull, holding high above his head what Toby assumed to be the other V-box. The men on board the Gull talked to the men on the sport-fisher. Then, someone went forward on the Gull and threw a line up and secured the Gull for towing.

Someone else went up to the crow's nest - high above the deck of the sport-fisher - with a pair of binoculars. Toby watched as he scanned the shoreline, starting at the North end of the bay. Toby hunkered down, so he couldn't be seen. When he thought it was safe, he peeked back out. The man in the crow's nest was pointing directly at Toby. The others were also looking at the exact spot where Toby and Laura had landed.

Toby was astonished. How could they possibly have seen him? He looked around to see if they had left a bag on the rock, and finally spotted a bright orange fender floating in the water just ten yards in front of him. It must have fallen off the bow of the Gull when he hit the rock. Now it was bobbing up and down - like a bright orange sign that said "We're over here!"

"My God!" Toby said. "They spotted us."

"How could they?"

"A fender fell off the Gull when we hit the rock. It's in the water right in front of us."

"A fender?"

"One of those big orange squishy things that go between the boat and the dock."

"You're sure they see us?"

Toby leaned out around the rock for another look.

The sport fisher had already released the line to the Gull and was underway, turning sharply back toward Toby and Laura.

"*Fuck!* They're coming. Let's go," Toby said.

Toby yanked Laura up roughly from the wedge between in the rocks. She yelped as her back and arm scraped the barnacle-encrusted rock. "Where's the backpack?" he asked.

"I've got it," she said, holding up her other hand.

Toby grabbed the V-box and looked at Laura. She nodded. "Take it. We can always leave it later."

They scrambled over the rock, broke through the shoreline underbrush and were immediately confronted by a nearly vertical fern-covered cliff.

"What now?" Laura asked in a panic.

"We go up - and fast," Toby said. "Give me the backpack. You go first, I'll be right behind you. You can grab the ferns, they'll hold."

Laura handed over the pack and started scrambling up the cliff. Toby stuffed the V-box in the pack, slipped it on his back and followed. "Just go straight up as fast as you can," he yelled. "And don't look back."

The cliff was steep enough to require handholds, but not so steep that there was a real danger of falling. The handholds were plentiful, mostly the dense tough sword ferns, but also some small vine maples and roots of the widely-spaced huge old-growth spruce and fir that had eluded the logger's saw due to the extreme slope of the hillside. Breathing heavily, they climbed fifty yards up the cliff before they first heard voices below them. "Stay low - but keep going!" Toby exhorted, in a loud whisper. He wasn't sure if they could see Laura or him amongst the high ferns. Toby kept expecting to hear gunshots. None came.

Finally, with chests heaving, unable even to speak, they crested the cliff to a worn-flat, ridgeline elk trail. Laura fell to the ground, rolled over on her back, and tried to catch her breath. Toby did the same. After a minute he crawled over to the edge of the cliff to see if he could spot their pursuers.

On hands and knees, Toby leaned out over the edge and peered down just as Joharu Jain, cousin and co-conspirator of Sanjay Jain and a former marathoner, parted the last ferns and looked up at Toby, just three feet away. Toby could only get up on one knee as Jain reached for the handgun on his belt and burst up the last few feet between them.

Toby grabbed Jain around the waist and spun him to the ground just as Jain pulled his gun out. They hit the rocky ground hard and rolled over once with Jain emerging on top. Jain got a knee on Toby's chest, pushing down hard to control him. Toby struggled, trying to grab Jain's wrists to prevent him from getting in a direct punch.

Laura sprung to her feet, picked up a football-sized rock, and rushed over behind the struggling men. She raised the rock above her, trying to hit Jain on the head. She stumbled at the last moment, missed his head but landed a hard blow directly on his right shoulder. She could feel it collapse as Jain fell off Toby and screamed in pain.

Laura looked around frantically for Jain's handgun. She spotted it a few feet down the trail, rushed over, picked it up and turned back to Toby and Jain just as another man scrambled up over the edge. Without thinking, she pointed the gun at the man and fired three times, hitting him in the chest. He didn't even have time to look at Laura before falling backward, over the edge, and tumbling silently down the cliff.

Laura stepped over to the still screaming Jain. He was on his back, lying next to Toby, who wasn't getting up.

"Don't fucking move, or I'll shoot you!" she yelled at Jain. "Toby, are you okay?"

Toby grimaced and said, "My chest - ribs maybe," he wheezed.

"Can you get up?"

Toby nodded and carefully raised himself onto his left elbow. "Give me a hand," he said.

Laura helped him to a sitting position and then onto his feet. Toby again yelped in pain as he stood. "My ankle ..." he said.

Laura tried to figure what to do next - deal with Jain, lean over the edge and start shooting, or help Toby. She opted for checking the cliff to see if anyone else was coming up. With both hands on the gun she got down on her knees, and then peered carefully over the edge. She could hear talking far below, but no gunshots, and no noises nearby. The man she had shot had probably given the others pause, as he bounced past them down the cliff.

Toby was gingerly hopping over to a log to sit.

"You okay for now?" Laura asked. Toby nodded and sat down.

Laura went back to Jain, who was now only moaning. His right side was grossly deformed. Laura's adrenaline-fueled smash had taken out his shoulder and collarbone, part of which was sticking out of his shirt.

"Don't move or I'll stomp on it again," Laura said as she bent over Jain and removed the rifle that he still had slung over his good shoulder. She took it and gave it to Toby. "Watch the hill," she said, and returned to Jain.

"How many of you are there?" she asked. Jain said nothing and continued moaning. "I'm not fucking around here you asshole!" she yelled. "I'll smack the end of that bone with this gun if you don't answer."

Jain sputtered and then coughed - the pain from the cough causing another round of moaning. "Six," he finally whispered.

"Have you gotten any of the vaccine out of these boxes?"

"No."

"Is there vaccine in the boxes?"

"Don't know," Jain said, groaning.

"Where's Dixon?"

"Don't know."

Laura walked over to Toby. "Don't move," she yelled back over her shoulder to Jain. She picked up the backpack, opened it and removed the V-box.

"Toby, can you walk?"

"A little, but too slow. You should leave me and go," he said in short bursts, breathing shallowly.

"You've been watching too many old movies," Laura said. "I'll leave this instead." She held up the V-box.

Laura walked back to Jain and placed the V-box beside him. She looked down at him for a moment and then raised the gun. Jain closed his eyes. Laura held the gun with both hands, aimed and fired twice. Toby flinched, pain shot up from his damaged ribs.

Jain opened his eyes and looked at Laura, wordlessly asking the question; "Why?"

"I didn't shoot you, asshole. I shot the V-box," she said.

Toby nodded to himself, relieved. Good move, he thought.

Laura bent over close to Jain's ear and said something to him. Then came back to Toby and helped him up. "First, let me look at the ankle," she said and knelt down to feel around the bone. "Can you move it in a circle?"

"Yup," Toby said. "I don't think it's broken, but it's a bad sprain."

"How about the ribs?"

"I think some are broken," he said, still having trouble breathing.

Laura looked both directions along the ridgeline elk trail. "This way," she pointed to her right. "We have to get away from here."

"What about the Indian?"

"He's going to try to climb back down. I told him to wait a few minutes first."

Toby put his right arm around Laura's shoulder and used the rifle for a cane with his left. "I thought I was supposed to be James Bond," he said as they limped slowly down the trail. "I don't think it's right for the girl to be James Bond."

Chapter 19

Three days later
Friday, July 10th, 2020
Malabar Research Farm, Central Oregon

Mark Dunn, the head of security for Dixon's four-man army at Haida Gwaii, broke into a trot as the smaller of the two garage doors banged shut behind a grey hybrid van. It was his military training: open the car door, stand back, salute the general. Of course there was no need to salute now; Mark was no longer in the military and the guest wasn't a general. Still, respect was called for.

"Mr. Secretary," Mark said as he opened the van door. "Good to see you."

"Thank you Mark," Secretary Solene said as he got out of the driver's seat and extended his hand. There were many things that could be said next, but instead, Solene held his grip for an extra moment and simply gave Mark a solemn nod.

Then the passenger door of the van opened, much to Mark's chagrin - he had gone to the wrong door. He was expecting Secretary Solene to be alone. A stately fiftyish woman, with short grey hair, emerged and gave him a knowing smile.

Mark moved quickly to greet her. "Dr. Contreras… I'm sorry, I didn't recognize you! Thank God you're safe!" Mark gave her an enthusiastic two-handed shake and smiled broadly.

"Yes I am, and thank you. These last few days have been quite an adventure. Right now though, I need to use the restroom. Can you direct me?"

"Sure, through that door and go right," Mark said, pointing over to the office section of the big warehouse.

"Nice place," Solene said as he looked around. "It's quite the little armory."

"It'll work."

"Give me a hand with these boxes," Solene said as he moved around to the back door of the van. "Where are we going to set up?"

"In the conference room, follow me."

A moment later, Mark leaned out of the conference room door to catch Dr. Contreras as she came out of the bathroom. "We're over here," he said.

"Can I ask about your appearance?" Mark asked Sofia, somewhat hesitantly, as she sat down.

Sofia gave him a weak smile. "At WHO – you know that I work for the World Health Organization, don't you?" She paused and Mark nodded. "At WHO, we often needed to go into countries where we were not welcome. And sometimes we needed to leave countries quickly. So, I have been provided with several false identities. Yesterday, I traveled back to Seattle under one of those identities, the passport of Dr. Silvia Montero, a woman with short grey hair."

"That was smart. Good work," Mark said.

"Manny called me several days ago to tell me about the danger. I feel now like a secret Interpol agent. I've used two identities, traveled to several countries, and finally ended up in Seattle this morning - as Manny requested."

"Were you able to drive on the back roads from Portland as we discussed yesterday?" Mark asked, turning to Solene.

"Yes, and it was a beautiful drive. No one followed us."

"What about the car?" Mark asked.

"I rented it in Seattle this morning. I told them I wanted it for a month," Solene answered.

"Good. We'll keep it here. I can park it in the corner and cover it with a tarp. It shouldn't be a problem." Mark nodded and smiled. "Well, excellent! It looks like you two are going to be safe now." He paused, waiting for

Secretary Solene to speak. He hadn't expected Dr. Contreras to be there and he was uncertain about how much she knew.

"Mark, you should know that Sofia has been informed about everything that is going on. We have discussed it all day on the trip down," Solene said. "And, before we call Professor Vanderham, I need to discuss an idea with you."

Mark took a hard look at Sofia. Now that he understood what she knew - he wondered what she thought.

"Okay, go ahead," he said, looking back at Solene.

"I'm a little worried about the two doctors at Malabar. The timing is tricky. They may start figuring things out before we are prepared to tell them what's really happening," Solene said. "I am thinking that we should add Dr. Contreras to that mix. I can tell Vanderham, as I tell him about the vaccine, that Dr. Contreras is from 'our benefactor's' biotech company, and that she is here to monitor the vaccine's effect."

"You're not going to tell Vanderham the truth about the vaccine are you?" Mark asked, somewhat alarmed.

"No, no. But I have to tell Vanderham something about the vaccine – in order for him to make sure that everyone gets it immediately. I'm going to tell him that our benefactor's biotech scientists have gotten word of a new flu that is emerging that may be very contagious. The scientists believe this experimental vaccine may prevent it. Given that, it would make some sense for Dr. Contreras to be here to monitor its use – as it is experimental."

"Don't you think that might spook them? Won't they think they're being used as guinea pigs to test new drugs?"

"Yes, and I hope that's exactly what they think," Solene said. "But that's fine. It will be a good cover. As they see the rest of the world get the flu, and that they don't – at least then they'll have a plausible explanation. In any case, they are already suspicious. I've received several emails from Vanderham asking pointed questions. But the belief that they may be guinea pigs could keep them off track and occupied for some time."

"So where does Dr. Contreras come into this?" Mark asked.

"Well, she will be with them. She can let us know if they are thinking about contacting the authorities. If they are, then we can go in and do the full disclosure. But I want to wait as long as possible before we tell them everything. That will be a difficult time."

"I suppose it would be good to have someone on the inside. We do have listening devices in several places. In reality though, they are pretty useless. We don't have anybody to monitor what we pick up."

"I was wondering about that. Where is everyone?" Solene asked. "Are you here alone?"

Mark nodded. "I'm by myself. Duval sent Pete out to be with Justice Brown. Pete picked her up in Dallas. She had decided at the last minute to go visit some friends. It probably saved her life. Pete's in D.C. with her right now."

"The others are with Duval then?"

Mark looked at Dr. Contreras. He wasn't sure what he could say in front of her. "After ... after..."

"Mark, I know what happened," Sofia said.

Before Mark could speak, Solene interjected: "But not everything, I have told her what happened, in general terms, but I haven't told her where or how."

"Okay," Mark said. He understood the reasons for the need-to-know partial disclosure. "Phil, Charlie, and Jacob, helped Duval with... with the final step. Jacob is now heading back up to the islands with Dr. Mothershed in tow, and Phil and Charlie are flying Duval to D.C."

"D.C.?" asked Sofia. "Is he going to pick up Justice Brown? That would be wonderful!"

"I don't know," Mark said. "It might be too visible for her to turn up missing. But I assume he's bringing her the vaccine."

"That's good too," Sofia said. "And now, can I ask about the others? Do you know anything about Laura and Dr. Benson?"

Mark inhaled slowly and then let out a deep sigh. "I do. I just found out this morning ... I'm sorry ..."

"Oh no!" Sophia gasped.

"Dr. Benson was using his debit card, so I was able to track his movements after he left the conference. He - and I'm assuming, actually I'm quite sure - he and Laura got on his sailboat in Anacortes and sailed around the south end of Vancouver Island into Barkley Sound. This morning I emailed to the Canadian Coast Guard out of Tofino to see if they could locate them. I claimed there was a semi-emergency. I got an email back almost immediately."

Mark grimaced, "Sorry to say, but yesterday they found debris from Toby's sailboat, including two life jackets, floating off the coast north of Tofino."

Sofia looked away, tears welling up. She covered her face with her hands, got up and walked to the far side of the Conference room.

"My God, do you think Jain and Patel did this too?" Solene asked.

"I think so. Other than Wyndi Rehn, and I don't have any idea where she is, everyone else is accounted for, either dead or inaccessible to them. Doctor Sundgren and Doctor Benson were the only people that they could still get to. Jain and his crew must be pretty desperate by now."

Mark looked at Solene, and somewhat hesitantly, asked "You know about the V-boxes don't you?"

"Yes, of course," Solene said. "And so does Dr. Contreras."

"And so does Dr. Contreras – what?" Sofia asked as she returned to the table, wiping her eyes. "I'm sorry, I missed that."

"Mark asked about the V-boxes, and if you were aware that they never contained any of the actual vaccine," Solene said.

"Yes, Manny told me this morning. Yet another one of Mr. Dixon's deceptions," she said, still sounding sad from the shocking news about her friend Laura. "Sometimes I wonder if any of you knows what is real and what is not."

"It was so stupid of us," Solene said, sighing. He stood up and paced to the end of the room and back. "The V-boxes, the bloody V-boxes …" he said, anger entering his voice. "I can't get over the irony."

"How so?" Mark asked.

Solene remained standing, arms folded in front of him. "When Dixon came up with the idea of the V-boxes, we thought it was so clever. For me, in fact, it was the reason I finally agreed to do the conference. Without the V-box idea, we would have no control over the group after they left Haida Gwaii. The V-boxes would – or so we thought – give Dixon the ability to take his time deciding. And since he never intended to put any real vaccine in them, it was risk free."

Solene threw up his hands. "Instead, they became so valuable that now many people have been killed for them. And because of that, Dixon had no choice but to act."

He slowly shook his head. "That's the irony – that they directly caused the exact thing they were meant to prevent."

"But it never for a moment occurred to me that Jain and Patel would do this. Did you see it?" Mark asked.

"No, not them specifically. But with so many people involved, something unexpected was almost a certainty. And now, I fear this is completely out of control."

"I don't think it's completely out of control," Mark said. "What do you mean?"

"How long do you think it will take the authorities to connect the dots between all these dead people and the conference at Haida Gwaii?" Solene asked.

"I don't know … weeks, maybe months," Mark answered. "And by then, they will be dealing with much graver issues."

"And how about this story we are about to tell Vanderham?" Solene asked, his composure showing unusual cracks. "I know, I know, same answer: eventually it won't matter. Sorry. I'm quite upset, as I'm sure we all are," he said and returned to his seat.

The three of them sat in silence for several minutes. Sofia had been experiencing the gamut of all possible negative emotions over the last few days – fear, despair, anger, confusion, even nausea. But now, she got up and went to Secretary Solene to console him. She stood behind him, placed her hands on his shoulders and said nothing, letting the contact speak for her. Solene reached up and put one hand on hers and held it there.

Mark went to the door, "I'll get us some water. Be right back."

After Mark had left the room, Sofia spoke calmly to the Secretary. "Manny, I'm going to repeat to you what you have been telling me. We can't stop this. We can only go forward now. Malabar Farm is all that really matters," she said, stroking his shoulder. "I haven't really said this, but I am so grateful to you for saving me and bringing me here."

Solene took a deep breath and then exhaled slowly, trying to settle himself. "Excuse my momentary lapse Doctor, and thank you for administering an appropriate treatment," he said, and smiled weakly up at her.

"We are going to need each other to get through this," Sofia said and made her way back to her seat as Mark returned.

Mark handed out the bottled water and walked over to the four boxes piled on the end of the table. He pulled several stick-on labels from his shirt pocket. "I printed these up this morning – fake shipping labels addressed to Vanderham," he said as he peeled off the backing and stuck one on each box.

"Why do we need those?" Solene asked. "Vanderham will know that I brought the boxes after he gets here and we tell him the story."

"Yes, he will, but the doctors at Malabar won't. They might notice. Remember, they won't know you were here."

"Good idea once again, Mark," Solene said. "You think of so many details. Thanks." He paused for a moment. "But do you ever worry about the things we haven't thought of?"

"All the time, sir… all the time."

Mark grabbed the speaker-phone from the credenza and placed it in the middle of the conference table. He uncoiled two thin wires with earpieces on one end. "Put these in your ears. It'll be like a speaker phone, except Vanderham won't be able to tell."

"Okay," he said when Sofia and Secretary Solene had their earpieces in place. "Are we ready to call Vanderham?"

"I hope he's there," Solene said.

"Me too," Mark said and dialed the number for the office at Malabar.

"Hello. I need to speak to a Professor Vanderham," Mark said, sounding official.

"Good," Mark said and gave the others a thumbs-up. Vanderham was there.

"Professor Vanderham, my name is Mark Dunn. You don't know me but I work at WPPS - the new building that was just built right outside the main entrance to Malabar Farm on the other side of the river."

Mark paused, listening to Vanderham. "Yes sir, that's the one. Anyway, I have some packages that were dropped off here by mistake. They are addressed to you and marked 'Urgent and Confidential'. I was wondering if you could drive down here and pick them up. I'm sorry, but I'm here alone so I can't bring them to you."

Mark paused again. "Actually no, Professor. And I'm sorry if you think I'm going a little overboard, but I'd feel more comfortable if you picked them up yourself. They look important."

"Okay then, good," Mark said. "I'll meet you out front in fifteen minutes."

Mark put the phone down and exhaled. "So far – so good."

"Nice job Mark," Solene said. "Now comes the hard part. I hope I can be as convincing as you."

"Manny!" Sofia exclaimed. "Remember who you are. Vanderham will be in awe. You could tell him anything – he'll believe it: trust me," she said. "And now, both of you roll up your shirt sleeves. I need to give you gentlemen a couple of shots before he gets here. And Mark, go get some packing tape, we'll need to reseal these boxes."

Fifteen minutes later, Vanderham pulled up in front of the completely featureless large metal warehouse.

Mark smiled and held out his hand as Vanderham approached the front door.

"I'm sorry, it's Mark isn't it?" Vanderham said, wrapping his bony oversized hand around Mark's. "Good to meet you. I've been wondering what this building was about – thought about stopping, but there never seemed to be anybody around."

"Good to meet you too Professor," Mark said, looking up at the craggy, smiling face of Professor Vanderham. Mark was charmed; the man certainly had charisma. Secretly, Mark was enjoying the possibility of getting to spend many years with him.

"Call me Vandy, I'm not a real professor anymore," Vanderham said, and stood back to take in the full blandness of the building. "So… what have we here? Looks like a self-storage place with all that chain link and razor wire fence. Looks like a good place to park RV's."

"No sir, we are actually a private security firm," Mark said.

"Security? What kind?"

"Well, we provide all kinds of security - events, private parties, traveling dignitaries. We are a small firm, only four of us, all ex-military. We travel a lot, mostly on the west coast. That's why you don't see many people here," Mark said and hoped it satisfied Vanderham's curiosity. The less said, the better.

"And you said your name is WPPS?"

"Yes sir, it stands for 'Willamette Professional Protection Services'," Mark said. He had made it up only two days ago, when he realized that Vanderham would need a name. It seemed perfectly meaningless to him.

"Well you picked an interesting name. You know what WPPS stands for to most people around here, don't you?"

Mark was getting concerned, and a little confused. "No ... I don't think so."

"You don't know, really?" Vanderham asked. "I guess you're a little too young."

"Sorry ..." Mark stammered.

"WPPS – Washington Public Power System - or was it 'Supply'," Vanderham paused, trying to remember. "Anyway, it was a nuclear power program in the state of Washington. They were going to build a bunch of power plants, but it all went to hell. It was the biggest bond default in U.S. history, and it was the end of the nuclear power industry in this country. Everybody called it 'Whoops' – a perfect name."

"I guess it was before my time," Mark said.

"Apparently so. I must be getting old. But I'm surprised no one else has ever said anything to you about it."

Mark was not surprised. Vanderham was the only person he had ever told it to. My god, Mark thought, it's scary how even the smallest, most innocuous things can go wrong. And now he had to tell Vanderham a more complicated lie.

"Sir, before you go in, I have a confession to make," Mark said cautiously. "I got you down here under false pretenses."

Vanderham stared at Mark and stepped back.

"A man and a woman came by earlier this morning and asked to rent my conference room and then asked me to make that call to you. That's really all I know. Well, except that the man is quite famous, and somebody that I couldn't say 'no' to. But don't worry, you are actually in for a remarkable surprise."

Mark stepped to the office door and held it open for Vanderham, "The conference room is down the hall to the right. You can't miss it."

Vanderham paused momentarily, trying to assess if he was in any real danger. Mark seemed sincere, even if he had admitted lying to him only a minute ago, and besides, he couldn't come up with any reason that someone might want to harm him. Vanderham nodded at Mark, and said nothing as he walked passed him into the warehouse.

As he entered the conference room, Vanderham was greeted by the smiling face and outthrust hand of the former Secretary General of the United Nations, one of the most admired men in the world, and a man that had been at the top of Professor Vanderham's list for over a decade.

"Professor Vanderham, so good to finally meet you," Solene said.

Vanderham took Solene's hand and shook it absently. His brain, momentarily shorted-out, finally stammered out some words. "Um yes, Mr. Secretary, it's a great honor to meet you – I think …"

"Professor, please, I'm very sorry to surprise you like this, my apologies. And this is Dr. Silvia Montero," Manny said, gesturing to Sofia, now Silvia.

Vandy gathered himself sufficiently to walk around and greet Silvia with his wrap around handshake. "Doctor," he said, with a nod.

"Professor, please call my Silvia."

"Yes, of course, and please call me Vandy."

"Have a seat. I'll try and get you back on solid ground professor," Solene said.

"Vandy," Vanderham said as he sat down.

"Excellent, and you may – actually, I insist – call me Manny."

"That will be difficult, sir."

"Manny," Solene said.

"That will be difficult," Vanderham paused, and smiled. "Manny."

"I said it was good to finally meet you just now because I am the anonymous 'Executive Director' of Malabar Farm. I hope you understand now why that could not be revealed."

Vanderham could only stare at Solene. And no, he didn't understand.

Solene continued, "I had intended, and still do, to come for an official visit later this year. I believe that I have it scheduled for the last week in September. At that time, I would like to stay for several weeks, perhaps a month, in order to get a complete understanding of the exciting program you have created here at Malabar Farm. And, I would appreciate a place to stay on the farm, if that is possible."

"Yes, of course," Vanderham said.

"I'm sure you are a bit confused. Is there anything I can answer for you right now?"

The moment he said it, Solene wished he hadn't. He knew that he couldn't let this conversation range too widely. He also knew he was not a good liar and that he might reveal too much.

Vanderham asked the right - and wrong - questions, "So you are the creator and owner of Malabar? This was your idea? You provided all this money?"

Solene stole a glance at Sofia. She was staring blankly back at him. Vanderham easily picked up on the tension.

"No, I'm not. As I believe I told you, the owner is a biotech billionaire. I simply work for him."

Click, click, click – the cogs in Vanderham's brain slid into place. He had always admired and had closely followed the career of Secretary Solene. He knew about WorldView, and he knew that Duval Dixon funded it. Click, click, click – and he of course knew that Dixon was a biotech billionaire.

"You're kidding me," Vanderham said. "Duval Dixon?"

Solene exhaled slowly, leaned forward and placed his hands, palms down, on the table. "I guess I could deny that, or refuse to answer, but that would be pointless, wouldn't it?"

"Well, Yes. I know about WorldView. So I know you already work for Dixon. If nothing else, it would be a conflict of interest to work for another biotech zillionaire. And I'm not sure that there is another one."

Solene paused a moment more, and then rose from his chair and walked to the end of the table opposite Vanderham. He stood there, arms folded, fixing Vanderham with an intense stare.

"Professor Vanderham, at this point I'm going to ask you to do something for me," Solene said. "I need you to keep all of this absolutely confidential. By 'all of this' I mean, this meeting, my role at Malabar Farm, and Mr. Dixon's involvement. And especially, what I'm about to tell you next. Can you do that?"

"May I ask why?"

"You may"

"Then, why?"

"I'm not going to tell you that now. I can say, however, that in time, you will know. Certainly by the time I return in late September. I can say this much. Mr. Dixon leads a very complex life, and right now he has a number of things going on that are, shall we say, 'ticklish'. It could be a problem for both Mr. Dixon and for Malabar Farm if word got out about his involvement at this particular time. This is true of my involvement as well. As you so quickly surmised, my involvement would lead directly to Mr. Dixon. So, you will simply have to trust me. Can you do that?"

Now it was Vanderham's turn to sigh. "Mr. Secretary, Manny, I guess I don't see why not. If I can't trust you, then ..." Vanderham paused, still trying to comprehend what was going on here. "I'm in shock a little I guess. Yes, of course, you have my word - no disclosure until you say so."

"Good, Thank you. Now on to the reason I'm here," Solene said, and returned to his seat. "We have a small emergency ..."

"Manny, may I take it from here?" Sophia interrupted.

Solene was momentarily startled. They hadn't talked about this beforehand. "Please do," he said, not wanting to get into a dispute, and happy to see Dr. Contreras becoming part of the program. Manny leaned back, folded his arms, and listened.

Forty-five minutes later, Vanderham said, "I understand." He stood up and walked over to inspect the boxes.

Sofia had dazzled Vanderham and Solene with a long, technically sophisticated, description of the new flu that she suspected was about to go global. She was able to call upon her long experience at WHO to include terms and protocols that neither Solene nor Vanderham had ever heard of. No one could have sounded more credible in her description of the experimental vaccine. She had been able to convince Vanderham that it was perfectly safe, brand new, and desperately rare.

Vanderham touched the boxes and looked up at Solene. "Perhaps it's a small price to pay - being guinea pigs for Dixon's biotech companies - in order to have Malabar Farm. I will say though, it's a little disturbing to hear that Dixon's intentions for this wonderful place are nothing more than to have a place to test new drugs."

The bobber went under; Vanderham had taken the bait.

Vanderham paused to decide how much more he should say. He decided to speak his mind. "On the other hand though, this will give us a completely free hand to do what we want here. And I will tell you that we will do amazing things. The combination of this incredible facility and the remarkable quality of the scientists you have assembled here, is unprecedented. Nothing like this exists anywhere else in the world."

Vanderham had worked himself into full lecture mode, something he excelled at. "And I hope you realize the value of the group of scientists you have assembled here. These are not students. Many, if not most, are already highly educated. The others are merely brilliant. You must understand that great things will be done here. These people are not expendable. Whatever plans you have in the future for testing drugs on these people, please bear that in mind."

Things were getting tense - formality was re-instated.

"Professor Vanderham," Solene said. "You have made too great a leap. Our intentions remain as we stated before. We wanted, specifically Mr. Dixon wanted, to create the exact facility that you have so enthusiastically described. We do expect that you and the scientists will do wonderful things. This vaccine is meant to protect this great asset, not to put it in danger."

Vanderham listened and was almost convinced, but he still had the killer question, the one that Dr. Jan had uncovered The one that Solene had never responded to.

"Mr. Secretary, do you recall the question I sent you a while ago? You never answered it."

"Yes, I know," Solene said. "I assume you received a response that said I was unavailable for the next six weeks?"

"I did, but now you're here, and so now you can tell me. Why is it that all – and I mean all – of the people at Malabar have no living parents? The majority of people at Malabar are in their late twenties and thirties. It is not possible for this to be a coincidence."

It was clear to Solene that Vanderham had completely bought in to the guinea pig ruse. So at this point, he wasn't sure how hard he should argue against it. But he did need to convince Vanderham that, at least, no one would be put in danger.

"Professor, I can't answer that for you. I didn't do any of the screening. Duval Dixon did it all. I can only say the Mr. Dixon has many unusual ideas. Often these ideas seem strange to us mere mortals. But in time, the reasons become clear. I suspect this is one of those times."

Vanderham looked over at Dr. Montero to see if she might give away something. She looked back passively. Vanderham sighed and sat down next to the boxes.

Silvia/Sophia spoke next. "Professor," she said, in her slightly accented and formal European manner. "I assume you believe Mr. Dixon is an intelligent man – do you not?"

"Of course."

"Did you believe Secretary Solene when he told you that Mr. Dixon screened these scientists himself?"

"If Secretary Solene says so, yes, I believe him."

"Then you must believe that Mr. Dixon is completely aware of the extraordinary talent he has assembled at Malabar Farm?" Sophia pressed on, now leaning forward with her hands on the table, as if she would jump across at Vanderham if he gave her the wrong answer.

"Yes."

"Good. Then let me assure you that finding human guinea pigs to test drugs on is a trivial matter. Most drug company executives believe that that is what Africa was created for. Thank goodness Mr. Dixon is not of that ilk. But there are many shades of grey in this area. So, understand that Mr. Dixon has no problem finding places to test drugs. Let me ask you this. Why would Mr. Dixon risk the extraordinary asset of Malabar Farm, and all these talented scientists, not to mention the large amount of money he has spent on all of this, *just to test drugs?*"

Vanderham stared at her, confused by the conflict between her very logical argument and the reality of the facts before him.

"What Dr. Montero has said is true," Solene finally said. "Even if you believe nothing else, please believe this – Mr. Dixon's only goal is to protect you and the others at Malabar."

"Okay, okay …" Vanderham gave up his inquiry, stood, and opened one of the boxes. "Doctor, do you have what you need to give me this vaccine right now?"

"I do," Sophia said, reaching into her bag for a syringe. "In fact, I gave Mark and Manny the vaccine just before you arrived."

Oops, Solene thought – another small slip. She had mentioned Mark.

"Mark?" Vanderham asked casually. "Who's that?"

"Ah," Solene said. "Mark. Didn't you meet him at the front door? We gave him a shot as a courtesy. He has been very accommodating to our needs."

Vanderham looked unbelievingly at Solene, but said nothing. He rolled up his sleeve and waited for the doctor.

"No, wait," Sophia said to Vanderham as he started to roll down his sleeve. "This vaccine is in two parts. I have to give you another shot."

"Two shots for everybody?" Vanderham asked, mostly making conversation.

"Yes," Sophia replied. "And a booster in ten days, to be safe."

"Could I get the flu from this? It happens sometimes."

"It is possible. But honestly, I don't know," she said, honestly.

"And when do you want to start giving the others the shots?"

Solene jumped in quickly. "Today - everyone needs to get the shots today. Our people tell us this flu could get here at any moment. There is no reason to wait."

This bit of news seemed reassuring to Vanderham. If they were just testing drugs, the urgency in Solene's request – and his voice, wouldn't be necessary. He began to think that this flu threat was real after all.

"How much vaccine do we have?" he asked.

"I'm not sure," Sophia said, looking to Solene for help.

"Two hundred doses is what I was told," Solene said.

"There are only about one hundred seventy scientists and staff at Malabar. Can we vaccinate some of the other people around here with the extra doses?"

"No, I don't think we should do that. Remember, this is an experimental vaccine. All the people at Malabar have signed contracts that have waivers for these kinds of things," Solene said, knowing it wasn't a good answer.

Vanderham took it in. The scales kept tipping back and forth. Were they guinea pigs or were they not? He kept staring down at the boxes, trying to sort this out.

"What are these?" he asked, pointing at the newly printed shipping labels.

"Glad you asked that," Solene said. "I had forgotten to tell you about those. We put them on so that the doctors at Malabar wouldn't be suspicious. Remember. We called you down here to pick up these packages."

Vanderham nodded and thought for a moment. "Then how do I explain how Doctor Montero got here? Was she delivered by the package truck as well?"

Sophia looked over at Solene and then looked up, rolling her eyes.

"If Doctor Montero flew in today, wouldn't she have brought the vaccine with her? And if it's so urgent, why would it be shipped like this?" Vanderham asked.

Solene looked up at Vanderham wide-eyed. It was obvious to Vanderham that he was groping for an explanation.

"See," Solene said, looking at Sophia. "Details ... and I thought Mark had this all figured out."

Sophia's astonished look sent Solene's stomach into full somersaults. This was why he had always had trouble believing in conspiracies. It was so damn difficult to put a coherent false premise together, much less keep it going. And that was another reason that he believed there may be other forces in play with the Eden Proposition. The fact that it had gotten this far always seemed to him to be an impossibility. On the other hand, there were all those dead people from the conference. The Indians were still out there trying to find the rest of them. Dixon was doing damage-control in D.C.. And now, the most critical thing in the entire Eden Proposition – vaccinating the people at Malabar farm - was quickly unraveling.

Vanderham sat down and stared hard at Solene. "Mark who?" Vanderham asked, for the second time in the last hour.

Solene was clearly flustered. The intense emotions of the past few days had his nerves frayed to the breaking point. He hadn't slept at all in the last forty-eight hours. He stood up and walked to the back of the room to buy some time. Finally, he had an idea. God, I hope this works, he thought.

"Well, I probably should have told you about this sooner," he said, smiling gamely at Vanderham. "Mark and his team here work for Mr. Dixon. Dixon is a little paranoid about security in everything he does, especially here, with all the time and money he has invested in Malabar. He's also a little old fashioned - out of touch really. He believes that all rural Americans are pot-growers or meth addicts. He wanted to make sure that Malabar and all the people here were safe. Mark and his security team are here to protect you."

Vanderham was approaching overload himself. The surprise of meeting Manute Solene, finding out that the Secretary was his boss, then this strange story of the flu virus, the mysterious European doctor, then the disclosure that Malabar Farm was the brainchild of Duval Dixon, and finally to find out that there was a private police force stationed at the front entrance of the farm – what in the world was going on here?

"I need to use the bathroom," Vanderham said. "Which way is it?"

"Down the hall, to the right," Sophia answered.

When Vanderham had left the room, Solene put his hands, palms down, on the top of his head. "Holy shit," he said.

"Manny," Sofia tried to sound in control, sensing that Solene was losing it. "Why not go ahead and tell him the whole thing right now?"

"No, my God, no," Solene said. "Don't you remember how you felt the first time you heard about the Eden Proposition? So, like that old joke, if we told him now we'd have to kill him. He'd never go along with it."

Solene walked around the table to the boxes of vaccine. "At this point, I have only one objective. I must get him to allow you to give out the vaccine – after that, it doesn't matter."

Vanderham headed in the direction that Dr. Montero had indicated, but in truth, he didn't need a bathroom break. He wanted to get out of that room and think for a few minutes. He passed by the bathroom and spotted an oversized door opening to the left, into the main part of the structure, and decided to do a little exploring.

Vanderham quietly opened the door and walked several steps into the open warehouse. He was astonished by what he saw there. Four black Hummers, that looked to be armored military models, each with a large gun mount in the back, were parked against the far wall. A helicopter, sans blades, sat on a pallet in the middle of the warehouse. Dozens of wooden crates were stacked against the back wall.

In the far corner, he spotted Mark, pulling a tarp over a vehicle of some kind. It appeared that Mark had not seen him enter. Vanderham quickly scanned the warehouse again, and then slipped back through the door before Mark could spot him.

Vanderham returned to the conference room, sat back down and said nothing about what he had seen in the warehouse.

"Professor, I know all of this seems a little odd to you right now. But, eventually, it will sort itself out," Solene said. "However, we need to focus on the critical issue at hand. We need to get these people vaccinated – right now, today! You must believe that this flu threat is real. Please trust me on that."

"Secretary Solene, I don't exactly know what to believe right now," Vanderham said.

"Professor," Sophia said. "It will be only a few days before we see this flu explode worldwide. And while I can't guarantee that this vaccine will work, I can guarantee that it will do no harm. Mr. Dixon has made our entire supply available to Malabar Farm. I've flown from Europe to work with you and to monitor its effect. Please – *lives* may be at stake, the lives of your people here at Malabar."

Vanderham swung back again. Dr. Montero sounded sincere and downright scared.

"Professor," Solene took up the argument. "I understand that this is confusing. Let me do this," he said and paused. "I will get in touch with Mr. Dixon, and ask him to come here and meet with you. He will be able to straighten out this mess that I have made. Understand though, that it can't happen right away - it may take a week or two for him to free up the time. Would that help?"

"Yes, of course," Vanderham said. "I'd like to meet Mr. Dixon. Who wouldn't?"

Vanderham walked over to the boxes and pulled off the labels. "Okay, let's go ahead with the shots. I can tell the other doctors that I got a call telling me to pick up Doctor Montero in Eugene. It's been long enough since I left, so we can go back at any time."

Solene sighed, "Good. And can you keep this meeting and everything else we discussed confidential until you meet with Mr. Dixon?"

"All right," Vanderham said. "Where will you be? Should I continue to use email to contact you?"

"That will be fine," Solene said. "I'm going to be traveling, so I can't guarantee that I will get back to you right away."

At the door, Vanderham smiled and looked back at Solene, "Dr. Strangelove – one of my favorite movies - have you seen it Secretary Solene?"

"Yes, it's one of my favorites as well," Solene said.

"Do you remember the part when Dr. Strangelove first hears about the doomsday device?"

Solene caught his breath when Vanderham said "doomsday".

"Yes," he said warily.

"You remember what Strangelove said?" Vanderham asked, and went on. "Strangelove said it made no sense to have a doomsday device, and then keep it a secret."

"Yes, I remember," Solene said, wondering where this was going.

"Well, this place - and the security team," Vanderham gestured at the big warehouse. "Is just like that," he said and, freezing Solene with a stare.

"What do you mean?" Solene asked.

"Well, how can you put a security team in place here to protect us?" Vanderham asked. "And then keep it a secret from us? How could that work?"

Chapter 20

That same day
Friday July 10th, 2020
Somewhere in Nootka Sound, Vancouver Island

They walked in silence through the dense, second-growth forest, working their way northwesterly on an elk trail that ran along the ridge line of yet another nameless hill. Fatigue had reduced their conversation to a minimum. They were tired and hungry, smelly and dirty, but at least the July weather had cooperated, they had stayed dry. For the last three days they had kept to the woods, up high along the ridgelines, avoiding all contact with people, fearing the worst from Dixon.

Toby stopped and studied an intersecting elk trail that headed down hill. "Let's try this one," he said, pointing down the trail. "The GPS shows a river down there somewhere, with an abandoned logging road alongside."

"Can you make it? It looks pretty steep?" Laura asked.

"I'll take it slow," Toby said, leaning on the crude crutch they had made days ago. His ankle was in bad shape and getting worse. All the walking had made it swell so grotesquely that two mornings ago they had had to cut the leather on his boot in order to get it on his foot. The ribs were no better, but no worse. Toby knew he could not go on much longer. Wherever this trail came out would be it.

For the next two hours he took one painful baby-step at a time down the steep trail. Finally, he limped out of the woods, his arm around Laura's shoulder, to a barely recognizable overgrown logging road.

"Toby, we need to stop and rest for a few days. I'm worried about that ankle," Laura said. "Just sit right here for a minute, I'll go look for someplace to stay."

Toby sat down against a tree, exhausted. It had been three days of pain and three days without food. He slid down the tree trunk onto his back and within seconds slipped into a stupor - not quite sleep, and not that far from a coma.

Laura tried to adjust his body so it looked more comfortable. She carefully placed the backpack under his ankle for some needed elevation. She stroked his forehead for a few minutes, wondering how badly he was hurt. She knew that the ankle would heal, but she had no idea what had happened inside his chest. It might be just broken ribs, or it might be something much worse.

She kissed him lightly on the forehead and got up, sighing and with tears in her eyes. She was near the end of her strength as well. Though not hurt physically, she was a wreck emotionally. She kept seeing the man she had shot. She saw him twitch twice and tumble backward down the hill. She had killed someone, shot him deliberately, and without hesitation. Of course she knew that that person would have killed her and Toby both if she hadn't shot him first. In her rational moments, that helped. But after three days without food, three days crazy-worried about Toby, three days sleeping in the woods – those rational moments were becoming hard to find.

Ten minutes later, she returned with some good news. Down the abandoned logging road only a few hundred yards, in a small clearing next to the river, she had found two small A-frame cabins. She had peeked inside the A-frames and they looked passable. And best of all, in one of them she had seen a shelf of canned goods - food!

"Toby … Toby, wake-up," she said, kneeling over the inert body. Toby opened his eyes, coughed, winced in pain and tried to move. Laura helped him into a sitting position.

"There's a place we can stay just down the road," she said, once his breathing had settled.

"A place? What do you mean?"

"Two A-frame cabins, right by the road, I have no idea why they're there. But they look abandoned."

Toby thought for a minute, but even simple thinking was becoming difficult. "It's a hunting camp," he finally wheezed. "Won't be used again until October – hunting season."

"Perfect," Laura said, smiling for the first time in days. "Can you make it? There's food in one of them."

Toby's eyes widened. "Food? You said the magic word. I'll crawl if I have to," he said and reached out for Laura to help him up.

A few minutes later Laura used the butt of the rifle to break the latch on the door of the A-frame. She helped the reeling Toby into the only room. She shook out a blanket over one of the four bunks along the wall and helped Toby lie down.

"Oh boy," Toby said as he carefully wriggled into a comfortable position. "This is good."

Laura found the propane tank, turned it on and got two cans of soup going on the camp stove. She ran down to the river and filled up the water jug. Soon they were both eating silently. They finished in seconds, out of breath. Laura made Toby drink some water and helped him get back to a comfortable position on the bunk. By the time she had removed his boots, he was asleep.

At that moment Laura came close, and for the first time, to believing in divine intervention. This abandoned hunting cabin had saved their lives.

She shook out another blanket, picked a bunk, leaned the rifle against the wall nearby and put the pistol under her pillow. "We're going to make it, dammit ... we're going to make it ..." she whispered to herself and then quickly fell asleep.

Part 3

Chapter 21

Two Weeks Later
Thursday, July 23rd, 2020
The CDC, Atlanta

Kyle Morrison wasn't sure when it started, maybe 1:00 am, maybe 1:30. But by 4:30 there were twenty people in front of his pharmacy counter doing a strange milling-about minuet. They all wanted to keep their place in line, but like magnets on repel, they didn't want to get too close to one another. Kyle had trouble keeping track of who was next. And whatever it was they had, Kyle knew he was going to get it. All the coughing had made the air around him humid with their virus-saturated mist.

Only a year out of college, Kyle had worked the night shift at the Drug-Mart-24 in Edmonds, Washington for the last nine months. Paying his dues, his dad had told him. And in those nine months, this was the first time that he had phoned Mr. Baxter, the store manager, with an emergency.

Baxter had sounded sleepy, but was polite. Kyle asked for help. He thought they should try to bring in another pharmacist right away. He told Baxter that within the hour he was going to run out of Tamistan, the over-the-counter flu remedy that was currently in favor, and asked that more be sent to the store.

Kyle remembered that during his orientation last year, something had been mentioned regarding the need to notify the CDC about unusual events like this. He asked Mr. Baxter how to do it. Baxter thought it should be in the procedures manual somewhere, but told him to wait until the other pharmacist showed up.

Then Baxter said something that alarmed Kyle even more. Baxter told him he was sorry he couldn't come in and help - he had the flu.

Kyle made an executive decision. He had John, the front checkout guy, come back and take all the remaining boxes of Tamistan up to the front counter in order to catch the "coughers" as they came in the front door. Normally Tamistan required a signature at the pharmacy counter, even though it no longer needed a prescription. Kyle told John to forget about the signature, and to put a sign on the front door when he ran out. This bought Kyle a few minutes so that he could pull out the procedures manual and find the instructions for reporting "unusual clusters", as they were called, to the CDC.

For the next half hour Kyle struggled through the user-*un*friendly reporting system of VISU - the Virological Influenza Surveillance Unit of the CDC. The system was called BioSense4-Pharma, supposedly designed for events just like the one going on in his store. Even so, the terminology was new to him. He did the best that he could, and then hit the key to send in the information.

The report went directly to the CDC in Atlanta. The Pharma queue in the Biosense4 system at VISU was deemed to be of lesser priority than the other health-care provider queues, so it was read only once an hour by one of the thirty-odd VISU analysts.

At 8:10 that morning Atlanta time – three hours farther into the day than Washington State - and only five minutes after Kyle had sent in his somewhat disjointed report, Berta Sosa, a first year VISU analyst at the CDC, checked the Pharma queue and found Kyle's report.

Andy Hobbs, the director of VISU, had walked by Berta's station with his morning coffee only minutes before. Since she knew he was in, and probably not yet busy, she decided to go tell him in person about this new and unusual Pharma queue entry.

"Mr. Hobbs … can I show you something?" she asked, standing in his doorway.

Dr. Maxwell Stanton, the director of the Influenza Division at the Centers for Disease Control, and Andy Hobbs' boss, arrived at the same time, also with coffee in hand. He had, in fact, run into Andy Hobbs on his way in to work that morning at a coffee shop in Clifton, the Atlanta suburb where the CDC was located.

Hobbs reappeared at Stanton's office door just as Max was reading his personal search engine's compilation of the previous night's news. Max always smiled when Hobbs appeared unexpectedly. Divito-esque, only five feet tall, rounded and balding, Hobbs inspired those around him to what would normally be unacceptable acts of affection: hugs, pats and even noogies.

"Did you see this thing in D.C. last night?" Max asked while scanning his personal news headlines.

"What thing? I haven't looked at my news yet," Hobbs said.

"It's the Pakistanis and the Indians again. They found five Indians dead in their beds in a burned-out house in D.C.. Two of them were apparently important scientists – one in biotech. A Pakistani terrorist group has already taken credit," Max said, shaking his head in disgust. "Won't those people ever stop killing each other?"

"Probably not. They've got hundreds of millions of reasons to keep exacting revenge," Hobbs offered as he came in and plunked himself down across the desk from Max. "I've got some official business. I think you should look at something. Call up the Biosense Pharma queue and look at the 8:05 A.M. entry from Edmonds, Washington."

Max pulled it up on his screen and read through the report. "Looks like we have an alert pharmacist," he said.

"That might be a first," Hobbs said sarcastically.

Max squinted at the screen, "Am I reading this right? This was sent in only ten minutes ago?"

"That's right. Berta picked it up right after it was sent and walked it over to my office."

"Well hell, he put his phone number in here, let's call him. He must still be there."

"I guess we could," Hobbs said. "Doesn't seem like proper protocol though. We are the government after all. We should take several days to make a decision like that."

Max dialed the number. It rang twice.

"Drug-Mart Edmonds, this is Kyle."

"Kyle, well good, I caught you," Max said. "I'm Maxwell Stanton. I'm the director of the Influenza Division of the Centers for Disease Control in Atlanta. Looks like you've had a busy morning."

Kyle was in shock. He looked over at the system that he had just used to send in the report, almost expecting Dr. Stanton's hand to stick out from it and motion "Over here…"

"Man, that was fast, I sent that thing in only a few minutes ago," Kyle said.

"Good timing. It just worked out that it got noticed right away," Max said. "So tell me, what happened this morning?"

"It's still happening," Kyle said. "A whole bunch of people all got the flu or a cold of some kind, all at the same time. I've never seen anything like it. But then, I've only been working here for about nine months."

"How many times normal would you say?" Max asked.

"Maybe twenty or thirty"

"And how about the night before this - anything unusual then?"

"No sir, and that's what struck me as being so odd about this. I'm pretty sure I didn't sell any Tamistan last night."

"Huh … that is odd. Is your store manager there?"

"No, I called him for some help. He's got one more pharmacist on the way here now," Kyle said. "But he said he couldn't come in because he thought he had the flu …"

"Okay, I want you to do something for me. I want you to go corral four of the flu victims who are in your store right now. But first go get four of your best thermometers, all the same brand. Then take their temperatures and write them down. Tell them this is a request from the head of the flu division of the CDC if they need encouragement. Then email me immediately with the results. You got that?"

"Yes sir, I think so. I've got a pencil – give me your email address."

"You're a good man Kyle. You did the right thing notifying us," Max said. "Get your pencil and do one more thing. Write yourself a prescription for the anti-viral Vistamacil-2 under my name - Maxwell Stanton. Double the first dose and take it right now, before you do anything else. Okay?"

"Yes sir, thank you," Kyle said hesitantly, not knowing if he should be grateful or scared. "The email address?"

"Okay, here it is," Max said, and gave him his personal address. "Send me your cell number too. And thanks again Kyle, good work."

"Going to do a little first person research are you?" Hobbs asked as Max put down the phone.

"This feels like it might be something important. I don't remember ever seeing a report like this from the Pharma queue, do you?" Max asked.

"I guess not. And the fact that nothing was going down the night before is bothersome."

"Not to mention that it is July, for Gods sake," Max said.

"Yep, it is July. You've got that part right at least. I'm going to go back and see if anything else has shown up."

"Good, and have your analysts check the queues more often, like every ten minutes. I think I'm going to send some people out there - to Washington."

"Really, it's a little early for that don't you think," Hobbs said with a surprised look. "You must be spooked."

"I am. Go check the queues, but come back in fifteen minutes, I want to know if you have anything else," Max said. He followed Hobbs out the door and sat down next to Mel Osborn, his administrative assistant.

"Mel, pull up the protocol for the expedited rapid deployment surveillance team," Max said and watched Mel's screen until he saw what he wanted. "That's it – RDST-E. What do I have to do?"

"Let's see," Mel said. "You have full authority, but you need to notify Director Lawrence, and the ASPHEP – that would be Assistant Secretary Ross at HHS. Then we need to identify and contact the on-call response team, and that's it – the response team takes care of the rest."

"How long does it take before they are in the air? I think it's less than an hour," Max said.

"The protocol requires forty-five minutes from notification," Mel said.

"Can you take care of this under my name?" Max asked.

"I think so," Mel said, still scanning down the document. "Looks like I need three things – the destination, the category of the infectious agent, and the BSL level."

"Okay - the destination is Edmonds, Washington. The testing needs to be for Novel type A Influenza, and they may be carrying BSL-3 specimens back with them," Max said and headed back to his office. "I'll be right here if you have a problem. Oh, and find out again when Laura is due back. I keep forgetting, but it should be any day now."

Dr. Sydney Lawrence, executive director of the Centers for Disease Control, happened to be in her office as the RDST notification from Max popped up on her screen. She had nothing scheduled until nine that morning, and thought that a short walk would be good for her.

"What's the deal Max – you out of coffee beans?" she said as she swept into Max's office and sat down.

"Who says that the wheels of government turn slowly," Max said with a smile. He checked his watch. "Twenty-five minutes."

"What do you mean?" Sydney asked.

"That's how long it's been since we got the initial report from Edmonds."

"You had better be kidding," Sydney said, not kidding.

"No, I'm not kidding. An alert kid pharmacist working the night shift in Edmonds, Washington, sent in a Biosense-Pharma report just twenty-five minutes ago."

"And you sent the RDST based on that?"

"Not entirely, I called him up and talked to him after I read his report. There's definitely something strange going on there. I asked him to check four people randomly for a fever. I just now got his email. All four were over a hundred. And besides, that's what that group is for. We're already paying them. Maybe we should make them do something."

"Okay, but it still costs money to fly the plane," Dr. Lawrence said. "Mostly though, Ross has to be notified, and he'll be all over me wanting to know when he should panic. It's not time to panic, is it?"

"Not yet, but stay tuned."

Andy Hobbs arrived at the doorway, and waited to be invited in.

"What have you got, Andy?" Max asked. "Come in, come in."

"Dr. Lawrence, how are you?" Hobbs asked. "Sorry to interrupt, but our friend, the pharmacist in Seattle, called around to a couple of the other Drug-Mart-24s in the Seattle area. It looks like a similar situation is occurring in Bellevue, Kirkland and Marysville – all northern or eastern suburbs of Seattle. He had them send in reports. They're in the queue now if you want to see them."

"Anything else?"

"Actually, there was one other similar report from the Sentinel Queue," Andy said hesitantly. "But ... it's from Chicago. A drive-up clinic had ten people waiting for them when they opened at seven this morning. All ILI's - Influenza like illnesses."

"Time to panic now?" Dr. Lawrence asked, getting up. "I think I will. I'm going to get my assistant over here, let's get set up in the conference room. I'll clear my schedule. I want a team assigned and a status meeting at ten in the conference room. Get as much info as you can before then. I'm going to go call Assistant Secretary Ross and give him a heads-up," she said, with her legendary take-charge skills on full display. She patted Hobbs on the shoulder as she headed out the door.

Hobbs gave Max a surprised look. "This isn't the way we usually work around here."

"Well, she's just being prudent. She probably didn't have anything to do today anyway," Max said. "We've been primed for a type A influenza pandemic for fifteen years now. Better safe then sorry."

Hobbs started to leave.

"Just a second, Andy," Max said. "Do a couple of things. First, follow up on the Chicago report – maybe try some pharmacies in the area. And then, just in case, call some other twenty-four hour pharmacies on the west coast - while the night shift is still on duty."

"Will do," Hobbs said and headed back to the VISU wing.

An hour later, Andy Hobbs and Dr. Stanton entered a packed conference room. There were more "liaisons" present then there were scientists. Max knew Becker, the liaison for Assistant Secretary Ross of the Department of Health and Human Services. And he knew the liaisons for WHO and the NIH. He thought the good looking women in the corner had something to do with the Office of the Surgeon General. And He expected that there were several coordinators of state and local public health departments. He also recognized the CDC media relations team. Panic indeed – Dr. Lawrence had turned over a lot of rocks to put this group together.

"Let's get started," Director Lawrence said, loudly enough to be heard above the chatter. "You all know Doctor Maxwell Stanton, the director of the Influenza Division. He'll deliver the briefing. But before he starts, let me make one thing crystal clear. No one talks to the media, except our own media team. I don't want us to pull a FEMA here. Everybody understand?"

Nods all around, everyone understood - no one wanted to pull a FEMA. Max stepped a few paces into the room, and in keeping with the "no wasted time" spirit of the morning's activities, launched directly into the heart of the story. "At 8:05 this morning we received a Biosense-4 report on the Pharma queue from a young man, the night shift pharmacist at a Drug-Mart-24 in Edmonds Washington ..." he began.

After relating the conversation with the young pharmacist, and the details of the deployment of the RDST, Max turned it over to Andy Hobbs.

Hobbs found a spot in the front of the room where everyone could see him - not an easy task - and began: "I won't go through all the details. We have started a new queue in the Biosense reporting system called 'Edmonds flu' ..."

Hobbs raised his arms. "Stop please," he said to the outburst of muttering in the room. "I know it's not my job to name this thing. This is just temporary. When all you important people go away for your weekend 'naming' retreat, we'll change it. Okay?"

"Anyway", he continued. "We will keep that queue updated as closely as we can to real time. Let me give you the highlights now. As of just a few minutes ago, we've drilled down in seven west coast cities. We've located pockets similar to the Edmonds story, in all of them," Hobbs said, and had to pause as the room energized.

"That's right – all of them," he said, again putting his hand up to ask for quiet. "And, we have some scattered reports in the Sentinel queue from the mid west. Several drive-up clinics are finding people waiting for them as they open up. Doctor's offices are opening up right now Central Time, so we expect more in the next few hours. But so far, we don't seem to be having any significant spiking at emergency rooms - though I can't vouch for that, as emergency rooms have never been very good at reporting to us."

"What's been going on before today?" A voice from the back of the room asked.

Max interrupted, "For the benefit of all you coordinators and media people – that's Helen Glick, one of our analysts in computer modeling for pandemic influenza."

"Thanks, Dr. Stanton," Helen said. "I'm just curious because outbreaks like this don't start in that many places at once. You must have seen other earlier reports. We'll need to know where they came from so we can track the history."

Hobbs looked over at Max, wondering if he wanted to handle that can of worms. Max nodded acceptance. "We have no earlier reports of anything unusual. That doesn't mean that there isn't a 'first case' out there somewhere. I know this is very unusual, but so far, we just don't have anything other than today's activity."

A distinguished looking gentleman in the front cleared his throat, announcing his intention to speak.

"I am Sander Gruenhoffer, the Director of WHO liaison activities here at CDC, for those of you who don't know me," Sander Gruenhoffer said, and smiled at the CDC media folks.

Max could see that the maneuvering for attention had begun. Everyone in that room knew this was going to be something big – potentially a career-defining event.

"Regarding the RDST deployment to Edmonds," Gruenhoffer continued. "I will remind you that we have a WHO collaborating laboratory located at the University of Washington Medical Center. I believe it's only a half-hour's drive from Edmonds. They have complete BSL-3 capabilities – that would be biosafety level three," Gruenhoffer said, again posturing annoyingly to the media team. "Perhaps the RDST could use that facility for a rapid assessment."

And now the squabble over territorial rights begins, Max thought.

"I think it will be just as fast to fly the swabs back here. And it's vital for us to start the virus isolation activities right away. We want to be as careful as possible with those cultures," Max said. "But I have a suggestion. Why don't you contact your lab, and see if they can send some people out to one of the other Drug-Marts to obtain independent samples for analysis. That way we won't have any issues with cross contamination."

That seemed to satisfy Gruenhoffer's need for something meaningful to do. "I'll get right on it. Dr. Lawrence, if I may be excused ..." he said, and gathered himself, nodding, and looking very important, as he left the room.

"Yes." Max pointed to a small man in the back who had raised his hand. Max introduced him to those who might not know him. "This is Sharif Baku, Chief of Molecular Pathology and Ultrastructure at CDC. He is in charge of our newest high-definition tunneling electron ultrascopes. Go ahead Sharif."

"Dr. Stanton, I want to let you know that our labs have been booked solid for weeks since we received these new machines. I'm not sure when we can free up time to look at your samples."

"Sharif!" Dr. Lawrence said. Her astonished look was all it took to get Baku backpedaling at top speed.

"I'll move things around. We'll figure it out," Baku said. "When do you expect to have the agent isolated?"

"Late this evening, maybe early morning, if all goes well," Max said. "And have your best people available to work all night, if necessary."

Dr. Lawrence stood, signaling the end of the briefing. "This looks very serious. Treat it appropriately. I want all hands on deck this afternoon and tonight if necessary. We will operate out of this conference room for the time being. Don't hesitate to offer ideas or opinions. Thank you all. Stanton and Hobbs – stick around for a minute."

Everyone else filed out of the room. Lawrence, Stanton and Hobbs stood at the end of the conference table until the room had emptied and the door was shut.

"So," Lawrence said. "What do you think? Is this the big one?"

"It's just too early to tell," Max said. "We don't even know what it is."

"We know what it's doing though," Hobbs said. "Nothing like this has ever happened. This is scaring the shit out of me, if you want to know the truth."

"Should we be doing something right away?" Lawrence asked.

Max, already annoyed at the multiple agendas on display in the briefing, spoke imprudently. "Are we talking ass-covering here or real steps?"

"I beg your pardon," Lawrence said stiffly. "Of course I'm talking real steps. Should we declare a quarantine? Should we limit travel? When do we alert the committee on Emergency Health Preparedness? All these decisions have to be made. And, by the looks of things, they have to be made soon."

"I'm sorry," Max said. "Some people in that meeting annoyed me."

"Get used to it," Lawrence said. "We live in a media-driven world. This could be a huge story."

"Okay, but it's still too early to answer any of those questions. First, we need to know what this is. Right now we can't even say for sure that it's influenza!" Max said, exasperated.

"Yes, of course you're right," Lawrence said with a long sigh. She looked over, and down, at Hobbs. "So Andy, you seem alarmed. What's your gut telling you."

"This isn't right," Hobbs said. "It doesn't add up. We've been preparing for pandemic flu for twenty years. But we don't have a script for what's happened this morning. It just can't start this quickly, with so many people, in so many places, without any warning. And it's July!" he said, almost shouting, waving his stumpy arms around. Max had never seen him like this before.

"Still - we need more information before you do anything," Max said, looking at Lawrence. "By two this afternoon, we can have a preliminary assessment. Andy will have much more info as well. Let's not do anything until then. That's still early enough to make the evening news."

"Okay, fine. I'll reconvene the group at two. And by the way, where was Laura? Why wasn't she at the meeting?"

"She's on vacation. She took two weeks off after that Duval Dixon conference on Vancouver Island," Max said. "She should be back any day now. We're trying to reach her."

Dr. Lawrence patted Hobbs on the head as she walked out the door.

Back at his office, Max stopped to ask Mel if he had been able to locate Laura.

"I talked to her admin person," Mel said. "He hasn't heard from her at all, not even after the Vancouver Conference. But she isn't due back from vacation until next Monday. He said he'd try to get in touch with her, though."

"Where is she?" Max asked.

"He didn't know."

"She didn't tell him where she was going on vacation?"

"I guess not."

"That's odd," Max said, and headed into his office. "Get the RDST on the phone for me please."

By one that afternoon, Andy Hobbs's VISU team was overwhelmed. Hobbs had reassigned all available personal to do proactive, anecdotal surveying. Though not scientific, it at least cut through the red tape and could create a very early picture of the situation. He had also recruited additional personnel from the admin pool and from the large staff of tech group analysts to set up and monitor TV feeds, internet news, and blogs from around the world. A picture was emerging from the fog of scattered information. It was far worse than Hobbs had thought only three hours earlier.

Hobbs walked into Max's office without the usual formalities, and plopped onto the chair across from Max's desk. "We're fucked."

"What do you have?" Max asked.

"Except for the east coast, and that's just a matter of time, or maybe were not calling the right places. Anyway…," Hobbs said, spitting out the words at a machine-gun clip, his voice an octave higher than normal.

"Whoa - take a breath, slow down," Max said.

"Sorry" Hobbs took one deep breath and exhaled dramatically. "There - better. We have over fifty people making calls. We have found pockets in virtually every large city west of, say, Ohio. We are even finding pockets in some medium-sized and small towns, especially on the west coast. And now, in the last half hour, we've got some indications in Europe – the Scandinavian countries. We haven't had enough people to call anywhere else in the world, but we'll try some other continents soon."

"Have you seen any WHO alerts?" Max asked.

"Not yet, but they're always slow to react. We usually don't even bother to call them."

"Small towns? Really?" Max asked, perplexed. Pandemics were supposed to follow a specific pattern, based on travel patterns. ILI's should not show up in smaller communities until several days later.

"Yup, Small towns: it's everywhere at once. There are so many things wrong with this, it's hard to know where to start," Hobbs said.

"Listen Andy – it is happening. We know that much. I assure you that the questions you have now are there only because we don't yet have enough of the right information. When we do, then we'll understand."

"I don't see how," Hobbs said. "And, by the way, the media is all over this. Local stations around the west have noticed that a lot of people are sick – probably in their own organizations. They're calling it a rampant summer cold. And a few Seattle blogs are reporting that a CDC team is in Edmonds."

"That was fast," Max said, checking his watch. "The RDST just called and said they were heading back to the plane at Paine Field in Everett."

"Good. What did they find out?" Hobbs asked expectantly.

"It's definitely the flu - not a rhino. Everyone they took swabs from had a low grade fever, but not more than one-oh-one. They'll be back in a couple of hours. Then we can run some RT-PCR tests and we'll know if it's in the books."

"It had to be a flu, so that's not big news. When will they be back?"

"Around three," Max said, "I'd better go see Dr. Lawrence, and warn her about the media."

Sander Gruenhoffer, the smarmy WHO liaison, was deep in conversation with Director Lawrence as Max stepped into the conference room.

"Is there news from the WHO lab in Washington?" he asked, pointedly. "And from now on you need to bring any information that you have directly to me."

Dr. Maxwell Stanton was the Director of the Influenza Division, not Dr. Lawrence. Though Sydney Lawrence was his boss, and the highest-ranking executive at CDC, she wasn't qualified for direct medical work. Dr. Lawrence was a political appointee. She was an excellent administrator, budget manager, and a no-nonsense leader, but she wasn't a medical doctor. Her PhD was in economics. She liked to call herself "Doctor" for all the obvious reasons, considering the place that she managed. Gruenhoffer didn't know; he was not a medical doctor either.

"That is correct, Sander," Dr. Lawrence stated. "Dr. Stanton is in charge of all things medical; I'm here to support him with all the rest. And we do need to be efficient. So please remember to make all of your reports directly to Dr. Stanton."

Max sat down and stared at Gruenhoffer, making it clear that, so far, he didn't like him.

"Yes, well, as I was saying," Gruenhoffer said. "Our lab at the university took your suggestion and ran with it. I must say I'm quite impressed with their enthusiasm. They returned to the lab a little over an hour ago with ten sample nose and throat swabs. They have run the RT-PCR tests – that would be the ..." Gruenhoffer paused, and looked down at his notes. "The Reverse-Transcription Polymerase Chain Reaction..."

"Gruenhoffer, I know what RT-PCR is," Max said, now seriously annoyed. "Stop right there. Get out your phone and call the person at the lab in Seattle who gave you this information. I want to talk to that person directly."

Gruenhoffer glanced over at Director Lawrence to see if by chance any relief would come from her direction. She was looking down at the desk. He pulled out his phone, hit the dial button, and without a word, handed the phone to Dr. Stanton.

A pleasant but harried sounding female voice answered. "Yes, what is it now?" she said, annoyed by what she thought was another call from Gruenhoffer. Max couldn't help but smile.

"This is Maxwell Stanton, the director of the Influenza division at the CDC in Atlanta. Who am I speaking to?"

"Dr. Stanton, wow, I'm sorry, I thought it was that annoying prick Gruenbiter - or whatever. This is some scary shit we've got going on here. As I'm sure you know."

"Well, I don't know nearly enough. Let's start again with your name?" Max said, still smiling.

"I'm Leslie, sorry, that's Doctor Leslie Pentilla. I'm the assistant manager of the joint WHO and State of Washington Lab here at the University of Washington Medical Center."

"Are you the person in charge?"

"No, the two managers, one for WHO, and one for the state, are both sick – ILI, influenza like illness, sorry, you probably already know that," Leslie said in a rush, sounding very nervous.

"Relax Leslie, I'm not like Gruenbiter," Max couldn't help himself and looked up to smirk at Gruenhoffer. "What have you found out?"

"Well there's good news, and that's probably the bad news," she said. "We had ten sets of swabs. We've run most of them through the rapid-typing tests. And the good news is that it's not H5, or any other known H subtype."

"You mean you had no matches at all?" Max said, coming out of his chair.

"Not yet."

"My God, what is this?" he said, mostly to himself. "You have full BSL-3 capabilities there, right?"

"Yes, we do. And we're up to date. It's first-class," Leslie said.

"I can't see any reason not to start a virus isolation right away. After all, it's not like it's going to get away from you. That's already happened."

"Well - that could be part of the problem, I'm not sure if everyone here doesn't already have this thing. I can't guarantee it won't get contaminated."

"True, but who cares? At least you'll end up with some virus to start the genetic sequencing with. If you need an official request from the CDC, I'll get it sent out right away."

"Probably, just to be safe. Usually the other guys do this stuff," Leslie said. "We also have good molecular equipment here. Not as fancy as your new toys, but it's still good enough to give us a picture of the bumps."

"Perfect. Get it all going."

"Any ideas about what I should say to the press?" Leslie asked.

"Nothing, for now."

"Too late for that. The State health department had to be notified in order for us to get involved. The Governor already knows. The press has been running stories about all the sick people for the last few hours. And now we have press trucks, lots of them, pulling up in front of the hospital. I'm not sure what travels faster – a new virus, or bad news."

"I have exactly the right person for you to talk to - hang on one second," Max said and handed the phone to Dr. Lawrence. "Here, talk to Dr. Leslie Pentilla. She has pressing problems. I need to talk to Gruenhoffer for a minute."

After listening for a minute, Dr. Lawrence began to shake her head. "You're kidding. Looks like we'll have to say something. You must have media people there at the hospital, go find them and think about a news conference at four, your time. I'm pretty sure we will have gone public with some kind of statement by then. And I'll have someone get in touch with your Governor in the next hour or two."

During the conversation, Max had sent Gruenhoffer off to get as many WHO collaborating labs into action as he could, including Europe and Asia.

After Gruenhoffer had left the room, Dr. Lawrence got up and stood with her arms folded and leaned against the back wall. "This isn't going according to plan. We are supposed to have more time. How could we have missed the initial stages?," she asked, a mixture of fear and confusion in her voice. "I was reviewing our own health emergency preparedness plan. More than half of it is useless. And the WHO 'six phases of pandemic flu' – I looked at that too. Do you know which phase we are in? We are already in the middle of phase six!"

"We don't know that yet," Max said. "Remember, we still don't know what it is."

"When will you know?

"I hope we can have something by tomorrow."

"What do I tell Secretary Ross then?"

"When are you talking to him?"

"When are *we* talking to him, you mean. We are talking to him at three, right after the briefing at two."

"Well, let's wait till we have the briefing then," Max said.

On that same day, July 23rd 2020 (day-one of the Eden Flu), and while panic was beginning to spread like a viral infection at the CDC, the President of the United States, Kathryn Pittman, was riding Misty, her feisty roan mare, up a steep hillside at her ranch in eastern Wyoming. The

Republican Convention was a little over ten days away. President Pittman had left D.C., along with almost everyone else – it was July, after all – to write the acceptance speech for her nomination to a second term. But that speech could wait; right now she was enjoying one of her favorite pastimes – driving the cattle back up the mountain to the high meadows where they would find fresh grass. She was accompanied by Pat Gathers, her ranch foreman, Lucy Kline, her sister and campaign manager and riding buddy since childhood, and two other cowboys. The four Secret Service men assigned to the ride, while adequate on horseback, had trouble keeping up. They were somewhere farther down the hill.

Pat Gathers stayed next to the President during the ride. He had been given the responsibility of carrying the secure walkie-talkie by the Secret Service. They had done this ride many times before and they knew that President Pittman would leave them behind. They assumed that was, in fact, her intention.

"Ma'am," Gathers said, sidling up alongside the President. "I've got a call for you."

Pittman took the device from Gathers and gave him a look that said "this better be important". "Yes," she said, trying to get Misty settled.

"This is Mitchell," said Cam Mitchell, her chief of staff. "I just got a call from Assistant Secretary Ross – he's in charge of Health Emergency Preparedness at HSS – I think you know him."

"Yes, of course I know him."

"He wanted me to give you a heads-up about some kind of flu outbreak on the west coast. Apparently, most of the west has significant pockets of this illness. Some spots in the mid west as well. They don't know what it is. They can't even say for sure if it's flu. It just started today."

"Is there something I should be doing," Pittman said. "Whoa! Hang on a minute!" she said as Misty flinched and then settled into a better spot.

"How far away are you?" Cam said. He was at the ranch house in the valley.

"About an hour, I think."

"You'd better head back. Ross couldn't offer any details. Like I said, they still don't even know if it's the flu. But Ross said that the people at the CDC were very concerned. If it turns out to be something serious, we don't want you out riding around chasing cows – not a week before the convention."

"Well, dammit!" Pittman said. "Okay, we'll head back in. Find someone at CDC that I can talk to first thing when I get back."

"Will do."

At 1:30 in the afternoon, Dr. Stanton walked over to the VISU wing to get the latest news from Andy Hobbs. VISU's conference room now had a dozen TV monitors sitting on the big table. Six people sat watching the national news and local stations from the west. Max walked to the door and asked was happening.

A young lady rose from behind one of the screens. "We just had the first national news story. You know how they are, 'Breaking News' and all that. They made it sound like a really big deal. And, they said the CDC had no comment on the situation. One of their people must have called here."

"I guess we won't be able to get away with that much longer," Max said. "How about the local channels?"

"Well, it's not even eleven out west. Mostly we are seeing teasers for the noon news. They're showing stuff like their own satellite trucks driving up to hospitals. I'm sure they're scrambling for information right now."

"Just like us," Max said, and headed off to find Hobbs.

The crowd was three-deep around the conference table for the two o'clock briefing. Dr. Stanton announced that the RDST would arrive back in about an hour. He described the early results from the WHO lab in Seattle. There were several questions regarding the preliminary finding that it wasn't a previously known H-subtype. The point was made by several people that that simply wasn't possible.

"Add it to the list," said Hobbs.

Hobbs reported that ILI's continued to be found in large numbers everywhere in the west. It was past quitting time in Europe; nothing new there would be discovered until tomorrow. Asia wasn't yet awake. And so far nothing had showed up on the east coast.

Gruenhoffer reported that seven WHO collaborating labs on the west coast were attempting to subtype the virus. They had no shortage of samples, as many of the lab personnel were already symptomatic. Gruenhoffer stated his anecdotal opinion that it didn't seem that this flu, or whatever it was, was making people "that sick".

"It's early yet," Hobbs replied.

Gruenhoffer also reported that WHO was considering issuing a level-three alert. He said that would mean health care workers should start taking the anti-viral medicines that had been stockpiled for them. WHO would decide within the next few hours. The question was asked if CDC personnel should start with the antivirals. Dr. Lawrence said yes.

The Media team reported that they were being inundated by calls from the news media, and from the state health departments. They felt it was imperative to issue a press release soon, or, even better, have a press conference. A half-dozen or so satellite trucks had already arrived at the front gate. Dr. Lawrence said she had no objection to a press conference, except for the fact that there was nothing to say.

"You could tell them that, so far, everything about this event is wrong," Hobbs offered.

Dr. Lawrence concluded the not-much-new briefing with the order for all necessary personnel to be available all night if necessary. She dismissed the group, but asked Dr. Stanton to stay.

"Go ahead and close the door," she said to Max as the last person filed out. "President Pittman is calling in five minutes. Any ideas about what to tell her?"

"We could tell her to drop out of the race," Max said.

Lawrence grimaced. "I don't have time for politics right now. I need to know what to tell her."

"You could tell her to declare a major health alert. Deploy the antivirals to the health-care community. Restrict travel, and ask people to stay home."

"Wait a minute. You've been the one arguing for more time to find out what this is. That's a level four alert you're talking about. It has major economic implications. Are you serious about this?" Lawrence was sounding a little nervous now. With so many things wrong about this event, and with so little information, and especially on such short notice, how could she possibly tell the President to issue a level four alert?

"Well, maybe it is still too early. And maybe Gruenhoffer is right, maybe people won't get that sick," Max said. "We're just guessing at this point. So tell her anything you want."

"She's at her ranch in Wyoming. Should we advise her to return to Washington right away?"

"Maybe she's better off in Wyoming," Max said. "But that stuff is up to her, or her handlers. As long as we can reach her, it doesn't matter to me where she is."

"Listen Max, you have got to forget politics now. This is too important. I don't care if you don't like her – get over it," Lawrence said sternly.

She stood up and walked over to the credenza for a glass of water. "I'm going to tell her that we recommend waiting until ten tomorrow morning to decide about declaring a health emergency. I'll tell her we will have better information by then. Okay?"

Max nodded.

The phone rang.

"This is Dr. Lawrence."

"Dr. Lawrence, this is the White House calling. Hold one moment for the President."

A moment later, "Dr. Lawrence, this is Cam Mitchell from the President's ranch in Wyoming. I have President Pittman on the call with me, along with Lucy Kline. Go ahead Madam President."

"Dr. Lawrence, how are you doing?" the President asked.

"Busy, Madam President, very busy," Dr. Lawrence said.

"I hear that something is going on. Tell me what you can," President Pittman said.

"Let me say first, that this is all preliminary information. This has happened very fast."

"How fast? When did you first get wind of this?" Pittman asked.

Dr. Lawrence's eye's rolled back. Damn pushy broad – I'll tell you everything, if you just shut up for a minute – was what she wanted to say. "We received the first reports this morning, from Edmonds Washington. An alert young pharmacist notified us at eight am, east coast time, that he was having a run on flu medicine."

"That's only a few hours ago. So what's the big deal?" Pittman asked, annoyed at being yanked back from her most favorite activity because of a few sick people in Washington State, of all places.

"The big deal is that this thing is breaking out everywhere. We have identified pockets of it in every city in the country, except on the east coast. Possibly tens, or even hundreds of thousands of people are symptomatic already."

There was a pause. Max assumed they were trying to assimilate these two incompatible pieces of information.

Cam spoke first, "That's not possible, is it? I remember from all of the briefings, that we would have weeks, maybe even months of warning before a widespread breakout would occur. Are you saying it's happening in less than a day?"

"Yes. That's right Cam," Lawrence said. "It's not possible, but it does seem to be happening."

"That's not very helpful." President Pittman said.

"I'm sorry. But believe me, we are more confused by this than you are," Lawrence said.

"Okay, so what is it? Is it the bird flu, or one of those pandemic flu's you guys are always panicked about?" Pittman asked.

"We don't know just yet," Lawrence said. "We have samples on the way to Atlanta right now. They should be here in an hour or two. We also have a number of World Health Organization labs on the west coast working on the isolation of the infectious agent. In the best case scenario, we should have it typed by tomorrow morning. Our strong assumption though, is that it is a pandemic type A flu of some kind."

"If WHO is involved, does that mean it's also in other countries?" a new voice - Lucy Kline - asked.

"There was some information that it was in Europe, but we'll know more in the next twenty-four hours," Lawrence said. "I'm only guessing now, but it must be other places if it's so widespread here."

"What is your recommendation?" President Pittman asked, her earlier annoyance now replaced with growing concern.

"I think we will have better information by mid-morning, tomorrow. We could issue a press release or have a news conference then. Worst case – you should consider declaring a public health emergency, so you can restrict travel, cancel events. Implement the appropriate 'social distance' strategies."

"Stay right there. We'll call back in five minutes," Cam said.

Max assumed that they wanted to talk politics.

Four minutes later, the phone rang. The same operator from the White House patched them through to Wyoming.

"Dr. Lawrence, It's still the three of us," Cam Mitchell said. "We've looked at declaring an emergency, and that seems likely, based on what you've told us. But we can take some steps to buy us one more day. Under the Public Health Service Act, we need to activate the 'Incident Management Team' under the direction of the Assistant Secretary of Public Health Emergency Preparedness – Mr. Ross. We will do that immediately. The President wants you to go to Washington D.C. today and join Ross as co-chair of that team. The President is also leaving immediately for Washington. We will issue a press release about the outbreak and announcing a press conference at 10 am tomorrow. You will be the main presenter, so be prepared. Go directly to the White House when you arrive. Any questions?"

"No sir, I understand, and I think that's an appropriate plan," Lawrence said.

"One more thing. The President and I will get off the line and begin getting ready to leave. But stay around, you may receive another call in just a few minutes – understood?"

"Okay," Lawrence said, somewhat puzzled by the request.

A few minutes later, the White House operator connected them once again to Wyoming.

"Dr. Lawrence, this is Lucy Kline. I'm by myself this time."

"Yes Ms. Kline, what can I do for you," Lawrence answered, raising an eyebrow to Max.

"Sorry for the 'intrigue' about this call. Cam Mitchell is a little too paranoid about this stuff. I keep telling him we are going to create a new cabinet level post just for him – the Secretary of Plausible Deniability," she said with a warm chuckle.

Max was impressed - she sounded like a real person.

"We have a question. Because this doesn't seem to fit any of our assumptions about a natural influenza outbreak, what are your thoughts about the possibly of this being bioterrorism?" Lucy asked.

"If I may," Max said quickly, in order to take Dr. Lawrence off the hook. "Terrorism doesn't make any sense. The influenza virus would be a very poor choice. Even a novel type A virus like the kind we would see in a worst case pandemic, would only kill two to maybe five percent of those infected. And it couldn't be controlled. For instance, if this is a pandemic that we are dealing with right now, the people of Iran, India, Israel – everyone, everywhere - would be infected. And it will be worse in those countries. Bioterrorists have much better choices than influenza. It just wouldn't make any sense."

"Okay. I'm glad to hear that," Lucy said. "But, you understand, we had to ask. And Dr. Lawrence, I'm sure you will have to deal with this question again in Washington – so be prepared."

"Thank you, I will. Anything else?"

"No, that's it," Lucy said. "I'll see you in Washington in a few hours. Dr. Stanton - good luck tonight. We are all anxious to know what we are dealing with."

"As are we," Max said.

The hospitals in the west were the first to act. Before the CDC issued any statements, before the state public health departments made any decrees, before WHO called for a worldwide alert, and while the President was still in the air heading for Washington D.C., the hospitals in all the major western cities dispensed their store of antivirals to their own health care workers, emptied as many beds as possible, cancelled all but the most critical operations and put their own emergency procedures into place.

By the evening of that first day, the flood of desperately ill victims of the still-unnamed influenza outbreak began to arrive: the elderly, infants, transplant recipients, those with various forms of immune system trouble - all the usual suspects for serious consequences of a dangerous type A Influenza.

At eleven that first night, Dr. Lawrence conferred at the White House with Secretary Ross, Cam Mitchell, Lucy Kline, and Felix Santana – the Director of Homeland Security - along with a half-dozen various staffers. They had moved the timetable up to nine am for the announcement of a national health care emergency. The information from Asia and Europe had confirmed a worldwide outbreak. WHO would be issuing a worldwide alert in a matter of hours.

At that same hour, on day one of the mystery flu, Dr. Maxwell Stanton was stretched out on the couch in his office at the CDC, not feeling all that great. The unmistakable first signs of a flu coming on had him in a quandary. Should he bail out and go home so as not to infect any other workers at the CDC, or should he stay on duty during this most important day?

"You don't look so good," Hobbs said, as he slumped into the chair in Stanton's office.

"I think I'm getting sick," Max said, with a sigh.

"Me too," Hobbs said. "It has arrived. I've had a dozen people go home in the last hour."

"Unreal. Maybe the antivirals will give us a little help. But at least we won't need to go very far for samples of the virus."

Max sat up and rubbed his face. He got up and walked over to his desk just as the phone rang.

"Dr. Stanton, this is Sharif. We have the first picture from the WHO lab in Los Angeles. You need to come over and look at this. It is most unusual."

"Why, what's so unusual?"

"I can't describe it, just come over immediately."

"Sharif, I'm coming down with something – probably our flu. Maybe I shouldn't go over there."

"Okay, I'll come to you. But it probably doesn't matter that much; I've had several people go home sick in the last hour."

Ten minutes later Sharif Baku, the Chief of Molecular Pathology and Ultrastructure at CDC, leaned over Max's desk and called up the picture from the Los Angeles lab.

"I could have put this on your screen for you, but I wanted to be here when you saw this."

Max looked at the first picture of a single influenza virus. It had the standard sideways-comma-shaped blobby main section. The second picture was magnified so that the two stacks of proteins that determined the exact subtype were visible.

"What the hell is that?" Max asked, with his finger on the H stack.

"It's the H stack," Sharif answered.

"Christ – I know that, but I've never seen one look like that. Can you count it?" Max asked urgently.

"Not very well from this picture. But I'd guess it's H13 or maybe H15," Sharif said.

"That's not possible, Sharif. We've never seen one above H9 before."

"I know," Sharif said. "Perhaps we should wait until we have the virus isolated here. So we can use our machines. Maybe this isn't accurate."

"How long will that take?"

"Three hours, maybe a bit less."

"Ok, I guess we can postpone our full-throttle panic for a few more hours. I think I'll try to sleep a little," Max said.

"That's a good idea. You don't look well," Sharif said. "You either," he said, patting Hobbs on the head as he walked out the door.

Chapter 22

**Day Two of the Eden Flu
Friday, July 24ᵗʰ, 2020
The CDC, Atlanta**

Four hours later, at 3 am Eastern time, on day two of the yet unnamed flu pandemic, Sharif Baku gently shook Max awake.

The coughing started immediately as Max sat up. "Yuk … bathroom," he sputtered as he exited down the hall.

Sharif had taken the precaution of wearing a mask, a good idea as Hobbs, working at the screen behind Max's desk, was filling the air with his own virus-filled droplets. Sharif also wished he'd put a dab of that autopsy cream under his nose as well - it didn't smell very good in there.

"Amazing, I slept a little," Max said as he returned from the bathroom. "I'm sure I have a fever," he said, breaking into another coughing fit.

"May I?" Sharif asked Hobbs, indicating he needed the screen.

"You might want some gloves," Hobbs said, as he moved out of Sharif's way.

"It doesn't matter. We'll all get it," Sharif said. "Several times in fact."

"What does that mean?" Max asked.

"You'll see," Sharif said and pulled up his latest picture of the virus.

Max studied it briefly. "Well, that looks a lot more likely. What's the number?"

"First guess is it's something like H5N7. We'll need to do more work to nail it down."

"Whoa – H5N7? That's not right either. We don't have an H5N7. I don't think that exists either," Max said as he stepped away for a cough.

"That's correct Dr. Stanton. It's new."

Sharif brought up another image. "This is from the San Francisco WHO lab. They insist it's an accurate picture."

Max leaned in for a look. "That's not the same …"

"No it's not," Sharif said. "It's H3N9. Also never seen before."

"What are you telling me?" Max demanded, and began to wonder if he was hallucinating. "Hobbs, are you getting this? Am I hearing this right? We have three novel type A's – all never seen before – dumped in our lap – nationwide - all on the same day!" Max was almost shouting.

"Not quite right, Doctor. There are two more, H5N2 and H11N5. We have five so far …" Sharif said.

"What is going on here?" Max sputtered. "Have aliens landed? Is this finally the wrath of God descending?"

No one spoke. No one had an answer. The three of them stared back and forth at each other waiting for someone to offer something intelligent that they all might cling to. Nothing came to mind.

Max broke the spell with a coughing fit. He stumbled, half bent over, into the hallway until it subsided.

"When can you confirm this?" Max asked.

"Do you want good science, or speed?"

"Both."

"Some of it depends on what we tell our own sick people. Do we want them to stay at home, or come back to work and gut it out, if they can? I'm assuming everyone will get it anyway."

"Are you suggesting we just skip all of our precautionary procedures? Everything we've ever set up to contain outbreaks here. Just give up and let everyone get sick?"

"Well, you two are sick," Sharif said. "Neither you or Hobbs should be here right now."

"Fuck!" said Max. It seemed to him to be the only appropriate thought. "Sharif, can you stay around until mid-morning? Until we can put together a story for the Lawrence and the President?" Max asked.

Sharif nodded, "I'll be in the lab." He patted Hobbs on the head as he walked out the door.

"Goddammit!" Hobbs said. "I'm going to smear snot all over me so that everyone who gives me a goddamn pat gets goddamn sick!"

"Settle down, big guy," Max said. "What's new in your area?"

"Well let's see," Hobbs said, and began coughing. "Hospitals in the west and mid west have already prepared for the worst. We'll have reports in the morning, but so far it doesn't look terrible. The east seems to be tracking with what we saw last night in the west. More people going to emergency rooms, probably because of all the publicity."

"There'll be a run on the antivirals soon," Max said.

"No shit Sherlock," Hobbs said. "Anyway - major outbreaks have been reported in Japan and New Zealand. Smaller pockets in the rest of Asia and Europe."

Max reached for more tissues as Hobbs doubled over from his first serious coughing fit. "Here," Max said, handing the box to Hobbs.

Hobbs blew, then he stood. "Here's how I figure it," he said, raising his stubby arms in the air and pacing back and forth in front of Max's desk.

"The minor pockets we are seeing right now, like in Europe and parts of Asia, are from travelers. Remember, the first people infected have been shedding virus for three days now. So, the minor pockets are from what we would normally expect from travelers. The major outbreaks though – those are from something that was dropped, e*n masse*, at those locations - maybe from aliens, maybe from God, or maybe something in the food chain. Likely something common like beer, or hamburgers, or cigarettes. Somehow – don't ask me how - but somehow something happened to get all these different viruses to these sites. I think the computer modelers might be able to at least sort out the initial locations from the rest. It won't matter though."

"At least that's a context that makes some sense," Max said.

"Yeah, maybe," Hobbs said, still pacing, stubby arms still wind-milling. "Now, if that is what's happening, then we're just seeing the beginning of the major outbreaks. Whatever it is that's carrying the viruses – let's say it's a cola for instance - then that contaminated cola is just starting to make it way around the world. The fact that it's already in New Zealand means it will probably go everywhere."

"So, we have two sources pumping this: the standard propagation through contact with those already infected, and then the initial contamination. The source of which, we haven't a clue," Max said, and stood up to join Hobbs's pacing. "And to top it off, we have five different novel type A's."

"We're screwed. That's my official position," Hobbs said. "That's all you need to tell Miz Prez. We're screwed."

"Succinct. Accurate ..." Max mumbled, and kept pacing. "So, following the 'we're screwed' line of thought. With five viruses, planted in millions of people worldwide – already planted, so there's nothing we can do about that now - and with several days' head start, we have to assume that everyone in the world will get sick. Several times, in fact. Everyone will get sick several times, maybe an average of three to five times each. And it will go on, wave after wave, for several weeks, maybe months. Holy shit ..." Max said, putting his hands, palms down, on the top of his head.

"You could add that to the report," Hobbs said. "Tell her – 'Holy shit, we're screwed'."

"Thanks," Max said, and walked over to his couch, suddenly overcome by the threshold of realization he had just crossed, not to mention the lack of sleep and the grip of a new type A influenza. "Since we're screwed regardless, I'm going to lie down for a couple of hours. If you're still around, wake me at eight. I'm scheduled to call the President at nine."

Dr. Maxwell Stanton woke at half past seven needing to clear his lungs. After coughing, blowing, and otherwise expelling as much crud as possible, he washed up and took his temperature – 100.6 – not too bad. He was sick, but functional. The antivirals were helping. He threw down another double dose, and chased it with as much water as he could handle.

He then sat down to prepare for his call. Sharif loaded up the latest pictures. Nothing new – still the five novel subtypes. Hobbs stumped in at eight with additional confirmation for his theory. At least now he had something to say to the President. At quarter till nine, he had Hobbs and Sharif Baku join him in his office.

Mel, Max's assistant, stuck his masked head into the room. Mel wasn't sick yet. "They want you on video in the conference room. It's all set, and the folks on the other end are ready for you right now. I saw the President, so you better hustle" he said. "But stop in the bathroom first – you all look like shit."

After a brief visit to the bathroom, the hair looked better, but there was no time to remove the beard stubble. The red eyes, nose and the box of tissues - looking strangely oversized due to it's placement near the camera - made it obvious that the team in Atlanta was sick.

Sharif busied himself with plugging his laptop into the video feed. Hobbs fiddled with the chair, raising it to its highest setting. Max blew his nose and began. "Good morning Madam President," he said, perhaps a bit too formally.

The President coughed.

Dr. Lawrence started, she sounded not-sick, "Dr. Stanton, what have you got for us?" she asked, without formality.

There were eight people in the room. Max recognized six of them - the three who had been on the call the day before from Wyoming, plus Ms. Lopez, the Secretary of Health and Human services, Assistant Secretary Ross, and Dr. Lawrence. Then there were two men, unidentified, neither one recognizable to Max. And apparently, they weren't going to be introduced.

"It's not good," Max began. "We have major outbreaks world-wide. Understand, we've only been tracking this for twenty-four hours, so we don't have good data. But based on reports from several sources, I'd guess millions are already infected. And it appears that it is already everywhere."

"How can that be possible?" President Pittman asked.

"Well," Max said, then sputtered and broke into a coughing fit. "Sorry. By the way – as you can see, many of us are sick here at CDC. So many that we have decided not to isolate or quarantine anyone. We have told the staff that if they think they can function, go ahead and come in to work. That's why we are still here."

"Three of us are sick as well," Lucy said, to low murmuring in the room. Lucy turned to the unnamed men. "We've had this discussion. The President is sick. There is no point in denying it. In fact, if millions of Americans are already sick – it won't hurt to be in the same boat."

"We are taking double doses of antivirals here," Max said. "It seems to be working. I don't feel good, but I can stay upright and function, at least for now. I'd recommend you all do the same. Drink plenty of water too."

"Thanks – I'll pass that on," Lucy said.

"Madam President," Dr. Stanton continued. "Sorry about the interruption. You asked how this could be possible. If you will give me a moment, I'll get back to that. We do have some ideas. But first – there is more bad news."

Max indicated for Sharif to put a picture of the H5N1 virus on the screen. "Can you all see this picture?"

Several people nodded.

"Good," Max said. "I'm going to give you a brief lesson on the influenza virus. Please stay with me - it's important."

"Are you sure this is necessary?" Dr. Lawrence asked, certain that it wasn't.

"Yes. It won't take long."

"Go ahead," the President said.

Max began the mini-lecture. "Influenza subtypes are determined by the two protein stacks that bump out of the surface of the virus – the H stack, for Hemagglutin – and the N stack for Neuraminidase. For instance, the avian flu that caused all the ruckus fifteen years ago was sub-typed H5N1. That's a picture of the H5N1 virus on the screen right now. What that means is its H stack was five high, and its N stack was 1 high."

Other examples - the 1918 pandemic was caused by H1N1, the 1957 pandemic was H2N2, and the 1968 pandemic was H3N2. There are a dozen other, mostly avian, known subtypes that have been studied and categorized at CDC. Several have occasionally cropped up in humans. H9N2, H7N2, H7N7, have been tracked for over a decade, but, like the H5N1, they never became human-to-human contagious.

"Now this is the important part. It is these stacks – the various subtypes – that determine how humans react to the virus. Our immune system recognizes these viruses based on their surface configurations. When a subtype is the same as or similar to a subtype that has already circulated, then the immune system already has the anti bodies. It knows that it is an influenza virus, and that it has to act to destroy it. For instance, H3N2, the 1968 virus that caused a pandemic when it first emerged, is still in circulation. But now, it's not a problem, as almost everyone's immune system has antibodies.

"Theoretically, the H stack could go as high as 16, but H9 is as far as any we have observed in any virus in nature."

Max paused to cough, Hobbs joining in.

"Everybody with me so far?" Max asked.

"Yes, go on please," Pittman said.

"Our first priority, at the moment we became aware of the outbreak, was to determine which influenza we were dealing with. In other words, what was the subtype – the H and N numbers - of this virus." Max took a drink of water and continued. "I won't go into the details of how that's done, but in the end we use the most sophisticated electron microscopes to get a picture. The picture is not fully determinate. We need to do other things, like gene sequencing, to get a final answer. But a picture still tells us a lot."

He paused and sighed, wishing he didn't have to tell them the next part.

"We got our first pictures around three this morning, from a WHO collaborating lab in Los Angeles. We now have over twenty WHO labs worldwide working on this," Max said, and nodded to Sharif. Sharif replaced the image of the H5N1 virus with a new picture – the H13N5.

"This is the first picture we got." Max sighed again. "For now, we are calling it H13N5."

"Oh my God!" Dr. Lawrence said. She understood the implications.

"I know. It scared us as well. This is obviously a brand new subtype, never seen before. It will likely cause a severe pandemic."

Hobbs excused himself to go out into to the hall for a coughing fit. Max blew into a tissue and tried to steady himself for what was coming next. Somehow, the act of telling the President this ungodly news made this even more terrifying.

"But, this is still not the bad news," Max said. He had their attention now. The eight people in the White House conference room looked at each other wide-eyed. How could that not be the bad news? What could possibly be worse?

"The bad news is that, so far today, we have identified five different new flu subtypes," Max nodded again. Sharif put up another picture. "This next one we are calling H11N2, the next is H5N7, then H5N2, and last, so far, is H3N9."

Max paused to let this sink in.

"Just a minute," the President said, blew her nose, and stood up slowly. President Pittman was a large woman, not exactly overweight, but large-framed, an Eleanor Roosevelt type, although somewhat handsomer. She moved slowly, but with dignity. She was the kind of woman who wore practical shoes.

She moved around to one of the unidentified men, bent over and whispered something into his ear. He nodded, got up, and left the room.

"Excuse me Dr. Stanton, I've asked to have the Vice-President join us. He's around here somewhere, so it won't be long. I'm going to cut off the video for the moment. Don't go anywhere. We will start again in five minutes."

The video link went blank. Max drank the rest of his water as Hobbs returned and sat back down.

"I think we've reached the 'Holy shit – we're screwed' part of the presentation. Would you like to deliver it?" Max asked Hobbs. "You have a way with profanity."

Hobbs coughed.

The video came back up. Max could see three more men standing at the back. One was the VP. He didn't recognize the other two.

"Are you there, Dr. Stanton?" President Pittman asked, now reseated in her original spot.

"Yes."

"I'm going to start where you left off. Let me see if I have this straight," the President said. "We have a worldwide pandemic that has infected millions already, everywhere on this planet. It started only yesterday. And this pandemic is caused by at least five, previously unknown, highly contagious subtypes of influenza."

"Yes, that's correct," Max said.

"What's going to happen?" the President asked. She had built her political persona based on her no-nonsense approach. It was now on full display.

Max inhaled, in preparation for a big sigh, but all he got was another coughing fit.

"Take your time doctor," the President said.

"Sorry," Max said. "Please, understand that I can only guess right now. There is so much we don't yet know. But I have thought about this over the last few hours. First of all – there is no point in thinking about containment. It's too late for that. What we need to do is think about care and treatment for the sick."

"How many sick will there be Doctor?" asked a voice from the back. Max guessed it was the VP.

"Well, everyone will be sick, several times, in fact. I'm guessing again, but I'd estimate everyone will get sick three to five times over the next two months."

"Everyone?" Dr. Lawrence blurted out.

"How many will die?" the President asked, cutting to the heart of the matter.

"Considering that everyone will get it, and more than once, and considering how many people have weak immune systems – people such as the elderly, infants, people already sick with something else, transplant recipients, people without resources for treatment - the list goes on and on. The point is that there are a lot of vulnerable people out there …"

"How many will die Doctor?" The President interrupted, wanting an immediate answer, not a lecture.

"A minimum of ten percent, perhaps as high as thirty percent."

"Are you serious?" the VP said, alarmed. "That's a minimum of thirty million dead in the next two months!"

"Yes sir, and those numbers are for the U.S. alone. The worldwide total could exceed a billion."

"Can't we do something, anything at all, to reduce all those deaths?" Lucy Kline asked. She was usually silent at these meetings. But now, she was no longer concerned with proper protocol.

"We can give the best treatment possible under the conditions. That will help considerably," Max said. "But if I may give some advice …"

"Please do," the President said.

"I think the tendency here would be to try to do too much," he said, struggling to find the right words. "And then, if you shoot too high, it might get completely out of control – sorry, I'm not saying this well. But let me give you an example. We need to be concerned about the secondarys, things like cholera and typhus. If we don't find a way to deal with all the corpses, we could start several dangerous secondary epidemics. So - right now - start thinking now about a plan for the bodies. It shouldn't be treated as an afterthought. And, if you are going to use troops, use them to keep the water systems and the sewage systems functioning. I guess what I'm saying is to think about falling back far enough to defend the places where we can have a positive affect. The flu will have its way regardless."

"Good advice, Doctor," Pittman said. "Now: Lucy, I'd like you, Dr. Lawrence, and Secretary Ross to go work on my speech to the nation. I don't want to scare people too much right now. But I want to be straight. We will declare a public health emergency under section 319 (a)."

Lucy nodded and excused herself together with Dr. Lawrence and Mr. Ross.

"Secretary Lopez, please start a task force on the points that Dr. Stanton has raised. The goal is to avoid the other diseases – typhus and cholera. Do not concern yourselves with the public's desire for proper burials. Begin planning for mass graves in all densely populated areas. I'd like a progress report by two this afternoon. *Understand please:* this cannot be government as usual. We need to cut through the crap. If you get resistance – just fire the assholes, and get on with it. And if you don't get this going quickly - I'll fire you. Clear?"

"Yes, very clear," Secretary Lopez said, and hustled out of the room.

"Vice President Baird, I want you, and your office, to coordinate all international issues. Please contact the Secretary of State and add her to your team. Take into account Dr. Stanton's assertion that containment is no longer an option. There is no point in any travel bans. That will be our official position. Understood?"

Vice President Baird nodded and left with his staffers.

President Pitman turned back to the camera, "Dr. Stanton, this is Milos Papadakas," she said, and pointed to one of the unidentified men, who then nodded to the camera. "Milos runs our FBI Bioterrorism Unit. The gentleman seated next to him has similar responsibilities at CIA. Milos will be joining you at CDC in Atlanta within a few hours. He will bring a team that will stay until further notice. Please find them adequate space. There could be as many as a dozen. Also, please be available to conduct another briefing for me at five this afternoon. Thank you Dr. Stanton."

The President nodded to someone off camera and the screen went blank.

"That woman is a powerhouse," Hobbs said, still staring at the blank screen. "Pretty impressive."

"I agree, very impressive," Max said. "I never liked her before, but right now, I don't think we could have a better person in charge."

Hobbs got up to go, "I'd better get to work before she fires me, too."

"Do you think they know something that we don't?" Max asked. "Sending in all those FBI spooks?"

"Maybe," Hobbs said, standing in the doorway. "It's a reasonable conclusion that someone has done this on purpose."

"But why the influenza virus? I still don't get it. If this 'person' has the resources to develop all these viral strains - and then has the resources to dump them everywhere in the world at the same time - why wouldn't he have chosen a more deadly virus? Surely, he could have come up with a better choice."

"I don't know why," Hobbs said, leaving the room. "And don't call me Shirley."

Chapter 23

That same day, Friday July 24th, 2020
Day Two of the Eden Flu
Malabar Farm

Sofia woke up feeling sick. After showering, she drove one of the electric carts down to the infirmary. She took her temperature, located the antivirals and took a double dose. A short time later the other two doctors came in to do the same thing. All were sick.

"Looks like we're in for a busy day," Doc Siefert said.

"So much for that experimental vaccine," Dr. Jan said, coughing.

"Are you okay?" Seifert asked, concerned, looking at Sophia, who was standing in the middle of the room, noticeably shaking.

Sad-eyed, with tears welling-up, Sophia looked at the other two doctors and tried to find something to say. "I'm sorry ... I'm so sorry," she whispered. She turned away and rushed out the door.

Sofia could not have been more frightened. She had watched the news the day before, with the heavy burden of knowing the truth, as the world came down with the flu. And now she had it. She had the flu. She knew what that meant: only one thing – certain death. Not only for her, but for everyone. No more illusion that Dixon might be right, that over time humanity would be better off with this severe culling of the herd. Once again Dixon had screwed up, miscalculated. The vaccine didn't work. Now everyone would die.

She walked in a daze, head down, across the bridge to the front gate of WPPS. She didn't know what else to do. She buzzed, hoping someone was there.

The gate clicked open. Mark Dunn appeared in the door as she walked up the drive.

"How are you feeling?" Sophia asked, as they sat down in Mark's office.

"Not good, I think I've got it."

"Me too. I need to get in touch with Secretary Solene. Do you know how I can do that?"

"He's here."

"In the building?"

"No, he's been staying in the farmhouse that came with this property. That's where we all live. He sent me down here this morning after he woke up sick. He thought you might come by."

"Well, good. Can you drive me there?"

"That's the plan. Manny was going to try to reach Duval after I left this morning. Maybe he has news."

They exited out the back and got into Mark's car. A short drive up the gravel road behind the WPPS building brought them to an old farmhouse, hidden from the road by a large mature woodlot.

Secretary Solene was sitting in a rocking chair on a large old-fashioned porch that ran along the entire front of the three story farmhouse. There were groups of wicker chairs, rockers, and double-seated couches spread around on the porch.

"This looks quite comfortable, and so do you," Sophia said, and managed a weak smile as she walked up the front steps.

"How are you feeling? Or need I ask?" Solene rose to greet the handsome doctor.

"The same as you, I presume."

Sophia picked out a comfortable looking wicker chair and sat down.

"I won't keep you in suspense. I imagine you are concerned, and scared," Solene said. "I reached Duval a few minutes ago. He told me what is going on here with us, and with the people at Malabar."

"I could have told you that: we have his damn Eden flu," Sophia said bitterly.

"Actually, we don't."

"What?"

"We don't have the 'Eden Flu'. We have a different subtype. It's the same one that caused the 1952 pandemic. But it's not a hybrid virus. It won't create prions. I guess you could call it a decoy."

"My God," Sophia said and started to cry.

Solene pulled his chair up close to her and reached out to hold her hand. "I'm sorry. It seems like a cruel trick, doesn't it?"

She looked up and nodded.

"But as you might expect, Duval has a reason for this deception," Solene said, releasing her hand and leaning back in his chair. "Malabar Farm would stand out like a sore thumb if no one got sick here. We would come under intense scrutiny. Who knows what would happen then?"

Sofia swept her tears away. "Actually, I have wondered about that," she said, sighing. "Sorry about this …"

"No need to be sorry; these last few days have overwhelmed me as well."

"Why didn't you tell me?"

"I just found out. Duval kept it from me, too."

"Why couldn't he have told us? This was total hell this morning. I don't know how much more I can take …" Sofia said, tears welling up again.

"I understand, I felt the same way. But he had a good reason not to tell us."

"He always does."

"It's not exactly good news. This strain of flu hasn't been around for a long time. The people here won't have much, if any, immunity. Especially those under thirty. Dixon told me to expect a mortality rate between two and five percent. In other words, five to ten people at Malabar could die from this. And since it was in that booster shot you administered a few days ago, he didn't want you to know."

"Oh no," Sofia said. "My God … I gave it to them? I told them it would keep them well. I convinced them. I stuck the needle in them. And now some of them will die?"

"According to Dixon, yes … some will die."

"Well thank you Mr. Secretary. You have replaced one black hole of depression with another."

"I'm sorry, I do understand," Solene said leaning forward to put his hand on her knee. "These last two days have been an emotional nightmare. Then this morning, I thought that Dixon had failed. That we all were doomed. That I was going to die. And now this news. It's very hard to take."

"Not to mention that we are sick," Sofia said, inhaling deeply, attempting to regain her composure. "That never helps. Are you taking antivirals?"

"Yes, we have some."

"I recommend taking more than the normal dosage, and have Mark come and get me if you think you may be in trouble."

"I'll be fine. Remember, I was actually around in 1952. I probably have some immunity."

"That will help," Sofia said, getting up to leave. "Well - I should get back. It's going to be a busy day. Are you going to stay here for a while?"

"I have no where else to go."

Sofia glanced around the porch and smiled, "I love this porch. After a time, I might be able to slip away and take an evening walk over here. Would that be all right with you?"

"Yes, I'd like that," Solene said, rising stiffly to walk her down the steps. Mark was waiting by the car.

Sofia turned and faced Solene as she reached the car. "I'm not going to let Dixon get away with this."

Solene was suddenly concerned. Was she going to go public?

"What do you mean?" he asked.

"I'm not going to let anyone at Malabar die. We have three excellent doctors, a well equipped facility, and a group of healthy young people. No one is going to die here," Sofia said confidently. "Not now … not yet."

Chapter 24

Saturday, July 25th, 2020
Day three of the Eden Flu
The CDC - Atlanta

They gathered in the conference room at the CDC on the morning of the third day of the still unnamed pandemic flu: four members of the FBI bioterrorism team, Dr. Stanton, Andy Hobbs, and Helen Glick. The entire FBI team, ten strong, had arrived the evening before. But the flu didn't care that they were FBI - two of the ten had been admitted to the hospital shortly after arrival, four others were in bed at the hotel.

"MPR?" asked Milos Papadakas, the head of the FBI's Bioterrorism unit. "Are you familiar with the term?"

Hobbs couldn't resist. "You listen to that crap? You don't seem like the type."

"M, that's M-PR," Papadakas said. There was no indication that he appreciated Hobbs' sense of humor.

Dr. Stanton didn't smile either, and gave Hobbs the look. Hobbs nodded. Max didn't want anymore wise-ass comments.

"MPR," Max said. "I understand the concept. Massive population reduction, right? Some radical environmentalists and the back-to-the-stone-age nut-cases have talked about it."

"There's a little more to it, but basically that's right," Papadakas said.

"You don't really believe those people could pull off something like this, do you?" Max asked.

"Like I said, there's more than just the extremists involved now. We are tracking over sixty groups and individuals that endorse the idea," Papadakas said. "Some are quite serious about it. Though we've never seen any evidence that they actually intended to do anything - other than talk about it."

"I'm afraid it would take a lot more than 'serious intentions' to have caused this event," Max said. "The manufacture of five unique subtypes of influenza would require considerable talent, a very sophisticated laboratory, and quite a long time to work on it. Are any of these groups capable of that?"

"No, to my knowledge, nothing close to that capability," Papadakas said. "And as I said, no one has crossed the line and actually advocated doing it. They just like to talk about it."

"My recollection of the MPR idea is that they intended to reduce the population a lot more than even the thirty percent that we might see, worst case, with this event," Max said. "I thought they were talking ninety percent or more."

"Yes, you are correct. Some even talk of reducing the human population down to the thousands, hundreds even."

The meeting went silent, except for the coughing. No one could explain the conflicting facts. The dots weren't connecting.

"The part I keep coming back to," Max said, attempting to break the awkward silence, "is why a group that has the capability to both create and distribute these viruses, would choose influenza. This current nightmare is the worst conceivable influenza event; far worse than anything we've planned for. And yet, even at it's worst, it will *only* kill thirty percent. With the capabilities that are necessary to do this, whoever is doing this could have chosen smallpox, or one of the hemorrhagic viruses – Marburg, or Ebola for instance - and had a much more devastating outcome. Why influenza? I still don't get it."

Papadakas sighed, rubbed his face and grimaced. "You sure there isn't something else I can take to make this headache go away?"

"Sorry," Max said. "We've given you the highest antiviral dose we can. Consider yourself fortunate. The average person will be lucky to get any at all."

Papadakas leaned back in his chair, closed his eyes, and rubbed his temples.

"Unfortunately, Brenner is our expert on the whole MPR issue. He's been tracking those folks for years," said one of the FBI team.

"Why isn't he here then?" Max asked.

"He is," Papadakas said. "He's in the hospital. He and Jenkins are both in the hospital. He was in rough shape by the time we landed yesterday. He's got a bad heart."

"Okay, then we can discuss MPR later," Max said. "What about regular old garden-variety terrorists?"

"I don't see it," Papadakas said. "For the same reasons that you have suggested. Other infectious agents would be more lethal. And perhaps more importantly, that with an uncontrollable influenza, their own countries would be hit even harder than us. We also don't have any chatter about it. We would have heard something if it was any of the usual suspects. And then there are the obvious challenges of the production and distribution of the viruses."

"How about another government, maybe North Korea?" Max suggested.

"Why? What would they gain from this? Besides, governments are more chatty than terrorists. I guarantee you we would have heard about an operation this big, even if it was North Korea. No way."

"So we are back to an accidental event, like some weird-science contamination of a cola syrup, or else an unknown MPR faction?"

"I guess," Papadakas said, wincing from his pounding headache. "Can you guys look into the 'weird-science' angle? The CIA will continue to track down anything from abroad – terrorists or governments. And we really need to wait for Brenner to get better in order to follow up on any MPR connections. He's the only person that ever paid serious attention to them. We'll keep you posted on that," he said and got slowly to his feet. "But right now, I've got to go lie down. I can't tell you how bad I feel."

"I think I can guess," Max said. "I'm worse too. I'm going to do the same thing. Bed is about all I can handle right now."

The meeting was abandoned, and with it all efforts to understand how it was possible for five novel type A influenza viruses to spring up everywhere at once. It would be another five weeks before that question would be addressed again.

Chapter 25

The next day
Sunday, July 26th, 2020
Day four of the Eden flu
The hunting camp, Vancouver Island

"Toby!" Laura screamed, "There's a car coming!"

The door of the A-frame slammed shut behind her as she ran in to get the rifle.

Toby was lying down. He jumped up, but a sharp pain from his still-healing ribs knocked him back onto the bunk.

After two weeks and a few days holed up in the A-frame, the ribs were much better, though any unusual movement might momentarily paralyze him with that electric-shock pain. The sprained ankle was almost completely healed. He had been taking long walks the last few days and expected to be ready to go soon. "Soon" had suddenly become now.

"Grab the backpack," Laura said, rushing by him. "I'll get the guns. Let's try and make it into the woods."

Toby grabbed the pack, shoved a few canned goods into it, checked to make sure the GPS was there, and followed Laura out the door as the gravel crunched from a vehicle close by. They had just enough time to crouch down behind a small woodpile at the back of the A-frame as a truck pulled in alongside the cabin. Two small boys spilled out followed by a man and a woman.

"We're going down to the river," one of the boys yelled over his shoulder as he ran past the woodpile - and then froze, spotting Toby and Laura.

"Dad, dad!" the boy screamed.

Toby and Laura had no choice but to stand up and walk into the clearing, trying to create some space between themselves and the pickup truck family. Toby held the rifle across his chest. Laura's pistol dangled from her hand, clearly visible.

The father saw them and reached back into the truck for his rifle. He stood behind the hood of the truck and pointed it in the general direction of Toby and Laura.

"Boys, get over here right now!" he yelled, keeping his gaze on the strangers.

The boys ran over and he shoved them down behind the truck. "Stay there!" he yelled.

"Who are you? What are you doing here?" he shouted at Toby and Laura.

"Are you the owner?" Toby asked, trying to sound calm.

"Yes, these are my cabins – my brothers and me," the man said.

"Look, we'll leave right away. We were lost and hurt and had no food …"

The man interrupted, "How long have you been here?"

"Two weeks," Toby said.

"Are you sick?"

"Sick? What do you mean?" Laura asked.

"The flu – do you have the flu?"

"No we're not sick," Laura said. "What flu are you talking about?"

"You don't know?"

"No, we haven't seen anyone for two weeks," Toby said.

The dad relaxed a bit, and pointed the rifle away from Toby and Laura.

"There's a big flu epidemic," he said. "Everyone has it, everywhere. We're going to hole up here till it goes away."

Laura looked at Toby. There was nothing that she could think of to say, so she just sat down on the grass and buried her face in her hands.

"We'll go now. We have a place north of here that we want to get to," Toby said. "Can you tell me how far this road goes, and how far it is until we get to other people?"

The man studied them for a minute, trying to figure out how friendly he should be. The sight of the distraught Laura tipped the scales toward sympathy.

"You sure you're not sick?" he asked again.

"No – it's the truth. We've been here for two weeks," Toby said. "I'm injured. I've got a sprained ankle and broken ribs, but no flu."

The man shouldered his rifle and started walking around the truck towards them.

"No … no! Stay there!" Laura yelled, and got back up. "We're not sick. But *you* might be. Please stay there."

The dad stopped in his tracks. "We feel fine. Nobody is sick."

"You won't know for three days," Laura said. "After that, you can relax. But if you are sick you are shedding virus now, even before the symptoms show up."

The man looked over at his wife - they had thought they were safe. Now, they had to spend three more anxious days before knowing. "You sure?" he asked, looking back at Laura.

"I'm a doctor," Laura said, and immediately wished she hadn't.

"A doctor?" the man said. "You should be helping. The next town, Salmon Creek, doesn't have a doctor, just a practitioner at the local clinic."

Laura knew the man was right: she should be helping. She looked over at Toby to try to read his mind.

"I can drive you there," the man said. "It'll only take a few minutes."

Toby answered quickly, before Laura could get tied-up thinking about the consequences.

"Okay, but we'll ride in the back of the pickup," Toby said. "How far did you say it was?"

"Fifteen miles or so."

A few minutes later, the truck pulled out of the woods, leaving the overgrown logging road to head north on a narrow, but paved, local road. A mile down the paved road they rounded a bend and came alongside a salt-water bay. A small house on the shore was the first sign of civilization that Toby and Laura had seen in weeks.

Toby knocked hard on the back window of the truck. "Stop here!" he yelled.

"Why?" Laura asked, confused.

"Later …" Toby said, stepping over the tailgate as the truck pulled over to the shoulder.

Toby walked to toward the man, but still stayed several yards away. "You're safer if you turn around here, before you get to any people."

"You got five miles left," the man said.

"We'll walk – thanks."

"Okay, why here?" Laura asked after the pickup truck had turned around and driven off.

Toby pointed towards the bay. There was a dock with a small gillnet fishing boat tied up to it. "We'll wait until dark and then go take the boat. We can probably get to the Dixon coordinates before it gets light."

"Toby no! That man's right," Laura said. "I need to go help."

"No! You can't do that. Think about it. How can you help?"

"Toby – it's the flu. I know what to do. I can save people, a lot of people," Laura pleaded.

"Save them for what? Save them so that a few weeks later they'll suffer an even more awful death? Is that saving them? They're better off dying now."

Laura stood, staring at Toby, her head twitching, as if her mind had short-circuited from this impossible violation of her physician's oath.

"And then," he continued. "Your reward for providing them the opportunity to die horribly will be, only weeks later, to get sick and die yourself."

Laura looked up at him and could think of nothing to say. Head down, she turned and started walking back up the road. Toby followed her into a small field where they found an abandoned out-building to hide in until nightfall.

At eleven, it was finally dark enough to go out. Toby and Laura made their way out to the dock, almost a half mile away. The gillnet boat was an old wooden-hulled single-hander, but seemed to have been recently used. A good sign, Toby thought - it was likely to be in working condition. Toby expected that it would not require a key, and he was right. The word "start" was hand-written above a silver button that only had to be pushed to get the two-stroke diesel fired-up. Toby pushed it - nothing happened. A quick inspection revealed that the boat's battery was missing.

"What's wrong?" Laura asked.

"No battery," he said, and sat down to rest his aching ribs.

"What now?"

"Well, I think that the battery is up at the house - the owner's security system."

"We can still walk," Laura said. "I don't think you should go up there."

"There aren't any lights on. Maybe nobody's home." Toby grimaced and got back up, "Give me the pistol. You stay here. I'll go have a look."

The garage was attached to the south side of the house and, luckily, was open. But it was even darker inside than the moonless night outside. Toby groped about, trying not to make any noise.

Suddenly, a dog began to bark only feet away, on the other side of the door into the house. The light came on in the garage, blinding Toby. The door opened and an elderly woman, red-eyed and sickly, stood there, trying to block her tiny dog from rushing into the garage.

"Young man," she said and coughed. "Thank god! I need your help." She slipped through the door, shutting the still yapping dog inside.

Toby backed quickly to the entrance of the garage and raised the pistol.

"Don't come any closer," he yelled. "Or I'll have to shoot you!"

"No, no, young man," she said. "It's okay, you can take anything you want. I don't care – really. I just need your help for a few minutes," she pleaded, stepping slowly toward Toby.

"Please stop!" Toby pleaded.

She kept coming.

"Verne's dead," she said. "He died this morning. I just need you to help me carry him outside." Tears flowed down through the valleys of her wrinkled cheeks. "Verne was a good man. He treated me nice for sixty years. He was a God-fearing man. All he asked before he died was to be buried out back. I dug a little grave. Hard work for a sick old lady. All I ask, is for you to help me carry him out there. I tried. I can't do it myself. Please, please, help me ..."

She kept walking toward Toby, her arms outstretched in a last silent request for help.

She didn't know how dangerous she was to Toby. How could she know? Toby was one of only a handful of people in the whole world who knew how dangerous she was. He didn't know what to do - his mind fogged up. The world around him turned milky white. He could barely see her now.

He raised the pistol and fired twice.

Her sad face looked confused for just a moment before she collapsed. It would be seared in Toby's memory forever. How could he have done this? Did human life mean nothing now?

Zombie-like and without hesitation, he stepped over the body of the old woman to fetch the battery that he had spotted on a wagon in the corner of the garage. He pulled the wagon out around the dead body and down the path toward the boat for several hundred yards. Then suddenly he stopped, paralyzed by the horror of what he had done. He fell to the ground, buried his head in his hands, and began to cry uncontrollably.

The crying convulsion finally passed, and in the distance he heard Laura approaching. He stood up, tried to settle himself, and shakily yelled to Laura, "I'm right here. I'm fine. Go back to the boat right now! I'll be there in about twenty minutes. I have one more thing to do."

"I heard shots. You sure you're okay?" Laura yelled back.

"Yes, I'm fine. Please, do as I say. Go back right now."

Toby now knew what he had to do to make it right. He left the wagon in the path, and went back up to the house. He would do what Mrs. Verne had asked. He would bury Verne. She would have died from the flu anyway in a day or two, and then she would have been the one not-buried. It was what he could do to make it right – bury them both in the back yard. And at that moment, he didn't care if it cost him his life. He deserved to die after what he had just done.

Toby grabbed a shovel from the garage and went out back to see where the old lady had dug. He was surprised to see that Mrs. Verne had dug an impressive hole; it would take only a few minutes to make it large enough for the two of them.

He completed the grave expansion to his satisfaction and went back to the garage. On the slim chance that he might avoid the virus, he put on gloves and tied a rag around his face. He spotted an old motorcycle helmet and put that on too. He went into the house and immediately gagged as the humid stench of the hours-dead Verne filled his nostrils.

Toby found him on the floor next to the bed. The old woman had apparently tried to move him and dropped him there. Toby went back into the living room, pulled a small rug out from under the coffee table, and placed it beside Verne. He rolled the body onto the rug, dragged it outside and rolled him into the hole.

Toby's helmet fogged up and sweat streamed down his face as he repeated the process for the old lady and then shoveled dirt over the bodies. He went back to the garage, pulled off the foul helmet, gagged and vomited. His ribs ached, his head was spinning, and he was in shock, but he had one more task to do. He found some good wood, and in a few minutes had fashioned two makeshift, but sturdy, crosses.

"Toby, Is that you?" Laura shouted as Toby stumbled up the dock, the wagon in tow behind him.

"It's me," he shouted back. "Stay in the boat – don't come out."

"Why?"

"Just do it!" Toby said, stopping ten yards short of the boat. "See if there are any spare clothes aboard the boat."

Laura went into the cabin, and emerged a minute later, holding up a pair of oil-stained coveralls. "How about these?"

"Fine. Throw them on the dock."

Toby stripped off all his clothes, walked past the confused looking Laura to the end of the dock, and dived in the water. He swam around as best he could with the damaged ribs, going under, rinsing his hair, and gargling the salt water. Then he realized that with the cracked ribs, he wouldn't be able to scramble back up on the dock, so he had to swim ashore, wade through the muck, and walk back up the dock.

Toby stood in front of Laura, naked, shivering. His arms wrapped around his aching ribs. "I killed an old woman," he said, his voice cracking, a mixture of sadness, fear and pain. "All she wanted me to do was bury her husband. They had been married sixty years …"

He sat down and began to cry again.

Laura started to get out of the boat to comfort him.

"No! Stay there! They were both sick. I buried them both. I handled the bodies. I've been exposed …"

Chapter 26

"This is it," Toby said, cutting the throttle back to dead slow. The "Mabes", the little gillnet fishing boat that Toby assumed was named after Verne's wife – presumably Mabel - motored slowly toward the opening of the estuary, a hundred yards ahead.

Five days earlier, after he had buried Verne and Mabel in the backyard of their house, Toby had insisted on going into voluntary quarantine. Laura told him three days would be enough, but Toby insisted on four. Laura stayed on the boat and Toby went back to the outbuilding.

To their great relief, the salt water cleansing must have worked. Toby had stayed healthy. But the four days of isolation had turned into an unexpectedly difficult emotional trial. Laura now seemed deadened, distant. She had spent the last eight hours sitting at the back of the boat, not sleeping, and speaking rarely, while Toby navigated the Mabes out into the ocean and then north to Nootka Sound.

After motoring all night to get to the river at Dixon's secret coordinates, they had had to wait two more hours at the mouth of the estuary for the tide to reach a full flood. The gillnet boat needed as much water under it as possible to wind its way up the shallow river. And at slack high tide, there would be no current to deal with. Toby was familiar with these meandering estuaries. He had paddled his kayak up many like this on the coast of Washington, though none was as long as this one.

Finally, with the tide right, Toby threw the little gillnet boat into gear and started up the estuary. The diesel engine chugged along, the little boat winding left and then right as the river snaked through the tall eel grass. Toby glanced back at Laura, "Do you remember 'The African Queen'? Bogart and Hepburn?"

She nodded.

"Just like this," he said, trying to sound cheerful.

Laura gave him a small smile, muted, but warm. A good sign, he thought.

After a few minutes, Toby could see they were coming to the end of the flat water. The forest loomed ahead. A landing of sorts came into view. Toby cut the engine, glided in, and threw a line around the old piling that marked the landing.

"Ready?" he asked Laura. "We'll have to jump."

They threw their weapons and meager gear onto the bank, jumped ashore and scrambled up to a small clearing that dropped to the marshland on the west and ended with the forested hillside to the east. A well-worn path led from where they were standing into the forest, alongside the river.

Toby checked the GPS while Laura stood guard, watching the path, pistol in hand.

"We're close. It's less than a hundred yards, directly up the path. You take the rifle and find a spot to hide. I'll take the pistol and go look."

Toby moved silently up the path, more curious now than apprehensive. The path circled uphill and brought him to the back door of a cabin, hidden so well among the trees that he didn't see it until he was only feet away. There was no clearing at all. He sneaked along the uphill wall, to the front porch. He stopped and slowly peeked around the corner – and then broke into a grin.

As Toby stepped out into view, the old man sitting in the far corner of the porch looked up from his book. "Ah, Dr. Benson," the old man said. "My Goodness! So good to see you!"

"Dr. Mothershed," Toby nodded. "One second - I'll be right back."

Toby didn't want to spoil the surprise, and so he said little to Laura about the cabin and who was there. As she rounded the corner to the porch, she dropped her bag, and snapped her head around to scowl at Toby. He smiled back.

"And Dr. Sundgren too!" Mothershed said excitedly. "How wonderful! How remarkable!"

"Remarkable is the right word," Laura said. "It's remarkable to be here. It's remarkable to find you here." She shook her head, smiled over at Toby, and stepped up onto the porch to give Dr. Mothershed a proper greeting.

Jacob Threelodges appeared at the front door just as Toby made his way onto the porch. "Wow! You're both alive!" Jacob said, and stuck his hand out to Toby.

"We are," Toby said. "Any more surprises? Is anyone else here?"

"No, just Dr. Mothershed and me."

"Dixon?" Toby stepped back, worried about what he might hear.

"He's in D.C. I believe. At least that's where he was heading a few days ago," Jacob said. "You guys look terrible, sit down, please. How long have you been walking?"

"We came by boat," Laura said, and threw her backpack on the floor.

"Good God, you look like you're starving," Jacob said, pushing a chair out for Laura.

"Yes - hungry, tired, dirty, and probably quite smelly," Toby said. "Is there room for us here for a while?"

"Better than that, we have another cabin, nothing fancy, but it will work perfectly for the two of you," Jacob answered. "We don't have electricity or running water. No cells or communications of any kind either - Duval didn't want any traceable signals. But I'm sure you'll get used to it - it's not bad really."

Laura looked over at Toby and rolled her eyes. She had been looking forward to a shower.

"I'll run down and get a fire going in the bath house. It'll take about a half hour to warm up the water tank. You'll love it - trust me," Jacob said. "Go ahead inside and eat anything you find that looks good. Toby, I'll bring you some clothes too."

Laura's spirits brightened. A bath house - now that sounded promising.

Jacob was right - Laura loved the bath house. It was perched on a steep bank above the small river that ran through the compound. Two Adirondack chairs sat on a covered porch that hung out over the creek. The porch led into the closet-sized changing room, no more than six feet by eight. The sauna was only a bit larger than the changing room. The heat came from an oversized wood stove in one corner, with a metal box, full of rocks, welded on top. Next to the stove was a galvanized water tank, gravity-fed from a pool upstream, and somehow heated by a tangle of pipes that passed through and around the wood stove. Two faucets next to the water tank regulated a showerhead mounted high on the wall.

The whole interior of the sauna room was made of rough-cut western red cedar. The floor had a waxy sheen from the hundreds of times that soapy water had slowly dried on it, and a slight tilt to allow water to run off and drain onto the rocks below. The whole place smelled of cedar and smoke and soap and humid heat.

Toby and Laura showered, sweated, and showered again. They used the remaining hot water to rinse out the two sets of clothes that now made up Laura's entire wardrobe, and the set that Jacob had provided for Toby. The ropes and clothespins that were strung along the ceiling of the changing room made it clear that the bath house doubled as a washer and dryer.

Finally, after cleaning everything that needed cleaning, they laid the towels that Jacob had provided for them over the chairs, and sat down on the cozy little porch - clean, warm, and safe for the first time in weeks.

"So?" Toby asked. "Three-star or four-star?"

"Five-star," Laura answered. "Definitely five-star. That was perfect."

Laura reached over and put her hand on Toby's arm. "My god, Toby, we made it. We're still alive. And, we were right - we figured it out. Dixon sent us here to be safe."

Toby got up and adjusted his chair so he could look directly at Laura. She was, after all, naked.

"Hey, pervert, knock it off," she said. "I look awful. My arms and legs must look like Zorro's practice dummy. Look at all these scratches. But then, I have lost some weight ..." she said, and smiled, her major dimples signaling encouragement.

"Well, what's going to happen next?" she asked, trying to sound serious.

Toby reached his right foot over to stroke her leg.

"I didn't mean next as in the next seven minutes next – I meant next as in the rest of our lives next," Laura said.

Toby continued stroking her leg.

She gave in, stood up and stepped over to Toby's chair, straddling him, a leg on either side of his outstretched legs. "They can't see down here, can they?" she asked.

"I'm sure Jacob knows better than to come down here anytime soon."

"Good. I guess I'm free for the next seven minutes. Got any plans?"

Two hours later, after a short nap, a swim in the creek and one more shower, they walked up the steps to the main cabin, dressed in their wrinkled, but now clean clothes. No one was there to greet them. Toby peeked in the front door and saw Mothershed asleep on the couch.

"Mothershed's taking his afternoon nap," he said quietly. "Put the clothes on the chair. Let's look around."

They stood back from the porch and took in the lay of the land. The cabin looked as if it had been dropped from a helicopter. The trees rose up within feet of the walls, on all sides, hiding it from every angle. There was no clearing, no yard at all, only intersecting paths coming together at the bottom of the front steps.

"Let's go up there," Laura said, pointing up an unexplored path.

It was well worn, but seemed to Toby to be too long for anything important, like the woodshed or that other cabin that Jacob had mentioned. Finally, Laura looked over at Toby and grimaced. To her right, an outhouse.

"I think they just lost a few stars," she said. "End of path, turn around."

Back at the cabin, they took the path that went straight out from the porch. A few yards down on the right, built into the hillside, and also surrounded by trees, were two large sheds. One was open and stacked full of wood. Toby, experienced in the ways of wood heat from his youth, estimated that it contained at least six full cords, an ample supply for the winter.

The other shed was larger and better built. Inside, dozens of large plastic storage containers were stacked along one wall. Toby peeled back the top of one, and found it full of canned goods. This was apparently the food cache.

Tools of various kinds lined the other wall, including chainsaws, and two small portable gas powered generators. Against the back wall, a dozen or more Coleman style and oil lamps sat on shelves. Beneath the shelves were four fifty-five gallon drums of an unidentified fuel. There was nothing fancy here, but there were enough basic supplies for an extended stay.

"The path keeps going," Laura said, as Toby emerged from inspecting the shed.

No more than fifty yards farther down the path they looked back, and could see nothing of the sheds. And only a few yards further on they came abruptly upon a smaller cabin. It was situated like the sheds – tucked into the hillside to their right and facing the path. The door was open and Toby could hear Jacob banging around inside.

"Hey," Jacob said, as they entered. He leaned on the broom with which he had been attacking the dusty floor . "How was the sauna?"

"Fantastic," Laura said. "Is this our new home?"

"Yes ma'am. Not fancy, but the price is right. I think you'll like it. I lived in it when I built the new cabin and the sheds, and the sauna."

"You built all this?" Toby asked. "By yourself?"

"Pretty much," Jacob said. "I started three years ago. Duval wanted a well hidden place. Nothing fancy."

"It is well hidden. You got that part right," Toby said.

"What have you seen so far?" Jacob asked, and set the broom by the front door. "You walked by the sheds. Did you go inside?"

"I looked in. It looks like you're prepared for an extended stay."

"There's plenty for all of us. You don't need to worry about that. I can show you the outhouse later. Let's go down to the water."

Jacob slapped Toby on the back as he slipped by and headed down the path. Jacob was a massive man, the kind with sloped shoulders above a tree-sized, though not fat, trunk. As he strode down the path on well-worn sized fifteen work boots, swaying slightly, he appeared to Toby to be rooted to the ground. If there was a sport called "North-woods-narrow-path Sumo" Toby guessed Jacob would be the world champion.

Jacob's black hair was pulled back in a long ponytail reaching to the middle of his back. And Dixon was right when he called him handsome. Toby wondered exactly how, and when, Duval Dixon's and Jacob Threelodges' worlds had intersected.

"How far?" Toby asked.

"A hundred yards maybe."

The path got narrow as it wound around a steep hillside and then widened as it opened up into the same clearing they arrived at earlier in the day. This time tough, it was different. This morning it had been a dangerous place. They had come ashore with guns drawn - tired, dirty and scared. Now, they were fed, clean, and safe, and they could see this spot for what it was - spectacular.

The clearing sat on a west-facing hill that sloped away on three sides, and was surrounded by the marshy estuary of the river that tumbled through the cabin property. The estuary seemed to go on forever. Toby guessed it went for at least three miles before emptying into the bay, barely visible in the distance.

"Wow!" Laura exclaimed. "This is beautiful."

Jacob stood aside as Toby and Laura walked on for a better look. Toby loved these places. They were like a huge sea of marsh grass. And they always remained wildly natural. The ground was too spongy for crops or livestock, and was slightly brackish as the entire area was tidal. The river that meandered in half-loops across the perfectly flat ground would rise and fall several feet daily, depending on the tides. A person couldn't even hike there, as many tiny waterways, some a result of the tides, and some the result of drainage from the surrounding hills, crisscrossed and cut up the marsh. This was one of the largest estuaries Toby had ever seen, and he wished he had his kayak here to explore it.

"This really is huge," Toby said, as Jacob ambled up.

"A little over two thousand acres."

"Who owns it – the logging companies?"

"No ... well kind of. My logging company owns it, and another thousand acres surrounding it, and then a thousand acres back up the river around the cabins."

Toby stepped back to get a new look at Jacob the logging baron.

"You're kidding," Laura said. "You own a big logging company?"

Jacob looked over at Laura and smiled. "Not big really. It's just me and those two chainsaws you saw in the shed."

"Ah ... Dixon," Toby said. "Dixon owns it?"

"Yup, five years ago he asked me to scout out a remote spot somewhere along the coast. I found this place up for sale by a logging outfit that went belly up. He didn't want his name on it anywhere so he set up Horton Resources to buy it."

"Horton Resources?" Toby asked. "Who's Horton?"

Jacob looked at Toby as if he had suddenly spoken a foreign language. Then it dawned on him. "Oh, sorry, that's me. My name is Jacob Horton. You're still thinking it's Threelodges – like Dixon said when he introduced me." Jacob chuckled.

Laura looked at Toby and shook her head one more time in disgust at yet another of Dixon's tricks. "'Threelodges' – get it? Dixon was giving us another clue. I was at the first lodge, the big one by Victoria, four years ago. We were at the second one at Haida Gwaii. And this is the third lodge. But how stupid of us - we missed it."

Toby grimaced.

Laura turned back to Jacob. "So - how do you know Dixon?" she asked. "Have you known him long? I'm assuming you're not really his maintenance man."

Jacob smiled and nodded as he tried to figure out which question to answer first. "No, I'm not his maintenance man, at least not for the other properties."

Jacob shuffled his feet and clasped his hands behind his back, preparing to tell the story. "I've known Duval since I was three. I'm thirty-eight now, so that's a long time. It was eighty-five; Duval was working in Dallas at MCI. His hobby at that time - and it was more than a hobby, he was both knowledgeable and passionate about it – was archeology, specifically the ancient Navaho culture. You might know it by the older name - Anasazi. The name Anasazi is out of favor now."

Toby interrupted, "Let's sit down - I'm a little woozy. But please go on, and tell us everything. We have plenty of time."

They found a comfortable grass-padded dry spot on the crest of the little hill. Laura sat with her knees pulled up to her chest and her arms tightly wrapped around them. Toby lay on his side, next to her. They both faced Jacob, who was appropriately sitting crossed-legged, framed by the spectacular vista of the long estuary to the west.

Then, as they settled in, something happened to Toby. He started to get dizzy and to drift away. He went out-of-body. He floated above the three of them, Castenada style. He watched from above as Jacob told the story of the early years of Dixon; the god, the time-traveler, the ancient Anasazi priest.

"Hey!" Laura said, shaking his shoulder. "You okay? Didn't you hear me?"

He looked at her blankly and took a deep breath, trying to return to her world. "Sorry, I just got a little dizzy. It was probably the sauna. What did you say Jacob?"

"Me? I haven't said anything since we sat down. Laura asked you if you were okay, and you kinda spaced."

"Wow, sorry," Toby said, wishing his little delusional moment was the real world, and that this world was the illusion. "I'd better sit up. Go on, I'll be fine."

"You were telling us about Dixon and the Anasazi," Laura said, priming the pump.

"Right. My mom ... her name was Kate, she's been gone for a long time now. She died when I was ten, cancer." Jacob paused and looked down for a moment. "My mom was an archeologist. But she didn't have an actual degree. She just picked it up over the years. At first, when she was young, she was a hired helper at the digs. But she was a smart lady and she studied hard. After a while, she was given more important jobs at the digs and started being the local person in charge. And that led to an official position with the tribe, as the tribes' on-site representative."

Jacob stopped for a minute and looked back, out across the open estuary. Laura reached out and placed her hand on his knee.

Jacob rubbed his eyes, turned back and gave Laura a wan smile. "Sorry, I haven't talked about her in a long time," he said quietly. "Anyway, at that time Duval wasn't a rich man. He had a good job and I'm sure he was well paid, but it wasn't like now. He would come to where we were, near Mesa Verde, in southwest Colorado. Do you know where that is?"

"I've been there," Toby said. "Where all the cliff dwellings are. It's an amazing place. Have you seen it?" he asked, looking at Laura. She shook her head.

"That's where we lived. And that's where the biggest population of Ancient Navahos had lived," he said. "I guess I should tell you this part, otherwise the rest won't make any sense. I never knew my dad. He was a real doctor of archeology from back east somewhere. He and my mom had a fling one summer while working together at a dig. She never told him about me, and he never came back. But for some reason, mom gave me his name – Horton."

Jacob plucked a stalk of grass, twirled it between his fingers and went on, "Duval would spend a month each summer at Mesa Verde. He did that for almost ten years. He and Mom became very close friends. But don't jump to any conclusions – Duval has told me that they were never ... you know, intimate. And I believe him. Then my Mom died.

"Duval still wasn't a rich man then, but he provided for me. I lived at Mesa Verde with my uncle. Duval would send him money – I never really knew how much. And every year he would take me on a trip somewhere; to New York, or fishing up here in the Northwest. I moved into Durango and lived with some cousins so I could go to a better high school. And then he paid for my college. I went to the University of New Mexico and got a degree in archeology. I have to confess though, I wasn't that interested in it. I did it for him, or them - my Mom too.

"Then, after college, Duval hit the jackpot with Switch.Net, so I went to work for him doing different things. I can tell you about that later if you're interested. And now this!" Jacob raised his hands and gestured in all directions. "Horton Resources!"

"Like a son," Laura said.

"Well, in some ways, yes. And in some ways, he's like a father to me. But not really," Jacob said. "He's always been kind to me, but he's never been affectionate. He stays a step away from that."

"How about you?" Laura asked. "How do you regard him?"

"Whew," Jacob said, looking uncomfortable. "I don't ever talk about these kinds of things." He took a deep breath and went on. "I've been around him for a long time, so I know him – in my world I know him well, maybe not in all of his worlds. But what I know is that he has enormous power. He makes things happen. People are drawn to him and want to help him, to work for him, to do what he wants. It's not like a cult, because he doesn't ever ask people to 'believe' in him – they just do. Because of who he is."

"So who is he?" Toby blurted. "A god? An ancient Navaho priest? An alien?"

Jacob recoiled. He looked at Laura for help and then back at Toby. "Huh," Jacob said. "I'm sorry, I didn't mean to make you ..."

"Where'd that come from?" Laura interrupted, looking sternly at Toby. "Are you sure you're okay?"

Toby rubbed his face. "Give me a minute," he said and stood up. He walked a few steps toward the river, stopped, stretched and did some belly breathing, trying to remove the cobwebs that lingered from his recent visit to the spirit world.

"Sorry, I'm a little dizzy; the brain is wobbly I guess. Probably lack of food and sleep, and that sauna. I'm going to need some rest soon, but I'm okay, for a while," he said, and sat back down next to Laura. "Please go on, Jacob."

Laura studied Toby for a moment and then turned back to Jacob. "Since you're so close to Dixon, you must know what's going on?" she asked, tentatively.

Jacob nodded slowly, staring at the ground. "Yes, I know."

"What happened with the Indians, Jain and Patel? Do you know if they were able to get any vaccine?" Toby asked.

"No, they didn't get any," Jacob said, and looked up. "I think I can tell you this now. The V-boxes never contained any vaccine."

Laura shook her head while muttering an inaudible obscenity. "Shakespeare should write this up. What a Comedy of Errors. Except it is about as far from funny as you can get. You mean to tell me that all those people were killed for useless boxes? And now *everyone* is going to die because of it?"

Jacob once again fixed his gaze on the ground in front of him and found another piece of grass to shred, choosing not to comment.

"Jacob, what do you think about this ... this, event? Not from what Dixon has told you. What do *you* really think?" Laura asked.

Jacob looked up and returned her gaze with equal intensity. "Understand that I am Navaho. I have a different view of the world – of earth – than you do. I regard the whole earth as sacred. We people are only a small part of it. We don't own it. But we *are* destroying it. This is obvious beyond any reasonable argument. Left unchecked, humanity will destroy the whole world. It will become as lifeless as the moon.

"The average person, even while accepting the fact that we are destroying our only home, will say things like: 'We will be better' or 'We will change our ways' or 'We will invent new things that will save us'."

Jacob put his palms on his knees, leaned toward Laura and continued. "So ... let me ask you something, Doctor Sundgren. Do you believe those claims? Do you think that humanity will change so radically, and so suddenly, that they will save our earth? Do you really believe that?"

Laura was speechless. Jacob had summed up the entire four week session at Haida Gwaii in a one minute speech. And now she had to answer. She had to get off the fence that she, and all the others at Haida Gwaii, had perched on over these last weeks. She looked at Toby, wondering if he could help. Toby remained silent, waiting for her to answer this primal question that they had somehow avoided asking themselves.

Laura brought her knees up to her chest and again wrapped her arms around them. Her head turned slowly back and forth. She stared first at the ground and then rolled her head back and gazed skyward. She gasped: a decision made, which now had to be spoken. It was the intellectual equivalent of giving birth, and every bit as painful.

"No!" she said forcefully. "No, I don't."

Jacob slowly shifted his gaze to Toby. Toby shook his head.

"Then, what would you do?" Jacob asked Laura.

"Don't ask me that. I can't deal with that question."

"Exactly the right answer, Doctor Sundgren," Jacob said. "And the same answer everyone else in this world would give. Everyone else! Everyone else except Duval Dixon."

Jacob gracefully uncoiled his legs and rose, towering above them, signaling the end of the interrogation.

"You see, I'm not upset that this has happened. From the beginning, I have believed it was the right thing - the only thing - to do. I think that if you are honest with yourselves, you will agree."

Jacob turned and they followed him silently back up the path.

"Jacob, thanks," Laura said, as they stopped in front of the small cabin.

"We can clean this up," Toby said. "Maybe you should check on Mothershed."

"Good, I need to start dinner anyway. You two try to stay awake for another hour. We are having a feast in your honor tonight – elk roast."

"Is there clean bedding in here?" Laura asked, anxiously awaiting the moment that she could finally climb into a fresh, real bed.

"Yup - inside. After a while, I'll come back down with some lamps and show you how they work."

"Jacob," Toby said. "Before you go - what do you know about the others? We know about Mallory, Rabinovich, Darby and Nguyen. What about the others?"

"Okay, I already told you about Duval. Justice Brown is safe. We don't know anything about Wyndi Rehn; no one seems to know where she is. Doctor Contreras is with Secretary Solene. He had her flown back from Europe when the killing started. They are both safely hidden at Malabar Farm - I'll tell you about that later. Dr. Mothershed is up at the cabin. I think that's it."

Jacob turned and disappeared up the path.

Laura reached out for Toby. She put her arms around him and they held each other tight in front of their new home. "I have one other confession to make," she said and pulled a step away.

"What was the first one?" Toby asked.

"The first one was that I agree with Dixon's decision - I can't believe I just said that. But somehow Jacob made me reach in and find my truth. Forget all the posturing. It is the only solution. I do understand that."

"Jacob made it simple didn't he?" Toby asked. "Maybe too simple."

"Too simple? You better not let Occam hear you say that," Laura said, a hint of a smile reappearing.

"So what's the second confession?" Toby asked.

"I decided this while we were resting after the sauna. Thinking about all we have been through in these past few weeks, I decided something else. I decided that I want to live. I don't want to die."

"Good, I don't want you to die either."

"No, no … it's more than that. I mean that I want to do whatever it takes to stay alive. Before, I thought about how I should go help people as this horror unfolds, you know – doctor's oath stuff. But now, I just want to keep myself, and you, alive. And if that means staying here for years, then that's what I want to do. Do you understand?"

Toby stared at Laura and tears filled his eyes. He could not imagine being more in love than he was at this moment. He walked back to her, grabbed her shoulders and said, "I love you! Let's get married!"

"Married?"

"Yes, married. All I have to do is carry you over the threshold – it's the new law. Then we'll be married."

"Okay," she said and kissed him hard. "I love you too!"

Toby picked her up, stepped up the porch stairs and through the door. "And tomorrow I want to tell you my plan for raising those squirrels."

Part 4

Chapter 27

The five weeks of the Eden Flu
Late July - August, 2020

Seemingly of its own accord - as if the mechanisms of the great machine knew where to draw the line - the United States conformed to the advice that Dr. Maxwell Stanton had given, and fell back far enough to protect the essentials. For the most part, the electricity stayed on. For the most part, the water and sewage systems continued to function. In America at least, typhus and cholera stayed away.

The world called in sick. Everyone stayed in bed, and yet the five strains of the Eden flu still managed to circulate. Regardless of any and all precautions, they flowed around the world, unrestrained. Wave after wave after wave surged through the human population, exactly as Dr. Stanton had predicted.

Travel, except by private automobile, ground to a complete halt. All social gatherings were canceled: all sports, all concerts, all meetings. Virtually all businesses were closed. Offices were dark. Restaurants were shut. The corner cleaner was locked up. The only local businesses that tried to stay open were grocery stores, pharmacies, and bars. But without deliveries, they soon ran out of stock.

Enough food kept moving thru the system, along with all the stockpiled supplies that each person had been exhorted to hold in reserve for the various potential natural disasters, and supplemented by the vast store of fat that most American's held around their bellies, to keep the people from starvation.

The electronic media kept functioning, but only just. The national news producers managed an hour of live newscast daily, with whomever on that day was well enough to deliver. The remainder of the daily broadcasting was recorded, either repeats or movies. The newspaper business, already on its last legs, had to shut down completely. There simply weren't enough healthy people to print or distribute the paper. The newspapers never returned.

The bloggers went nuts. Conspiracies abounded, and rumors circulated at the speed of light. The president had died over a dozen times already, though she eventually survived.

People perished in great numbers. Famous people, babies, doctors, policeman, soldiers, scientists, parents, children — no one was safe. Being sick could not be avoided, so no one tried. The only goal was to survive. In the end, sixteen percent of America's population, almost fifty million, and over twenty-two percent of the world's population, failed to reach that one-and-only goal.

The dead were buried without ceremony. Mass graves, some holding over a hundred thousand bodies, were carved into Mother Earth, then filled in by herds of bulldozers driven by space-suited men. Unmarked and cordoned-off, no one would or could bring flowers. No visitors would ever be allowed.

President Pittman survived, as did her sister. But Cam Mitchell, who had received a new liver only a year earlier, was one of the first to go. Congress was hit exceedingly hard. The automatic re-election that incumbency had come to guarantee had raised the average age of all Congresspersons to over sixty. Fully half of the Senate, and almost that same figure in the House of Representatives, perished. The TV talking-heads and the bloggers claimed that the radical pruning of Congress was the biggest single benefit of the pandemic. Unfortunately, the mortality rate of lobbyists held closer to the average.

Dr. Sydney Lawrence and Secretary Ross were killed in a car crash on the Potomac Parkway. A feverish, hallucinating, ninety-two year-old Senator from Mississippi lost control of his SUV and hit them head-on.

Then, five weeks later, and almost as suddenly as it had began - it ended. Because it had started everywhere at the same time, everybody was on the same cycle. Except for those still fighting for their lives, the survivors as a group looked up one day, saw the sun, and said "Wow - I think I'm better". Their overwhelming emotion was euphoria, not sadness as might have been expected. "It's over and I survived" was the dominant view. Of course, everyone had friends and relatives who had perished, but for the survivors, these were unavoidable - and thus guiltless deaths. Parents of lost children had the biggest problems. But some surviving spouses, in their most private moments, saw the loss of their partners as an opportunity.

The people quickly went about the business of restarting the machinery of mankind. There were jobs in abundance. Cheap housing, furniture, and cars flooded the market. The activity in real estate was unprecedented. Of course, not all segments of society participated in the boom, but in general, the mood of the world, and especially of the U.S., was positive. "It's over and I'm alive" was forefront in the hearts and minds of the survivors.

And yet the biggest question of all remained unanswered. Where did it come from?

Chapter 28

Week five of the Eden Flu
Tuesday, August 25th, 2020
The CDC, Atlanta

"I guess congratulations are in order Dr. Stanton," said Milos Papadakas, head of the FBI's bioterrorism unit, as he and his depleted team of six seated themselves in the same conference room they had last occupied almost five weeks earlier.

Dr. Maxwell Stanton, the newly appointed Executive Director of the CDC, nodded acknowledgement. He, Andy Hobbs, and Sharif Baku, along with the six FBI agents, had finally resumed their discussion of bioterrorism. Brenner and Jenkins, the two agents who had gone straight to the hospital five weeks ago, had not survived. Nor had Helen Glick, the computer modeling lead in Atlanta.

Dr. Stanton and Hobbs had been healthy, and back at work, for over a week. The CDC had sustained less than five percent casualties, probably due to the practice of significant overdosing of the readily available antivirals.

But to Max, the losses were still significant. Besides Glick and Dr. Lawrence, Laura had not returned from her vacation. She had never even been heard from. And since no one knew where she had gone, nothing could be done to try and find out what had happened to her.

So Max invented his own story: Laura on a remote beach in Mexico, working day and night to help the locals survive the flu. Then, completely exhausted and very ill, she lay down on the beach and died. The tide came in and washed her out to sea – a Norse burial of sorts.

Though physically drained from fighting the various viruses, the FBI team was charged-up emotionally. They had the responsibility of finding out the answer to the big question: Who had done this awful thing? They desperately wanted to be the heroes that brought the person, or group, responsible for killing 1.5 billion people to justice.

"Let's get started," Papadakas said. "I've read your reports. So, is it your conclusion now that the weird-science option we discussed before is not possible?"

Max nodded and exhaled slowly through pursed lips. "Every scientist we have asked to look into this can't see how it could happen. They can't imagine a situation where five viable novel type A influenza viruses could be created spontaneously and accidentally."

"How sure are you?" Papadakas asked.

"Well, hell, I'm completely sure. It could not have happened that way. Period, the end. You can take it to the bank."

Papadakas smiled. "I appreciate your confidence."

"So, what does that leave us with?" Max asked. "What about the terrorists?"

"It's not terrorists, or at least not any of the usual suspects," Papadakas said. "No one has taken credit for this. In fact, everyone has gone out of their way to distance themselves. As far as we're concerned, no one we know of could have pulled this off anyway. So, in the spirit of certainty - it's not terrorists. One hundred percent sure."

"Another government, then?"

"Same answer: no way. Another government would only do something like this as a smoke screen for some other action, like an invasion. Nobody has done anything like that. And we absolutely would have heard something through our surveillance assets."

"That leaves God, and the Aliens, as the prime suspects then?" Hobbs asked.

"God, Aliens, and the mysterious MPR radicals," Papadakas said. "So, based on this new short list of suspects, my group has been assigned the MPR angle. The MPR concept is the only context where any of us can see a motive for this."

"So who's got the Gods and Aliens detail?" Hobbs asked.

"Don't laugh," Papadakas said, smiling. "Langley actually has a team looking into the Alien possibilities. And we did talk about a team to explore

God's role, but we could only think of one way to get a meeting – and no one would volunteer. If you're interested, Mr. Hobbs, I could recommend you."

Hobbs had been had. "No Thanks," he said. "I'm needed here."

"We could find somebody," Max said, piling on.

Max turned back to Papadakas. "So, MPR: what can we do to help?"

"We have a couple of things to discuss," Papadakas said. "Can you tell us anything else you've learned about the viruses. We have your latest reports, but they don't help much – too technical. But can you think of anything else – gut feels, hunches? Anything at all?"

"Is there any way to determine how it was made, or where?" One of the other agents interjected. "What I mean is – is there such a thing as a marker, some piece of it that could give us a clue as to it's origin."

"Other than the H and N numbers – and I think you already understand those - there are eight RNA segments that carry the viruses' genetic information. But these eight segments frequently get combined, mixed, with other flu viruses' RNA segments. We call that 'reassortment'. And because of that process, we don't have any standard blueprints to follow," Max said. "So, the answer is no. Other than the fact that these viruses are unique to us, there is nothing else that could be considered a clue."

"So there's nothing else that you've found?" Papadakas asked again.

"Look, we've only been back at work a few days. Give us a little more time," Max said. "Believe me; we're doing everything we can. We have several things we want to look into. For instance, there is one thing I just noticed yesterday."

"What's that?" Papadakas asked.

"I was looking at all the latest pictures of the five viruses, and I noticed an anomaly on the surface. All five seemed to have the same anomaly - a third bump, like the H and N bumps, but smaller. It will take us a while to figure it out. But that's just one example of the kinds of things we intend to follow up on."

"Good - keep us posted," Papadakas said. "And I do understand that you have just gotten back to work. The same is true for us."

Papadakas opened a file he had in front of him. "I've got one more question, then we'll get out of your way."

"Shoot."

"I told you that Brenner was our only analyst tracking the MPR crazies. Now that he's gone, we have a lot of catching up to do. But the night he was hospitalized, he left me a short note. He died early the next morning, so I couldn't ask him anything about it."

Papadakas handed the note to Max. "Do you know anything about this?"

Max took the note and read it. It said: "Milos - I remembered something, might be important. Look up the file on Ruth Kald."

"No, never heard of her," Max said, passing the note to Hobbs. Hobbs read it quickly and shook his head.

"We looked up the file, but unfortunately there wasn't much in it. It only contained a request for our field office in Seattle to try to locate Kald, and the results of that attempt," Papadakas said.

"This is all we know: sometime in 2008 Kald put up a web site that included the text of her book – a book that was never published anywhere else. Also on the web site was an interactive forum discussing the concept of her book. That's about all we know, except that Brenner thought it was important enough to send a team from the Seattle field office to look for her."

"Did they find her?" Max asked.

"No, they never found out a thing out about her. Ruth Kald didn't exist, at least as Ruth Kald. And the web site, after being up for only a few weeks, just disappeared. The FBI team couldn't find any remnants of it. They finally traced the location of the server. According to them, it was on a machine in an outbuilding, a shop, on a farm north of Seattle owned by a farmer named Chuck Métis.

"Métis was an amateur techie. He had a couple of servers that he used to host neighbors' and friends' web sites and a couple of local environmental sites, things like that. He said that he had never heard of Ruth Kald. After looking into it, the FBI team determined that Métis had no knowledge of Kald's site. Kald had somehow dropped it on his server without his knowledge. He didn't really pay much attention to his machines."

Papadakas paused and took a drink. "But here's where it gets a little interesting. The site disappeared because Métis' shop burned down. No

cause for the fire was ever found. Métis though it was suspicious. And then
- that's the end of the trail. We can't find any other mention of Ruth Kald,
or of her book, anywhere."

"Doesn't seem like much to me," Hobbs said. "Is that really worth
looking into?"

"No, it's not much at all," Papadakas said. "But Brenner though it was
important enough to write me a note about it before he died. That must
not have been easy for him. And there was one more thing that caught my
interest: Kald's website, and her book, had a name. She called it '*The Eden
Proposition*'. Ring any bells?"

Max and Hobbs shook their heads. But it did sound ominous, Max
thought.

Chapter 29

Later that same day
Tuesday evening, August 25th, 2020
Malabar Farm

"Still no word from Dixon?" Dr. Contreras asked.

Justice Martha Cartman Brown had re-seated herself on the porch across from Contreras and Secretary Solene, after bringing out a round of gin and tonics. It had been a warm day in central Oregon. The G & T's and the shaded porch were a welcome relief, especially for Contreras who had just hiked the three miles from her Malabar Farm cottage to Solene's farmhouse. This was the fourth consecutive Tuesday evening that she had made the hike. It had become the highlight of her week.

That first week, a week after she had made her pledge to not let anyone die at Malabar – a pledge that she had honored, so far – she had been delighted to find Justice Brown seated on the porch with Secretary Solene. Dixon and his henchmen had faked Justice Brown's death – an easy thing to do at that time – and had spirited her out to Solene's farmhouse hideout. They had agreed then that Dr. Contreras would sneak away every Tuesday evening to give them an update on the progress of the flu, and other things, at Malabar.

"No nothing yet," Solene said, answering Contreras' question about Dixon.

After faking Justice Brown's death, the two security men then did the same for Dixon. He had died in Dallas. His body had joined many others in one of the mass graves. Or so the story went.

The security team then drove Dixon to Santa Fe, and, at Dixon's insistence, they dropped him off there alone, at a motel. Then they went on to Malabar, where they joined Mark Dunn at WPSS, bringing Malabar's armed forces up to full strength – all four of them. Queried after returning, the only thing they would say was: "Dixon said he would be in touch."

"So how is week three of your house arrest going?" Sofia asked Justice Brown.

"Well, I'm still here, and thank God for those book tablets," Justice Brown said.

"I don't have one yet. Do they really work?" Sofia asked.

"Beautifully," Solene said. "They're well lit. You can make the font any size you want, and download a book in a minute. You can mark your place, highlight and extract passages. I love mine. It's the best thing since the iPod."

"The tablets Dixon left here have over ten thousand titles," Justice Brown added. "The hardest part is deciding what to read. Or have read to you - if you don't mind a slight Scandinavian accent."

"And over in storage at the commissary there are several copies of the entire Harvard project. I can't remember the name, but it theoretically contains everything ever published. Well, not everything, but everything deemed valuable. Something like a hundred thousand titles."

"Only English titles I presume?" Sophia said.

"I think that's correct," Solene said.

"No matter now, I guess," Sofia said. "In less than a year, there will be no other language."

"Also correct," Solene said, and took a long pull at his drink.

That evening, Professor Gil "Vandy" Vanderham watched the woman he knew as Dr. Silvia Montero walk past his office on her way toward the river. He thought this might be the third or fourth Tuesday evening she had made that walk. He knew for a fact that she took the same route last week, as he had watched her from his kayak on the river, upstream of the bridge. He already decided to follow her if she went that way again and so he grabbed his binoculars and headed quickly down to the river.

It had been four weeks since that strange meeting at WPPS with Secretary Solene. Vanderham kept silent about the things he heard, and the things he thought, after the meeting. Mostly because he and everyone else at Malabar had gotten sick, though not as bad as the rest of the world - the "experimental vaccine" must have done some good. But now, there were even more questions. Duval Dixon was dead, and Secretary Solene had not returned his emails and was reportedly missing, another presumed victim of the flu.

So if Dixon and Solene were both dead, why was Dr. Montero sneaking over to WPPS every Tuesday evening? Vanderham thought he had better find out.

He slipped across the river and into a field north and west of the WPPS shed. A car was just leaving the building, driving on the back road up to the old farmhouse on the hill.

During his four years at Malabar, Vanderham had visited that farmhouse several times. The former owners, Hugo Maltby and his wife Emma, had invited him up for dinner twice. Vanderham guessed that they had wanted to know what the hell was going on at Malabar. Maltby was retired and wanted to sell, just like all the others up the road. Eventually, he got his wish.

Vanderham knew a way to get to the farmhouse by circling north, through an abandoned field, though he felt silly running in a crouch behind the Scotch Broom bushes that had grown up in Maltby's unused pasture. He came up on the house from the backside, behind the old woodshed.

He then had a decision to make. He could stay behind the woodshed and listen, or he could try to creep out across the yard to get a view of the porch. But the lawn option could result in his being seen, and he already felt foolish enough just being there, so he opted to listen.

There were three different voices coming from the porch, two were female, and the other was the unmistakable voice of Secretary Manute Solene. Vanderham would now bet money that Solene had been at the farmhouse the whole time, hiding. That's why he had been reported missing. But why?

Vandy took a deep breath - only one way to find out he decided. He hid the binoculars behind the shed, and then circled back far enough down the hill to intersect the driveway. Then he marched up the driveway to the farmhouse as if he had been invited. This should be interesting, he thought.

Solene saw him first. "Well, Well," he said with a wry smile. "We have a visitor." Sofia looked wide-eyed at Justice Brown. It was too late for her to slip away.

Vanderham's long slow-motion gait took him up the porch stairs two at a time. Solene barely had time to walk over and offer his hand.

"Professor Vanderham," Solene said smiling. "What a surprise."

Vanderham noted the lack of the word "pleasant" in Solene's greeting. "Good evening," Vanderham said. He nodded to the ladies, who remained seated.

"Professor, this is Martha Cartman Brown – Justice Brown," Solene said. "Professor Vanderham."

"An honor – and a surprise to meet you, Madam Justice," Vanderham said, accepting her outstretched hand.

"And of course you already know Dr. Contreras," Solene said. The "oops" light went on immediately.

"Dr. Contreras," Vanderham said. He walked over and extended his hand. "Perhaps we haven't met after all."

Solene's voice changed to a resigned, no-bullshit tone. "Have a seat, we'll get you a drink," he said, walking over to the screened door. "Mark, could you do me a favor and bring out another round of G and T's? Four this time."

"Well now, this is … fascinating," Vanderham said when Solene sat back down. "You're dead," he said, looking at Justice Brown. "You're missing," he said to Solene. "And you're someone else," he said, smiling at Dr. Contreras.

"Very confusing, I imagine," Solene said.

An awkward silence followed; neither Solene or Vanderham wanted to go next. The women deferred. Mark appeared with the drinks and then walked out to sit on a bench under a tree in the front yard. Vanderham guessed that he was out of hearing range, but he did have a clear view of the proceedings. Vanderham had also noticed the holster bulge under his sweater. This may not have been such a good idea after all, he thought.

Vanderham took a sip of his drink, and then looked directly at Solene. "Why don't you just tell me what is going on here? The truth, this time, please," he asked, trying to strike the balance between "forceful" and "non-threatening".

Solene looked at the ground and then back to Vanderham. "I don't see that we have any alternative. Do you?" he asked and then looked at the others for approval, or perhaps another story that might work - he was fresh out of ideas.

"You could have him shot," Justice Brown said, and took a sip from her drink.

Vanderham looked at her and stopped breathing. He didn't think she could be serious, and yet it didn't appear that she was trying to be funny. The hair stood up on the back of his neck.

The truth was that Justice Brown had not yet accepted her position in this horrifying event. Dixon had convinced her to come to Malabar. She had agreed reluctantly. She was the last of the Haida Gwaii participants still in circulation. Dixon insisted that it was inevitable that the authorities would figure it out. It would be very difficult for her if she ended up being the one with the all of the blame. And besides, it wouldn't make any difference to the final outcome – that die had been cast.

She understood the logic, and so she had agreed to come, and now found herself sitting on the front porch of the Malabar safe-house. But she had not resolved her anger. Besides the obvious – the Eden Proposition itself – she still seethed over the killings of the people who had been at Haida Gwaii, especially Dixon's brutal and unapologetic murder of the Indians, Jain, Patel and their cohorts.

Then there was the matter of the vaccine. Dixon had said he wouldn't give it to her unless she agreed to come to Malabar. Survival is always a strong argument. But any illusion that she and Dixon had a special relationship was destroyed. More fuel, several pounds of plutonium worth in fact, for her free-floating anger. So, her comment about having Vanderham shot was really directed at Solene – just another way to express her overall disapproval. Of course, Vanderham didn't know this.

Solene waited a few seconds before speaking. Let Vanderham sweat for a moment, he thought. You never know, it might be useful.

"I'm pretty sure she's kidding," he said, with a smile.

Justice Brown gave Solene a smirk. Vanderham couldn't tell if it was the humorous variety or the fuck-you variety. He had never been very good at reading women.

"I don't think I want to be part of this conversation," Justice Brown said, rising from her chair. "The two of you can handle it without me. I'll be in my room," she said and walked away without another word.

"Well, where to start ..." Solene began. "Dr. Contreras, why don't you give Professor Vanderham a full explanation of the flu – all of them. Full disclosure, please. I'm going to go in and speak with Justice Brown, just to make sure she's okay. I'll be right back," he said, grabbing the glasses as he went in.

"It's Sofia," Dr. Contreras said. "My real name is Sofia Contreras. I'm sorry about the deception. You will understand why it was necessary when we finish. It's a long story I'm afraid ..."

Chapter 30

Two Weeks Later
Tuesday, September 8th, 2020
The CDC, Atlanta

"Sorry for the short notice," Papadakas said. "I'm glad you were here."

"You got lucky," Max said. "I've been mostly in Washington since you left. It's only been a few weeks, but I already hate this job. Come in please."

Papadakas stepped into the conference room trailed by two of his team and a third man dressed in camouflage. "This is the gentleman I told you about on the phone," Papadakas said. "Dr. Stanton, please meet Robbie Olds. Robbie, this is Max Stanton, the new head of CDC - but maybe not for long."

Olds was a large man, strong not fat, tanned, mid-seventies, and sporting a crew-cut – the first one Max had seen in quite a while. "Call me Robbie, please Dr. Stanton – none of my friends do," he said, flashing a compelling smile that surrounded a full set of too-white choppers.

Max smiled back. He already liked this guy.

"Have a seat everyone," Max said. "We have water on the table. Robbie: this is Andy Hobbs, my sidekick."

Olds stuck out his hand. "Good to meetcha Doctor Sidekick," he said and sat down heavily.

Stanton wondered if Olds was trying to be funny, or was just hard of hearing. He hoped it wasn't dementia, although it seemed possible. Dr. Sidekick? He'd have to use that one – Hobbs had just gotten a new name.

"Let me get you up to speed. I'm anxious for you to hear what Robbie has to say about Ruth Kald," Papadakas began. "Since our last meeting, we had made no progress finding out anything about Kald. Then, last week, someone suggested trying to find Robbie. Robbie was Brenner's boss until 2008, when he retired. It was a bitch trying to locate him, though. Yesterday we finally found him in the Nevada high-desert. He made us promise not to tell exactly where."

"Don't even think about it," Robbie said. "I'd have to kill you all, if anyone found out."

"Robbie – we were there yesterday," Papadakas said.

"Better watch your back then," Robbie said.

Now it was clear to Max that not all the cylinders were firing behind those bright white choppers.

"Anyway, Robbie remembered some things about Kald that sounded important. Some things that might help you. And, frankly, some things that scared us," Papadakas said. "So Robbie, before you shoot us, tell us what you know about Ruth Kald."

The pasted-on grin disappeared from Olds' sun-weathered face. He suddenly looked competent.

"I read the book, Kald's book – *The Eden Proposition*. I thought it was damn good, in fact," Olds said. "This was back in oh-eight I believe," he said and paused.

It looked to Max as though he went away for a moment.

Olds returned and went on, "It was the year before, that would be oh-seven, that we started tracking the MPR people. They had been around before that, but some bigwig in D.C. got a wild hair and thought we needed to have someone assigned full time. It fell into my DBS group - that's Domestic Bioterrorism Surveillance - and I assigned Brenner to be the agent in charge. He was competent, but not an original thinker, if you get my drift.

"Anyway, one day he came into my office and showed me *The Eden Proposition* web site. He'd followed some threads from some chat rooms that were talking around the fringes of MPR and bumped into it. The website was well done, very professional looking. And it was from what we called the 'radical' MPR faction."

"What does that mean?" Max asked.

"Well, we put the MPR people into two groups; the pragmatists and the radicals. The pragmatists thought any significant reduction in population was a good thing. The basic idea was it would reduce the demand for resources and buy time until a better solution came along."

"Sounds pretty radical to me," Hobbs offered.

"No, not compared to Kald's group. The radicals argued that the population needed to be reduced to only a handful of people, fewer than a thousand. Their premise was that the basic systems, that's what they called them – systems," Olds said, and drifted away again.

After too many moments had passed, Max wanted to go over and whack Olds' head, like a balky blender, to get him going again, but settled instead for a question.

"Systems – what systems?"

"Sorry, I was just trying to remember," Olds said. "They were talking about the systems that supported the culture: the economic system – free markets, the system of government – democracy, organized religion. Those were the systems. The radicals thought that these were the problem. They believed these systems needed to be changed in a significant way in order to establish a culture that could be sustainable over the long run. And, they believed that these systems were like a virus themselves: that their primary goal was simply to continue to exist. Therefore the system itself was designed to resist any meaningful change. Probably easiest to see in something like the organized religions of the world. May I?" Olds asked, pointing to a bottled water on the table.

"Of course," Max said.

Olds took the bottle and slipped it into one of the large pockets in his camouflage pants.

"That night, I decided I'd take a look at Kald's book. I finished it the next day. It was realistic enough to be scary. The premise was that this mega-wealthy, slightly eccentric man, one of those internet billionaire types, decides that the radical MPR concept is the only hope for the planet, and therefore the only hope for human beings to survive in the long term. He decides that the government would never do such a thing, or any other institution for that matter, and that it would take someone like him to do it: an individual with the financial resources, and the guts, to pull it off," Olds said. He pulled the bottle of water from his pocket, opened it, took a drink, and placed it back on the table.

"But he doesn't know how to kill everybody, so he gathers a group of scientists, people who know this stuff, together on a ranch somewhere and gets them to figure it out for him. He tricks them by making it into a game of some kind ..."

Max shot straight up out of his chair. "What?" he shouted. "What did you say - a game?"

"Yes, I said he had them play a game of some kind, to trick them," Olds said, looking bewildered. "Is there something wrong with that?"

Max stood and stared angrily at Papadakas. "What is this! Are you fucking with me?"

Hobbs stood up and moved to the back of the room. He thought Max might be going postal.

Papadakas was seriously confused. Instinctively, he also stood up and moved back a step.

"What's the problem?" Papadakas asked. "Dr. Stanton – are you all right?"

Stanton looked over at the cowering Hobbs and realized he was scaring them. He folded his arms and paced along the wall, trying to think.

He stopped next to Hobbs and turned back to Papadakas, who was frozen in the same spot. "Okay, I don't have time for any bullshit. I've had it up to here with bullshit lately, so tell me what is going on. Mr. Olds, are you telling me the truth and are you sure it was in 2008 that you read this book?"

Olds had his competent look on. "Look, I know that I'm not always on top of things these days. I'm not an idiot. And to be frank, I have more trouble with the present than I do with the past. The past is pretty damn clear. And yes, it's the truth - and yes, it was 2008."

Max put his hands, palms down, on the top of his head. "Holy shit," he said and walked slowly back to his seat. Dots were springing up everywhere in his mind. Not all the connections were made yet, but he knew they would be soon.

"Okay, finish the story please," Max said. "Then I'll tell you who is responsible for this flu."

"You know who did it?" Papadakas said, incredulous.

"I think so, but I want to hear the rest of the story."

Papadakas sat back down, "Robbie, go on."

"Well, after the conference of the scientists, this rich guy goes away for several years and develops a virus, from the info he got from the scientists. A virus that can kill everybody. Once he has the virus in hand and actually has a way to kill everyone, except for the few he'll keep alive to start the 'second age' – that's what she called it – then he has to decide if he should really do it."

"Let me guess," Max interrupted. "In order to decide, he calls together another conference of big names: senators, religious leaders, people like that. A sort of trial for mankind."

"I thought you hadn't heard of Kald. Did you read the book?" Olds asked.

"Am I right?"

"Yes, that's exactly what happens. That's where the book ended, and the web site took over. The great debate about whether it was time to start over was held on the web site. It was interactive. Anyone could pose an argument, and others would debate it. It was well thought-out stuff. And it seemed like quite a few people participated. Then, a few weeks later, the web site just disappeared. And that was it," Olds said. "So - you *have* read it then."

"No, I haven't," Max said. "What about the virus, what did Kald say it was?"

"I don't recall exactly. But remember, my job was bioterrorism surveillance, so I was interested in what she proposed for the virus," Olds said. "It seemed to me that Kald had done only enough research to be able to use a few technical medical terms. You know - so she could create something plausible to the average reader. But even with my level of knowledge, I could tell she was just making up stuff that couldn't really be done. That wasn't her point. All she wanted to do was to set up a believable context in order to hold the big debate on her web site."

Max nodded; that made sense.

"But I do remember that she called her virus a 'Trojan Horse,'" Olds said, leaning forward and putting his elbows on the table. "It looked like one thing when you caught it, and then it did something else once it was inside you."

"That's the part that scared us," Papadakas interjected. "Is that possible?"

More dots, more connections.

"Yes, it's possible. And as of right now – I'll bet its even likely," Max said and exhaled slowly. "Mr. Olds, you are a hero. You've connected all the dots. Now I know who did this and why," he said, and turned to his sidekick. "Just like I told you Hobbs – once we had all the information, this would all make sense."

Max stood again and walked to the back wall, hands on top of his head. "My God ..." he muttered under his breath, and turned back to the group with another dramatic exhale.

"Duval Dixon," he said.

Papadakas, Hobbs, and the others stared at Dr. Stanton in disbelief. Duval Dixon? How could that be true.

"It's Dixon. He's done this. And I'll bet you anything that our flu viruses are exactly as Robbie just said – a Trojan Horse. My God ..."

"Please Dr. Stanton, settle down, sit down and fill us in," Papadakas said.

"Just one moment," Max said, turning to Hobbs. "Go find one of our network geeks, break into Dr. Sundgren's vmail, and bring back a screen with the last two vmails from Duval Dixon on it. And do it fast."

"Aye-aye, sir," Hobbs said with a mock salute and hustled out the door.

Max turned back to Papadakas and began, "Dixon held both of those meetings. The ones that Robbie said were in *The Eden Proposition*," Max said. "The first meeting, the 'game' Robbie mentioned, took place four years ago on Vancouver Island. One of our epidemiologists, Dr. Laura Sundgren, was there. Dr. Sundgren and I are friends, so she told me about it in some detail. It always seemed odd to us – but we just assumed it was odd because Dixon was odd, and let it go at that."

Max dropped his head and sighed again. The realizations just kept bubbling up. Now he wondered if Laura might be somehow involved. She had been at both meetings, after all.

"The second meeting, the 'trial of mankind', took place in early June of this year. It lasted six weeks. Then, no more than a few days later, the flu descended upon us. Wait till you see the vmails - they'll make your hair stand on end."

"Dr. Stanton, you do know that Duval Dixon is dead, don't you?" one of the FBI team asked.

"Is there a body? Has anyone confirmed the DNA? I'll bet you his entire fortune he's alive somewhere. We'll, actually, I know where," Max said. "He's at his 'Eden.' Wherever that is."

"It seems unlikely that he would give up a hundred billion dollars by faking his own death. There must be a thousand lawyers working the probate by now," the FBI agent said.

Max gave him the don't-be-such-an-idiot smirk. "What the hell good is money when there are only a few thousand people left on Earth? He doesn't care. He's probably watching and laughing at the greedy bastards right now."

A few minutes later, Hobbs returned with a screen. The group gathered around Max as he called up the vmail from Dixon.

They watched Dixon describe the session on "population issues". Reading between the lines, it fit perfectly with *The Eden Proposition*. Max then called up the bio's of the attendees.

"Wait a minute – someone please write these names down," Papadakas said.

"Okay, let's go through the names," Papadakas said after watching the entire vmail. "Read them off please."

"Senator Mallory."

"He died a while back, remember?" an agent said. "Right before the flu started."

"Rabinovich?"

"Same thing," said another agent.

"Do we have a trend here?" Hobbs asked.

They went through the list. No one knew about Mothershed, Contreras, Nguyen, or Benson. All of the others were either known dead, or known missing.

"I'll tell you right now, you won't be able to find any of those four," Max said.

"This is unreal," Papadakas said, shaking his head.

"Robbie, can you recall anything at all in the Ruth Kald investigation that might connect her, or her web site, to Dixon?" Max asked.

"No sir, I can't. I've been trying to connect him ever since you brought up his name. But I can't come up with anything."

"Well, keep trying," Max said. "No way was this a coincidence. Somehow Dixon read *The Eden Proposition*, fell for it, and then made it go away before it became well known."

"We'll put some people on it. We'll try and track down Métis. And maybe someone, somewhere knows who Ruth Kald is. We didn't try that hard to find her last time," Papadakas said. "Dr. Stanton, I know Dixon was a big player in the biotech business, especially in India. What else can you tell us about that?"

Max stared at Papadakas. India, biotech - more dots, more connections.

"Dr. Stanton ..." Papadakas said. Stanton was staring right through him, lost in thought.

"My God, it all fits," Max said. "You need to get over there right away and find out as much as you can."

"To India?"

"Yes, India. Obviously, that's where he built the viruses," Max said. "Wasn't it last year that some Pakistani terrorists blew up that biotech building. Dixon's biotech building! The one where all those scientists died?"

"Yes, last year, but it was terrorists who did it," Papadakas said. "How is that connected?"

"It wasn't terrorists. Dixon did it to cover his tracks. To keep the work secret. He had all the people that worked on making the viruses killed. That's how he could pull this off," Max said. "That part had always mystified me."

"What part?" Papadakas asked.

"The science part - it would take an enormous effort, with a lot of people, to manufacture those five viruses. How can you keep that many people silent? Obviously, that so-called terrorist attack killed them all. Remember, how 'unfortunate' the timing of the explosion was because there was a big meeting of some kind going on in the building at the time?"

Papadakas nodded. It made sense, but that explosion had been investigated. It was a high-profile event, so Papadakas assumed that many smart people had looked into it. His recollection was it was an open-and-shut case. The terrorists had done it, and had even taken credit for it. Papadakas was hesitant to dispute someone else's conclusions. But, then he quickly decided that this was far too important for professional courtesy to apply.

"We'll get together with the CIA later today – it's their turf," Papadakas said. "And, we'll get some teams going to locate the participants, and Dixon. It won't be easy, though. You know that the mass graves cannot be disturbed. the President just made an official decree to that effect. It was heading toward chaos very quickly over that issue."

"What about those Indians that were killed in D.C. right before the flu started?" one of the FBI men asked.

Papadakas nodded, "Right, good call. We need to find out if they were connected to Dixon."

"Gentlemen," Olds interrupted. "I don't mean to go old-school on ya, but this is pretty explosive news. What do think would happen if this Trojan Horse idea got out and people started thinking everyone was going to die. It could be a real mess: anarchy, riots, who knows what else. You had better keep a tight lid on this – if you still know how."

Papadakas hesitated; there were simply too many thoughts swirling around inside his head at that moment. But yes, secrecy - another element to be managed. Olds was correct.

"Of course," he said. "This has to be absolutely secret for the time being. Disclosure of any of this will be decided by the President. I'll brief her tonight. Dr. Stanton, please be available. I'll call you later with a time."

"Milos, you have a lot to do," Max said. "We just have one thing now. We need to find out what's inside that Trojan Horse, before it gets out."

"You'll need to get the NIH involved won't you?" Papadakas asked.

"I'm afraid so," Max said. "They have most of the talent for this sort of thing."

"For the moment however, hold off on contacting them," Papadakas said. "The more I think about the point that Robbie made about the chaos this could inspire, the more I think we need to be extraordinarily careful about who gets involved, and who knows about this. For instance, I'll have to keep it from our esteemed FBI leader, Mr. Moss. He leaks so bad he leaves a trail of water wherever he goes. Somehow, I'll have to get to the President directly."

"I could contact Lucy Kline," Max said. "I think she'll take my call."

"Good, do that," Papadakas said. "Have her figure out how to meet with me privately. And then call me back with the details."

"Maybe I can come up with a story for the NIH that won't involve telling them everything," Max added. "I'll work on that, but I will still need to have someone on the inside that understands the gravity of the situation."

"Okay, we'll get you a name," Papadakas said and stood up to go. "Dr. Stanton, Robbie - this has been extraordinary. My head is spinning. I keep wanting to think that we have made some silly mistake in our reasoning. I keep wanting to think that it couldn't be Duval Dixon who was responsible for killing over a billion people. And, I keep wanting to think that it's not possible for him to have created this 'Trojan Horse' that Ruth Kald imagined. I keep wanting to think we must be wrong. But it's clear - we're not wrong. And we don't have the luxury of second-guessing the conclusions we have come to today, so let's get to work."

"What about me?" Robbie asked.

"You're coming with us," Papadakas said. "As of now only six people know about this. Dr. Stanton understands the reasons for secrecy, and Mr. Hobbs – I'll personally shoot your nuts off if you say anything. Robbie, you're the wild card here. So, your reward for solving the crime of all the centuries is to be placed under arrest."

"I figured," Robbie said. "Probably won't make much difference though. We're all gonna die soon anyway."

"Don't be so sure, Mr. Olds," Max said, rising to walk them out. "A lot of 'maybes' remain. Maybe we are wrong. Maybe Ruth Kald and Dixon have nothing to do with this. But if they do, then maybe Dixon's 'Trojan Horse' won't work. The science behind this concept is a stretch, after all. And if it is Dixon, and his virus does work, then maybe we can figure it out in time to stop it. We've come a long way today. Nothing says we can't go a long way tomorrow, and the next day. So, don't give up yet. And thank you. You are a hero." he said, and gave Olds a vigorous handshake.

Chapter 31

Early October, 2020

At FBI headquarters in Washington D.C., Papadakas worked hard, and successfully, at keeping a lid on the Ruth Kald/Duval Dixon/Trojan Horse story. And as Dr. Stanton had predicted, the other unaccounted-for participants of the Vancouver Island conference could not be found, and were declared missing. The FBI found out that Chuck Métis had died in a tractor accident in 2009. No investigation or autopsy had been done, so there was no way to know if it was suspicious. The investigation of Ruth Kald went nowhere. The FBI confirmed that the Indians killed in D.C. were connected to Dixon.

The CIA sent people to India, but they were not officially allowed to investigate the bombing of Dixon's buildings. The Indian government made it clear, no matter what might be found out, that the terrorist story would not be changed. It was vitally important to them that Pakistan be blamed.

At the White House, Dr. Stanton became a regular visitor. Within a few weeks of the Dixon discovery, he was spending half his time with the President and Lucy Kline. He became the President's most trusted advisor on the situation, so she kept him close by. He stayed at the White House while in D.C., and before long, he got even closer to the center of power. He and Lucy Kline began sharing a bed.

At CDC and NIH, scientists struggled to understand the five flu viruses. Under normal circumstances, work like this might take years. The concern for speed seemed a little strange to many of those working the problem. But so far, the real reason for the urgency managed to be kept secret.

At the "third lodge" on Vancouver Island, Toby and Laura were trying their best to prepare for the long, wet, dark winter that loomed, now only weeks away. Neither of them had gotten the flu, and no sick straggler had managed to find the way up the long estuary to their hidden compound. Their plan was to stay put for at least another year, until the hosts for the Eden Flu were all gone. Then they might venture out, carefully, to see what had happened.

They felt that the winter wouldn't be too bad. Dixon had provided book tablets with thousands of titles. Dr. Mothershed and Jacob Horton were interesting companions. The surroundings were beautiful. And, best of all, they each had a warm body to snuggle up to. It was a simple place, a simple life, and they were in love – and alive. It could be much worse.

At Malabar Farm, the Tuesday night cocktail gathering at the farmhouse front porch now included Gil 'Vandy' Vanderham. He had been a startlingly easy convert to 'The Eden Proposition' plan. Like many people with an interest in ecology or related fields, Vanderham had come to the conclusion that the health of Mother Earth was in great jeopardy. He had also come to the conclusion that there was no solution to the problem – until he heard 'The Eden Proposition.' And like all the others on that front porch, the plan was considerably more acceptable to him as long as it didn't include his own death.

The Tuesday night group decided to wait and watch for as long as possible before informing the other residents of Malabar Farm of their great good fortune. The farther into the event that they could hold off telling them, the better chance they had of preventing the outside world from finding out about Malabar. No one had a clue what might happen if the rest of world found out about them, though it was a favorite topic on the farmhouse porch after a round or two of gin and tonics.

Justice Brown's despondency and anger bottomed out, she seemed to be getting better. Dr. Contreras and Secretary Solene both knew they would be sharing one of those charming cottages at Malabar Farm soon, though it had not yet been discussed between them. And even Vanderham was feeling the stirring of the pairing urge. He had his eye on the keeper of his Abe hat. He had managed to sneak her in for the vaccinations.

Waiting and watching – these next weeks would pass slowly for them. And for Solene, "wondering" was added to the mix. In the back of his mind, he couldn't help but wonder if

Dixon had told him the truth. Solene couldn't be certain that the flu they all had caught was indeed benign. Maybe they were all doomed.. With Duval Dixon, Solene had well learned, you just never knew.

And no one had heard a word from Dixon.

Chapter 32

Later that month
Thursday, October 15th, 2020
The CDC, Atlanta

"Dr. Stanton; I have Senator Kiefer of Texas on the line for you," Mel said as Max walked by on the way into his office.

"Put him through," Max said.

"Yes, Senator. What can I do for you?" Max asked brusquely, hoping the Senator would get the message and would keep this conversation short.

"Dr. Stanton, this is Duval Dixon, sorry about the senator story. I need a few minutes of your time, but don't bother trying to trace this call - it can't be done. Are you alone?"

Max caught his breath. He looked at the receiver, as if it might have Dixon's smiling face on it. "Mr. Dixon, is this really you? This isn't some prank that Andy Hobbs has staged? I don't have time for that kind of crap."

"I can give you a few words from the vmail I sent Laura before the conference if you like," Dixon said.

"No, that won't be necessary." Max had recognized Dixon's unmistakable voice.

"For starters, obviously I'm not dead."

"We know that."

"Really?" Dixon said, sounding surprised.

"We know a lot more than you might imagine. We have found Ruth Kald. We know you are responsible for this flu and we are well on our way to discovering the contents of your little Trojan Horse," he said, embellishing a bit about Ruth Kald, and hoping it would get a reaction from Dixon.

Dixon didn't respond immediately. Max prayed he wasn't going to hang up.

"Well, good for you. I'm impressed," Dixon finally said. "This is helpful; it will make this conversation easier, not to mention shorter."

"Please tell me everything, Mr. Dixon. It's not too late, is it?" Max said, and instantly wished he hadn't begun to beg quite so soon.

"I'll tell you enough. But please, don't give me any more bullshit. You don't have Ruth Kald. It's not possible. Though I must say, I am impressed that you know the name."

"All right, no bullshit. And I expect the same from you," Max said. "First, let me ask about Laura. Is she alive?"

"Honest answer: I don't know. I think it's unlikely, but I can't say for sure."

"You didn't kill her, and all the others?"

"No, I didn't kill her. The others you speak of are Mallory, Rabinovich, Darby and Nguyen I presume?"

"Yes – and the other missing people from your little clambake."

"I can't tell you anything about the missing people, but Mallory et al, were killed by a group of Indians who mistakenly thought that those people possessed a vaccine. They didn't, so it was unfortunate."

Dixon continued, "There's no vaccine, of course. I didn't do this to preserve a core of humans. I did this for all the other species who live on this planet. Humans are the virus, and soon Mother Earth will be rid of it, and then she can slowly return to good health."

"These were the Indians that you killed in D.C.?" Max asked, deliberately ignoring Dixon's little diatribe.

"Yes, very good Dr. Stanton."

"So they killed Laura as well?"

"I told you, I don't know what happened to her. But enough small talk," Dixon said, shifting gears. "I need to tell you what's going to happen. You are correct about the 'Trojan Horse', though you are lying about being close to finding it. I know you are not. And, trust me, it wouldn't make any difference. The game has been over for some time now."

"Are you going to tell me what it is?"

"In a minute. First I'm going to tell you what to do. Listen *very* carefully. There are only a few weeks left until the symptoms start appearing. Between now and then, the people of the world need to take significant actions to make sure they don't kill Mother Earth on their way out the door. They, and you, must think this through with great care. *Please* listen carefully."

Dixon continued, "Nuclear power plants need to be shut down and made stable. Refineries and chemical plants need to be shut down in a way that they won't spread toxins at some point in the future. Gas lines need to be shut down, otherwise all the cities will go up in flames. Ranchers need to open their gates so the animals can move freely. Zoos need to euthanize their animals so as to not artificially introduce species into foreign environments. There are many other things, but you get what I'm driving at. Humans need to be responsible - *at least this once*. They need to leave this place the way they found it."

Max now believed that Dixon was truly insane. Until this moment, he had thought Dixon was caught up in the MPR concept. And to be completely honest, there were times when Max thought MPR was not entirely unreasonable. It was a solution, after all. But this – total extinction of his own species – how could anyone get his mind to that place? Dixon must be completely nuts.

"Who should I tell this to?" Max asked, stalling until he could think of something better to ask.

"The President. She can take it from there."

"I'll do that. Now tell me about the Trojan Horse," Max said, hoping that he was being sufficiently subtle.

"*Listen to me, goddammit*!" Dixon barked. "Carrying the message that I just gave you to the President is the most important task you - or any human being, for that matter – has ever been given. Quite literally, the fate of this planet may depend on it. Tell me you understand!"

"I'm sorry," Max said. "This is coming at me a little fast …"

"Tell me you understand – *now*!" Dixon shouted the command into the phone, frightening Max.

"Yes, of course … I understand."

"Okay," Dixon exhaled, "Good. Now, the Trojan Horse, as you call it," Dixon said. "There is a third anomaly on the surface of the viruses, as I'm sure you've noticed."

"Yes we have. It's a part of a protein, as best we can tell. We felt it was possibly an artifact of your production process."

"No it's not," Dixon said. "It is a precursor protein for PrPsc - the pathological prion protein. Each individual flu virus that existed in your system will, at some point, have a normal PrP protein latch on to this precursor prion, and then fold itself into a PrPsc prion. And then, as you well know, that new mis-folded PrPsc protein will do the same thing, starting the chain reaction that leads to CJD – mad cow."

"We all have CJD?" Max wheezed, seriously unnerved.

"Yes we do," Dixon said. "As you know, the incubation period for CJD is substantial, usually two to four years, sometimes as long as thirty years. But that incubation period is a function of how many of the pathological prions you start with in your system. The more you start with, the shorter the incubation. In this case, since everyone has had millions of flu viruses rattling around their systems for many weeks, everyone has started out with a massive dose of the PrPsc prions. Therefore, the incubation period has been shortened substantially. You will start to see symptoms within a matter of weeks now. Death will come within two to four months. We know this for a fact: it's been comprehensively tested."

"But there's no treatment for CJD," Max said, still reeling.

"Of course. That is the whole point."

"My God Dixon, this is unbelievable!" Max said, his voice an octave higher. He started running through the characteristics of CJD: can't be cured, can't even be detected, creates immobility long before death, one hundred percent fatal. This is far worse than all of the previously imagined worst-case scenarios, he realized.

"Yes, it is unbelievable. A good point," Dixon said. "In fact, many people won't believe you. There is no diagnostic test, as you know. So - my suggestion is that you get a large number of autopsy teams together and go examine people who have died for other reasons. Look for the scrapie-associated fibrils and the floral plaques in their brains. You will find that everyone has them in very advanced form. There are experts at NIH, and in England, that can confirm my claim that there is only a month or so left before serious symptoms emerge. That is why the message that I gave you to take to the President is so important."

"So there's nothing that can be done?" Max asked.

"Nothing. As I said - that is the point."

"What about the 'Eden' in The Eden Proposition?" Max asked. "Isn't there an Eden?"

"No Eden, sorry."

"What about you?"

"I'll be gone too," Dixon said. "And if you don't have any more questions, I'll be gone now."

"Can I contact you later?"

"No."

"I just don't know how you could do this …"

"No, of course you don't," Dixon said, and hung up.

Part 5

Chapter 33

November, 2020

Dixon's message to the President got through - loud and clear. Duval Dixon had no way of knowing, but Dr. Stanton had more than the President's ear, he had the President's sister, and she had both of the President's ears.

It took several weeks to confirm Dixon's claim. The first autopsies revealed that everyone was infected with the deadly prion disease. More teams were dispatched, this time world-wide. They found the same result. All of the experts on prion-based CJD and chronic wasting disease agreed that every one of the autopsies showed advanced progress of the disease.

How could it be possible? Everyone would be dead in a matter of months? Many skeptics remained. So – yet another, this time wider and even more comprehensive, circle of autopsies finally confirmed the horrifying conclusion to everyone's satisfaction. No one could now logically dispute that the end of the human era was near.

In the first week of November, the leaders of all nations gathered at the U.N. in New York. President Pittman delivered the finest speech of her career. She spoke passionately about the need to be responsible in our exit from this Earth. She implored the leaders of the world to focus all of the remaining energies and the remaining days of their people on the task of atoning for centuries of abuse to Mother Earth. Let's leave her as we found her, she begged.

The side-bar message, delivered in the hallways and in private meetings during those days at the U.N., was that this focus on an orderly shut-down would have the additional, and significant, benefit of giving the people a higher purpose to cling to as their time ran out. Perhaps it would help to alleviate the despair, and the possible chaos of those final weeks. For many, that side-bar message became the stronger argument.

And it worked. The people had a purpose. But then they went far beyond being purposeful. Because the influence of competition - in all its forms - competition for resources, competition for territory, for markets, for jobs, for lovers, for respect - all became unnecessary, the people came together at a level that could not have been anticipated. Though there was the inevitable despair, confusion, brutality, and chaos in many places, for the most part, the human species departed Mother Earth with unexpected grace and dignity.

On February 7th, 2021, Rodrigo Sato, a half-Japanese, half-Chilean fisherman, who lived on a rocky remote island off the far southern coast of Chile, lay on the deck of his modest wooden fishing boat surrounded by dozens of squawking, expectant gulls. His eyes fluttered and closed, he spasmed-in his last shallow breath, and then he silently slipped away. It was the last breath taken by the seven billion, four-hundred sixty-one million, six-hundred fifty-four thousand, two-hundred and twelve victims of Duval Dixon's Eden Flu.

Chapter 34

Wednesday, February 17th, 2021
Vancouver Island

Toby sat on the crude bench that he had chain-sawed out of a Douglas fir stump and tried yet again to sketch the spectacular estuary before him. He had always wanted to draw - living most of his life in Astoria had given him a case of artist-envy. Astoria had a gallery on every corner, and in order to participate in any good conversation at the pub, you needed to be either preparing for a show, or currently having a show, or be exhausted from having just had a show. Toby's drawing talent was emerging slowly, although he could see that it was a learned skill. It would take time, and fortunately that was something he had in abundance.

Several seconds passed before he realized the importance of the barely audible sound coming from the west. Before, it had been a common sound, so his brain initially filed it under background noise. But then it went "oh-oh" and raised the alarm. It was the distinct sound of an outboard motor, and it was coming up the estuary.

They had talked about how to handle this situation. Laura and Toby hadn't been vaccinated - they couldn't risk contact with anyone from the outside world. The plan was to go fetch Jacob. Then, armed with a handgun hidden in his pocket, he would greet the stranger. Laura and Toby would hide in the woods in a place where they could back him up with a hunting rifle.

Toby ran back up the path and found Jacob in the storage shed. Jacob raced up to his cabin for the bulky jacket and gun. Toby got Laura, grabbed the rifle and headed back down the path, joined by Jacob. Toby and Laura went to the spot that they had prepared for this possibility just as the boat emerged from the nearest bend in the river and motored up the last hundred yards to the landing.

Only one person was in the boat: an older man with a full grey beard, sunglasses, and stringy grey hair falling out from under a green and yellow "John Deere" cap. He pulled up to the landing smiling. Toby watched as Jacob helped him secure his aluminum work boat and then helped him out of the boat and up the bank to the clearing. The man had taken off his hat, and with the bushy full beard, and the limp grey hair, he was only two Kleenex boxes short of achieving the full Howard Hughes look.

But the smile was unmistakable.

Duval Dixon gave Jacob a hug as Toby and Laura got up from behind the stump and walked out into the clearing.

Dixon was genuinely surprised. He clapped his hands and raised them in the air. "You are here! You made it. Excellent!"

Laura took a step back as Dixon walked over to greet them. "Duval, don't come any closer. We haven't had any vaccine. Are you contagious at all?" she asked.

"No, don't worry, I'm well. I never had the flu," Dixon said. "And besides, you've had the vaccine. Well, not the complete version, but it probably would have worked. Do you remember those awful tasting Tom Collins drinks I made you drink up at my cabin?"

Laura shook her head in disbelief. Toby nodded.

"Goddammit Dixon," Laura said angrily. "You should've told us. We could have done something – we could have helped. Instead we hid out in the woods like cowards."

"Now wait a minute," Dixon said. "Who knows what might have happened to you out there – nothing good, I can tell you that much. You should thank me for taking that decision out of your hands."

"Well you always know best, don't you," Laura said sarcastically. "So – did it work? Did you kill everybody?"

"Yes, it worked," Dixon answered, without emotion.

Laura stared at Dixon for a long moment, folded her arms, sighed, then stepped away and headed back to the cabin.

Dixon watched her walk away, then turned back to Toby and Jacob. "How is Mothershed?" he asked hesitantly, fearing bad news.

"He's fine," Jacob said. "He's up at the cabin reading."

"Good."

"Are you okay?" Toby asked, reacting more to Dixon's appearance than his apparent energy level.

"I'm better. I took a couple of weeks off before I came up here," Dixon said. "I'll tell you about it tomorrow - on our way out. I'd like to spend a little time with Dr. Mothershed right now. Tomorrow we'll leave early. Be packed and ready to go by first light."

Toby nodded. "Where are we going?"

"You'll see tomorrow," Dixon said, then clasped Toby's arm. "I am extremely happy that you two survived and made it here. I'll bet it's a good story – also on tomorrow's agenda."

Chapter 35

Thursday, February 18th, 2021
Vancouver Island to Decatur Head

Wrapped in hooded Gore-tex jackets against the steady rain, with the first light barely discernable from the night, Dixon's little tribe huddled in the aluminum workboat for the trip to the nearest village. An hour later, the first leg of their journey over, the five of them threw their wet raingear in the trunk and crammed themselves into the mid-sized sedan that Dixon had dropped off there the day before. It would have to do until they could find something bigger.

Twenty miles down the road they found a van in Gold River, picked up some supplies, and broke out the firepower - three handguns and two rifles with scopes. Just in case, Dixon said. Dixon told them he had not actually seen anyone on the trip up from California, but he had seen indications that some stragglers might still be moving around. Dixon broke out a vial of booster vaccine. Also just in case, he said. Laura administered the shots.

After a slow winding trip up and over the backbone of Vancouver Island they picked up Highway 19, the main road along the eastern shore of the massive island, and headed south. For the rest of the morning they traveled on Highway 19, mostly in silence, and arrived at Victoria on the southern tip of the island at two in the afternoon. Jacob drove, Toby and Laura sat in the back. And because the steady rain reduced visibility to a minimum, the ride seemed oddly routine.

The plan was to find a boat in Victoria harbor, spend the night, and then motor over to Anacortes in the morning. They would grab another car in Anacortes, and proceed down I-5 until they reached their destination, the location of which Dixon had not yet revealed.

The harbor offered a large selection of fine motor yachts. They settled on a forty-eight foot Tollycraft, the deciding factor being the keys left in a drawer near the wheelhouse. There were enough canned goods and wine on board for a decent meal, so Toby suggested they leave right away and make way to an anchorage in the San Juans. A good idea, Dixon agreed - it would be safer. So, after running the big diesels long enough to feel confident, they threw off the lines, and with Toby at the helm, they rounded the breakwater and headed due east into the San Juans.

Toby knew these waters well, the limited visibility didn't bother him. He knew his destination too - Decatur head, where he and Laura had started this journey in what felt like decades ago. But this time he expected they would have the anchorage to themselves.

Over dinner, Dixon had Toby tell the story of their escape from Jain and Patel, and their trek to Dixon's secret cabin. Laura continued to be distant. She hadn't recognized the anchorage. She didn't ask about it, and Toby said nothing. She excused herself early and went to bed, saying she didn't feel well. She didn't look well either, Toby thought.

Chapter 36

Friday, February 19th, 2021
Decatur Head

The next morning, Toby got up early to an empty bunk. He found Laura in the galley, finishing a can of Spaghetti-os. "Feeling better?" he asked. Toby put his hands on her shoulders and administered an affectionate little back rub.

"A bit," she said. "I must have eaten something bad yesterday. We need to be careful what we eat. Some things may be getting a little too old."

"See any coffee?" Toby asked.

"No, I looked in the cabinets, but didn't see any."

"I threw it out last night," Dixon said, startling Toby, who hadn't noticed him sitting in the shadows at the dinette.

"Threw the coffee out?" Toby asked, not sure if Dixon was even speaking to them.

"Yes, the coffee," Dixon said. "I'm afraid you're going to have to give it up."

"Give up coffee – why?" Laura asked, now alert, as she sensed another Dixon mind-twister on the way.

"The Eden Flu – it's in the coffee," Dixon said. "And the vaccine won't help you if you ingest the virus directly. The ingested virus will cause you to start the prion chain-reaction. It won't be as fast, but it will eventually have the same result. Stay away from coffee from now on."

"Coffee? No wonder it started so fast, and in so many places," Toby said. "How did you do that? How did you get it in the coffee?"

Dixon put down the marine atlas he had been studying, folded his hands in front of him, and prepared to deliver a short lecture.

"About ten years ago, a fungus got into the coffee industry system. It spread everywhere before it was detected. You couldn't see it, but it affected the taste, and reduced the shelf life of the roasted beans. A treatment was developed - a fungicide that was dusted on to the beans after roasting. It was thoroughly tested, and had no harmful health issues for humans, so it came into wide use.

"The fungicide had one important active chemical ingredient that was produced by only two chemical companies. I bought one of them many years ago, and the other one had a mysterious fire last year – which took them offline, and made my company the sole provider. The fire also reduced the available inventory, so my production was in high demand. It was used as quickly as we could make it."

Laura was now interested, there were some medical questions here. "But how did the virus survive the heat from brewing the coffee?"

"Ah - good question doctor," Dixon said. "Encapsulation. As you know, some viruses exist with a kind of natural protein encapsulation. We just incorporated that into our design. Actually, I think it was some of the best science we did in the entire operation. The brewing was, in fact, necessary. It released the viruses."

Laura shook her head and clenched her teeth, once again disgusted with Dixon's violation of all things sacred.

"The morning coffee?" she asked. "So when someone inhaled that first steam off the cup, they exposed themselves to a massive dose of the virus? My God Duval, somehow that makes this even worse."

"I never liked that part either," Dixon said, unemotionally, as if he were discussing the weather. "But it was all we could come up with. You must admit though, it was effective."

Two hours later, they abandoned the Tollycraft at the gas dock in the inner harbor at Anacortes. After some difficulty finding a vehicle that was both big enough and had keys, Jacob finally pulled up to the end of the dock in a large black SUV. Jacob once again drove.

The rain had stopped. Toby and Laura could now look out at the empty world as they drove east on highway 20 toward I-5.

"Duval, what are those signs on the lawns?" Laura asked as they drove slowly through the residential streets of Mt. Vernon, the little town at the intersection with I-5.

Dixon glared back at Laura with the intense look that had frozen them so many times at Haida Gwaii. "Jacob, take a right at the next block and then pull over."

At Dixon's request, they all got out of the car and stood in the street of what had been a typical residential middle class neighborhood. Almost every house had a crude sign, often painted on boards stuck into the ground by the curb, or nailed to the mailboxes. The boards had letters spray-painted on them; some had a "D", almost all a had a "C", one house had a "K". The letters all had a black slash through them. The houses had fresh digging in the lawn – clearly graves.

"This is what I've been doing for the last two months," Dixon said. "I started in New Mexico, but then went to Fresno, where I was needed more." He paused and looked absently down the street. "I was what was called a 'driver'. A simple term - I guess it started as people became unable to drive, the healthier ones would drive for the others. But then it became something quite different."

Dixon walked over to the car, reached in, and brought out a handgun.

"Jacob, take this and watch for dogs," Dixon said. "I haven't seen any yet, but if we stay here long enough, they'll show up. Don't hesitate to shoot them; you never know what they'll do. They seem to have collectively gone a little nuts."

Dixon walked slowly over to the curb, looking at the mound of fresh dirt in the front yard.

He turned back and continued, "As the end approached it became imperative – a compulsion of sorts, but still necessary - to make sure that you and your family were buried. No one wanted to die in bed and end up being eaten by the family dog, or rats, or birds. And Laura, as you know, when the prion disease took hold, it became a guessing game. If you waited to long, you'd become both disabled and disoriented, and unable to end it on your own terms. You could wind up on the ground in the street, unable to move, with dogs chewing on your body while you were still alive. Everyone feared that kind of end."

Dixon walked out to the middle of the street and gestured down the block. "But you don't see that here. And, mostly, you won't see it anywhere else. These lettered signs are the reason."

In the distance, dogs could now be heard barking.

"Should we get in the car?" Jacob asked.

"We could, but don't drive. I want to finish the story."

They got back in. Dixon sat in the front passenger seat, turned, and continued. "As I said, I was a 'driver'. I drove a back-hoe through neighborhoods like this. The 'D' on the signs means 'Dig'. Those people needed help digging the graves – as you see, most people were buried in their own yards. Some church groups did the Jonestown thing - you remember - mass suicide, leaving a few to bury the rest. But for the most part, people wanted to be buried at home."

"What's the slash mean?" Laura asked.

"I'll get to that. The 'D' was a request for the next driver who passed by to stop and dig. So I'd pull up, ask them where, and how big – how many caskets. Then I'd dig the hole. Nothing fancy, there wasn't enough time. After digging, I'd used a can of spray paint to slash the 'D', so no other driver would stop. Same thing with the 'C.' 'C' meant cover. It meant that the family was dead, usually by their own hand, and were in the coffin, or coffins. My job was to go in, put the cover on the coffin, if there was one, and then fill the hole with dirt. Then I'd slash the 'C' on the way out. They were done."

"My God Duval, you did that? For how long?" Laura asked.

"Six weeks, maybe more. Understand: at first there were quite a few drivers. It was a noble thing to do. Then, of course, the drivers themselves would get sick. But I never got sick, so I kept going until the end. Whenever I saw a backhoe or tractor parked somewhere, I went to find out if it was a driver who couldn't go on. Usually it was, so I had to take care of him as well."

"And the houses where the siding is ripped off or the porch torn up?" Toby asked. "Wood for the caskets?"

Dixon nodded. "Yes. Plywood went fast, but a lot of people tore up their houses so they wouldn't have to drive. Driving was one of the first skills to go."

Dixon rolled down the window and listened. "I don't hear any dogs. I want to get out for a minute. I need some air. Let's go, I'll finish the story outside."

Mothershed stayed in the back seat but they kept the door open and stood in a circle around him.

Dixon looked ill; a pale cloud had come over him. He took a deep breath and continued. To Toby it seemed as though Dixon needed to get whatever it was that he had to say, out. And it was going to be painful - like passing a kidney stone.

"If you look farther down the road, there is another sign, a 'K'," Dixon said, and pointed several houses down on the opposite side of the street. "Understand that suicide has always been considered a sin by many religious people – one that would keep them out of heaven. And, as you can imagine, that caused quite a dilemma for the true believers. So, the vast majority of religious organizations did some fancy footwork and decreed that suicide was acceptable under these extraordinary circumstances. Most even said it would be acceptable to 'assist' within your family, or your church."

Dixon paused, considering his words. "But the Catholic church ..." he paused again and nodded to himself, now looking angry. "The Pope refused to grant absolution for suicide. Sanctity of life and all that, and then he promptly died, leaving no one to countermand his decision. Confusion reigned within the church. Some cardinals – many in the U.S. – did grant absolution, within the limits of their authority. But as the disease took hold, and people's thinking ability began to deteriorate, it became pure chaos. Dozens of temporary Popes were appointed, all issuing conflicting decrees. In the end, the poor mass of Catholics were left with wildly confusing instructions."

Dixon walked a few steps into the street, took a deep breath, turned and walked back. And in a blink, he had returned to his normal self. Somehow, he had fought his way out of the clouded place he had been in since starting this discussion.

Toby watched him regain his composure and understood. It wasn't that Dixon felt the need to be 'strong', or to be a 'man' – at least not in the normal sense. Toby knew that Dixon simply felt he had no right to express emotion. He had done this monstrous thing, so he had forfeited any rights he had to be affected by the horror that he had himself created. That was why he became a 'driver'. Not to atone. And not to try to look better in anyone else's opinion, but simply because it was necessary, and he had no right to refuse.

Toby knew this because he felt the same way. He was too much a party to this event to be able to express disgust. He too had forfeited his rights.

Dixon continued. "The 'K' solved the problem. It meant 'kill'. My title was actually 'black driver'. We were the drivers that were willing to shoot people."

Laura gasped. Jacob turned away. Toby and Dixon held eye contact for too long.

"Like the other black drivers, I wore a black head scarf, and my backhoe had a pole with a large black flag on it. I'd pick up handguns from the places where the family had already taken care of their own business. I always had ten or twenty on hand."

"You shot people? *Families ..., little kids...?*" Laura stammered.

"Yes, many – hundreds. Maybe a thousand or more. I didn't count," Dixon said. "That's why I went to Fresno; it had several large Catholic neighborhoods. You understand don't you? This way it wasn't suicide for them. They were murdered. They could go to heaven."

"Why do you care? You don't believe in heaven!" Laura demanded, almost screaming.

"I don't care," Dixon said. "They did. But stop now – I know it doesn't make sense. After all, I caused all this suffering, so why should I help relieve only a tiny bit of it? I can't tell you why. I just did it. You asked about the signs, I told you. They were a good thing. It meant a lot to people to be buried at home."

Dixon nodded to himself and looked briefly down at the ground.

"No mas. I'm finished with this now."

Dixon walked around the car and got back into the passenger seat. Laura shook her head. This alleged human being, this Duval Dixon, could not have confused her more.

Jacob started the car and looked over at Dixon. "Which way?"

"Head south on I-5. Take the I-405 cutoff around Lake Washington, and keep going south all the way to Oregon. I don't think we should go through the city. Puget Sound used to be home to several submarines. It's possible one of them may be lurking there, somewhere off Seattle."

"Eden is in Oregon?" Laura asked.

"Dr. Sundgren," Dixon said, turning to look directly at Laura. "I'm not going to tell you where Eden is until we get there. You may remember that I said, up at Haida Gwaii, that I have always been a little paranoid. You see - I know that you want to live a full life with Toby. I'm assuming therefore, that you want to get to Eden. I'm also assuming that, given the chance, you just might pop a cap in the back of my head."

Laura clenched her jaw and returned Dixon's stare.

"So this is a little like the V-boxes," Dixon continued. "It is now in your best interest to keep me alive."

"You know what they say, Duval," Laura finally said, after a momentary stare-down. "It's not paranoia if they really are after you."

"As I thought," Dixon said and turned back.

For the next hour they drove south, down the empty freeway. There were cars and trucks on the shoulder, and sometimes in the right lane, but they hadn't yet encountered a complete blockage. Toby noticed that you couldn't see in the windows of some of the cars. They were covered with something from the inside. Then came the grizzly realization that someone had died inside, and was still in there moldering.

In Marysville, a startling site appeared. Laura saw it first and told Jacob to pull over. To the west of the freeway, in the parking lot of a large casino, they saw a metal barrel with a fire in it. Next to the barrel were two RV's parked end to end. The first one had a sign that read "Vote for Mary" and under it, "The next President". The banner on the second RV said, "Voting today!" and under it another banner said, "Friday, Feb. 19".

"That's today," Toby said.

"We should get back in the car and go – right now," Dixon said. "Nothing good can happen here."

"No way," Laura said. "Someone is over there, maybe others. We need to go see."

Dixon reluctantly acquiesced. He didn't want to argue with Laura anymore. "Okay, we'll go. But we are going to be very careful."

"Jacob, park about fifty yards away, in a spot where you can see the front of those RV's, and where you can get a clear shot," Dixon said as they pulled off the freeway and into the casino parking lot. "Then get around behind the car and put a scope on us – or whoever shows up. Laura, you stay in the driver's seat and be ready to pull out. Dr. Mothershed, can you fire a handgun?"

"No, I don't know how," Mothershed said.

"Well then, just lie down on the seat," Dixon said. "Toby, you and I will go over and vote for Mary."

"Women still have a right to vote," Laura said. "I'm going too."

Dixon said nothing.

After Jacob pulled up to a good vantage point, the three voters walked warily over to the RVs. There was an open tent along side the far RV, like those the big stores would put outside their front door for special sales. A long table with two chairs was set up outside the tent and another table, with two boxes on it, was just inside. It must be the voting booth, Toby thought.

The door to the far RV opened and a wild looking creature emerged.

"Voters – good, good, good!" she yelled, her head shaking erratically from side to side, like an exaggerated Parkinson's spasm. "Over here," she said and waved them in to the tent.

She walked up to the outside table. It had a large tarp over it that went down to the ground. "I have to sit here," she said.

Still twitching, she sat down and stuck both her hands under the table. "You go vote over there."

The three looked at each other and nodded. They could see that Mary was way off the rails. They'd vote, and then they'd get the hell out of there.

Laura smiled politely and asked, "You're Mary – right?"

"You're god-dammed right, you blond bitch. I'm Mary. I'll be your next President! Then you'll see," Mary said with her head still jerking from side to side, her arms out of sight under the table.

Laura looked frightened, and stepped back. Dixon moved over to the voting booth and took a piece of paper off the pile. Toby followed him, then glanced back at Mary - just in time to see her pull a double-barreled shotgun out from under the table.

She leveled it at Dixon, then in an instant, Toby was deafened, stunned by the roar of the shotgun. Disoriented, he watched a large chunk of the far side of Mary's head come off and fly across the pavement, landing twenty feet away. He stared at the odd head-chunk, but could see out of the corner of his eye as Mary tumbled off her chair and at the same time flipped the shotgun over the table. Toby followed the shotgun as it bounced at his feet and landed by Dixon, who was spinning to the ground. Dixon did a complete turn and landed face-down. His head hit the asphalt with a sickening "thunk".

Toby stood paralyzed, his ears ringing. He could see blood pooling out from under Dixon's head.

Laura was now at Dixon's side. She picked up the shotgun lying at his feet, and Toby watched, still confused by the bizarre events unfolding before him, as Laura put her finger on the triggers and pointed the shotgun at Dixon's head.

Toby took a quick glance over his shoulder, now expecting Jacob to blow Laura's head into chunks. But Jacob was busy crab-running toward them while keeping his gaze, and his gun, pointed at the RVs.

Laura looked up at Toby as he turned back. Toby finally regained his motor skills, shook his head 'no', and stepped toward her. Laura took one more look at Dixon - trigger finger still poised - then threw the gun away, and knelt down beside him to see how badly he was hurt.

So, Toby thought, this is it. This is how it ends for Duval Dixon. After all the things Dixon had done. After all the things he had survived. It ends right here. Gunned down in a casino parking lot by an insane bag lady. Who is writing this fucking script anyway, he wondered.

Jacob arrived, breathing hard. "How is he?" he asked, still watching the RVs.

"I don't know," Laura said. "Toby - help me roll him over."

They quickly got him onto his back. Dixon was still breathing. A moment later his eyes fluttered open. Laura dabbed the end of her shirt on his forehead in order to remove enough blood to see how badly he was cut.

Dixon's eyes came into focus He looked at each of them in turn, getting oriented.

"Duval, Duval!" Laura shouted.

"Whoa," Dixon wheezed, taking in a deep breath.

"Where are you hurt?" she asked, again in a loud voice. All of their ears were still ringing.

"My arm hurts - maybe in the fall."

"Toby - go get the first-aid kit and bring back the car," Laura said.

When Toby returned, they had Dixon sitting on a chair, his jacket and shirt off. Toby could see blood on his left arm.

"It looks like you had a few pellets go through the upper part of your arm, but that's it," Laura said, looking up at Jacob. "Jacob, that was unbelievable! Another millisecond and she would have cut him in two with that thing."

"Yeah, lucky," Jacob said, his rifle still trained on the RVs. "Let's go. I don't think anyone else is here, but those guns made a big noise. Maybe someone will come. I think we should get out of here right now."

"All right," Laura said. "He's fine, I'll finish the bandages in the car."

"Toby," Jacob said. "You drive, I'll ride shotgun."

Dixon, holding a bandage tightly to his forehead, was able to walk to the car and slide in next to Mothershed, with Laura right behind him. Toby got in the driver's seat. Jacob got in next to him, gun pointed out the window. They sped out of the casino parking lot and back on to I-5, heading south.

A few miles down the road, and several deep breaths later, the group's collective blood pressure returned to survivable levels. Jacob turned back to face Laura and Duval. "Everything okay doc?" he asked.

"He's fine," Laura said. "The head wound is superficial, no signs of a concussion. I think he's going to need stitches though. Do you think we should risk going to a hospital so I can get a suture?"

"Can it wait for a few hours?" Duval asked.

"Sure, I can bandage it. But it might make a bigger scar."

"Let's wait then. We can still make our destination by evening if nothing else happens."

"Okay, but you need to tell us where that is – right now!" Laura said. "What if crazy Mary hadn't missed? What if you were dead? Where would we have gone then?"

"Don't worry about it," Dixon said. "I told Jacob."

Toby looked in the mirror and caught Laura's eye. She was shaking her head. Toby wondered how this might have turned out if Laura had known that one simple, little fact. Would she have killed Dixon? Would Jacob have killed her? And, to make this even more surreal, Toby couldn't shake the image of Mary's head blowing apart, the big chunk flying off to land on the asphalt, like a discarded half-eaten Macdonald's hamburger.

Just keep breathing, he told himself, in and out, and keep driving. Maybe we'll find something close to sanity at the mysterious Eden. Or maybe not.

Five hours - and no further incidents later - Dixon tapped Toby on the shoulder. "Our exit is next; get off and head east on highway two-twenty-eight. It will take about half an hour I think."

"You think?" Laura asked. "Haven't you been here before?"

"Once. But it was a long time ago – six years, I believe."

Toby drove carefully down the rural two-lane road, and for long stretches the countryside appeared normal, the scenery sometimes spectacular. Wildflowers were growing up along the road, and the pastures were returning to grass. Then abruptly, they would come upon a field or barn littered with dead livestock and the stench would be overwhelming.

After the half hour had passed, and with anticipation growing, they rounded a bend to see a bridge blocked by a tanker truck that had jackknifed mid-span. Several cars had been abandoned by the end of the bridge. Toby thought it looked dangerous, possibly a trap. He stopped about a hundred yards short of the bridge.

"Any ideas?" Toby asked.

"I think we're close," Dixon said. "Let's sit here for a while and see what happens. Laura - hand Toby up the other rifle."

"'See what happens'?" Laura asked. "What's going to happen?"

"If there is anyone up at Malabar, I expect they have a camera and sensor-alarm of some kind at this spot. Let's give them a few minutes to drive up," Dixon said. "Laura, you and I will get out, maybe they'll recognize us. Toby and Jacob stay in the car and keep the scopes pointed at the other side of the bridge."

As Dixon had predicted, ten minutes later an armored Hummer came slowly down the road from the opposite direction and stopped fifty yards short of the bridge. A helmeted man in body armor got out and trained his binoculars on the group. Then he waved and yelled, "It's Mark!" and walked quickly down to the bridge. He got in the tanker truck, and after a few back and forth moves, got it straightened out, drove it up the road, and parked off to the side, next to the Hummer.

Mark had his helmet off and a big grin on, as they drove up beside him. "Unbelievable! Dr. Sundgren, and Dr. Benson, you're alive! We'd given up any hope that you two had made it. There will be some happy people back at the farmhouse."

Dixon leaned forward from between Laura and Mothershed and asked the question that he had been too frightened to even contemplate until this moment: "How is it at Malabar?"

Mark's smile gave away the answer before his words could.

"Good - things are good," Mark said. "Everyone survived the initial flu. Somewhere around thirty people went away during the end times to help friends or family. Most have returned."

"And Solene?" Dixon asked.

"He's fine, and Justice Brown and Dr. Contreras are here as well."

"Sofia's here?" Laura asked, surprised.

"Yes. She's not at the farmhouse – she's at Malabar, but we see her every week," Mark said.

Laura looked over at Dixon, "What is Malabar? Is it close?"

"It's what you have been calling Eden," Dixon said. "It's only a few miles up the road. But we won't see it until tomorrow."

Dixon leaned out and asked Mark, "Can you reach Vanderham and have him bring Dr. Contreras over to the farmhouse right away? He knows what's going on, doesn't he?"

"Yes, he knows, and I'm pretty sure I know where I can find him."

"Mark - ask Dr. Contreras to bring sutures when she comes," Laura said.

"Will do," Mark said. "I was about to ask – are you okay?"

"I'm fine," Dixon said. "Let's head on up. Lead on Mark, we'll follow."

Two hours later, the group assembled in the spacious dining room of the farmhouse - Dixon, Dr. Contreras, Vanderham, Secretary Solene, Justice Brown, Dr. Mothershed, Laura and Toby, all seated around the old table, drinks in hand. Toby and Laura had been greeted with astonishment; no one had expected to see them again. Dixon's wounds had been cleaned and sutured. Salmon from last winter's catch were on the barbeque, tended by two of the security team, Pete and Phil. Only Jacob, Mark and Charlie were missing – they had gone down to the WPPS building.

Over dinner, Toby sat back and listened to the conversation. He noticed a new tone, a new attitude emerging. They could have discussed the events of the last three months – stories of survival, stories of death, the horror of it all. Instead, the conversation centered on Vanderham's and Sofia's impressions of Malabar Farm, on the extraordinary people there, and the great beauty of the place. A future had suddenly appeared - young, healthy and promising. The necessary process of turning away from the sink-hole of their shared past, and embracing a hopeful future, had begun.

Toby wanted to bury the past even more than the others. He daydreamed the image of a "Driver" approaching his past, a large "C" painted on a board next to it, his unwitting role in the unspeakable events of the last year now being covered by yards of dirt. Someday it might happen, he hoped. Tonight's dinner conversation had helped. And tomorrow, he and Laura would move to a cottage at Malabar Farm. A new start, and likely to be the place where they would spend the rest of their lives. He wished the "Driver" would pass by soon. That promising future would come more easily with the past well buried.

After dinner, Dixon and Vanderham retired to the den for a private conversation. Vanderham had insisted it was time to rally the people at Malabar. For the last few weeks they had been stuck in a kind of purgatory, halfway between the end of the First Age, and the beginning of the Second. Vanderham wanted to gather all the people in the auditorium, introduce the "dignitaries", and deliver a stirring speech - a call to action - officially declaring the beginning of the Second Age. The farmhouse group, Dixon included, had agreed. Dixon's only condition was that he would not speak. That responsibility fell to Vanderham, although Dixon had a few things he wanted Vanderham to say.

Finally, after a complex rearrangement of the sleeping assignments at the farmhouse, the group retired. It had been a long day for the travelers from Vancouver Island.

Chapter 37

Saturday, February 20th, 2021
Malabar Farm

The next morning, as always, Toby rose early. He slipped on his clothes, and quietly walked down the stairs. It was still dark out at this hour, just after five, but a light was on in the kitchen.

Dixon and Jacob were there, Dixon pouring coffee into a thermos. They had jackets on and were obviously about to leave.

"Morning," Toby said. "Where you guys going?"

Dixon looked over at Jacob, who took the hint, excused himself and headed out the front door.

"Can I pour you a cup?" Dixon asked.

"I thought we couldn't drink coffee anymore."

"They stocked up here before it was contaminated."

"Sure, I'll take a cup."

Dixon pulled a cup out of the cabinet, filled it, and handed it to Toby. "Follow me."

They walked down the driveway, around the bend and out of sight of the farmhouse, where two Hummers were parked, facing downhill. Charlie, Mark and Jacob were leaning against the front one, drinking coffee. Dixon stopped just out of earshot.

Dixon turned to face Toby. "The four of us are leaving. I'm sure you can see that my presence here would be a major problem for the people at Malabar. So now, as long as you keep Solene's, and perhaps others, role in the Eden Proposition unspoken, then you can blame it all on me. The rest of you were just innocent bystanders, duped into the event. Leave it at that. As we discussed last night, it's time to move on."

Toby nodded. He understood. "Where will you go?"

"Everywhere," Dixon answered. "I want to check on the Inuit on Hudson Bay, the Antarctic outposts, the nomadic people of Tibet, the submarines. I want to know who is still with us."

"You're not going to … to …"

"Perhaps," Dixon interrupted. "It might be necessary, if my task here is not yet complete."

A chill went up Toby's spine. He had expected a different answer, although he didn't know why.

"Before you go, I need to ask you something," Toby said, apprehensively.

"No need. Yes, it was me."

Toby nodded, of course he knew that. Now the more important question; "Does anyone else know?"

"No," Dixon said. "No one else. I told Solene you were important, I never told him why."

Toby said nothing and stared at Dixon.

Dixon paused, nodded at Toby, then turned to his band of explorers, "Let's go boys!" He grabbed Toby's elbow and escorted him over to the vehicles. Mark and Charlie got into the lead Hummer. Jacob stood by the door of the other.

"Will you ever come back?" Toby asked, choking up, surprised by the lump in his throat.

"In a few years, someone will return, but not me," Dixon said. "It might be important for the people at Malabar to know who else is traveling with them on this spaceship."

Dixon squeezed Toby's elbow, then reached up and gripped his shoulder. He took a step away, produced the green John Deere cap from his back pocket, slipped it on, and turned to Jacob.

"Okay Woodrow," Dixon said to Jacob. "Saddle up, let's head out."

Jacob got in. Dixon walked around the front of the Hummer, glanced back at Toby, tipped his cap and gave him the perfect Duval Dixon crinkled-eye smile. Years later, Toby would swear it was a cowboy hat, and not the green cap, that Dixon wore as he rode off down the drive.

Vanderham put the word out for everyone to assemble in the auditorium at one o'clock that afternoon.

At twelve forty-five they began to arrive, casually chatting and laughing, the usual noisy entrance of a crowd going into a theatre. But then the indifferent noises changed to hushed murmurs and pointed fingers as they first saw the strangers sitting with Vanderham, and then to silence and astonished stares, as they recognized the famous people - Secretary General Manute Solene, Justice Martha Cartman Brown and Dr. Sessions Mothershed. They seated themselves quickly, sensing that they would finally hear the true story, and perhaps even the meaning, of their miraculous survival.

Vanderham began by first introducing the new arrivals, including Toby, Laura, and Mothershed, and then Solene and Justice Brown, who had not been seen by anyone from Malabar while in hiding at the farmhouse. He also introduced Pete and Phil, though many had met them during the last few weeks. Vanderham made no mention of Mark, Charlie or Jacob.

Vanderham understood the importance of this day, of this speech. He paused and looked up and around at the expectant group. The auditorium at Malabar resembled many of the large classrooms at OSU in which Vanderham had regularly lectured over the past decades. Vanderham stood at floor level, behind a wooden podium, in front of an arc of seats in three sections, rising steeply for fifteen rows. It seated three hundred when full. On this day, it held one hundred fifty-two.

Vanderham was in his element here; few could match his skill at commanding a room such as this. The people at Malabar had heard him speak in this auditorium many times over the last year. Though they were familiar with his skill, they never tired of it. But for the distinguished newcomers, it was their first chance to hear this seemingly shy and awkward "Lincoln" impersonator speak before an auditorium. Even for Solene, a man who listened to blowhards for a living, Vanderham was one of the best speakers he had ever heard.

Vanderham stood erect, feet apart, his bony hands wrapped around the front corners of the podium. His deep, modulated voice needed no amplification.

Vanderham told the story of the Eden Proposition. He told the story of Duval Dixon. He dropped the revelation that Dixon had been at Malabar the night before, and had gone out early this morning to survey the world.

He made the case for "Massive Population Reduction" in such a logical and convincing way, that even Justice Brown could understand it. Then he stepped away from the podium and moved forward so that he was only a foot away from the people in the front row. He clasped his hands behind his back, leaned slightly down, and then abruptly straightened up, making eye contact with those in the back row.

"The future of the human race belongs to us," he said, his voice filling the auditorium, his arms outstretched. "We are all that is. We - the people in this room - will decide the culture of the Second Age of Humankind. Our choices, our decisions, will set the course for generation, upon generation, *upon generation!*

"The opportunity we have been given, cannot be overestimated. It would be easy to go forward by simply repeating the past. But, we cannot allow that to happen!" he boomed, and stepped a few paces to the side.

"We must step back and rethink everything. *Everything!* Even the little things. Should we teach our children soccer or baseball? Piano or electric guitar? Do we pass on to them science - or superstition? Do we teach Spanish, French, or only English? Do we redefine the art of dying, and 'walk the earth' as the original Americans did. Or do we maintain the keep-me-alive-at-all-costs methods of western medicine? What do we do with the abundance of 'things' that have been left behind? What should be preserved, and what should be discarded?"

Vanderham paused, looked around the auditorium, and walked back to the podium.

"These, and a thousand other questions need to be asked and answered. And while we must understand the lessons of the past – we must not be bound by them! Everything needs to be questioned, everything examined, everything seen in a new way. We must clearly understand our responsibility, and the opportunity that we have to correct the mistakes of the past and to set a positive, *sustainable course,* for the generations who follow us.

"How we do this – this is our first task," Vanderham said, holding up a sheet of paper he had put on the podium earlier. "As a starting point,

I've put a list of thirty committees up on the network. Each committee has space for twenty people. Each committee addresses one of these questions. Sign up for as many as you want, until all are full. And – just so you don't think I have assumed the role of dictator - five of these committees are tasked with coming up with a better, or different approach. This is just a way to get started."

Vanderham paused again, looking around at the mesmerized auditorium.

"We will start today!" he spoke loudly, dramatically. "This day – February 20th, 2021, will hereafter be known, and celebrated, as the official anniversary of the beginning of the Second Age. Today, let us all declare the First Age over, and put the past behind us. The future … is now *ours* to create!"

Vanderham nodded to himself, and again surveyed the silent group. Someone started clapping and they all rose to their feet. Vanderham motioned to them to stop. He had one more thing to say.

"And my last act as the head of this former school, is to give out a homework assignment," he said, smiling. "Without a doubt, the best homework assignment I've ever given."

He stepped out from behind the podium, raised his hands above his head - a benediction. "Now, I beseech you all – go forth and procreate. The survival of your species demands this!"

Maggie MacDonald took it upon herself to organize a party at the basketball court. She would roll over a sufficient number of kegs. Someone decided that the supply of salmon on ice at the commissary should be sacrificed on the barbeque. The party was deemed by all to be a necessary first step for the homework assignment they had just been given.

Toby, Laura, Sofia, and Manny toured the housing area and picked out two neighboring cottages high on the hill. Toby wanted the sweeping view from the front porch. They spent the afternoon moving their few possessions from the farmhouse and from Sofia's former cottage. After several trips to the commissary in the electric carts, they had assembled the beginning of their new homes.

Late in the afternoon, before the Second Age anniversary celebration had begun, Toby and Manny joined Mothershed for a tour of Malabar's extensive labs and greenhouses. Sofia took Laura down to the infirmary and introduced her to Doc Siefert and Dr. Jan.

The Second Age party became a true celebration. Vanderham's speech had lifted the cloud of despair that had hung over everyone for the last several months. The call to focus on the future gave them an exciting new challenge to grasp. And the homework assignment added a heart-pounding additional dimension.

Toby and Laura retired early, Laura still not feeling well. But they stayed long enough for Laura to observe that the infirmary would be busy delivering many babies before the next Second Age celebration.

Chapter 38

Sunday, February 21st, 2021
Day two of the Second Age
Malabar Farm

On day two of the Second Age, Toby slept in. The "Driver" that he had wished for had finally come. Dixon's departure, together with the knowledge that no one else knew, had done the trick. Toby's unspoken role could now be buried. The relief of that burial, added to the exhaustion of the past few days, conspired to keep him snuggled up to his tired companion until almost ten in the morning.

Laura nuzzled him awake. "Don't get up," she whispered in his ear. Toby wasn't sure if he had the energy for what he thought she had in mind. But it wasn't that. Instead, she said she had something to tell him.

Laura got up on one elbow so she could look squarely at Toby. She smiled radiantly, and waited long enough to get his full attention before saying anything.

"What?" he asked, turning on his side, now curious.

"I talked to Doctor Jan at the infirmary yesterday. I wanted to see if she had any ideas about why I've felt so bad lately," Laura said, still smiling. "And guess what – she figured it out."

"Great," Toby said. "Well, I mean great, if she can help."

"No, she can't help," Laura said. "But it's still great."

Laura leaned over and kissed Toby.

"We're going to have a baby."

Toby sat up, confused. He pointed to his chest, and squeaked, "Me ...?"

Laura laughed, "Of course, dummy. I guess it wasn't one in a million after all."

Toby jumped up. "Holy shit!" he said, his hands on the top of his head.

"Doctor Jan told me one more thing," Laura said, and sat up cross-legged on the bed. "This will be the first baby born here."

"Adam?" Toby said absently.

"Not a chance - don't be silly," Laura said. "But we do need a name."

"How about Mugsey?" Toby asked. "He was my favorite basketball player growing-up."

Laura laughed, "Good one. But the baby could be a girl, you know."

Toby sat back down on the bed. "Okay - I can give you a serious answer for that," he said with a wry smile.

He leaned over and kissed Laura gently on the neck, then whispered in her ear.

Laura leaned back, a bit curious about the whisper, and studied Toby for a moment. "Well, it's not one of the usual suspects these days – but nice. Is it a family name?"

Toby paused for a moment, then decided that those dots could never be connected now. "Sort of," he said.

"I do like it," Laura said. "It's strong. Okay then, if it's a girl, we'll name her Ruth."

The End

2427175

Made in the USA